Merry Christmas

Mary Jane Burgoine

NOW I LAY ME DOWN TO SLEEP

NOW I LAY ME DOWN TO SLEEP

Mary Jane Bergoine

Eloquent Books
Durham, Connecticut

Eloquent Books
An imprint of Strategic Book Group
P. O. Box 333
Durham, CT 06422
http://www.StrategicBookGroup.com

ISBN: 978-1-60911-843-3

Book Design by Julius Kiskis

Printed in the United States of America
18 17 16 15 14 13 12 11 10   1 2 3 4 5

Dedication

To my Husband and Family, who have put up with me through
it all, enjoy.
I love you all.
MJB

one

IRENE- 1944

The sun was shining brightly as Irene bounced down Rose Avenue on her way to school; she was meeting Brenda, her very best friend, along the way. They had known each other since first grade and had done practically everything together ever since. Irene could hardly contain her excitement, it was nearly Graduation day, but Graduation was not the only thing making her feel the way she did. She and Roland had made plans to elope the very same night as the Graduation dance. They were both eighteen now and couldn't wait to start their lives together. She desperately wanted to share her news with her little sister Donna, but she didn't dare. Donna was so easily tricked into telling everything she knew especially if prompted by one of their parents. She was only fourteen and as sweet and honest as they come and Irene loved her dearly. She couldn't tell her older brother, Jake, either, because he would feel it was his duty to protect her from making a mistake and she was afraid he would try to stop her. He'd tell her she was too young to get married and to wait a few years, she could just hear him. Jake was always protecting her and Donna and Mama as well when he could manage it, sadly for Mama though most times it simply wasn't possible for any of them to protect her, she shook her head, she didn't want those dark thoughts interfering with how

1

wonderful she felt.

She was so excited; she thought she might burst, and she wasn't sure just how she was going to make it through the entire day. Her mother had instructed her to hurry home after school, so they would have time to walk downtown to Martha's, which was just the best dress shop in town. Martha's carried all the latest fashions, just like the ones she and Brenda drooled over so often in the magazines in the Five & Ten store downtown. She was thrilled she was going to be able to buy a gown there, but she was elated by the knowledge that she was marrying Roland so soon, that it was taking precedence in her every thought. She thought in utter amazement, it's even diminishing my excitement over shopping for my gown, today.

The town of Sarnia, Ontario, was quite small, but Irene loved it, she'd grown up there and had not really known anything else. She'd been a baby when her mother and father, Elinor and Otto Giles' farm had burned to the ground and her parents, her older brother Jake and she had moved into town so her father could look for work. Within a few days, he'd found a job at the Oil Company and had been fortunate enough to find a home only a few blocks away that they could rent enabling him to walk to work everyday. Eventually, after saving and just plain doing without her parents had managed to buy the house from the estate after the property owner had passed away. Irene had grown up in that home and loved it, but now she was looking forward to a better life with Roland.

Irene knew Mama had been saving to buy her a gown for graduation for a long time now, skimping here and there so she could put money in the jar marked for special occasions. Donna was coming with them this afternoon too, she was almost as excited as Irene was about the ceremony and Irene's new gown. She was going to be wearing a dress Irene had worn to a wedding a couple of years back, it was quite fancy and Donna loved it. She had always dreamed of the day when it would be hers. She loved inheriting Irene's clothes, they were always so beautiful, Irene had such good taste and Mama always altered them expertly so they fit her perfectly, but this dress fit her so well, when she'd first tried it on, it seemed as if it had been made just for her.

Irene met up with Brenda just two blocks from the school, the short walk that remained, did not allow them enough time to bring each other up to date on their plans for the big day. Brenda had her gown, already; it was a lovely shade of pale yellow and was strapless. She would be wearing it with a gorgeous shawl that she'd borrowed from a friend of her mother's, it matched the gown perfectly and a pair of high heeled shoes, borrowed from one of her aunts, they were almost the exact colour as the gown and Brenda was lucky, as they were just the right size too. She was going to be wearing her mother's pearls, the ones her mother had worn on her wedding day years ago.

Brenda's date was Harold, he was so handsome he had a full head of dark thick hair that shone in the sunlight, and Brenda had secretly admired him since she'd first laid eyes on him in the eighth grade. She was thrilled when he asked her to be his date for the dance. She'd already been imagining a wonderful future with him; she secretly hoped Harold felt the same way as she did.

Irene was going with Roland, of course. He was gorgeous and incredibly smart; Irene knew all the other girls were jealous; he was even going to be Valedictorian at Graduation. Irene just loved being the object of the other girls' jealousy. When they had first started dating, she'd been afraid that he would be bored with her. She knew she was no match for him intellectually, not then or now, but she hoped her sophisticated manners would get her by. He wanted to be a doctor and Irene liked the sound of that. She was so sick of living in near poverty, always having to scrimp and save for everything, even the essentials. She knew she was better than that, she thought with a quick toss of her head. Roland was perfect; she knew he would make her very happy and not only was he good looking but one day he would be quite wealthy, she smiled at the thought. She had secretly told Brenda all about her hopes and dreams involving Roland, and the upcoming wedding, she did leave out the part about the money he would make though, after all, she didn't want her best friend to think that was all she cared about. Brenda had told Irene all about her fantasies regarding Harold as well. They were fast friends and had no secrets from each other, well almost none, Irene thought with a sly smile.

Brenda and Harold were going to stand up with them at their wedding. They were all going to wear the same clothes that they were wearing to the dance. All Irene had to do was find a gown that was suitable for both the dance and her wedding. She hoped Mama wouldn't make her buy something different from what she really wanted and needed. She just couldn't imagine getting married wearing a bright colour; she needed a soft sophisticated colour and she would have to make sure she found one.

School was going so slow, it seemed that all her classes today were just dragging by. Her last class of the day, English, was the only one she really looked forward to because she sat beside Roland, that was the only class they shared. Roland was in the advanced classes and she was in the commercial course. She was taking shorthand and typing in the hopes of landing a secretarial position after graduation. Roland was taking Math classes like Trigonometry and Algebra, he even knew how to use a slide rule properly, she could never quite figure out just how those things worked. He was taking Latin as well since that was a compulsory subject for admission to medical school. They would sneak long looks at each other and Roland would sometimes put his hand on her thigh when no one was looking. Irene wasn't sure how to respond to that, it made her feel funny inside.

She and Brenda had talked about all the things Irene would be expected to do after she married Roland, at least all the things they'd found out about from sneaking a look at some pictures that Brenda's father had hidden in the basement. They were mostly just pencil sketches, of men and women having sex and doing things that the girls thought were really awful and hoped they would never have to do. They knew enough about marriage to know, they would be expected to do whatever their husbands wanted. They had learned this from their friend, Laurie, who was a couple of years older than they were and had been married for a year already. She didn't go into detail but she had told them, "Wives are expected to make their husbands happy." She had gone on to say, "Not just keeping the house clean and making meals, that's the stuff they teach you in Home Economics at school; but in the bedroom as well," and of course they didn't teach that in school. After looking at the pictures and talking to Laurie, Irene hoped and prayed she knew enough not to disappoint Roland. She wondered if he had any experience with sex, she would never dare to ask him, she would be far too embarrassed.

Roland and Harold walked the girls home from school and like the perfect gentlemen they were, they even carried their books for them. Brenda's house was the closest to the school and once they arrived at her front yard, they sat on the grass and began talking about their plans for the ceremony and dance. They listened to Roland practise his Valedictorian speech and all of them agreed it was amazing, he had done a wonderful job composing it. They talked about where they were going to meet after the dance. They decided they'd take a room at a hotel, a few miles, outside of town in the village of Stratford. Roland had already arranged for the Church; they were to be there by one in the afternoon. They weren't taking any chances that someone might know them and tell their parents, which could easily happen if they chose a Church here in town. They were afraid their parents would try to stop them. They were planning to go to each of their parents' houses and tell them that they were married after their wedding, and then go home to the small apartment they'd rented over the butcher shop. It was at the end of the street that Roland's parents lived on, Mutton Street, just before the railroad tracks. They knew it would be noisy but they also knew that was the reason the rent was so affordable. Irene only hoped she would find a job soon so she could help with the expenses. Roland already had a decent job, he worked after school two days a week and on Saturdays and they'd promised him that he could work full time in the summer; it was at the same Oil Company that Irene's father worked for. Roland worked in the Lab and Irene's father worked in the yard.

Irene frowned and suddenly jumped up from the grass, she just remembered her mother would be waiting for her, wondering where she was. She quickly told her friends, "I need to get home fast, I was so caught up in our plans, I forgot all about going shopping for my gown." She laughed and said, "Goodbye, see you later," and she and Roland ran all the way to her house. Mama and Donna were sitting on the porch waiting for her. Mama looked at her crossly, but didn't say anything until Roland left, and then with the annoyance she felt evident in her voice, she asked, "What took you so long to come home?" Irene thought quickly and told her, "I had to stay after school to help with an article for the school paper." She felt guilty lying to her mother, but how could she tell her she'd lost track of time making plans with her friends for her wedding. Oh well, Irene thought, soon enough I won't have to make up stories, or explain my whereabouts to anyone, except maybe Roland and I can handle that.

They walked along talking easily about their days. It was so easy talking to Mama when Father wasn't around. Irene and Donna talked about school and Mama told them about the casserole she'd made for dinner, it was their favourite, chicken with vegetables and dumplings. She said, making their mouths water, "It's sitting on the sideboard just waiting to be warmed up when we get home." They hoped Father would not be cross, about dinner being late. He knew how much buying this gown for Irene's Graduation meant to Elinor. He also knew how hard she tried to manage on less so she could put a little aside, each payday for things the girls needed. Elinor closed her eyes silently praying, that he would remember those things and not be too upset.

They reached Martha's Fashions and Irene noticed all the beautiful gowns in the window, there were two in particular that she really liked, but she wasn't sure if they'd be too expensive, so she decided to be quiet and see what Mama picked out and then she could look at the prices of those ones and get an idea of what price range she would have to work with. With fingers crossed, she reluctantly snuck a peak at the prices of the gowns in the window and then looked at the prices of all the gowns Mama was suggesting she try on. She bit her bottom lip, the prices of the ones she liked were substantially more money.

Irene dutifully tried on everything Mama asked her to, but Mama noticed that none of the gowns seemed to be exciting Irene, and since she wanted her Graduation day to be perfect for her, she finally asked, "Is there a particular gown you would like to try on, Irene?" Irene looked at the floor and timidly replied, "I really liked two dresses in the window." She explained, excitedly, "I noticed them when we first walked up to the shop," and she animatedly described them to her. Mama walked outside to look and Irene watched her, thinking to herself, "yes" she knew just how to manipulate Mama to get what she wanted. She only hoped that Mama had enough money with her. When Mama came back into the store, she asked the shop girl, "How much are they?" Mama frowned when she heard the prices, but she thought, I have the grocery money in my purse, if I skimp just a little more on this weeks meals, I can do it. She swallowed, thinking, I hope Otto, won't notice, he gets so cross if I spend too much on the girls. She thought it would be worth it if she could make Irene's Graduation special and she knew Irene truly wanted one of these gowns. She asked the shop girl, "Please bring them to the fitting room, my daughter would like to try them on."

The first one didn't look good on her at all it was too long in the waist and made Irene look dowdy. Irene's heart sank, she was afraid the other one wouldn't fit her either, but as she slipped the silky soft fabric on, she felt goose pimples rising on her arms, she turned and looked in the mirror and smiled, she knew that this was the gown for her. She hoped Mama would approve. When she walked out of the fitting room, Mama and Donna both gasped, Irene looked stunning. The gown was a beautiful cream colour with small rosettes in such beautiful shades of pinks and roses with small green leaves and stems and tiny little pearls sewn in rows all around each group of rosettes. The gown was strapless and came with a matching shawl. It was a perfect fit and even the length was just right. Mama said, smiling, "I'm sure I have a pair of shoes that will match it perfectly," she added excitedly, "And a necklace as well." They were the ones she had worn on her wedding day and they still looked just like new. Irene hated the idea of wearing anything "cast off" but thought that, in this case it would be perfect because she would now have something "borrowed" and "old" she just had to work on something "blue" she thought maybe I can get away with blue underwear or something, she shook her head, she would have to think about that one. Irene was not normally superstitious but she thought, better safe than sorry.

Irene changed back into her own clothes and came out of the fitting room with the gown draped over her arm. Mama took it from her and went to the counter to pay for it; Irene watched her counting out her money in small bills and coins and had to look the other way she was so embarrassed. She felt humiliated; she was going to make damn sure she would never have to do that. She knew that doctors made exceptionally good money and that they were respected in their communities, she couldn't wait, she had always dreamed of being a "somebody." She hated being poor. She desperately wanted to be able to buy anything she wanted. Roland was the perfect answer.

Donna chattered all the way home about Irene's beautiful gown and how she hoped that it just might be hers one day. "Could I wear it for my own graduation?" she asked Mama. Irene had to smile, her little sister was so easy to please, for some reason she never wanted more than she had and she was never embarrassed to wear hand-me-downs. Irene was so glad she was the eldest girl, because she could not see herself wearing anything someone else had grown out of and handed down to her. She felt she was so much better than that.

When they reached home, Irene took the gown out of the wrapping and hung it on the door of the bedroom she shared with Donna. She was going to have Brenda come over after school tomorrow to see it and she wanted it to look perfect. She was smoothing out the fabric and plumping the crinoline underneath it when she heard Mama calling her for dinner.

She ran down the stairs and washed her hands in the kitchen sink. She sat down at her place at the table and waited for Father to come in from the living room. He always had to sit down and say grace before anyone was allowed touch anything on the table and if you did you were sent to your room, without any supper. Some days it was so hard not to touch, especially if she was hungry, she could smell the food on the table but she had to sit there until Father finally came in, sat down, and said grace, and then they had to wait for him to serve them. They always had enough to eat, but just enough. There never was much money for extras, they pretty much had three meals a day, but when it came to snacks they were not allowed because they might be eating something that was meant for the next days meals. Tonight Irene was starving, she hadn't eaten her sandwich for lunch; she recalled she'd nearly thrown it in the trash before she remembered that Roland might like to have it. His parents didn't have much money in their family either. Sometimes Roland didn't have any lunch at all and if he did, it wasn't always enough for someone his size. Irene seemed to keep forgetting that, she was always thinking about the things that mattered to her and the future she was determined to have. She knew that they would have a few lean years in the beginning of their marriage, but that it would all be worth it later on. Roland was going to do well and they would be very wealthy. It was a good thing he had such high marks in school because he was now in line for a scholarship and without that he wouldn't be able to afford to go to medical school. Irene jolted back to the present, she wanted to make sure he thought she was very considerate and reminded herself to think of him more often so she wouldn't make silly mistakes, like nearly throwing away her lunch, without asking him if he wanted it. She didn't want him to think she was selfish. She really didn't think she was, she knew she should think of others more often, but she was just so focused on not being poor anymore she sometimes forgot that other people had needs too.

Donna and Irene cleaned up after dinner and as they were washing the dishes, they could hear the muffled voices upstairs growing louder and sounding more impatient. Mama and Father were upstairs talking, as they sometimes did after dinner, whenever Father thought there was something to discuss or if he was suspicious that Mama might not be telling him everything he thought he should know. Father was like that sometimes, you never quite knew just what he was thinking or when he would lose control and strike one of them. The girls knew that he was becoming extremely upset because his voice was getting louder. They jumped when all of a sudden they heard him yell, "You spent what!" and then heard him ranting about how hard he worked and how Mama just threw his money around. Irene and Donna exchanged worried glances and just as the yelling seemed to have stopped, they both gasped as they heard a loud, slap and then heard Mama cry out in pain. They looked at each other in horror and tried their best to appear busy with their cleaning chores when they heard their Father stomping down the stairs. Their hearts pounded in their chests when he appeared at the kitchen door, he glared at them for a few seconds, then turned and headed down the hall. They held their breath as they watched him walk down the hall and storm out the front door. They breathed easier once they knew he was gone, they were so frightened of him. He would come home eventually and things would be normal again, Irene thought, it always was. That knowledge helped her not to feel too guilty about the pain her mother had just endured for buying her the gown she wanted. After all, she thought I didn't actually ask Mama to buy it; she did that on her own, so that's not my fault, at all. Thinking that way made her feel a little better.

When Mama finally came down the stairs a while later, her face was puffy and she had a huge red welt on her cheek. Irene winced at the sight of her, but decided she could do nothing to make things better, so she smiled at her and pretended not to notice anything was amiss. She quietly finished her chores and told Mama, "Roland is coming by for a little while. We'll just be sitting on the porch talking," and quickly made her way outside.

Donna noticed how Irene had acted as if nothing was wrong; and thought Irene seems so cold and uncaring sometimes. She went over and kissed Mama; she gave her a hug and asked, "Can I get you a cup of tea?" Mama answered, softly, "No, I'm fine, but thank you," and picked up her mending basket, and started to work, darning a sock with a hole in it that belonged to Father.

Donna went upstairs to her room. She looked at the gown hanging on the door and wondered, why does Irene have to have such expensive things, anyway. She knew she would have paid more attention to the price tags, because she knew that money was scarce and she hated it when her poor Mama was always paying the price of Father's rage over the things Irene seemed to "need." Donna was so different from her sister, she sometimes wondered if Irene had any real feelings for the hardship of others at all. She didn't think she did. Donna knew that as long as her sister got what she wanted she just didn't care about anything or anybody else. Donna lay down on her bed and silently sobbed. She couldn't stand thinking about what Mama went through just to make her sister happy. She vowed that she would never do anything that would hurt Mama like that; in fact, she would do everything in her power to help her with the chores and to make life easier for her. She was determined to do her best to make sure Father was happy as well and hopefully that would help to ensure he didn't lose his temper so often and just maybe, she thought, Mama would be safer. Father seemed to take out most of his frustrations on Mama; he didn't strike her or Irene very often anymore since they had become teenagers and now that Jake was grown, he didn't hit him at all anymore.

The next day after school Brenda and Irene talked excitedly, about their gowns, all the way to Irene's house. Irene couldn't wait for Brenda to see her's, she knew it was exquisite and so much more expensive than Brenda's, but she thought since she was going to be somebody one day she deserved it. Irene felt only the slightest twinge of guilt for what it had cost her mother, but she wouldn't let herself think about that now.

When Brenda saw the gown, she squealed in delight, "Oh my God, it's the most beautiful gown I've ever seen; it's just like that one in the magazine! Remember?" Irene thought, yes, she's right. She knew it had seemed familiar but hadn't been able to place it. Now she knew for sure she would be the envy of all the other girls at the Graduation dance, because all the girls at school looked at the photos in the fashion magazines at the Five and Ten store too and they would all recognize her gown, she smiled at the thought.

Later that day, Irene packed the things she would need for her wedding day and for the wedding night. She had to make sure no one was around and that was no easy task, since she shared a bedroom with Donna. Today Donna was over at her best friend Jenny's house, Jenny's mother was teaching them to knit. That was something Donna really wanted to learn and Mama didn't seem to have time to teach her.   At least Irene didn't have to worry about Jake, he was always working and when he wasn't working, he was with his friends. He never stayed home long, just long enough to eat and sleep otherwise he was gone. She knew he wanted to move out so badly, but he worried, he felt he needed to make sure Mama was okay and by coming home every night to sleep he could do that. He'd told Irene he thought that she and Donna were safe, Father didn't hit them very often anymore; he mostly just used Mama as his punching bag now. Irene was packing a very skimpy nightie, she had made it herself by cutting and sewing an old dress that was too short for her, she had removed the lining so the nightie was almost see through. She'd seen nighties like this in magazines worn by voluptuous models. When she dared to try it on and stepped in front of the mirror, she realized she looked just like those models. She had full breasts, thin arms, legs, and a small waist with rounded hips. She imagined if she let her hair down, she would look very sexy indeed. When she held her hand mirror and stood backwards in the full-length mirror to see the back of the nightie, she realized she had a very nice bum as well. She practically purred as she said softly, "Roland will love this nightie, it's really sexy." She was proud of the job she'd done, making it out of an old dress. She thought, I know how to be thrifty; I just don't like the fact that I have to be, then whispered, softly, "Not for long though."

   She had to admit that she was extremely nervous about their first night; she and Roland had not done much more than kiss so far. She recalled Roland had tried to touch her breast one night when they were kissing on the side porch, out of view of anyone, but she hadn't been ready for that and she'd moved his hand back to her waist. She also thought about the last dance, Roland had taken her to, they'd gotten a little too close on the dance floor and one of the chaperones had come over and sternly warned them to keep their distance. Once the dance was over, on their way home, they'd found a quiet place behind some houses where they were out of view and Roland had pulled her into his arms. They had kissed so passionately and Roland had held her very close, she'd felt his excitement. She remembered how that had made her feel all tingly, that had been so exciting. Roland had rubbed her leg with his hand gradually working his way up until his hand reached the edge of her panties. Then he'd lifted the elastic just enough so he could get his hand inside, she'd waited just until he touched her and she heard him groan, then she stopped him even though it had felt so good and she really hadn't wanted to stop. She realized coming out of her thoughts, soon we won't have to. She wondered, under her breath, "I wonder what making love feels like." She thought of what Laurie had said, that sometimes it felt good, but she'd also warned her that the first time would hurt. Irene was afraid of that, but she knew Roland was very gentle and she didn't think he would ever hurt her. She finished packing and put the suitcase under the bed. She and Roland had arranged, that tomorrow night before she went to bed, she was to put her suitcase outside under the side porch. Roland would come by late at night, fetch it and put it in the car that he was borrowing from his Grandfather, to take them to the dance. His Grandfather had no idea he wouldn't get the car back for a couple of days. They were taking it to Stratford to get married. Roland had said his grandfather rarely drove it anyway; he said he walked everywhere he went, because his legs got too stiff if he didn't walk everyday. She recalled, Roland had said, he wouldn't feel too guilty about not returning the car promptly. He had told Irene, nervously though, that they'd have to make sure they took very good care of it.

Irene thought, smiling, Roland is such a considerate person; honest as the day is long, I just hope that won't be a problem someday, because although she knew honesty was a good thing, it could be carried too far, especially, she thought, if it gets in the way of things that I want. I'll just have to wait and see. She was almost certain she could handle him, most of the time. She knew she could convince him to do the things she wanted him to do. Funny, she thought most of the time he even thinks those things are his own ideas; she smiled to herself at that thought. She knew she already had him wrapped around her finger.

two

ROLAND

Roland was in a hurry to get to school today and had been everyday since he'd started dating Irene, almost a year ago, he just couldn't get enough of her. He was content to simply watch her talking and laughing with her friends, to Roland, Irene was perfect. He thought, as he hurried along the sidewalk, she has a beautiful face and a luscious body, although she's not very tall, she's gorgeous. He thought of her dark hair, she wore it pulled back in a ponytail, as all the girls at school did, he remembered the first time he had seen her with her hair down. He'd called around to her house unexpectedly one evening and recalled that when she'd answered the door he nearly couldn't speak, she looked so beautiful. Her dark brown hair framed her flawless, heart shaped face and made her bright turquoise blue eyes seem even more brilliant. The dress she'd worn hugged her curves and was a tad too short and he couldn't help but notice her exquisite legs. How he'd longed to be alone with her, that night. She'd come out, sat on the swing on the front porch, and talked to him for a while. She'd apologized for the way she was dressed, rags, she'd called them, she'd said she and her sister, Donna, were helping their Mama put up pickles in jars. They'd picked the cucumbers from the garden patch in the backyard. He thought she looked wonderful even though she did smell of vinegar and dill and he'd teased her about it. He'd dreamed of how she had looked on several occasions after that, he'd even had a dream where he was taking off that clingy dress she was wearing and discovered she had nothing on underneath. He wondered if she would really look like she did in his dream, he couldn't wait to find out.

Roland had only ever been intimate with one woman and that was when he and some of his friends had snuck a couple of bottles of whisky from the cellar at his friend Randy's house. They'd had a few too many drinks that night; they'd been celebrating his seventeenth birthday. When his friends found out that he was still a virgin they'd found a young attractive prostitute and paid her to have sex with him. He'd been too drunk and naïve to comprehend she was actually working; he'd thought she was simply attracted to him. She'd taken him to a room in an old house and as soon as she'd closed the door, she had taken off all her clothes. Roland had been shocked and a little embarrassed but he'd also been amazed, she really was quite attractive. He remembered her full breasts and nicely shaped hips. He'd stolen glances at her and had noticed her pubic hair was blonde and curly. She'd caught him looking and he'd been even more embarrassed. He'd been stunned, though when she said, "Look all you want, your friends paid me quite well for tonight, they wanted me to take my time and teach you everything you need to know." She'd smiled at him as she walked towards him and said, "They said you're a virgin." He could still hear her say those words and even just thinking about it he was embarrassed all over again, which he knew was silly, after all this time, but he couldn't help it. He remembered looking at her body, he'd really wanted to have sex with her, and so he'd pretended that he'd known all along that she was a prostitute. She taught him how to make love and he figured he must have learned well since she'd been moaning in delight at times. When they were getting dressed afterwards, he asked her why she did this. She said that she came from a poor family and that she desperately wanted to go to college one day and she didn't know of anything else she could do to make as much money in so little time. Roland had felt both guilt and pity, so he'd given her a few extra dollars that night, because he hadn't know what else to do for her. He remembered walking home that night and feeling a twinge of remorse for what he'd done and knew he'd need to go to confession before he could receive Communion on Sunday. He recalled telling the priest in the confessional of his sin, he'd called it adultery and he suddenly remembered Father, had corrected him and told him it was called fornicating since he wasn't married. He didn't remember the whole lecture he'd received that day from the priest, but he sure remembered how totally mortified he'd felt.

Roland had been born in Detroit, Michigan, his parents, Clancy and Alma Petersen, had moved to Sarnia when he was only eight years old and Melissa, his little sister, had only been four. Melissa was the light of his life, until he met Irene and now he was very much aware that Melissa felt she wasn't as important to him anymore, because he didn't spend as much time with her as he used to. He'd tried very hard to be with her as much as he possibly could; he even took her shopping one day and surprised her with a new dress. Melissa was thrilled she was going to wear it to his Graduation ceremony. Roland's part-time job at the oil company paid him quite well and he was able to afford a very nice, dress for her.

Melissa was a little jealous of the time Roland spent with Irene, even though deep down inside she knew he still loved her, and that he still liked to spend time with her, when he could. She thought I could probably get over my feelings of not being quite so important in Roland's life anymore, much easier, if Irene was a different sort of person. She thought Irene is two faced and a little too showy; she always wants the very best for herself. Moreover, it seemed to Melissa that Irene always knew just how to get exactly what she wanted, especially from Roland. She also seemed to think she was better than everyone else was. Melissa couldn't believe it when, she learned that Roland had scrimped and saved to buy Irene an expensive hope chest. She recalled, Roland told her that he and Irene had been passing by the furniture shop one day walking home from the movies and Irene had noticed the hope chest in the window and told him how much she wanted it. He told her that she had said, "I'd be so happy if only I could have that." Irene must have known that Roland wasn't making much money at the time; he'd just started his job and hadn't been making the same hourly wage as he was now or working anywhere near as many hours then, either. Melissa wouldn't have even known about the hope chest except that the day before it was to be delivered to Irene, Roland had asked her to go for a walk with him and they'd stopped in at the furniture store so he could make the final payment. He'd wanted to show her the "present" he'd bought for Irene, he'd been so proud and happy that it would finally be delivered to her. Melissa couldn't help but notice, that hope chest he'd bought her was the most expensive one in the store. When she'd commented on the price, Roland told her the story of how much Irene wanted only that particular one. He had actually thought it was sweet. She thought her brother could be so dumb sometimes. That was when she had first started to worry about him being with Irene. Her parents loved Irene though, they couldn't see through the façade as she did, but even though she had her doubts about her, she couldn't deny the fact that Roland was head over heels in love with her. She knew she was probably stuck with her, because she was pretty sure that Roland would ask Irene to marry him someday.

Roland was in Rosen's, which was one of the nicer men's stores downtown, picking up his suit, the tailor wanted him to try it on one more time, so he could make sure it was just right. Roland had already tried it on a few times before, when he'd initially enquired about renting it, and again later to make sure the jacket alterations were accurate but the trousers had not been finished at the time. Now all the alterations were complete and he wanted to be sure the suit was perfect as well, not so much for Graduation, although that was important enough, he wanted it to be perfect for their wedding. He wanted Irene to be proud of how he looked, he knew she would look perfect, she always did. He smiled thinking about her, he couldn't wait to make her is wife.

He left Rosen's with his suit in a garment bag and walked down the street to Danforth Jewellers, he had to make the final payment on Irene's engagement ring. She didn't even know he'd bought it, he thought with a smile. She'd been hinting about wanting one and had even shown him which one she wanted, just in case he was somehow able to afford it one day. When she'd showed it to him his only reply had been, "Maybe one day." Then as soon as he had taken her home, he'd raced back to the Jewellers and put the ring on lay away. He'd felt bad for her and thought she deserved to have it even though he really couldn't afford it, along with all the other things he had to pay for before the wedding. He would have done anything in his power though, to make sure she got it. He'd even gone without lunch sometimes so he could make the payments on it. Irene thought he was without lunch because his parents couldn't always afford it, which was true of course, but he made good money and could have easily afforded to pay for his own lunches, which he usually did, however lately he'd had to make payments on the hope chest, the engagement ring and the wedding rings. Irene didn't have a job so he'd bought both their wedding rings, at her insistence. She'd said, pouting, the day they'd picked out hers, "You're mine and I want everyone to know it once we're married," so he'd relented and purchased his own ring too. He also had to make the first rent payment on their apartment, and of course, he'd purchased all the furniture, dishes, and everything else they needed to set up house. His wages had been stretched to the limit, but he thought it was well worth it, he wanted so much to make her happy; he loved her so much. He did wish sometimes though that she didn't have such expensive tastes. He would have been happy with used furniture, but Irene wouldn't hear of it, she had been shocked at the mere mention of it. She'd said, "I think we should have a fresh start," and of course that meant having everything new.

Roland felt his life couldn't have been more perfect, until last week when he'd gotten a letter from the US Army, telling him he was to report for duty in September, he was drafted. Roland hadn't told anyone yet, including Irene, he didn't want to spoil his or her Graduation, or so he told himself. The truth was he was afraid that if he told her she might not want to marry him right away and he knew he couldn't live with that, especially if he had to go to war. War was a place he didn't want to go anyway, but he knew he had to defend his Country even though he was terrified just thinking about it. He would need to know that she was waiting for him when he returned home. He hoped she would forgive him if she ever found out that he'd actually known before their wedding and had deliberately not told her. He needed her to understand, he did plan to tell everyone after they were married, including her. Roland worried about Melissa as well, the two of them had discussed the possibility of his being drafted at length on several occasions, however, since he lived in Canada and had turned eighteen last November and hadn't heard a single thing from the US government, they had assumed he was safe. They hadn't even spoken about it for a couple of months now. Roland closed his eyes and willed himself not to think about it anymore, he told himself he had better things to think about today.

He walked to over to his best friend, Randy's house and asked him, "Hey, buddy I need a favour from you, would you be my best man at my wedding?" Randy's eyes almost popped out of his head, he said, "You're kidding right, I didn't think you'd go through with it." He clapped him on the back, but his face grew serious and he said, "I'm so sorry, Roland but I can't." Roland felt as if he'd been slapped, "What?" He said a little too loudly. He was so disappointed when Randy said, "My brother Paul is travelling all the way from Manitoba, to see me graduate. You know I'm the youngest and the only one in my family to graduate from high school so all of my family's coming." He continued, "Paul is especially important to me though, since we were always so close. I've been looking forward to spending a couple of days with him since he's only going to be staying for three days and then returning home to his wife and new son." He asked, "You remember, Roland, I told you about the baby? It's only a month old and Paul said he thought the trip would be too long for his wife and the baby, so they're both going to stay behind." Roland simply shook his head and told him, "I understand, don't worry about it." When he left Randy's he didn't know who else he could ask.

Irene suggested, "Harold can take Randy's place as best man," when Roland told her of his dilemma later. She said, "He's Brenda's date and you know I'm having Brenda as my maid of honour, which means Harold will be there anyways, so why not?" Roland thought a minute and decided, "Yeah, why not, that's a great idea," and kissed her on her forehead. He knew Harold, although not as well as Randy, but he liked him, knew him well enough to know that he could keep a secret and that was very important to both Irene and him. Roland asked Harold to be his best man that same day as soon as he left Irene at her house.

Later that day Roland was packing clothes into a small suitcase; he didn't need much, just some travelling clothes and his toiletries. They were going to change in the janitor's closet at school after the dance while everyone was milling around talking and saying goodbye. After they changed, they planned to sneak out to the car. They were going to cover their good clothes with garment bags, so they would still look neat for their wedding the next day. Roland had to remember to pack the wedding rings and the marriage license they had obtained last week, as well. He wanted to make sure their wedding was as perfect as it could possibly be, so he was making certain he didn't forget anything. He'd even ordered a bouquet of roses for Irene to carry and he'd made sure a photographer would be there at the Church; the priest had assured him there was always one at the ready on Saturdays for the weddings and baptisms. They were getting married in the little Catholic Church in Stratford, called St. Anne's.

Roland was so proud of Irene; she had endured four weeks of catechism classes so they could be married in the Catholic Church. Roland was a devout Catholic and would only marry in the Church. Irene had objected at first, she didn't think there was anything wrong with the United Church that she'd practically grown up in, but she relented when she realized just how important it was to him that she become a Catholic. She also realized that if she didn't they couldn't marry in the Catholic Church and Roland refused to marry outside of the Church. She loved him and didn't want to lose him, so she agreed to go to the classes, even though she'd had to lie to her parents and tell them she was studying at Brenda's the whole time. She'd asked the priest to please not tell anyone and he had obliged, saying he understood her predicament. Irene had been confirmed three weeks ago, and was now ready, in the eyes of the Church, for the Sacrament of Marriage.

Roland thought finally, there would be nothing standing in the way of their getting married. He ran through all the things he needed to accomplish in his head and mentally checked off each one. There was nothing else to do; tomorrow was Graduation Day, at last. He decided to rehearse his Valedictorian speech one more time. He set off looking for Melissa, she loved to listen to him, sometimes he couldn't figure out why, but he had to laugh

at her, she was just so special and she would do anything for
him and he knew it. He knew she would be upset with him for
not telling her about his upcoming marriage to Irene. He just
hoped she would forgive him in time. He made a mental note to
see Harold later, just to make sure he was ready and was up to
speed on their plans. Harold was a very reliable sort of person,
but Roland had to be sure, he didn't want anything to stand in
the way of making Irene his bride.

Melissa was delighted to hear Roland's speech; she was amazed
that he could recite it without even so much as a glance at his
cheat sheet. She made him do it three times and he never made
a single mistake or even had a single hesitation throughout the
whole thing. She hugged him, she was so proud; she said, "You're
going to make the whole school proud."

Roland walked over to his Grandfather's house to pick up
the car, Gramps was watching out the window waiting for him.
He was a few minutes late, but when he told Gramps it was
because Melissa wanted him to recite his entire speech three
times just to make sure he was really ready, Gramps just laughed.
He walked outside with Roland and gave him the keys. Roland
was impressed when he saw the car, and said, "Wow it's so clean
and shiny, you didn't have to do that, but thank you." Gramps
was so proud of Roland and all his academic accomplishments;
he wanted his Graduation day and evening to be perfect. He said,
"That was the least I could do for you," he hugged him and told
him, "I'm so proud of you I could burst." Roland shyly looked
at the ground, then up at Gramps, and smiled before he hopped
in the car and started it up; as usual, it purred like a kitten, he'd
known it would, Gramps always kept it tuned up. He waved to
Gramps as he backed out of the drive.

It was beginning to get dark; Roland wanted to stop by
Harold's before it got too late. He pulled up in front of Harold's
house and jumped out of the car. He was just about to ring
the bell when Harold appeared at the screen door. The two

boys went down to the curb to admire the car and discuss their plans. Roland smiled when Harold informed him; he already knew exactly what to do and what time to meet. By the time, he left Harold's he was beginning to calm down.

He just had one last thing to do tonight, which it was now finally dark enough for him to do. He had to pick up Irene's suitcase from under her side porch. As he neared the house and noticed that the only lights on inside her house were the ones in the room that Irene shared with Brenda. He knew that her parents went to bed early because Irene's Dad started work very early everyday and had to get up at five each morning. He left the car a few houses down from hers' on the street and walked the short distance back to the house. He quietly walked to the side porch and found the suitcase exactly where Irene had said she was going to leave it. He hurried back to the car with it and put it on the back seat, he didn't want to take a chance opening and closing the trunk, he had to make sure he didn't make any unnecessary noise and risk being caught, just in case anyone should hear and look out the window, he knew neighbours tended to talk. Roland knew he was being overcautious but this was so important to him that he couldn't help himself. He had never in his life had to sneak around like this before and feared he was probably not very good at it. He sighed thinking; being married to Irene was going to be worth all of it and more.

When Roland got home, he put both his and Irene's suitcases in the trunk, under the blanket that Gramps kept there for emergencies. When he finally went to bed he was asleep almost as soon as his head hit the pillow, he was both exhausted, from all the meticulous planning and excited at the same time. Now that everything was taken care of, he could finally let himself rest.

The next morning he awoke to the smell of breakfast cooking. He was starving all of sudden, he thought of how funny that was, sometimes he only had to smell food cooking and he became ravenous. The smells were different this morning, usually it was just toast and coffee he could smell when he got up. Today he could smell bacon and eggs and that was usually a, "just on Sunday" treat. He pulled on a tee shirt, he was already wearing pyjama bottoms, he hurried into the bathroom to brush his teeth and comb his hair, he figured he would bathe later. Breakfast smelled too good and he had to get to it.

When Roland entered the kitchen, Melissa and Mom yelled, "Congratulations," at exactly the same time. They'd made this special breakfast in his honour and he was pleased as punch that they'd gone to all that trouble just for him. His Mom said, "Since you're the only one so far in this family to graduate from high school, we wanted to make your day as special as we could." She said, "I'm sorry that Dad couldn't be here, but he's getting the afternoon off to attend the Graduation ceremony, so he had to go to work extra early this morning to make up the time." The three of them talked and laughed all through breakfast, Roland enjoyed their company so much he suddenly realized he actually felt calm and smiled thinking about how wonderful his family was. He was determined that he and Irene were going to have this kind of family themselves. He often felt sorry for her; she didn't have a very happy home. She didn't talk about it much, but he could sometimes hear her father ranting when he came to pick her up for a date. He had to admit he didn't care much for the man.

three

THE CEREMONY
AND DANCE

Irene walked to school alongside her parents with Jake and Donna walking directly behind them. They had to be there by two thirty, the Graduation ceremony actually started at three, but the Graduates needed time to put on their gowns and caps and assemble backstage. Donna was practically skipping along. She just loved the dress she was wearing, she felt so grown up in it. Irene was wearing a navy skirt and white blouse, which was what they were supposed to wear under the Graduation gowns so they would all look the same. The boys were to wear dark pants and white shirts with dark ties.

Irene looked at her family and thought that they looked very special in their best clothes; she was so excited about today, but even more so about tomorrow, her wedding day, every time she thought about that she got goose pimples. She was having trouble containing herself; she was almost giddy. Her parents thought she was simply excited about the ceremony and dance. She wished she could tell them, but she didn't want to risk them trying to stop her, and she knew Father certainly would; besides she had promised Roland she would tell no one.

When they reached the school Irene ran backstage to look for Brenda and Roland, as her family went to find a seat in the auditorium. Irene found her friends and they chatted excitedly

27

as they pulled on the gowns they were given to wear for the ceremony. Their homeroom teacher instructed them, to line up the same way they'd practised at the rehearsal. Irene thought everything was moving so quickly. It seemed the whole month of June had been nothing but a blur.

Suddenly, the music started playing and the teaching staff filed out onto the stage. The principal began speaking, he was talking about how hard all the graduates had worked all year long and really deserved their Diplomas. Irene waited anxiously and finally heard the principal call her name, she walked out onto the stage to accept her diploma. She noticed her parents as she turned, before she walked down the steps to sit in the seat she'd been assigned to, they looked so proud, even Father. Irene felt so happy. From her seat in the front row, she watched Brenda and Roland receive their diplomas as well as all her other classmates. Once each graduate had received their diploma and was seated in their designated seat, the Principal introduced Roland, the Valedictorian, to the stage. Roland was fantastic; when his speech was finished, there wasn't a dry eye amongst the graduates or anyone else for that matter. Irene was so proud of him, she thought he was going to make an exceptionally good doctor one day and she thought with a contented sigh that she was going to be the best doctor's wife ever.

After the ceremony, pictures were taken and everyone was drinking punch and having a great time. Dinner was served at five thirty and it was delicious; they ate chicken, roasted potatoes, peas and carrots. There was a beautifully decorated cake for dessert it had been decorated to look like a Diploma. Everyone had a wonderful time and after the dinner was finished; they all hurried home so the graduates could get ready for their big dance that evening. Irene couldn't wait to put on her gown and go to the dance with Roland.

When they arrived home, she hurried up the stairs and once in the bathroom, she stripped off her clothes and ran a warm bath.

Donna insisted on adding scented bubbles, which Irene playfully pretended she didn't want, she enjoyed teasing Donna. The bath felt so good, she could feel some her nervousness melting away. She had to try hard to calm herself; she didn't want her family to start wondering what was going on, after all the ceremony was over, the dance and party were supposed to be the fun part. Her family wouldn't understand why she was so nervous now and she certainly didn't want them to start thinking about it too much. She knew it wasn't just tonight; she'd been acting strange a lot lately. She had often been distracted, and sometimes didn't even hear what was said to her. Everyone thought she was just excited about Graduation, although she did catch Mama looking at her suspiciously one evening when she'd been daydreaming and hadn't heard the question she had asked her. She thought who wouldn't be distracted and nervous with their wedding day tomorrow. She wished they could tell everyone and have a real wedding, the kind she'd always imagined having. Unfortunately, she and Roland both knew that his parents wanted them to wait until Roland was finished school and Irene's parents wanted her to enjoy life as a single girl for a while. They had wed so young themselves and said they felt they had missed some of the fun they should have had; at least that was what Mama said. Father, didn't even like the idea that she was dating. She thought he sometimes forgets that I'm grown up now; I'm eighteen, for Heaven's sake. That was another reason she couldn't wait to be married and living in their own home, they would have total freedom; they could do what they wanted to, when they wanted to and no one would tell them they couldn't. She couldn't wait; she hated living at home and being ordered around by her father.

Irene stepped out of the bath and dried herself off. She applied a little scented powder to her body and brushed out her hair. Mama came in to help her pin it into an upswept do with pins and clips. Irene looked in the mirror, once Mama was finished; she loved the style Mama had created. She had skilfully wrapped small strands of hair around her fingers and pinned them in place with bobby pins, she made Irene's straight hair look like it was curly. Mama did such a wonderful job; Irene especially loved how she used tiny golden clips with little flowers that looked the same as the flowers on her gown. Sometimes Mama really outdid herself. Irene thought something was missing though and asked, "Mama, would you mind if I used some of your rouge on my lips and cheeks, tonight?" Mama smiled and left the room, when she came back she handed Irene a little box tied up with a golden ribbon. She said, smiling, "I bought this for you." Irene opened the box and discovered Mama had bought her, her very own pot of rouge. Irene was thrilled; she hugged her and said excitedly, "Thank you, so much, for everything." She smiled as she thought; now I won't have to find a way to sneak hers. Once Irene had applied the rouge to her lips and cheeks and was satisfied with the result, she and Mama went to her bedroom; Donna was already waiting there for them. Mama helped Irene into the gown and zipped it up as Irene stepped into the shoes. Donna helped fasten the necklace Mama was lending her; it was a small pearl on a gold chain and had matching earrings. When Irene looked at herself in the full-length mirror in the hall, she couldn't believe how wonderful the gown looked with the shoes and jewellery. Mama brought the shawl and placed it around her shoulders, saying, "Look! It looks wonderful with the shawl, too!" Irene looked into Mama's eyes and said, "I really appreciate everything you've done for me, thank you." Mama replied, "Don't you worry about that." She smiled and added, "And stop saying thank you, I want you to have a wonderful time tonight." Donna was jumping up and down with her hands clasped together, saying, "You look amazing!" Irene smiled and as she started down the stairs, she noticed Father, he was starring up at her; he waited until she reached the bottom and to her astonishment said, "You look beautiful, I'm very proud of you, tonight." He added, "Now that you're a grown woman, I hope you won't be in an all fired rush to get married, I want you to enjoy the single life for a little while, because you won't have the same freedom once you're married." Irene swallowed and smiled at him thinking, if he only knew. She thought nervously, if he did, he'd hit me, probably a few times and send me to my room; he wouldn't allow me to go to the dance. She swallowed again but kept smiling, hoping he wouldn't notice how nervous she was becoming.

Roland was almost finished getting ready, he'd bathed and shaved and so far had his shirt and pants on. He was just tying his tie, when Melissa banged on his door, asking, "Aren't you ready yet?" He laughed and told her, "Come on in." She was so excited for him, she was still wearing the dress he'd bought her and said, when she saw him looking at it, "It's too pretty to take off just yet." He just smiled at her, he was glad she liked the dress so much. She helped him with his tie and the cufflinks on his shirt, she even put his good shoes next to the bed so he could step into them. When Roland finally put on the jacket, Melissa jumped up and down clapping; she said, "You're more handsome than the movie stars I see at the theatre." He looked down at her and kissed her cheek. He said, "You, my dear, are not exactly impartial in your opinion," but he laughed, he loved being her idle. Roland headed out of his room to the full-length mirror in Mom and Dad's room to make sure he looked okay. Once he saw he had everything in its proper place, he headed to the kitchen; he needed to collect the corsage he'd bought for Irene, earlier. Mom had carefully wrapped it in a tea towel and put it in the icebox to keep it fresh. Roland looked it over and was impressed; it looked just as fresh as it did when he'd purchased it from the flower shop earlier today. He said, "Thanks Mom" and kissed her cheek. On his way to the front door he passed by the living room where his Dad and Gramps were smoking cigars and talking, they both agreed, he looked dapper. He felt good; he kissed his Mom and Melissa again and shook hands with his Dad and Gramps. He headed out to the car, as he slid behind the wheel; he put the corsage on the front seat beside him. He took a deep breath and started the engine. He waved to his family, as he pulled away from the curb, thinking the next time you see me, I'll be married and Irene and I will be telling you all about our wedding.

Roland pulled up in front of Irene's house and took the corsage from the front seat. Donna was watching out the window and starting yelling, "He's here, he's here!" Irene just laughed. When she heard the doorbell ring, she felt a little twinge of excitement as she always did when she knew she was going to see Roland. Father answered the door, he wasn't quite rude, but he certainly wasn't warm and inviting either, he said gruffly, "Wait here, Irene'll be right out." Ronald stood on the porch feeling a little uncomfortable but didn't know what else to do. When Irene came to the door, he just about fell over, she looked so beautiful. Her shoulders were bare and the dress allowed just a little of her full breasts to show, as he took in the full length of her, he once again noticed she had the most shapely legs peaking out of the bottom of the dress. He caught himself gaping and immediately held himself in check; he wanted to appear the perfect gentleman tonight, of all nights. He stammered, "Hello, you look gorgeous." Irene had noticed the look on his face when he first saw her and was very pleased with herself; that was just the effect she'd hoped for. Roland remembered the corsage and held it out to her saying, "This is for you." She noticed it went with the gown perfectly, she looked back at her mother and Mama smiled. Irene knew then that Mama had helped Roland by telling him the exact colours that the corsage should be. Mama pinned it on her dress and they were ready to go. Roland walked her out to the car and opened the passenger door for her. He helped her in, went around, and got into the driver's side. They waved to her parents and Donna as they pulled away from the curb. When they'd gotten round the corner where Irene's family couldn't see them anymore, Roland stopped the car, pulled Irene into his arms, and kissed her. He asked, "Are you sure you're ready to marry me tomorrow?" She smiled tenderly and said, "Yes, I can't wait to finally be your wife," and they kissed again. As he drove away, he was smiling, that was exactly what he wanted to hear.

When they arrived at the dance, they were excited to see all their friends, they all talked at once and the girls complimented Irene on her gorgeous gown, one of the girls asked, "Is it the one in that fashion magazine, the one in the Dime store?" Irene was thrilled that she'd noticed, she said simply, "Yes, as a matter of fact it is." She noticed some envious looks from some of the other girls, who had overheard. She smiled up at Roland and as she did she spotted Brenda and Harold, they had just arrived, when she told Roland, they excused themselves from the group and rushed over to greet them. Irene and Brenda complimented each other on their gowns and shoes and talked about how excited they each were about tomorrow. Brenda asked Irene, quietly, "Are you really going to go through with it?" Irene assured her saying, "We most definitely are." When all the couples started to move into the hall, they decided they would too.

The hall was decorated beautifully and they were all a little awe struck by it. Most of them had never been anywhere fancy and felt out of place as they looked around shyly. There were tables and chairs encircling a huge dance floor decorated with silver streamers and flowers were everywhere. There was a band on the stage playing softly. They were instructed to wait until everyone was seated and then as they'd been told, the principal would announce that the dance was to begin and at that time he'd instruct the band to begin to play the dance tunes and only then could they actually begin dancing. The music they played while they waited was soft background type music.

Roland and Irene were seated at a table chatting with Brenda and Harold and several other classmates and their dates, when the principal announced the beginning of the dance he nodded

to the band to begin playing and turned back to all of them and
told them to have fun. The band started to play and couples
started moving out onto the dance floor. Roland took Irene's
hand and led her out onto the floor, they started dancing a slow
dance and it was all Roland could do to keep her at a respectable
distance. He wanted to pull her into his arms tightly and kiss
her. Irene was wishing the very same thing. Roland whispered,
"I love you," into her ear and told her, "I can hardly wait for
tonight." Irene blushed and told him shyly, "I love you too." They
were planning to have their honeymoon night tonight since they
couldn't afford two nights in the hotel room. They also knew
that their parents would worry too much if they disappeared for
two nights; one night was going to be bad enough. They hoped
their parents would simply think they'd partied a little too long,
as was the custom after graduation dances. They'd been told,
that they were adults now and not to drink too much or do
anything foolish. They weren't quite old enough to drink legally,
but their parents knew they probably would anyway.

Irene and Brenda thought the dance was spectacular, and
couldn't stop talking about it, the whole time they were changing
their clothes, in the janitor's closet; they had to whisper so they
wouldn't be caught. The girls had both brought plain skirts and
sweater sets consisting of a short-sleeved pullover sweater and
matching cardigan and bobby socks with saddle shoes. When
they finished changing, they looked at each and both drew
in a sharp breath and exclaimed at the same time, "We could
almost pass for twins; I didn't know you were going to wear that."
Brenda suddenly thought of the noise they must have made and
said, "Shush, someone might hear us." Wide eyed, Irene clapped
a hand over her mouth. They quieted down immediately and
packed their gowns into cloth bags to protect them. The two of
them were very excited about spending the night in the hotel.
Irene was going to be sharing a room with Roland, and of course,
she thought that was okay since they were getting married the

following day, but Brenda was planning to share a room with Harold and Irene was worried that someone would find out and poor Brenda's reputation would be tarnished. Brenda was head over heels in love with Harold though and had told Irene, "Don't worry," when Irene had mentioned it earlier. She said, "I think that Harold might feel the same as I do." Irene quietly asked Brenda, "But are you still sure you want to spend the night with him?" Brenda said, "Oh, stop worrying! Harold told me that if I didn't want to do it, that it would be okay with him." Brenda continued in a serious manner, "I really do want to go all the way though." She said with her face growing more serious, "Since we aren't children anymore we should know what it's like to sleep with a man and since I want to marry Harold one day, anyway, I think its okay." Irene wondered though, she herself would never have agreed to go all the way with Roland if they weren't getting married. Sure, they fooled around and teased each other, but she always stopped him before they went too far. Irene had to admit that she was looking forward to not having to stop him anymore, even though she was nervous about it.

Brenda and Irene opened the door of the janitor's closet and peaked out, all was clear; they hurried down the hall and ran out the side door. The boys were waiting at the car and as they stowed their gowns in the trunk, the boys rushed inside to change, they used the same janitor's closet since it was out of sight and easily accessible. They were quick though and as soon as they could see no one was roaming about they left the closet and sprinted down the hall and out the side door to the car as well, they stowed their good suits in the trunk with the girls' dresses and hopped in the car. The girls were talking animatedly about the wedding tomorrow.

Roland barely heard their conversation, he had other things on his mind, he was suddenly having second thoughts about telling Irene about the Draft Notice, he felt guilty keeping it from her. He struggled with the guilt feelings, he didn't want to lose her and he was afraid he might if he told her. He'd overheard her quite sometime ago; she had remarked to a group of her girlfriends that she wouldn't wait around for any man to come home from the war. She'd explained to her friends that she didn't like the stories she'd heard from her grandmother about women waiting for their men and some of them never making it home. She'd told them she thought that was so sad. Roland knew that was a while ago and hoped she would feel differently now. He thought I might have to take that chance, since I'm not sure I can handle the guilt keeping it from her. He pulled away from the curb and looked over at her, she'd been watching him, and she was smiling; she seemed so happy. As he drove towards Stratford, he thought I have to keep her smiling and happy as long as possible, September is a ways off, telling her can wait.

four

THE NIGHT BEFORE

The four of them finally reached the hotel and the girls checked in with the front desk and told the clerk that they had a room reserved; the boys did the same. Their rooms were on the third floor, at opposite ends of the hall. Once they got off the elevator, they said goodbye to each other, Irene and Brenda hugged each other and they agreed they would all meet for breakfast in the hotel restaurant tomorrow at ten. They each went to their own rooms, Roland and Irene to one and Brenda and Harold to the other.

When they reached their door, Roland unlocked it and put the bags inside, and then he turned to Irene, picked her up and carried her across the threshold. Irene was so surprised, she laughed at the awkward way Roland tried to negotiate the doorway while carrying her, when he finally placed her on her feet inside the room and closed the door they were both laughing. Roland pulled her to him and hugged her tight, the warm, soft feel of her body made him stop laughing and he leaned down to kiss her. He kissed her lips lightly and then abruptly stopped, he said, "Since we only have this night in the hotel, I want it to be special, I ordered a bottle of champagne to be sent up to our room." Irene smiled and said, "Why don't we get things ready for tomorrow while we wait for the champagne." Roland replied,

37

"That's a good idea." He looked at her intently for a moment and continued, "Then we can have the rest of the night to do other things." Irene blushed and they started hanging up the clothes for their wedding the next day. They were excited but nervous as well and talked non-stop as they hung and smoothed the garments making sure they would look just right for tomorrow. They arranged their shoes and got all their accessories ready, her jewellery and his cufflinks. They even got out the undergarments they were going to wear and placed them in a drawer in the bureau across from the bed. The room was small consisting of only a double bed, a bureau, two night tables, a desk and a small loveseat. They weren't too concerned with the furnishings though, they would only be here for tonight and they planned to make it as special as they possibly could.

Once everything was taken care of for tomorrow, Irene kissed Roland's cheek and went into the bathroom, on her way she said, "I want to freshen up, I won't be long." She was just stepping out of the tub when she heard a knock at the door. She heard Roland answer it and thought that it must be either Harold or Brenda. She wrapped herself in a towel and cracked open the bathroom door asking, "Who is it, Roland?" Roland strode over close to the bathroom to answer her and noticed she was shy, he said, "Don't worry, that was just the champagne I ordered." Irene laughed, nervously, and said, "I forgot about that, how did you do that anyway? We aren't really old enough to drink." He said, smiling, "They never asked me any questions, I ordered it when I reserved the room." Irene smiled at him; she'd always thought Roland could pass for older than he was; he had such a confident air about him, that no one ever questioned him or his actions. He was looking at her very intently and she couldn't help being caught up in his gaze, she noticed his dark eyes seemed to be getting darker and much more intense. Roland moved toward her and slowly pushed the door open, Irene stood to the side, clutching the towel. She forgot all her shyness as Roland took her by the shoulders and looked into her eyes, as he moved closer she could feel his breath in her hair and on her face, her whole body was tingling. Their mouths just seemed to find each other's and they kissed with a passion they had never dared before. He pulled her so close she didn't think she could breathe. All of a sudden, he swooped her up in his arms and took her to the bed; where he gently laid her down, never taking his eyes from hers. He started unbuttoning his shirt and she sat up to help him, but he kissed her and laid her back down, saying, "I just want to look at you." She lay there watching him undress; she'd never seen a naked man before, except in those pictures, the ones Brenda's father had hidden. She was shy but also amazed at how wonderful his body looked. He had a muscular chest, covered with black hair, broad shoulders and a slim waist and hips, but as he removed his shorts, Irene gasped he seemed so big, for the first time she started to worry. She didn't know much about sex, but she knew where that was supposed to go and she couldn't imagine how it was going to fit. Roland sensed the uneasiness in her and as he bent down to kiss her, he told her, "I won't hurt you." She seemed to relax a little and he kissed her deeply. Their tongues met and he seemed to fill her mouth with his, she could feel his hands starting to remove the towel and felt just the slightest twinge of embarrassment and then she felt his hand on her breast, as he moved his lips down her neck, she melted. Roland's mouth explored every inch of her. She felt herself grow hotter and limper as his lips and tongue found her, she groaned and felt her hips move upward, involuntarily as she exploded with pleasure, she had never experienced anything like this before. Roland stopped and slid on top of her, she thought his whole body seemed warm and hard both at the same time. She could feel him slowly entering her little by little, as he kissed her. He kept his mouth tightly over hers as he thrust into her. She tried to cry out, but he kept his mouth over hers, he knew the pain would only last a few seconds, he'd remembered to ask his doctor about it, the last time he'd been in to see him. She tried to move her hips downward into the bed to ease the pain. He kissed her fervently and pushed hard once more; she tore her mouth from his and cried out in pain. Roland lay still inside her until she began to relax. He found her mouth again, tenderly kissed her, and murmured, "It will be alright now," and when he started gently moving inside her again she felt unbelievable pleasure. They began moving together finding their own rhythm until they both exploded in pleasure. They lay in each other's arms for what seemed like ages, fully satisfied.

Roland got up and found the champagne and the two glasses that the bus boy had delivered to the room, while Irene went to the bathroom to find the nightie she'd packed. She felt comfortable naked while they were making love, but she didn't think she'd feel too comfortable just yet to sit and drink champagne that way. She freshened up and slipped on the nightie, it was very revealing; she knew Roland would love it. She removed the pins from her long dark hair and let it fall about her shoulders. She liked what she saw in the mirror. She opened the door and walked out of the bathroom, Roland was just pouring the champagne in the glasses. He turned around to face her when he'd finished, his eyes grew dark with passion again at the sight of her, she looked beautiful. He walked over to her, took her in his arms, and kissed her. He ran his hands through her soft, long hair, continued down over her body and under the nightie, and found her again. She could feel his excitement against her abdomen and felt herself grow weak again. She lifted her arms, at Roland's prompting and he pulled the nightie off over her head and once again he started kissing her everywhere working her into such a state she couldn't wait for him to enter her, this time. In all her excitement, she suddenly remembered the pictures she saw in Brenda's basement and wanted to try to give him the same amount of pleasure he gave her. She gently pushed him onto the bed and started kissing him. When he thought he couldn't take anymore without exploding, he turned her onto her back and moved on top of her, with one thrust he was inside her. They found their rhythm once more and again they exploded this time with even more pleasure than before. Irene was thrilled that it hadn't hurt at all that time.

They picked up their glasses of champagne and moved over to the love seat, this time she didn't care that she was naked, she felt comfortable with him now. They drank their champagne in happy silence, both thinking how perfectly suited they were to each other. Roland couldn't believe how wonderful she was in bed and Irene couldn't believe how wonderful he made her feel. She'd never experienced anything like it. She knew she was going to love being married to him.

When they started talking they realized how tired they were. They decided they should probably go to sleep, they knew they'd promised Brenda and Harold that they would meet them for breakfast in the morning. Roland took her glass from her, picked her up, and carried her to bed. He walked around to his side of the bed and as he lifted the covers to climb in he caught a glimpse of her naked body. His gaze travelled up to her face he noticed she was looking at him too, their eyes met and held as he got into bed and slid over to her side. As he kissed her, she held him tight and they felt the excitement rising once again. They made love once more and promptly fell asleep in each other's arms. They were so happy together. Irene had the sweetest dreams that night. She didn't think she'd ever been as happy as she felt with him right now.

Roland slept fitfully he kept dreaming that she was unhappy and crying and for some reason there was nothing he could do about it. He awoke in a sweat, fully aware of the fact that his dream might be coming true. He was so afraid to tell her about the Draft Notice, he really didn't want to do anything to cause her to be unhappy. He suddenly remembered he'd forgotten to give her the engagement ring. He quietly slipped out of bed being careful not to wake her. He fetched the ring from the pocket of his trousers and when he got back into bed, he slipped it, ever so gently onto her finger. He fell asleep again holding her close and listening to her soft, even breathing, he knew she would be ecstatic when she saw the ring in the morning.

five

THE WEDDING

Roland and Irene awoke to the sound of someone knocking
on the door. They were both so sound asleep it took
them a few seconds to realize that it even was someone
at the door. Roland jumped out of bed, pulled on his trousers
and went to see who it was. Harold had been just about to walk
away when Roland opened the door. Harold said with a smirk,
"Hey sleepyheads, it's a quarter past ten." He continued, "What's
taking you two so long?" He said, with a smile, "Brenda and
I have been waiting in the restaurant, we can't drink any more
coffee, are you two coming down?" He asked, "Is everything
okay?" Roland assured him that they were fine; he said, "We just
slept in, we stayed up too late last night." Harold tried to hide
his growing smile, Roland could tell he didn't believe they were
sleeping, but he had the good manners not to say so, especially
when he knew Irene might hear. Roland told him, "We'll be
down in a few minutes."

When he closed the door, Irene was already in the bathroom
brushing her teeth, all of a sudden, she noticed the ring on her
finger, and she let out an excited shriek. Roland started and then
suddenly remembered the ring he'd slipped on her finger while she
slept. She ran to him and threw her arms around his neck, saying,
"Thank you so much it's beautiful." He told her, "A beautiful ring

43

for a beautiful lady." Irene blushed and smiled up at him. She asked, "Who was at the door?" He said, "It was just Harold, he and Brenda are wondering when we're coming down for breakfast." She said, "I wonder if Harold and Brenda got along okay last night." Roland playfully told her, while kissing her neck, "They couldn't possibly be as good together as we are." Irene laughed and kissed him and that was enough to start them again. They made love once more, this time rather quickly and then laughed the whole time they were getting dressed; neither of them could believe how they didn't seem capable of keeping their hands off each other. They finally made it down to the restaurant.

When they sat down, Irene noticed that Harold and Brenda were smiling rather understanding smiles and she was a little embarrassed, but she knew Roland would never say anything, she trusted him completely. Brenda suddenly noticed the gorgeous ring on Irene's finger, and shrieked, "Oh my God, that's beautiful! Can I see it up close?" Irene obliged proudly. She told her, "Can you believe it, it's the one I showed him ages ago, at Danforth Jewellers. He actually remembered!" The girls stood up and hugged each other. Brenda told Roland, bowing playfully, "You have excellent taste, sir."

Once they'd eaten breakfast, Irene and Brenda decided, and the guys agreed, that they would use one of the rooms to get ready and the guys should use the other. That way they could help each other with their dresses, since they were sure the boys didn't know how to do them up properly. They also wanted to help each other with their hair. Irene wanted all of them to look perfect for the pictures they were going to have taken after the ceremony.

While the girls got ready, they discussed the previous evening. They were so excited the dance had gone well and were amazed they had all actually been able to sneak out of the dance without calling any attention to themselves. They marvelled at how they were able to change their clothes and meet at the car and no one was any the wiser. They also discussed their nights in their rooms. Irene said shyly, "Sex was fantastic way better than I ever expected." She told Brenda, "I can't believe I could possibly feel that way, after the initial pain was over, it felt wonderful." They both laughed about that, because Irene hadn't even believed that it would hurt. Irene asked Brenda, reluctantly, "Did you and Harold sleep together?" Brenda shyly admitted, "I got scared at the last minute." She went on to say, "Harold was wonderful, though. He held me when I cried and told me not to be silly, when I told him I was crying because I didn't want to disappoint him." She laughed and told Irene, "He laughed at me and then, very seriously he told me I meant far too much to him to let that bother him, and then he said, that whenever I was ready that would be just fine with him." Brenda confessed, "We got dressed again and slept side by side on the bed without doing anything except kissing and holding each other." Brenda said dreamily, "Irene, he was wonderful and after last night, I know for sure that I really do love him." Irene smiled and said, "I'm not surprised." When Brenda looked puzzled, she added, "I've watched you, for ages, you just sparkle whenever Harold's around, I even notice how your voice goes up a notch whenever you talk about him." Brenda laughed and said, "Oh my God, I hope no one else notices that, I wasn't even aware I was doing it." She was quiet for a second and then demanded, "Why didn't you tell me?" Irene smiled and told her, "I thought it was cute, and don't worry no one knows you as well as I do, so I'm sure no one else would even have noticed." Brenda gave Irene a hug and told her, "Enough fooling around or we'll never be ready."

They were finally dressed in their gowns and started to do each other's hair. Irene finished brushing out Brenda's and pinned it partially up and secured it in the back with a gold clip, it was an attractive style and when Brenda looked in the mirror she exclaimed, " I love it." Brenda started brushing Irene's into a gorgeous upswept do, she said, "Since you're the bride, I think you should wear it up in a sophisticated style." Irene, knowing Brenda had excellent taste and was quite skilled, as well as knowledgeable regarding the latest hairdos, answered, "I trust you completely." As Brenda worked she asked, "Does it ever bother you that since Roland is American he could be drafted, soon?" Irene shook her head in answer and Brenda told her, frowning "Hey don't do that, I can't put the pins in with you moving your head all over the place, just a simple, yes or no will suffice." Before Irene could say anything, she continued, "I read about young men being drafted as soon as they finished high school, in the States." Irene shrugged and said, "I trust Roland and he would have told me if that were even a possibility." She added, "Roland told me a few months ago that since his eighteenth birthday had come and gone in November, he was sure he didn't have to worry about it. He said, he thought, maybe it was because he was living in Canada." Irene didn't know much about being drafted anyway, and since she didn't think it would ever be important to her, she never gave it much thought after that. She preferred to think about their future together and how happy she was going to be with him. She knew they were going to be wealthy one day, since Roland was going to be a doctor. She couldn't wait to be wealthy.

Brenda was watching Irene; she'd become quiet suddenly and seemed to be in another world. When Brenda said, "There, all finished!" It made Irene jump. They both laughed, Brenda told her, "It's your wedding day you have every right to daydream." Irene looked in the mirror at the two of them, Brenda was standing right behind her, and they looked wonderful. Irene turned and kissed Brenda on the cheek and hugged her. She said thank you to her so many times for all she had done today and for helping with all the planning and for keeping the wedding a secret. She told Brenda, "You're the best, best friend anyone could ever wish for." Brenda blushed and hugged and kissed her back. She told Irene, "I feel exactly the same way about you." The two girls promised each other, they would always remain best friends, no matter what happened in their lives.   They were just about to leave the room to meet the boys when Brenda suddenly said, "Wait a minute, do you have something borrowed, something new and something blue?" Irene laughed and told her, "I'm way ahead of you, I am wearing my mother's shoes and necklace, that covers the borrowed and something new is a little clip in my hair that I didn't wear last night and the something blue is my underwear, they have a little blue flower on the side." The girls laughed and Irene said, "Well, I couldn't think of anything else to wear that was blue because if the blue showed it wouldn't match my dress." They laughed harder; they only stopped when they heard a knock on the door. Harold and Roland were in the hall, when the girls opened the door; they told them, "We could hear you laughing from down the hall," and asked, "What's so funny, anyways?" That made the girls laugh even more, they didn't want to tell them about the blue flower on the panties. Therefore, they just told them, they were laughing about old wives tales and superstitions about weddings. The boys rolled their eyes and Roland said jokingly, "I don't want to hear about any of those, some of those superstitions make me think too much and I don't want anything to ruin this day." He winked and they all laughed again shaking their heads as they left for the church.

They were standing by the car, just about to climb in, when Roland handed Irene a beautiful bouquet of roses in the exact shades of pinks as the roses on her gown. Irene was so thrilled that she jumped up and down, she couldn't stop herself, she was so totally and pleasantly surprised, she hadn't expected to be carrying a bouquet. Roland placed his hands around her waist to calm her down. She looked up at him and told him, "You're just the most perfect husband," she added laughing, "To be, I mean". He whispered back, "And you will be the perfect wife." He was happy that Irene was pleased with the bouquet; he'd tried so hard to pick out the colours based on what he remembered were on the dress.

He and Harold had run down the street to the florist as soon as the girls had gone to their room to get ready this morning. Roland had ordered the bouquets a couple of weeks ago, but at the time, he hadn't known the colours so the florist told him he could choose them once he was here in town. He said he would order roses in several different colours just to be sure. Roland chose the colours and he and Harold waited anxiously for the florist to make the bouquets. They dashed back with the finished bouquets, which they deposited into the car and then hurried back into the hotel to get dressed. They'd had a small nose gay bouquet made for Brenda to carry it was made of white daisies with yellow centres to match her yellow dress; it had been easy to pick out the flowers for her bouquet. Brenda thought it was just perfect. They even remembered to pick out flowers for the boutonnières they were going to wear. The ones from last night were pretty messy now.

The little church was so small; it was a tiny white building with a black steeple and cross on top. There were only two small steps, before a set of beautiful polished solid wood embossed double doors that had been painted a glossy black to match the black steeple. Irene was thinking as they approached, these steps will be a beautiful place for photographs after the ceremony. They entered the church; they were about fifteen minutes early. The priest walked down the isle, to greet them. He asked for the marriage license, which Roland gave him and he reminded Roland to make sure their rings were with the best man and the maid of honour, so they could hold them until it was time for him to bless them, before they placed them on each other's fingers once they'd exchanged vows. Brenda asked, nervously, "How will we know when it's time to give them to you." The priest smiled and told her, "Don't worry, I'll ask them for them." Brenda looked slightly embarrassed by the simple answer. She was worried about making things awkward and spoiling Irene's wedding; she wanted it to be as perfect as it could be. The priest sensed Brenda's feelings and said, "Why don't all of you take the next few minutes and try to calm down, I can see that you're nervous," he added, "Everything will be just fine." He winked as he turned and walked back up the isle. He had to get things ready for the Wedding Mass.

The priest had been right the ceremony was easy to follow and was over almost before they knew it. They all seemed to be in a daze as they walked down the isle afterwards. Irene and Roland were just beaming, they were so happy. Harold and Brenda were proudly walking behind them. There were a few people who had come to church for the mass, they were sitting in the back pews and they smiled as they watched them walk by looking so happy.

When they opened the doors to walk out a photographer was already there and he began snapping pictures. He had them pose in front of the church; he took one of Roland and Irene kissing. He also took a picture of just Irene and Brenda and one of Roland and Harold. He said, "Most people want those in their albums." When he finished he told them, "Come back and see me in about a week and I'll have these ready, for you to look at. You can choose which ones you want and I'll put them in an album or I can frame them if you want, that's up to you."

They went back to the car and once inside, Roland and Irene began to relax. They looked at one another and Roland said, "Well Mrs. Petersen, should we go back to the hotel and change into our traveling clothes and go home?" Irene was smiling from ear to ear at the sound of Mrs. Petersen. She couldn't believe she actually was. Harold and Brenda were watching from the back seat exchanging smiles. Harold hoped that they would be next.

When they arrived at the hotel, they quickly got out of their clothes and as Irene was just getting ready to pull on her skirt Roland snuck up behind her and turned her around, he pulled her into his arms. He kissed her hard and passionately and she could feel his arousal. He undid her bra and slipped it off and laid her gently on the bed as he started to remove her panties he noticed the little blue flower and smiled as he slipped them over her hips, he followed with his mouth kissing her abdomen. He continued delivering little kisses, driving her mad as he slipped the thin material off completely with one hand and opened her legs with the other. His lips caressed her and she reached for him, she wanted him now. Roland's kisses were now moving up her body until he reached her breasts, he took each nipple in his mouth one at a time and coaxed it until it was hard and erect while his fingers continued to stroke her. Irene thought she would go mad with longing. He moved his lips up along her neck and then up to her lips as he kissed her mouth he thrust into her. The two of them easily found their rhythm and before long, exploded together in pleasure. They lay in each other's arms afterward and suddenly Roland noticed the time, it was fifteen minutes to three and checkout time was three o'clock. He and Irene dressed in a hurry and joked about not looking at each other so they wouldn't start again.

They packed up their things and raced to the front desk. Roland couldn't afford to pay for late checkout fees; he needed to be sure that he'd have enough money left for groceries. Of course, he still had the money he always kept reserved in the extra pocket of his wallet. He called that his "just in case" money, he never used it. It was only for real emergencies. He paid the bill and hand in hand, they walked out to the car. Harold and Brenda were already standing on the sidewalk, waiting for them. Harold had paid for his own room. Roland told him, "I was going to pay for your room; I fully intended to pay for both rooms, since I was the one getting married." Harold assured him, "It's okay; I wanted to pay for it." He told Roland, quietly, "It's the only wedding gift I can afford to give you." Roland smiled, squeezed his shoulder and said, "Thanks, I appreciate it, but just your being here was a gift in itself." Roland was thinking as he climbed into the car, that'll give us a little extra cash, just in case we need it.

six

GOING HOME

Irene and Roland looked at each other with dread; they were sitting in the living room of their own apartment, over the butcher's shop. They had just dropped Harold and Brenda off at their own houses and gone straight home. They needed time to figure out what they were going to say to their parents and his Grandfather, when they returned the car. Roland broke the silence with, "Funny how we were so caught up in the excitement, ourselves, we didn't give so much as a thought to how we would tell our families, or to how they would react to the news." Irene nodded in agreement. They sat for a while longer and finally decided that they couldn't possibly prepare since they had no idea what to expect. They hoped their parents would be happy for them, but Irene doubted it would happen that way, at least not with her family, maybe someday, but she didn't think they'd be too happy about it right now.

Driving to Irene's house they checked the time, Irene's father would have just arrived home from work and her mother would be preparing supper. They decided to just tell them as quickly as possible and get it over with; they discussed it and thought it would be better that way instead of beating around the bush. They would tackle the chore of telling Roland's parents next, Roland thought it would be much easier telling his family. They were so much more forgiving than Irene's were. He didn't want to say that to her though and risk hurting her feelings.

Roland stole glances at Irene sitting beside him in the car, as he drove. He was trying to picture her reaction once he told her he was drafted and that he'd known for a week before the wedding. He hoped she would understand why he waited to tell her. No matter what though, two years of service was a long time. He wished he didn't have to go. He reminded himself he needed to put that out of his mind for now and concentrate on the task at hand and he knew it was going to be no small task.

They arrived at Irene's house and parked at the curb directly in front of the house. Irene saw Donna standing at the front window watching the car and smiled when Donna finally noticed that she was in the car; within seconds, she came flying out the front door to greet her. Donna hugged Irene and whispered in her ear, "You're in big trouble for not coming home last night, please be careful." She squeezed Irene's hand and said, looking frightened, "Father was really angry this morning when he left for work." Irene stiffened and stood a little straighter. Roland heard what Donna had said and went around the car and took Irene's hand in his, he whispered, "Don't worry I'm here," and squeezed it slightly. Irene glanced up at him and together they reluctantly followed Donna into the house.

Mama was in the kitchen and as soon as she saw Irene she wiped her hands on her apron and hurried out to see her, it was then that she noticed Roland. She stopped, surprised by the sight of the two of them holding hands and looking very nervous, she said nothing but her eyes portrayed the fear she felt as Father came out of the kitchen. He'd been washing up after work and as he came into view he said, "You'd better have a damn good excuse for worrying your mother and me like this." He suddenly stopped speaking when he noticed Roland his gaze drifted to their tightly clasped hands. He asked them, suspiciously, "What do you two have to say for yourselves?" Roland spoke up; he said,

"Mr. & Mrs. Giles, Irene and I would like to talk to you." Irene's father held out his hand, pointing the way, and nodded toward the living room, his eyes portraying his simmering temper; he said, sharply, "Sit down." Irene and Roland sat close together on the couch, Father sat in his favourite chair and Mama stood behind it. Father said, "If you want to say something, just say it and get it over with." Roland took a deep breath and blurted out, "Irene and I were married today." Both Father and Mama looked stunned and all of a sudden, Mama started to cry. Irene looked up when she heard her mother's soft sobs, she was so nervous she'd been looking at the floor the whole time. Father told her, with a mean glance, "Be quiet and stop your blubbering," then he yelled, "Get to the kitchen, that's where you belong if you can't stop crying."

Roland looked shocked, he glanced at Irene and then back at her father realizing that this was normal in their house and this was what she'd grown up with, he was appalled. Irene's father got up and paced around as if he wasn't sure of what to say. Irene held Roland's hand a little tighter and Roland put a protective arm around her shoulders as they waited for him to say something. Finally, he said, "I wish you would have told me a little sooner." He asked gruffly, "Why were you in such an all fired rush anyways?" His eyes narrowed to slits and he asked, "Is there something else you want to tell me?" Roland was the first to speak. He said, displaying a confidence he didn't entirely feel, "I love Irene and she loves me and we didn't want to wait to start our lives together." Father looked at Irene and cocking his head in Roland's direction, asked her sternly, "Is that how you feel?" Irene couldn't look at him; she kept her head down, in fear and muttered, "Yes." Just then, Mama came back in the room, she looked at Father and waited, he nodded his approval, and said, "I'm very happy for you both." And added, "However, I'm a little disappointed I would have liked to have seen your wedding, you're my eldest daughter, it would have been nice to celebrate with you as a family." She asked, "Why didn't you tell us?" Irene answered, "We didn't want anyone to stop us, but we also didn't want to hurt anyone we just want to be together." Mama smiled then, she could see the love between the two of them. She said, with a smile surfacing on her lips, "I wish you a long and happy life together." Father interrupted and asked with a scowl on his face, "Just where are you two planning to live?" Roland thought, thank God not with you, but told him, "I rented an apartment above the butcher's shop on the same street as my parents' house." Father only shook his head, then said, in a mean voice, "I see you two have been planning this for some time, you seem to have everything sorted out." However, determined to find fault in some other way, he looked at them tauntingly and asked Roland, "Just how do you intend to support my daughter?" Roland replied, "My job at the oil company is full time for the summer and we'll save as much as we can this summer." He added, exuding a newfound confidence, "I have a scholarship to pay for school." Father already knew he planned to become a doctor. Mama interrupted and asked, "Will you stay for supper? There's plenty for everyone." Roland replied, "We'd love to, but we still have to tell my parents." Mama nodded and told them, "We understand."

Donna was peering around the corner in the hall. When Irene noticed her, she went to her and hugged her. Donna said, "I overheard the news, I'm going to miss sharing a room with you." She started to cry and Irene consoled her by telling her, "We're going to be living within walking distance and you can walk down and visit anytime." Jake just barked, "Congratulations," gave Irene a quick hug, shook hands with Roland and went out the door. He had to go to work, "I'm on the late shift," he said as he left.

When they got back in the car, they breathed a sigh of relief, looked at each other, and laughed even though there was nothing funny about the confrontation they had just been through. It seemed it was better to laugh than cry. Irene asked, "How do you think your parents will take the news?" Roland assured her, "They'll love you and they'll be just fine with it."

When they pulled up in front of his house, his Dad was sitting on the porch and they noticed Gramps was with him. They both stood up as they pulled up to the curb. The two of them started down the front steps and stopped abruptly when they saw Irene getting out of the car. Gramps just stood there looking at the two of them. Roland's Dad turned and flew back up the steps. He poked his head in the front door, and hollered excitedly, "Roland's home." His Mom came barrelling out of the house and was down the steps in a flash, but she stopped as soon as she noticed Irene. Roland reached for Irene's hand, and that's when his Mom noticed the glint of the wedding band on his finger, she quickly looked at Irene's left hand, which was partially hidden behind her skirt and noticed what looked like an engagement ring and a wedding band as well sparkling on her finger. She looked back and forth between the two of them and quietly said, "Congratulations," and tried hard to hide her smile.

Gramps and Roland's Dad looked at each other and then at his Mom. Gramps asked puzzled, "What did we miss?" His Mom laughed and said, "You two can't see past the nose on your face." She told them, nodding in Irene and Roland's direction, "I believe these two have an announcement to make," and smiled at the two of them. Roland looked at Irene and said, happily, "Yes we do." He continued, "We want to tell you that we got married this afternoon." Roland's Mom reached out to Irene and pulled her into a warm embrace, she kissed her cheek and said, "Welcome to the family." His Dad gave Irene a hug too and welcomed her to the family as well. Gramps took his turn; he said, "It'll be good to have another woman in the family, especially one so pretty." Irene blushed she'd never felt so happy and so welcome. Roland looked at her and smiled; he leaned down and whispered in her ear, "I told you they'd love you." As they went up the steps and into the house, Roland's Mom took Irene's arm and told her, "Please call us Mom and Dad now," and she smiled the warmest smile Irene had ever seen.

When they got into the house, Mom had dinner ready and they sat down at the table. Mom hurried to set another place beside Roland's usual spot for Irene; she'd already had a place set for Roland, just in case he made it home in time for dinner. She'd thought he might be hungry when he finally finished celebrating his Graduation. She never dreamed he would be late because he was at his own wedding. Dad had been rummaging through the cupboard and finally found what he'd been looking for; he turned to show them a bottle of wine. He usually kept one for special occasions. He found the glasses and started pouring. He said, smiling, "We're going to drink to the Bride and Groom! The new Mr. & Mrs. Petersen."

Melissa came bounding into the kitchen talking a mile a minute about something she and her friends were doing, but stopped before she finished as she looked from Roland to Irene and then at her parents and Gramps. She blurted out, "What's going on?" Mom laughed and told her, "Sit down and Roland will tell you." When she sat down, Roland told her, smiling, "Irene and I were married today." Melissa looked at Irene and then back at Roland. She saw the smug look that crossed Irene's face just before she turned it into a broad smile and said, "Well, now I have another little sister." Melissa felt like screaming, she didn't want to be her little sister, she didn't trust her, she didn't even like her. She thought Irene was the most selfish person she'd ever met, funny, she thought, most people didn't seem to figure that out. When she'd told Mom how she felt about her, Mom had only told her that she had to try to get to know Irene better and that she must be a nice person, after all Roland had fallen head over heels in love with her. She knew that Irene had fooled everyone, but she was determined not to be fooled, herself no matter what. She decided to watch her closely, not that it would do any good now, Roland had already married the witch. Melissa caught herself. She didn't want her thoughts to show too much on her face. Mom always said she was transparent and had explained to her that it meant she could read her thoughts, by her facial expressions. She noticed Roland was looking at her strangely, so she pouted and said, "Don't look at me like that! How did you expect me to take the news? I wasn't even invited to my only brother's wedding!" Mom interrupted and told her, "Calm down, Melissa." She explained, "Roland and Irene decided to get married by themselves, without the fanfare of a big wedding and we'll just have to accept it." She added, "Sometimes it's better to start out a marriage without the added expense that a large wedding can entail."

During the meal, they talked about their plans for the future. Irene told everyone, now that she had graduated; she wanted to become a legal secretary. She was an excellent typist and had gotten very good grades in shorthand as well. She felt she was more than qualified for such a position. She even said that she planned to stay working, so she could help Roland get through Medical school. Everyone was very impressed with her, except Melissa, she was trying her best not to make faces at her.

Roland talked about his position at the Oil Company and how they'd given him a raise in pay and increased his hours for the summer; he would now be working full time. He said, "I plan to save as much as I can so that going to school won't be so much of a financial hardship for us." He really wanted to be a doctor; he even thought he might like to specialize. He wanted to deliver babies, and he told everyone, "I can't think of a happier occasion than delivering babies and I would love to be a part of making so many families happy." He loved children and wanted to have lots of them; he told everyone, "I've even toyed with the idea of having nine kids, so I could have my own baseball team." Irene went white. Roland looked at her and laughed and so did everyone else. While everyone was laughing and talking, Roland thought to himself, Irene and I have never actually discussed how many children we'd like to have, he was getting an uneasy feeling. He was beginning to wonder if maybe they should've talked about it. He knew Irene had mentioned having a baby later after they were established; Roland wasn't sure just what that meant. Oh well, he thought, dismissing the uneasiness, he was just being silly, of course Irene wanted to have more that one child. He decided that he wouldn't worry about it; he had plenty of other things to worry about right now anyway. His mind began to wander, that Draft Notice was really getting to him. He'd always had something else to occupy his mind before, but now that the wedding was over and Graduation was over as well, he knew he'd be thinking about it all the time now. He wondered how he would tell everyone, especially Irene. He was dreading it. He thought about just saying it aloud right now and getting it over with, but he knew he owed Irene more than that. She was his wife now and he should tell her first, in the privacy of their own home. Then he'd deal with the rest of the family, hers and his own after.

seven

HOME

They walked the short distance to their new home, hand in hand. Irene was quiet, she was thinking of the distinct differences between her family and his. His was so much fun, even at the dinner table they were able to laugh and be themselves. They could say almost anything to each other. She thought of her own family they were so quiet at the table, everyone was so afraid of upsetting Father that they said very little. They usually only spoke when they were spoken to most of the time. It was so nice to be able to be yourself; she envied Roland a little for having such a wonderful family. She hoped that they could be like them if they had a family. She'd do her best to make sure of it.

Suddenly, she thought of the conversation at dinner, when Roland had said he wanted nine children, she wasn't sure if he'd been serious or not. She decided to be brave and just ask him, so without looking at him, she casually asked, "Hey were you serious about wanting lots of kids?" Roland explained, "I love children, I'd like to have as many as we can. What about you?" She thought about it and said, only, "Yeah, I love them too," and smiled up at him, thinking I'm going have to find out what I can do to prevent having any though, until I'm good and ready, and I'm not sure if I ever will be. It wasn't that she didn't like kids;

she did, but someone else's. Then she could visit them and when she got tired of them, she could just go home to peace and quiet. Children always seemed to be so noisy and busy. She'd have to make sure that he never knew how she really felt and that shouldn't be too much of a problem, she thought. She'd need to think about how she would approach her doctor to get the information she needed on how to prevent becoming pregnant, without raising any suspicions. Just then, Roland asked her, "What have you been thinking about?" He had been watching her and said, "You've been so quiet for the last little while." She told him, "It's been such an exciting day; I was only trying to digest everything." He laughed and said, "I don't think we'll see another day quite like this one again." He pulled her close and kissed the top of her head. Irene felt so loved by him and with the love that she felt for him she thought she just might burst.

They finally reached their new apartment and climbed the steps to the front door. Roland opened it, scooped her up in his arms, and carried her into the apartment. He kicked the door shut and took her straight into the bedroom. As he laid her on the bed, he started unbuttoning her blouse. She reached out and unbuttoned his shirt and as she started to undo the buckle on his belt, she slid her hand down and was surprised to find him aroused already. She heard him groan at her touch. He practically tore off the rest of her clothes and his too. He lay on top of her and he couldn't help himself, he just had to have her right now. He knew she was as eager as he was and before long they cried out in ecstasy together.

Time passed quickly over the next few weeks. They were such a happy couple; they made love every night and talked for hours about anything and everything. They had made love in every room of the apartment, even the kitchen. They sometimes didn't get through dinner without undressing each other and making love right there on the spot. They laughed about it afterward. Their life together seemed like a, happily ever after, fairy tale they enjoyed every single minute they were together.

Roland went off to work every day, he loved his job, he worked in the lab and found it so interesting, he thought just maybe, he might like to become a Chemical Engineer, but since he wasn't sure yet, he decided to keep it to himself.

Irene had found a job at a legal firm, just two blocks from their apartment. She was so excited, she talked non-stop about it, she loved her new job. Roland watched her as she told him all about it and was glad she was happy. He wanted her to have something to do, that she truly enjoyed, while she waited for him to return from the Services. He would have done anything not to destroy that happiness, but he knew that time was passing quickly and he had to tell her about his Draft Notice. He had to report for duty in exactly six weeks and two days. He'd already informed his boss and was told they'd have a job for him when he returned. He decided that he would tell Irene tomorrow night after dinner.

Irene was getting dinner ready the next evening thinking that their life together couldn't possibly be more perfect. She started thinking about Roland going to school, she thought I can't wait for him to become a doctor, and then maybe I could have someone help with the housework. She was making imaginary plans for their future, she knew they were going to have a large home and entertain every week since Roland loved to have company over; he was such a "people" person. She was also dreaming of all the lovely things she could buy for her house. Then she thought we might like to travel as well, whenever Roland was able to take time away from his practise, of course. She also wondered about all the ladies' shops she'd read about in the magazines, she would finally be able to afford to shop in some of them. She loved dreaming about her life as the respected wife of Dr. Roland Petersen. She smiled at the thought of being introduced to people as Dr. and Mrs. Petersen. Irene was so caught up in her daydream she never heard the front door. When Roland came up behind her with a huge bouquet of flowers and kissed her neck, she jumped, dropping the potato she was peeling in the sink, it landed in the bowl of water she was using to keep the peeled potatoes from turning brown. Water splashed up soaking her and Roland too. She let out a scream and Roland wrapped his arms around her in an effort to soothe her, telling her, "Its okay its okay, it's just me, I didn't mean to scare you." Irene's heart was beating a mile a minute, but they both broke out in peels of laughter, when they realized what had happened, she told him, "I guess I was daydreaming and didn't hear you come in." She looked at the flowers and playfully asked, "What's the occasion" then frowned and kidded him with, "Or did you do something you shouldn't have?" He pretended to be hurt, "Can't I bring my best girl flowers, just because I love her?" She smiled up at him and said, "Thank you, they're lovely." She suddenly remembered the "best girl" part, she pretended to pout and said, "I hope I'm your only girl." She took the bouquet from him and couldn't help but notice, the flowers smelled wonderful, there were lilies, carnations, roses, daisies, stock and baby's breath encircled with mixed greens all tied up with a delicate pink bow. She didn't know too much about flowers, but she had never seen such a beautiful bouquet and she told him so. Roland smiled looking very pleased with himself. She thought he was just about the most handsome man she had ever seen. She reached up and brought his head down so she could reach to kiss him. As she kissed him he said, "That could be dangerous," she laughed; he scooped her up and headed for the bedroom as the beautiful bouquet landed in the sink with the potatoes.

When the two of them returned to the kitchen, Irene noticed the flowers had at least landed in the water so they were still fresh. She took a vase down from the shelf, filled it with warm water and untied the ribbon that held the bouquet together; she placed the flowers in the vase and rearranged them a little. They were absolutely gorgeous. She tied the pretty ribbon around the vase and set them on the table inhaling their lovely aroma, then went back to making supper. Roland watched her with a proud smile on his face. Every time he looked at her he nearly burst with pride, he thought he was so lucky to have her for his wife. He sobered thinking of how he dreaded having to tell her anything that would upset her. She was just so beautiful when she smiled. He decided they would have a nice dinner, and then after they cleaned up the dishes, he would sit her down in the living room and tell her about the Draft Notice. He said a silent prayer asking that she would understand and not be too upset with him.

Roland helped with the dinner and the clean up afterward, he always did. He loved that time together. They always talked about their day, laughed, and had a good time while they tidied. He thought all men should help with things around the house; it gave couples more time to be together and made for a happier home. His own Dad helped his Mom whenever he could and Roland could see just how happy they were. He thought of how Irene's Father never lifted a finger to help her mother around the house and if he did lift anything, it seemed it was only his fist. Roland detested men who hit their wives he thought they were cowards. No woman deserved to be hit, he thought couples should be able settle their differences by talking to each other. He was so glad his parents had taught him, by example, how to be a good husband. Roland couldn't remember a time when he saw his parents angry at each other for long, they always stopped whatever they were doing, went to their room, and discussed the problem. Sometimes they shouted at each other but when they finally came out of their room, they had settled whatever the problem was. Roland had discussed this with Irene and she was flabbergasted that any marriage worked that way. She had told him how things were with her parents and how she'd always thought that was just the way couples lived, until she grew up, and then she admitted to him that she started to resent her father for what he did to them. Roland felt sorry for her and for her mother. Irene had cried when she told him how her father was always hitting her mother and saying mean things to her.

They sat down in the living room on the couch; it was a lovely shade of brown with cushions of green, yellow, orange and brown on a cream background, tucked into the corners. Irene thought they helped add some colour to the room; she hated drab surroundings and tried her best to brighten things up with coloured accessories and cushions. She bought a huge plate that contained the same colours as the cushions, for the centre of the coffee table and they'd found a pole lamp with the cream and brown colours on the shades. They loved it, they didn't have any other lamps in the living room and they liked the fact that they could turn each of the three lights on it to different angles and light up the room quite nicely. It worked well when they had company and needed a bit more light. Their company consisted mostly of Brenda and Harold, who were now engaged, and their parents. Sometimes Melissa or Donna came over for dinner and a couple of times both girls even came over at the same time. Irene and Roland were pleased at how well they were getting along. They had even started getting together to go to movies or knit or just talk; they seemed to genuinely enjoy each other's company. The girls said they had a lot in common with each other. It was nice to have their families get along.

Their parents were so different, yet on the one occasion they'd invited them to dinner at the same time, they had gotten along pretty well. Irene's father was not as friendly as Irene thought he should have been, but she couldn't do much to change him and he at least hadn't offended anyone, as he had a nasty habit of doing. Their mothers got along famously; they'd laughed and talked as they helped clean up. Irene and Roland thought that was especially nice. They weren't planning to have them both at the same time too often but it was nice to know they could if they wished. Their place was a little small for too many people at once. Their kitchen table seated six but it was rather cramped, it was really only meant for four, and even that was tight, but they'd found two extra chairs and painted them to match the others for those times when they just might need them. The little living room only had a couch, so they had to bring in the kitchen chairs whenever they had company. They had two bedrooms but one was really tiny and they hadn't furnished it yet; they used it to store the two extra kitchen chairs and other miscellaneous items. Their own bedroom wasn't large either, it consisted of a double bed and dresser, there wasn't much room for anything else. They used TV tables as night tables, they were small enough to fit beside the bed, but still were able to hold a lamp and an alarm clock. They would bring them out into the living room to serve as side tables for drinks and snacks when they did have company. The bathroom was small; the bathtub was right next to the sink, which made it hard to get in and out of without bumping into the sink. They joked that if they got too fat, they would never be able to have a bath. Even with all its faults, they thought the place was perfect for them, especially right now. They could certainly make do with it until they could afford something better.

Roland looked at Irene; she was sitting beside him smoothing her skirt, he thought she seemed anxious. She sensed he was looking at her and turned and looked up at him. She smiled but reluctantly asked him, "What's the matter?" He was surprised and said, "What makes you think something is the matter?" She looked at him and turned her head to the side, the way he loved and told him, "Your face seems to be tight and it only ever looks like that if something is bothering you." He was astonished; he didn't think she noticed little things like that. He took a deep breath and told her, "I need to tell you something and yes, you're right, it has been bothering me for sometime now." He said, "What I have to tell you is very serious and not good news." She looked panicked, but said nothing; she waited for him to continue. He said, "I have put off telling you because I wanted you to be as happy as you have been for as long as possible." Irene's face seemed to change Roland saw fear in her eyes. He reached out to take her in his arms but she pulled back and pleaded with him, "Please, Roland just tell me, what's wrong." He swallowed hard and told her, "I've been Drafted; I have to report for duty Thursday, September 6th." Irene looked as if she would faint. Roland caught her up in his arms and stroked her hair as she started to cry, the crying turned into huge sobs. He held her tighter, whispering, "I wish I didn't have to go, I just want to stay with you and never leave your side." It took Irene quite a while before she could speak. She asked him, "What are we going to do?" Roland assured her, "With the money I've saved and your job you'll be able to stay here in the apartment if you want to." He said, "If you want I could arrange for our furniture to be stored at a friends and you could move back with your parents, if you would feel better there." Irene looked at him in horror and screeched, "Never! I never want to live there again!" He said, "Okay, calm down, it was just a suggestion, I only want you to be happy." Then he added, "Would you like to live with my parents? You could have my old room, it's empty and Mom would love to have you." Irene thought about this momentarily, but told him, "I think that's the least of our problems right now." She hugged him and asked, "Do you have to be gone for two whole years?" He replied, "I'm afraid so, that's what the Draft Notice says." She asked, suddenly. "Could I see it?" Roland felt as if a huge weight had landed squarely on his shoulders, he dreaded showing her the notice, he knew she'd see the date on it and she'd know that he had known before the wedding. He decided he needed to be honest with her; she had a right to know. He gently moved her arms from around his neck and said, "I'll go and get it." Irene read the Notice, aloud and after she finished she said, "I guess I was hoping it was all a mistake, but there is no getting around this, is there?" Then before Roland could say a single thing in reply, he watched as her facial expression changed from one of despair to anger. She looked at him with pure rage in her eyes. She screamed at him, "You've known about this for weeks now, why didn't you tell me?" Roland looked at the floor his eyes filling with tears; he knew she was angry and hurt at the same time. He tried his best to explain, "I love you and I didn't want to ruin our Graduation or our Wedding." He didn't tell her he had been afraid of losing her. She wept all over again murmuring, "I thought we had no secrets between us, this hurts!" She said, "It feels sort of like," she seemed to be searching for the right words, "Not being trusted." She went on, "I love you and I want to know everything about you especially things like this. I could have been there to help you deal with it, but I feel like I didn't matter to you, that you didn't need my comfort or didn't think I could provide any. I don't like feeling like this." She breathed deeply and continued, "I know you love me, but I need you to tell me things and not hold anything back, in case you haven't noticed, I'm a big girl now." She hung her head in defeat, tears running down her cheeks, and whispered, "I'll miss you terribly when you're gone. I'll pray for you every day and I'll look forward to the day you finally come home."

Roland's heart soared, he could not have been more relieved then when he heard her utter those words. He knew he had done wrong by not telling her sooner and seeing the raw pain in her eyes when she looked at him felt like a knife was being jabbed into his heart.

Each time they spoke about his leaving for the Services, over the next few days, she seemed to be coming to terms with it and understanding a little bit better, just why he had waited to tell her. She now fully understood how much he loved her and wanted to protect her from anything that would hurt her. He felt a strange sort of comfort and relief as well, just knowing that.

Over the next few weeks, she didn't cry quite as often and they seemed to be almost normal in their day-to-day routines.

They still made love everyday, talked non-stop about anything and everything, and tried their best to keep each other smiling and laughing. They knew they were going to have a tough time when it came time for him to go. They had become far more than husband and wife, they were best friends as well as soul mates.

eight

ALONE

Irene watched agonizingly as Roland boarded the bus, she knew that she wouldn't see him again for two whole years, if he came home at all. She had to stop thinking such terrible thoughts; she'd had nightmares about him being shot and never returning. She needed to keep telling herself, he was going to come home. She noticed the small bag he was carrying, the army would issue everything he would need in the way of supplies and clothing, so he wasn't taking much else, they didn't allow it. She'd given him a small picture of the two of them to take with him; he already had a picture of her in his wallet, he carried that everywhere. She wanted him to have something to remind him of their love for each other. She remembered how he'd smiled and assured her that he wouldn't need anything to remind him of how he felt about her. As the bus pulled away, she waved until she couldn't see him any longer. She felt like running after it but instead turned to walk back home, she felt as if a piece of her heart was missing. Roland's Mom put her arm around her shoulders and told her she was taking her home for lunch. Irene looked up at her with tears streaming down her face, she was the kind of mother she had always dreamed of having, one who would understand when you needed her. Her parents had said goodbye to Roland the day before when they had been at their house for supper. They probably wouldn't have even remembered if she hadn't called and reminded Mama the day before. She couldn't believe that her parents were so insensitive that they didn't think that she would need them today. She sighed; wishing wouldn't make them any different. She looked up at Mom, smiled through her tears, and told her, "I'm so glad I have you to talk to." Mom looked at her with so much love and understanding that Irene's tears started flowing all over again, but this time it was because of the comfort Mom provided, it felt so good. She felt so loved by his family, except for Melissa. Irene had no idea just what the problem was there, but she knew she didn't trust her. It was hard to trust someone when you knew they didn't like you. They walked slowly back to Mom's house, talking quietly about Roland and how much they were all going to miss him. Irene had been calling her "Mom" for quite some time and felt comfortable with it now; she was ten times the mother her Mama was. She always knew Mama loved her but hugs, kisses and real comfortable conversations had been practically non-existent when she was growing up. Her family simply didn't display any emotion. It was as if they thought it was a disgrace of some sort. She thought of how it still felt strange calling his father "Dad" though; she hoped that eventually that would change as well. Irene knew how close Roland's family was and that they would all miss him terribly, as would she. She also knew they would be there for each other and for her as well, she felt so fortunate to have them.

Irene helped Mom get lunch ready while Melissa set the table and then hurried outside to pick some flowers to make a centre piece for the table to help cheer everyone up. Mom had always said that flowers could cheer anyone up, in any situation, Melissa wasn't sure about that but she thought it couldn't hurt. They could certainly use any help they could get right now. She couldn't remember a time in her whole life where everyone was this sad. Melissa looked at Irene and felt sorry for her she looked lost and so terribly sad. She knew how close her Brother and Irene were, she could see it every time she looked at them. When they were together, it seemed that they completed each other somehow; Melissa figured that must be what love was all about. She still didn't like Irene very much and she didn't trust her yet, but she had to admit she certainly did make her brother happy.

During lunch, Mom asked Irene, "Will you feel comfortable in the apartment by yourself?" She told her, "We all discussed this and we would love for you to stay with us while Roland is away." Irene felt blessed, but said, "I really appreciate the offer, but I am going to try to live there for a little while." She told them, "I hope you understand, I think it will be easier if I try to lead an almost normal life for the first little while and try not to make too many changes." Mom nodded, she seemed to understand, but she said, "As soon as you're ready, just come on over, we will all help clean out the apartment and store your things, you can have Roland's room, I already have clean sheets on the bed, so it's ready whenever you are," and she smiled at her.

Irene felt better knowing that there was a place to come to if she needed it. She helped Mom and Melissa clean up after lunch then kissed and hugged everyone goodbye. She knew she had to face the apartment by herself and get used to Roland not being there. She planned to write him a letter right away. He had given her the address for his mail for the next six weeks of training. He was going to be in Florida. She didn't know much about that place only that it was supposed to have exceptionally warm weather and she knew that it was far away. She had never travelled anywhere except to the small towns surrounding Sarnia. She reminded herself, once Roland is a doctor we will be able to afford vacations to nice places, like some of the elite people I read about in my magazines do, that helped her feel a bit better.

When she entered their apartment, she felt the loneliness immediately the feeling was overwhelming. She started to cry huge tears that seemed to be coming in torrents, she cried for the rest of the afternoon and into the evening. Just as dusk was setting in and she was closing the drapes in the living room, she noticed her reflection in the windowpane. She was shocked she looked dreadful. She went to the bathroom and splashed cold water on her face to take some of the puffiness away. She took a long look in the mirror and talked herself into taking things just one day at a time and maybe she thought I might be able to get through this. She thought of Roland and knew that he must be both lonely and frightened. He was too proud to admit the fear, but she'd seen it in his eyes when he looked back at her just before he boarded the US Army bus. She reminded herself that he was going to need her support not her constant crying and complaining.

She straightened and walked out of the bathroom, she decided that she was going to write letters to try to help him get through. She was going to talk to him in her letters as if he was sitting right beside her. She would tell him all about her days, lunch with his Mom or shopping with her friends, she would write about anything except sad things, she wanted him to smile each time he read her letters.

She went to her room and found the writing paper she kept in her dresser drawer. She'd received this stationary set as a gift from a woman she used to baby sit for when she was younger, but she'd never had anyone to write to until now. She looked at the paper with the lovely flowered border and thought it was perfect for writing cheery letters that would make Roland smile, as well as letting him know that he was both missed and loved. Irene resolved to write him a cheery letter every other day. She smiled as she sat down and busied herself writing about the lunch at his Mom's and of her returning to work tomorrow. She would make sure she ended every letter with the words "I love you and I miss you, please keep safe." Before she put the letter in the envelope, she dipped a cotton ball into a little of her perfume and lightly rubbed the paper with it. She wanted him to feel that she was there with him when he read it; she even wanted him to smell her perfume. She put the letter in the envelope and sealed it.

Thankfully, time passed quickly, Irene worked all day at the lawyer's office and volunteered to stay late whenever they needed someone. The firm really appreciated all the hard work she put in and gave her a very nice raise in pay. She was especially glad because it allowed her to put aside even more money. She was determined to save, so when Roland returned they would have a substantial amount in their savings account to help them out, they would need it when he went to school.

Both Melissa and Donna came for visits; they even came over together a few times. She would shop with Brenda and spend time just talking with her, Brenda was such a good listener, which truly helped her over the rough times. She visited with Mom and Dad and the odd time she would go and see her own Mama and Father, they never came out to see her, she felt very hurt by that. Roland's Mom and Dad were so supportive and constantly invited her over or stopped by just to make sure she was okay. She was growing so much closer to them and she leaned on them at times for support, they were so caring, such a contrast to her own parents, she thought. She would have given anything to have grown up with parents like them.

One morning about a month after Roland had left, Irene felt a little under the weather when she woke up. She brushed it off as some sort of bug at first, but it was happening repeatedly and sometimes she even felt dizzy. After discussing how she felt with Brenda, she told her, "It's probably some bug you picked up but you might need some medication to help you get rid of it." Irene suffered with it for a few more days and when she wasn't improving, she decided it was time to make an appointment to see her doctor. She just couldn't seem to shake this bug herself, and thought Brenda might be right, she probably did need some help in the form medication.

She hurried across the street on her lunch break to see her doctor. Irene wondered why she was even bothering now, she seemed to feel so much better in the afternoon, and was thinking she probably should have cancelled the appointment. It was mostly in the mornings that she felt dizzy and nauseous and she was sure it would soon pass. She walked into the reception area where the nurse greeted her and asked her to have a seat for a few minutes. Irene sat and picked up a magazine and started reading about the war, since Roland would be over there fighting soon she tried to read everything, she could on the subject. The nurse called her name, and showed her into the doctor's office. She sat down and told the doctor how she felt and all that was happening to her. He examined her and sent her for blood tests. He also asked her to bring a urine sample the next day; he told her it must be first thing in the morning that she take the sample. Irene left his office and checked her watch; she had just enough time to have her blood drawn, before she had to return to the lawyers' office. She wouldn't have time to eat her sandwich, but she wasn't very hungry these days anyway.

The next day she dropped off the urine sample on her way to work. It took three days before the doctor finally called and told her he would like to see her again. Irene stopped in on her lunch hour the following day, and when she did, she told him, "I actually feel much better, the nauseous feeling is getting much better and I rarely feel dizzy at all anymore." Her Doctor smiled and told her, "Don't worry, you aren't sick," he paused, smiling even wider, "You're pregnant!" Irene felt the room spinning and the colour was draining from her face. Concerned, her doctor asked, "Are you okay?" He said with even more concern evident in his voice, "Don't you want to have this baby?" Irene bolted to her senses, "Of course I do," she managed, "It's just that my husband is going to be fighting in Korea and I didn't expect this." She said with wide eyes, "I'm sorry I know that doesn't make sense ..." the doctor interrupted her sympathetically, saying, "I understand, and I'm sorry that he won't be here when the baby is born." He reassured her, "I'm sure that there will be lots of family to help you, between his and your own." He also said when he noticed she still seemed to be a little shocked, "I'll be here for you as well." Irene thanked him and left the office. She had to go to the drugstore and get the vitamins he'd prescribed and then return to work, her lunch hour was almost up.

She felt like she was in a daze but thought the walk to the drug store might do her some good. She returned to work afterwards and somehow managed to get through the day. She was so glad Brenda was coming over for supper that night. She really needed to talk to her. She didn't want to have a child yet and she had no idea what to do about it. She'd heard if she took a hot bath, she could possibly lose baby. She'd overheard this in a conversation some of the girls at work were having. She'd been busy at the time and had only heard that particular phrase, she wasn't sure if there was more to it or not and of course she didn't dare ask any of those girls or they might guess what she was trying to do. She thought she would try it anyway; who knows, she thought with a sigh, it just might solve my problem. She thought it couldn't hurt, if anything it would probably help her aching back, that was something else that had recently happened, but her doctor told her that it was quite a normal occurrence during pregnancy.

When Brenda came over that evening and she told her the news, Brenda thought it was wonderful. She said, "Roland would be so proud, if he was here." Irene thought about that and realized she was right. Roland really wanted children; maybe this would somehow help to ensure he came home safe. All of sudden she hoped that the hot bath she'd taken when she arrived home from work wouldn't make her lose this baby. She thought to herself, wow three months pregnant. She was trying to figure out just when it might have happened. She wasn't sure exactly, but they had never taken any precautions. Irene had forgotten all about it, she hadn't thought that she would get pregnant so soon. As with everything else that had to do with sex and pregnancy, she was totally in the dark. She didn't really know very much at all. She said, "Funny, isn't it, how things seemed to happen for the best." Brenda told her, "Don't worry just try and be happy and write to Roland as soon as possible and let him know." She said, "You have so much support from family and friends that you won't have to worry about anything." She said, thoughtfully, "You should start thinking about where you want to live, though." Irene looked surprised and Brenda told her, "Well, think about it you'll have trouble living here when you have to quit work to look after the baby, how will you pay the rent?" Irene hadn't even thought about that. She loved her job and really wanted to stay. She knew though, that "good mothers" stayed home with their children. She hadn't seen many mothers working, unless they were widows and even then, most of them didn't because they had pensions. She would have to give these things a lot of thought. She still had a couple of months, she hoped. Her doctor told her that usually with the first child it takes a while to show because the abdominal muscles are so strong. She hoped he was right.

Irene went to work the next day and immediately after work walked to Mom and Dad's, when she walked in the side door and found them in the kitchen, she announced, smiling, "I have some news." Mom and Dad both looked at her expectantly. Irene asked, "Where's Melissa?" Mom said, "She's in the garden picking flowers again, she said she had a rough day at school and needed cheering up." Irene smiled and ran to the back door and called her to come in. She came running with a lovely bouquet of fresh picked flowers. Irene said, "I understand you had a really bad day." Melissa just nodded and Irene said, "Come on into the kitchen, I have something to tell all of you and hopefully it will help cheer you up." Melissa followed her she was quite curious now. When they reached the kitchen, Irene said smiling, "I can't wait anymore, I have to tell you or I'll burst! I'm going to have a baby!" All of them looked stunned and then one by one they started smiling and huge broad smiles covered their faces. Dad said, "Roland will so pleased." He asked, "Have you told him yet?" Then remembered and corrected himself, "I meant have you written him yet?" Irene smiled and said, "Yes I posted a letter right away as soon as I could after I found out." She thought that was almost true, they didn't have to know about her thoughts of not wanting to have the baby. Mom hugged her close and kissed the top of her head. Melissa took her turn and hugged her too, asking at the same time, "Can I baby sit sometimes?" Irene laughed and said, "Let me work on having this baby first." They all laughed. Mom said to Irene, still smiling, "Your parents and Donna must be thrilled too." Irene looked at the floor and Dad stated, more than asked, "You didn't tell them yet did you?" Irene shook her head, but a tear slipped from her eye and she struggled to get a hold of herself. She was afraid to tell her father. She didn't know what his reaction would be. Dad put his arm around her shoulders and told her, "We can go with you if you want." Irene said, "Thanks Dad, but I know I have to go alone, I don't want them to know I actually told you first." Irene looked at Melissa and then asked her, pleadingly, "Please, keep my secret and don't tell Donna you knew first." Melissa replied sincerely, "Of course I'll keep your secret, I promise," and she crossed her heart. Mom said, "I'm so glad you feel this close to us, because we love you as if you were our own daughter." She added, "We will always be here for you, I hope you know that." Melissa nodded her agreement, as did Dad. Irene felt truly loved, even more so now, than she had before.

Irene walked slowly to her parents' house. When she arrived, Donna was sitting outside on the front porch with a few of her friends they were talking and playing a game of cards. Donna dropped her cards when she saw her and ran over and gave her a great big hug. Irene looked surprised and asked, "What was that for?" Donna said, "I miss you and I wish you could come back home until Roland comes back." She said, "I'd love to have my big sister back again." Irene hugged her and asked, "Are Mama and Father home?" Donna nodded and told her, "Mama's washing up after dinner and Father is reading the paper in the living room." Irene asked, "Would you come in for a few minutes with me?" She continued, "I want to tell all of you something." Donna looked puzzled and told her friends to play without her for a few minutes.

Irene and Donna walked into the house, arm in arm smiling at each other, Mama looked up from the sink and smiled, she said, "To what do we owe this surprise visit?" Irene walked over and gave her a kiss on the cheek and Mama winced. That's when Irene noticed the purple bruise. She closed her eyes for a second, in an effort to clear her head, she'd seen this same thing all her life and yet she never got used to it. She hated her father sometimes for what he did to them. She told Mama, "I have some good news to tell you." Mama whispered, "Your father is not in a good mood, maybe now is not a good time." Irene just looked at her and said, "I want to tell all of you this news tonight, it's important." She walked into the living room and looked over at Father sitting there in his chair; he hadn't even so much as acknowledged her yet. She blurted out, before she lost her nerve, "I have something I want to tell all of you". Father looked up at her and muttered grumpily, "Make it some other time!" Irene took a deep breath and persisted, "I want to tell you that I'm expecting a baby in March." Father just glared at her, without saying anything. Mama came over and gave her a hug. She said through her tears, "I'm so happy for you." Donna said, "I can't wait until March," she asked excitedly, "Will it be the beginning or the end of March?" Irene said, "Well, the doctor thinks it will be somewhere around the middle. He said he would give me a more accurate date on my next visit, next month." Donna asked her, "Is it okay if I tell my friends?" Irene smiled, "Yes, you can tell anyone you want to." Father suddenly bellowed at her, "Sit down!" Mama said in a concerned tone,

"Otto please." Father yelled at her in reply, "Get out of here! Go back to the kitchen where you belong." Irene cringed but said nothing. Father looked at her in disgust. Irene felt herself shrink back in the chair for a second, and then reminded herself that she was a married woman now and she didn't have to take this from her father, anymore. She sat up straighter in the chair and met his gaze, she tried her best to exude a confidence she didn't feel. Her father must have noticed her change in posture because he said, "I know you're married now and can do as you please, but keep in mind you're having a child now and you won't be able to work anymore, so just how do you think you are going to support yourself and that bastard you're carrying." He continued with a vengeance, "You'd better rid your self of that attitude of yours because soon you'll be forced to come back here and if you expect me to feed you and that brat, you'll listen to me and do as I say. You never should've married that man. He knew he was drafted before he married you, he probably had this all planned, he just wanted to make sure that he would have you to come home to." He added, to help make his point, "If he comes home, he was probably afraid that some other boy would marry you before he got back." He added, throwing his head to the side and narrowing his eyes, "He most likely only wanted to have sex with you anyway and you were stupid enough to agree." Irene who had heard enough, jumped off the couch and for the first time in her life, she actually talked back to him. She hissed, "You can think whatever you like and now that I know how you feel, I'll make sure you never see me again and you'll certainly never see this baby you call a bastard." He hollered at her, "Don't you talk to me like that." Her eyes bore into his and she told him, almost in a whisper, "You have no control over me anymore." She started for the front door but stopped long enough to tell him one more thing. She said, "You're a mean and unhappy man, you can't stand to see anyone happy, because you are so miserable yourself," and she walked out the front door and down the walk, as she did she heard Father yell at her, "Don't you ever come back here again." Tears sprang to her eyes and she tried hard to swallow the lump in her throat, she looked back over her shoulder, fearful that he might come after her and practically ran all the way home. She cried harder when she realized her Mama would be the one who would bear the brunt of his anger.

When she reached her apartment door, she quickly unlocked it, walked in closed and locked it immediately. She collapsed on the couch in a flood of tears. She hated her father now more than ever and couldn't have cared less if she ever saw him again, but she wanted Mama and Donna to be a part of her life especially now. She wanted her Mama there when she had her baby and she knew Donna wanted to spend time with the baby, she was afraid she'd made things even worse for them, now. She thought about Jake, he would probably want to see the baby as well; she knew he wouldn't either though because he wouldn't risk Father's temper. Jake knew he would take it out on Mama. She started to regret what she had done. She knew her father well enough to know that she wouldn't ever be able to go back there, if Mama and Donna wanted to see the baby and her as well, they would have to do it without his knowledge and she knew that, that could be very dangerous for both of them.

She wasn't able to stop crying and decided to write a letter to Roland. That will cheer me up, she thought, because I promised myself that I would never write anything that might upset him. She set out her stationery and pushing her father out of her mind, she concentrated on only good things and she told him all about those. She wrote of how Melissa wanted to baby sit and about how his Mom and Dad had offered for her and the baby to live with them until he returned. She wrote about how she was feeling exceptionally well now. She even joked about getting fat and she told of how she wanted to work for as long as she was able, provided the lawyers would let her stay. She finished off the letter, as always, with the words, "I love and miss you. Please come home safe." She put some of her perfume on the paper, put the letter in an envelope, sealed and addressed it. She slipped on her sweater and walked down to the corner to mail it.

She'd just tucked her letter into the mailbox when she noticed Mom walking quickly in her direction. Irene smiled, Mom was just the person she needed right now, she was always such a comfort to talk to. Irene waited until she caught up to her and hugged her. They walked arm in arm to Irene's place, on the way Irene asked her, "How did you know I needed you tonight?" Mom answered her with, "I just wanted to make sure that things went all right with your parents today." When Irene looked up at her and she could see the pain in her eyes, she draped her arm around Irene's shoulders and told her, "I'm here and I'll listen if you need someone to talk to." Irene told her everything that had happened including how her mother had a huge bruise on her cheek and was so obviously afraid of her father. She told her how he'd even sent her out to the kitchen and told her that's where she belonged, again. Mom listened and when Irene finished she told her, "Don't worry, we'll figure out a way for your mother and Donna to see the baby, if your father won't allow them to." She said, "I'm sure your father will come around, it may just take some time." Irene felt better; she always did when she talked things out with Mom.

Mom went into Irene's little kitchen and put on the kettle to make tea. She even found some cookies that were leftover from when Irene had Brenda over for dinner the last time. They sat at Irene's little kitchen table and talked about what they would do to get ready for the baby. Irene told her, "I'm planning on working as long as I can." Mom said, nodding, "I think that's a good idea, it will keep you busy until it's time to start getting things ready for the little one." She smiled at her. Mom was so excited about the baby. She said, "Roland will be so happy when he finally gets that letter." They knew it took several weeks sometimes for him to receive the letters they sent. It took that long for them to get the ones he wrote, as well.

Mom told her, excitedly, "Gramps is making a crib and playpen for you." Irene knew he was an excellent carpenter and made gorgeous furniture. He'd made some of the pieces in Mom and Dad's house and they were beautiful. Mom said, "He said he was glad to have the chore. He told me he loves making things and that this was going to be extra special." Mom explained to Irene that he was making the playpen so it would fold in half, making it easier to carry if she needed to. Irene thought that was a great idea. She was really looking forward to seeing the crib and playpen when they were finished. She knew he would do a wonderful job. Mom glanced up at the clock on the wall and said, "I better be getting home, Dad will wonder if I got lost." She laughed, and said, "You should go to bed, you need your rest, you have to get up early for work in the morning." Mom washed the cups and spoons and Irene dried them. They put them back on the shelf above the sideboard.

Mom walked through the apartment and once she'd opened the front door she turned to Irene and told her, "Everything will be just fine, you'll see," and gave her a hug. Irene watched Mom walking home from her porch up on the second floor; it was up so high that she could see her walking almost all of the way to her house. She came back inside and locked the door. She went straight to the bathroom to get ready for bed. She knew she would sleep better now that she had talked to Mom.

Irene worked until she was almost ready to deliver. She finally quit at the end of February. The lawyers had let her stay as long as she wanted to. They felt sorry for her with Roland being at war and she worked in the back office anyway so they didn't have to worry about clients thinking poorly of the firm. After all women who were in a "family way" didn't work outside of their homes. Irene thanked God every night in her prayers for the wonderful lawyers she worked for, because if she didn't have her work she knew she would have gone crazy.

She moved into Mom and Dad's house the week after she quit work. Mom and Dad helped her find a place to store her furniture. Dad had a friend at work with a large garage on his property and he said the kids could use some of that space. Irene's friends helped her with the packing and Harold's friends moved the furniture to the garage with the help of a borrowed truck from one of Harold's friends whose father had a delivery service and let them use the truck to move Roland and Irene's things. Irene felt so grateful; it seemed everyone wanted to help her. She didn't always like the looks of pity on their faces, but she knew their hearts were in the right place.

Mom, Dad and Irene were sitting in the kitchen having tea one evening after dinner. Irene was getting quite uncomfortable her baby was due any day now and she was having trouble sleeping, and doing almost everything, she felt huge and awkward. She'd just gotten up to use the bathroom for the umpteenth time this evening when Gramps knocked at the door. He opened it and hollered in, "Got a delivery here!" A few of his friends had come with him to help carry the crib and playpen he'd made. He said, "I wanted to make sure Irene had these in place, I know that baby is due anytime now." When Irene came out of the bathroom, she noticed the beautiful crib and playpen set up in the living room. They were made of solid oak and were simply gorgeous. They were polished to a shine and the headboard and footboard were decorated with little inset animals that Gramps had actually engraved in the wood on the crib, she was speechless looking at it, it was just beautiful. She found her voice and exclaimed, while jumping up and down, "Thank you, oh thank you." She stopped abruptly and cradled her huge belly in her arms. Mom said, laughing, "Be careful." Irene laughed and hugged Gramps; she said, "They are absolutely gorgeous!" He replied slightly embarrassed, he wasn't used to this kind of attention, "I hoped you'd like them." She exclaimed, "Like! I love them!" Gramps and his friends chuckled at her obvious appreciation. His friends suggested that he should go into business since he was so good at it. Gramps replied, shaking his head, "An old man like me should definitely not go into business. I know I'd just forget things and go belly up before long." They laughed at that, but they all knew that his memory was not what it used to be.

nine

THE BABY

The same evening Gramps delivered the crib and playpen,
Irene went into labour. Mom took her to the hospital
and waited outside the room for hours, before a nurse
appeared and told her to go home and rest. She said, "It will
likely take a while, first babies usually do." Mom finally relented
went home and napped for a few hours but came right back.
Dad joined her after work looking worried. Mom told him, "The
first child can sometimes take quite awhile." He reminded her,
"Roland was born in only eight hours and this has been close to
fifteen now." He no sooner got the words out when a nurse came
out with a tiny bundle wrapped in a pink blanket. They beamed
with pride as they looked at their new granddaughter, for the
first time. The proud looks on their faces lasted all through the
evening. They visited Irene, once she was settled in her room
but a nurse poked her head in the door and told them, "You
can't stay long because the doctor ordered complete rest for her
tonight," so they kissed her goodbye and smiling, said, "We'll
be back tomorrow." Irene smiled and whispered, "Thanks" and
promptly fell asleep.

They walked home quickly, knowing Gramps and Melissa
were waiting anxiously to hear the news. They sat down in
their living room and told them all about Irene and the new

85

baby girl. Mom and Dad suddenly looked at each other; they knew they were both thinking the same thing. They had to at least, make an effort to tell Irene's parents, Elinor and Otto, no matter what Otto had told Irene about her never coming back. He could have changed his mind in the meantime besides Alma and Clancy thought that they had a right to know, Irene was still their daughter. They decided they'd walk down right away before it got too late and they might have to worry about them being in bed for the night.

When they reached the Giles house, they could see the lights were still on in the living room. They reluctantly knocked on the door. They had no idea what to expect. Otto answered and they both cringed at the look on his face when he recognized them. He asked gruffly, "What brings you two here?" Clancy ignored his rude demeanour and spoke up, saying, "Your daughter Irene, just had a baby girl; we thought you and Elinor would like to know." Clancy glared at them and then said, shaking his head, "Thanks for your trouble, but we don't have a daughter named Irene, anymore," and he slammed the door in their faces.

Alma gasped and Clancy put his arm around her shoulders and guided her down the steps of the Giles front porch. As they turned onto the city sidewalk, Alma looked up at the house, through her tears, she saw Elinor in the upstairs window, and it was obvious she was crying because her shoulders were shaking violently. Alma cried all the way home. Clancy also had tears in his eyes. The two of them just couldn't understand how they could abandon Irene like that and their new granddaughter now as well. Clancy thought it was a damn shame. He feared for Elinor and Donna, because he knew that they would try their best to see the baby and Irene. He was afraid of what would happen if they did and Otto found out they'd disobeyed him. The thought was inconceivable.

The next day Mom and Dad visited Irene in the hospital they brought Melissa with them, but since she wasn't old enough yet to visit, she had to stay outside. "You have to be eighteen to visit someone in the hospital," the nurse at the desk briskly told them, when she saw them approaching. Melissa barely looked her age of fifteen, so they knew trying to sneak her in would be out of the question. They planned to have Irene wave to her from the window though since Melissa was upset that she couldn't see her. Mom told her, "I'm sorry, but you'll have to wait until Irene comes home to see the baby."

They brought flowers and of course, a few clean nightgowns for Irene. Mom brought the sweater and hat set she had knit for the baby. It was so tiny and just beautiful; Mom knit it in white so it could be used for either a boy or girl. Irene told her, "You're going to have to teach me how to knit now too." Mom replied, "Of course I will. Now that we know it's a girl, we can start making things in pink," She told her, "Melissa is already making something special, she started it as soon as we told her it was a girl." Irene smiled; she knew her own sister was probably doing the same thing only she would have to hide it from her parents, especially Father. She asked, gingerly, "Did you get a chance to tell my parents?" Mom and Dad looked at each other and Irene caught the expression on their faces. Tears filled her eyes and spilled onto her cheeks as she asked, "Are they coming to see me and the baby?" She already knew the answer, but she had to ask, just in case. She was still hopeful that Father might forgive her. Mom came over crying openly, sat on the bed, and held her. Dad went over to the window, but Irene and Mom both noticed his eyes were glistening; they knew he was crying, too.

Irene was pretty sure Father told them he wouldn't be coming and she was quite sure that he hadn't been nice about how he'd said it either. She wanted to ask but she was afraid of the answer. She hoped Mama and Donna could somehow manage to see her and the new baby soon, she really missed them. She had to admit though, she didn't miss Father at all, and in fact, she didn't care if she ever saw him again. He was such a mean, cruel person. Irene reminded herself that she needed come to terms with the fact that if her family didn't want to see her anymore, then she would just have to accept it. She was bound and determined to make a good family life for her new little girl. She sat up straighter in the bed, kissed Mom on the cheek and looking from Mom to Dad, said, "Thank you both, Mom and Dad, for being here for me." She noticed Dad was waving to someone out the window. She asked him, "Who's out there?" He said, "Melissa, she's anxiously waiting for you to wave to her, she's too young to visit, we tried to sneak her in, but we got caught." Irene smiled and got out of bed as quickly as she could muster given the stitches and soreness. She smiled wide and waved at Melissa, she could see her waving and smiling back at her. Irene felt such a warm feeling just knowing that this family was also hers now and that they would be there for her no matter what. She resigned herself to think of them as her only family from now on.

Irene turned from the window and announced, "It's time to give this baby a name." She started rhyming off all the choices that she and Roland had discussed in their letters over the last few months and then asked them, "Do you like the name Cassandra Elsie Petersen, "Cassie" for short?" Mom and Dad smiled and Mom said, "It's perfect." They knew she had chosen Elsie, because it was her mother's nickname. She told them, "Cassandra is Roland's favourite name, according to his letters." She decided that she would write him a letter later and tell him that she agreed with his choice. She also wanted to tell him of the name she'd added as well. She knew he wouldn't mind.

Irene was discharged from the hospital eight days after Cassie was born; her doctor said, "You should be happy that you're getting the rest you need to recover." He reinforced, in response to her constant pleading to go home, "You will be very busy once you have to cope with the baby on your own." Irene knew that she would have plenty of help. Mom, Dad, and Melissa

couldn't wait to help her. She had even chosen to bottle feed
Cassie, instead of breast-feeding so they could help as much as
they wanted. When Mom questioned her on that decision Irene
told her that the doctor had advised her to, since she wasn't
producing adequate amounts of milk. She shrugged thinking
about that little white lie, but she knew Mom would never know
that it wasn't true.

Irene was all packed up, sitting on the chair beside the bed
waiting for Mom and Dad to arrive, she was ready early, it was
only ten thirty, and discharge time was eleven. She sat there,
thinking about being a mother and how her life was going to
change, drastically. She supposed she felt all the feelings that
a mother was supposed to feel but she still worried. When
the nurses brought Cassie in for her feedings during the day
she found herself getting frustrated if Cassie cried too much
or sometimes she just felt bored and wanted to put her down.
She was always afraid that if she didn't appear to be thrilled
with her new baby each time they brought her in, people would
think poorly of her and Irene cared too much, about what others
thought of her to let that happen. She'd watched the woman
in the bed next to hers, when the curtain wasn't drawn. She'd
noticed how excited the woman was to see and hold her new
baby boy, she even breast fed it. Irene couldn't believe anyone
would want their life disrupted like that all the time and shook
her head at the thought. This woman already had two other
children, one was five and the other was three. Irene thought,
maybe this motherhood thing takes time to develop. She wasn't
sure if she would ever feel the way this woman did, but she was
sure she would find out. She knew Roland wanted more than
just this one child, so maybe she would feel differently after she
had the next one in a couple years after he returned home. In
the meantime, she might have to keep pretending, if her feelings
didn't change soon. Her doctor had spoken to her about new
mothers needing time to adjust, she shrugged, maybe this was

what he meant. She hadn't wanted to ask him though, just in case he thought she wasn't fit to be a mother.

Suddenly Mom and Dad appeared in her room, they were excited, telling her that Dad had borrowed Gramps' car to take Cassie and her home. Gramps was keeping Melissa company at home. Mom and Dad had allowed Melissa to take the day off school; they knew she was far too excited to make it through the day knowing that Irene and Cassie were at home, besides they thought Irene needed the sense of "family" today of all days they knew she would be missing her own sister and mother. They were determined to make up for that the best way they could.

The nurse appeared with the wheelchair and another nurse followed behind her with Cassie, they'd dressed her in the nightgown Mom brought in and the sweater set that Mom had knit; it had a little hat and booties. She was wrapped up in a little blanket. Irene thought she looked like a doll. Once Irene was settled in the wheelchair the nurse placed Cassie in her arms. Irene kissed the tiny head and smiled up proudly at Mom and Dad. Dad picked up the suitcase beside the bed and they headed out to the elevator. The nurse followed pushing Irene with Mom at her side. They reached the car which Dad had parked in front of the hospital and Irene settled in the backseat holding Cassie, Mom crawled in beside her. They waved at the nurses, standing on the curb, as Dad drove off.

Melissa was sitting on the porch steps and Gramps was in the one of the chairs on the porch. They both stood up smiling and waving frantically when they caught sight of the car. Melissa came running down the drive, tripped, and skinned her knee. She got up so fast and kept running, they had to laugh, normally she would have been nursing that skinned knee and crying, she wasn't much for any kind of pain. She was so excited that she didn't even seem to feel it this time. When Dad stopped the car in the drive Melissa tore open the door on Irene's side and asked, "Please, I can't wait any longer, can I see Cassandra." Irene laughed and pulled back the blanket so she could see her. Melissa melted, and said, "Awe, she's so small and so cute!" Irene told her, "If you wait until I get into the house you can hold her, if you want." Melissa started to yell, "Yes, yes" in excitement and then quickly covered her mouth with her hand, she didn't want to startle the baby, but it was already too late, Cassie started screaming. Melissa felt so bad she looked like she would cry herself. Irene said, sympathetically, "Oh, don't worry about it, Cassie is just going to have to get used to our happy family," and smiled.

Mom took the baby so Irene could get out of the car, she snuggled her and soothed her by humming a little song that Irene had never heard before, she wasn't good with children and didn't know any children's songs, she thought she'd better listen closely to the ones Mom sang and maybe she would learn them. Cassie quieted down immediately and Melissa felt much better. She chattered away as they walked into the house saying, "We're going to have to remember not to make sudden noises and startle Cassie." They all smiled at each other, they knew she was the one that was going to be guilty of that most of the time." Gramps looked at the baby and said, "I'll wait my turn to hold her." Irene heard him and thought this family is simply incredible.

When they were all settled in the house everyone took a turn holding Cassie and Mom fed her and burped her. Melissa helped Mom change her and they put her down to sleep in the new crib. She looked so lost in it she was so tiny. Mom said, "I have a little bassinette that you could use if you want to keep the baby beside you at night until she grows a little." She said, "I used it for Melissa when she was born and I carefully wrapped it up so Melissa could use it for her first baby, but she's insisted that you use it for Cassie." Irene thanked both of them. Melissa suddenly remembered the little blanket she'd made and ran to her room to get it. She returned out of breath and handed it to Irene saying, "I made this for you." Irene was amazed at how beautiful it was. She noticed the detail in the stitching and how perfectly the satin edging was stitched on. She asked, amazed, "Melissa, did you make this all by yourself?" Melissa nodded, and Mom said, "She worked on it as soon as she finished her homework, every night while you were in the hospital, she wanted you to have something pink, once she found out it was a girl." Melissa also gave Irene the yellow receiving blanket she'd knit before she'd known that it was a girl, and it was equally as beautiful. Irene hugged her and said, "Thank you so much, they're beautiful"

Over the next few weeks, Irene was beginning to feel closer to Cassie and she was amazed at how much the family helped her with the baby's needs. Mom did all the laundry, Melissa fed Cassie and held her every minute she possibly could. Brenda came over often and held her and fed her as well. Irene thought, just maybe, she could manage this "mother business" after all. She had to laugh thinking of her apprehension in the hospital. She was actually enjoying being a mother, most of the time now. She was getting a bit restless though, she felt she needed something else to do. She asked Mom, "Could you teach me how to knit?" Mom told her, smiling, "I would be more than pleased to." Irene learned quite quickly and was really enjoying making little hats and sweaters for Cassie.

Irene was sitting on her bed writing a letter to Roland one afternoon, when she heard a knock at the door. She didn't think anything of it since Mom and Dad had neighbours and friends that dropped in all the time. Irene rather liked it; they were usually such fun, interesting people. Irene kept writing and the knocking grew louder, she paused with her pen in midair listening, and just then, remembered Mom and Dad had taken the baby for a walk and no one was home but her. She ran out of her bedroom to the back door only to realize that the knock was coming from the front door. She ran to the front thinking, Mom and Dad's friends always use the back door and they just knocked and walked right in and shouted, "Anyone home". When she reached the front door, the knocking grew louder still. She tore open the door and found Donna standing on the porch in tears. Irene grabbed her and threw her arms around her. Donna just sobbed. Irene waited for the sobbing to subside a little and then asked her, "What's wrong?" Donna said, gasping for breath, "Mama and I got ready to come and see you, we were going to tell Father that we were going to the store for groceries, but Mama suddenly changed her mind and said she wanted to tell him the truth before she left. She said it might be better just in case he somehow found out. She told me to wait inside and she went outside to talk to Father; he was up on the ladder nailing down something on the roof that had come loose in the wind. It seemed like Mama was taking ages to talk to him, so I decided to go look out the door and make sure she was okay, as I walked to the door, I heard Father yell, you're not going anywhere! Get back in the house and tell Donna to get to her room. Then as I reached the door, I saw Mama walking closer to the ladder and, Irene," she screwed up her face as if in pain and said, "She pushed it! And I heard Father scream, Elinor NO! Mama looked up and saw me as I ran out onto the porch. She stared at me for what seemed like ages. Then she told me, run to Irene, she'll take care of you. She said she was going to take care of Father." Donna whispered, "Irene, I don't even know if she knows that I saw her push the ladder." She asked Irene, pleadingly, "What should I do?" Irene held her saying, "Quiet now, try not to be too upset, Mama was just protecting herself, she knew he would beat her when he came down from that ladder. Maybe she just couldn't face another beating. She probably thought you were in danger too. I think you have to keep what you saw a secret. You can never tell anyone. Okay, promise me?" Irene lifted Donna's chin, waiting for her answer. Donna replied, "I promise," she thought because Irene, who was so much older and smarter than she was, said that they needed to protect Mama, she would do as she said. Irene confessed, "I may have done the very same thing if I was the one being beaten all the time." Donna asked Irene,

"What is Mama going to do when Father gets better? Won't he just beat her then?" Irene shook her head and said, "Don't think about that now." She told Donna, handing her a tissue from her pocket, "Dry your eyes." She said, "We should go back and see if Mama's okay," she added almost as an after thought, "And see how Father is, too."

Irene ran back to her room to get her coat and a piece of paper to write Mom a quick note to let her know that she had to go out and that she'd explain when she got back. When she finished the note, she grabbed Donna's hand, "Let's go," she said, as they hurried out of the house and down the street on their way to their parents' house. Irene was worried about Donna she looked so pale.

ten

A Welcome Surprise

When Irene and Donna reached the house, they could see what looked to be Father, lying on the grass under the ladder, he was almost completely hidden by the large cedars that grew under the window, but they recognized the red plaid flannel shirt he wore. Mama was nowhere to be seen; as they drew closer, they could see Father was face down in the dirt with what appeared to be something on his head. The neighbour Mrs. Sanderson came hurrying out of her house and prevented them from getting any nearer. She put an arm around each of their shoulders saying, "Come, come, your mother's in here," and steered them towards her house, next door. She didn't want the girls to see what happened to their father. She took them into her kitchen, "Sit down" she said as she pulled two chairs out for them, and said, "Help yourselves," as she poured tea into cups and motioned, with a nod towards a plate of cookies on the table. She went on to say, "Mr. Sanderson has gone to get help." The girls looked at each other in shock, they both knew, without asking, that Father must be dead. Irene reached out and held Donna's hand.

The two of them hurried into Mrs. Sanderson's living room, when they heard Mama's voice. They saw her sitting on the couch, weeping and ran to her and hugged her. They held her tightly, until they heard a voice call out, from behind them, "Sorry to bother you." They looked up startled and realized it was Mr. Sanderson, he said sadly with his head down, "The police would like to know if they can speak to you, Mrs. Giles." Their Mama answered, to the girls surprise, she said in a shaky voice, "Yes, fine I'll talk to them." She asked when the police officer appeared in the living room, "Is it okay if my girls stay with me?" The officer nodded his approval and asked, gently, "Please tell me in your own words what happened." Mama started to cry, "It was entirely my fault," she said as Irene and Donna nervously looked at each other. Mama continued, "I told him I was going to go out with Donna," and motioned with her hand, indicating which of her girls was Donna. She continued after drawing an uneven breath, "I must have distracted him... he was hammering some tiles on the roof...when I turned to go back into the house, he fell and landed behind the cedars." She drew in a ragged breath as she said, "The ladder fell and then the hammer, fell on top of him." The police officer turned to Donna and asked, "Were you there when your father fell?" She said, almost too quickly, "I was in the house, I didn't see anything." She told him through her tears, "Mama told me to go to Irene's; she said she was going to help Father." The police officer thought a moment, but seemed to be satisfied with that because he rose from the couch and put a hand on Mama's shoulder, in comfort, then he squeezed Donna's shoulder slightly, and said, "I'm so sorry I had to ask those questions, I don't believe I'll need anything else." He said again, "I'm sorry," and he left with a sombre expression on his face.

They stayed at the Sanderson's for quite some time after he left. When they did go back to Mama's house, Father's body was no longer there, and the ladder and tools had all been put away. Mr. Sanderson had cleaned up everything as best he could, after the body had been removed.

Irene stayed and comforted Mama and Donna until they

quieted down. The doctor had come out to the house and given
them some medicine to help them relax and sleep and they were
resting now. Jake came home from work quickly when Irene had
called him. He said to her, after checking to make sure neither
of them had woken, "I'll take care of them and make sure they're
okay, you go home and take care of Cassie." She kissed his cheek
and told him, "I need to get back not just for Cassie, but also to
tell Mom and Dad what's happened." She said, "I told Mama not
to worry about arranging anything. I told her that I would make
all the arrangements for the funeral." She hoped Mom and Dad
would know what to do, because she sure didn't. Jake hugged
her and said, "Thanks, sis, I'm glad you're looking after that," he
sighed and a sad sound escaped, he said sorrowfully, "I know I'll
have my hands full taking care of Mama and Donna."

As she walked home she thought of what Donna had said
about Mama pushing the ladder, Irene wondered if maybe it had
only appeared that way from where Donna had been standing,
inside the house. She shook her head thinking she just couldn't
imagine Mama doing anything like that on purpose. Suddenly a
thought crept into her head, Mama is finally free she will never
have to suffer another beating from him again, Donna won't
have to be afraid to go home and Jake can finally get a place of
his own, as he has been wanting to do for quite sometime now.
Irene thought even I will be better off because I won't have to
put up with the humiliation of him calling my little Cassie a
bastard ever again." She smiled a slow smile as she approached
Mom and Dad's front walk, thinking maybe this surprise is a
"welcome surprise" after all.

When she opened the front door of Mom and Dad's
house, everyone was in the living room; they looked up at her
questioningly, as she walked in. Mom seemed to know instantly,
something was not right. She asked, "Irene, is everything okay?"
Irene was surprised that tears actually sprang to her eyes as she
told them what had happened that day. She hated her father for

what he did to her Mama. She hated him for the way he spoke to her as well. She was glad he was dead, but she knew she'd have to pretend that she was mourning his loss, she thought people might get the wrong impression if she didn't. She kept up the pretence, sniffling and crying for a while longer, she didn't want anyone to think she was insensitive, especially her newfound, wonderful family. Mom and Dad came over and held her as she cried, and told her, "Don't worry we'll take care of everything, you won't have to do a thing." Irene breathed a sigh of relief; she knew she could count on them. Melissa had been watching suspiciously from where she was sitting on the couch. She'd noticed Irene's distant stare as she told them what happened, she was sure something wasn't quite right. She'd been looking out the window when Irene was coming up the walk, she could have sworn that Irene had been smiling. She thought she'd ask Mom about it later.

The funeral was held at the same United Church they used to attend as a family when Irene was growing up. Irene's mind wandered, as she stood there only half-listening and looking around the familiar building. She was thinking, that lately only Mama went to church, she didn't even make Donna go with her anymore and Father, she knew hadn't been there in several years, he'd said countless times that he thought it was a waste of time and Jake, he simply said church wasn't for him. Irene attended the Catholic Church every Sunday with Mom, Dad and Melissa, she even took Cassie, who was always good as gold during Mass. She began looking around at the people in attendance and noticed almost everyone Father had worked with was there for his funeral, as well as neighbours and a couple of Mama's friends. Irene wondered if they came because they liked him or if they wanted to make sure, he was really dead and wondered if he'd been mean to everyone he knew or if that was something he'd reserved just for his own family. Brenda and Harold came to pay their respects as well. They visited the house afterward and brought a casserole. They told Mama they'd be more than willing to help her with anything she needed and told her to call them anytime. Almost everyone brought food; Mama wouldn't have to cook for quite some time and that would be a blessing Irene thought; she'd always worked so hard keeping the house and making meals. Father had never appreciated her efforts, Irene thought with a shake of her head.

The Oil Company Father worked for paid for the whole funeral, they'd learned from a Company representative that he'd been paying into some kind of fund that not only paid for the funeral, but also paid Mama a small pension, as well. Irene was so glad to hear that Mama wouldn't have to go to work to support herself. She could if she wanted to, but she wouldn't have to in order to eat. The house was paid for, which meant she would only have to pay the utilities, taxes and food. That will give her time to decide what she wants to do, Irene thought.

Irene and Mama were talking in Mama's kitchen one day, several weeks after the funeral. Cassie was playing in her playpen; she could almost sit up by herself now. She was adorable and Mama loved looking after her. Irene asked, "Mama, will you be all right financially?" She told her, "I have been so worried about you, but I didn't want to pry." Mama was surprised, she smiled and said, "Oh goodness, don't worry about me; I am the sole heir of your uncle's estate, since he never married and never had any children." She continued, "He named your father and me as his heirs in his will. He was quite well off and the last letter I received from the lawyer said the cheque would be here soon. So believe me you don't have to worry, I'll be just fine, financially." She added excitedly, smiling widely, "In fact I'd like to give you and Roland a gift. Roland will be home next year and the two of you will need your own home." Irene looked at her mother in astonishment she couldn't believe her ears. She thought now we won't have to struggle when Roland goes to Medical School. She jumped up and gave Mama the biggest hug, saying, "Thank you, thank you."

Irene noticed that Mama often seemed preoccupied and asked her one day, "Are you having trouble dealing with being alone, I mean without Father?" Mama said, "No, I know this sounds terrible, but I'm actually enjoying the freedom of being able to be myself without the fear of him not liking something I said or did and being beaten for it." Irene hugged her and told her, "I understand, Mama." She couldn't help wondering though, if Mama might be feeling a little guilty, she still couldn't get what Donna had told her she'd seen that day, out of her mind.

When Mama was lying in bed that night, she asked God once again to forgive her for the terrible thing she'd done. She cried herself to sleep almost every night, she felt so guilty. She'd gone over that day in her mind repeatedly and she was almost positive that Donna had seen her push that ladder, even though she had never said a thing. She knew for sure that she had seen Father fall. She remembered yelling at her to go to sister's immediately; she'd told her that she would take care of Father. She recalled looking down at him and noticing that he couldn't move, he'd knocked the wind out of himself when he hit the railing on the side of the porch on the way down and he couldn't breathe. She remembered jumping with a start when the hammer hit the ground so close to his head and then when the ladder fell on top of him, she'd jumped again. She recalled looking around to see if anyone was nearby, and saw him fall. There was no one and they were hidden from view of the neighbours by the cedars. She watched him as he tried to move a little and was suddenly gripped by fear. The realization of what he would do to her when he got up, finally dawned on her. Without even thinking about what she was doing, she'd picked up the hammer and hit him in the head with it as hard as she could. She stood up never taking her eyes from him; he was perfectly still, laying face down with the hammer wedged into his head. She hadn't meant to but she'd hit him with the pointed side of the hammer, the side that was used to pry and it was now imbedded in his head. She knelt and reached for his wrist feeling for a pulse, she'd managed to find a very weak one, so she waited behind those cedars until she could feel no pulse at all. She remembered she'd gotten up, forced herself to cry, and went screaming over to the Sanderson's house to get help, or so everyone thought. She sighed deeply; she knew she could never let anyone know what she'd done. She would have to try to live with it and hope the good Lord would forgive her. She knew if she'd allowed Otto to get up that day he'd have beaten her badly and most likely Donna as well. He'd forbidden both of them to see Irene or the baby. She'd lived with him long enough to know how he thought and she knew he'd have thought it was his duty to punish them and severally at that. He had told her enough times over the years that he thought it was a man's duty to keep his wife and kids in line. Mama thought she'd go mad thinking about it. She hoped and prayed her children would never find out, she was terrified they'd hate her for it. She consoled herself thinking, if Donna had witnessed what really happened surely she would have talked to me about it by now. She had to keep telling herself this in order to keep her sanity. She was so sure she'd done the right thing to protect both Donna and herself. She thought Jake and Irene seemed to be happier since Father was no longer around. Donna was hard to read, she appeared to be tense all the time. Mama reached over to the night table and picked up the bottle of sedatives the doctor had prescribed and swallowed two. She was only supposed to take one, but she was quite sure that two wouldn't hurt, too much; she knew one would never be enough to enable her to sleep tonight. She couldn't stop thinking about that horrible day.

Donna also lay awake in her room, down the hall she was thinking about that day, too. She kept going over and over the images and sounds that were engraved in her mind. Mama's face, filled with hatred, as she looked up at Father, when he said,

"You're not going anywhere." Mama pushing the ladder, with what she thought, from where she stood, was all her strength. She could still hear Father's panicked shout, "Elinor, No!" and then the sound of him hitting the railing on the end of the porch and the ladder falling on top of him. When she ran out of the house and Mama told her to run to Irene's, Donna was sure out of the corner of her eye, she'd seen him move as she reached the city sidewalk, she was certain there wasn't any blood at that time or any hammer sticking out of his head. She wondered did the hammer fall off the roof after she'd gone. How could that be? When she and Irene were in Mrs. Sanderson's kitchen, they'd overheard a police officer say that the hammer was embedded in his head. She and Irene had looked at Father on their way up the walk, but Irene had blocked her view and then Mrs. Sanderson wouldn't let them see either. She recalled how she and Irene had looked at each other in shock when the police officer had made that comment about the hammer. She just couldn't shake the thought that something terrible had happened that day and she couldn't ask Mama about it, because she'd promised Irene, she wouldn't upset Mama anymore than she already was. She'd lied to the police officer when he had asked her it she had seen or heard anything, she'd told him she didn't. She'd said that she was in the house, which was true, but it wasn't the whole truth. She'd worried so much that he would know she was lying. She was shaking and crying so hard at the time. She remembered Irene holding her tight, and that she was crying too. The police officer just kept saying, "I'm so sorry, I know how hard these questions are right now, but please, I have to ask them," and she and Irene had simply nodded.

With considerable guilt, she had to admit it was a relief not to have to worry about Father suddenly losing his temper and striking her or worse yet Mama. He always hit Mama harder and rarely just once, he usually kept hitting her and kicking her, until he finally grew tired and then most times he left and went out.

She recalled how she and Irene used to lay awake and listen for him to come home. They were always afraid he would start in on Mama again; sometimes he would hit her even though she was already asleep. They could hear him sometimes, shouting loudly, "That was just to make sure you got the message, in case you missed it the first time." Donna and Irene were never sure what that message was supposed to be. It had become worse since Irene had married and left home; she was so afraid sometimes. Jake would often sneak into her room and tell her, "Be quiet, don't cry or Father might hurt you too." He always said, "It's too late to help Mama, but it will hurt Mama more if Father hurts you too." Jake must have known it was harder for her since Irene wasn't there anymore, she was going to miss him, he was going to be moving out soon. He said he needed to start a life of his own and he told Mama that he was too old to be living at home now. He said she'd be much better off if she didn't have to cook for him anymore. Donna knew he just wanted out; he'd only stayed at home this long to make sure they were safe, but with Father gone now, he didn't need to protect them anymore. She hoped he'd be happy on his own. She planned to visit him often and she teased him about it, telling him he probably would starve because he couldn't cook. He'd just laughed and said, "You can visit anytime you like, little sis, and you can cook for me if you like," and ruffled her hair.

eleven

CHANGES

Mama was visiting Irene practically every day now; she was thrilled that she could finally be a Grandma in every sense of the word. She was always taking little Cassie out for walks and buying her cute little clothes and tons of toys. Irene couldn't have been happier, even Donna was coming over almost every day after school to see her and Cassie. It seemed only natural that since Mama and Donna were over at Mom and Dad's so often, that when Mama suggested, one afternoon, she should move back home until Roland returned, that she said, "Yes." Mama told her, excitedly, "Jake's room's empty now and a crib will fit nicely beside the bed. It will be perfect for you and Cassie." It seemed so right to Irene since Mama was alone, except of course for Donna but she was busy with school and friends, as she should be at her age. Irene thought Mom, Dad, and Melissa, they all have each other, and Mama needs someone too. Irene also thought Mama could use some cheering up and she knew her little Cassie, was just what she needed. She told Mama, smiling "Yes, I think it will be perfect too, thanks."

Mom and Dad were sad to see her go, but they understood her reason, even Melissa said she understood. That night after everyone was in bed, Irene sat down to write Roland and tell him all about where she had decided to live, she was sure he would be okay with her moving.

A few weeks after Irene moved into Mama's house, Mama noticed that Irene seemed bored; she just didn't seem to have enough to do. Mama suggested, one day, after giving it considerable thought, "Why don't you see if those lawyers you used to work for need some help." She told her, "It might help you pass the time until Roland comes back, I'd be more than happy to watch Cassie for you and Donna can help me after school, too." Irene thought, it makes sense, and replied, "I am bored, thanks Mama, that's a good idea, I'll go and see them tomorrow." The next day she walked over to the lawyer's office and was surprised when they welcomed her back and told her she could even choose the hours that she wanted to work. They said she could start out part time and increase to full time if she wanted. They even said that they would pay her the same hourly wage as she was making when she left. Irene was thrilled, she'd always loved working for them, they were so good to her and the work she did was so interesting. She couldn't wait to get home and tell Mama the news. She thanked them and when she left, she practically ran home.

Mama was excited for her and noticed the positive changes in her mood, improving each day she'd come home from work, smiling and eager to see Cassie. Mama had been worrying about her, she had even wondered for a short time if Irene even enjoyed being a mother, but now that she had something to occupy her mind, she seemed to be doing fine. Mama decided she probably didn't have to worry after all, she thought Irene was more than likely missing Roland and needed the distraction that this job provided, in order to cope. She had also noticed that Donna was happier at home now since Irene had moved back with Cassie. She smiled thinking, everything's wonderful, I'm so busy with the little one all the time I have very little time anymore to think about "that day" which felt so good, I finally have a little relief from the constant guilt and my family is happy, I'm certain now that I did the right thing.

Irene was getting used to working and coming home and playing with Cassie in the evening, she far preferred this life; it was so much more fun than just staying at home. She loved to wear nice clothes and to socialize with the people at work. The girls went out for lunch regularly, even when they ate the brown-bagged lunches they brought from home, they still talked and laughed and had a great time. Irene wondered if Roland would mind if she continued to work once he came home. Mama seemed to be having the time of her life looking after Cassie and Cassie had grown very attached to her, which didn't bother Irene in the slightest. She liked to play with her daughter, occasionally, but she thought if the truth were known, she far preferred to do her nails or read a good book. Mama and Donna were more than welcome to do all the work involved with Cassie; that was just fine by her. Irene could tell that Mom and Dad weren't too pleased about her working though because Mom would say things like, "You really should be home more with Cassie; she's going to think her Grandma is her Mommy." She usually went on to say; "Maybe it would be possible to cut back a bit on your hours and just work a day or two each week." Irene would smile and reply, "I'll see about that," but she couldn't even imagine actually doing it, she loved her job and told everyone that she needed to work to help distract her from constantly worrying about her husband so much. She said, to Mom, "I'm not as depressed now that I'm working and busy, please try to understand." The statement was true enough, but she also knew she didn't want to reduce her hours. She wasn't sure what excuse she would use once Roland returned home. She knew she didn't want to quit work, though, so she would have to think of something.

Time passed so quickly and Cassie was growing like a weed, she was almost eighteen months old now and was beginning to walk. Roland was going to be coming home in just three weeks time. Irene and Mama had been showing Cassie pictures of him and telling her he was, "Daddy" in the hopes she would say it to him when she saw him. They prayed she wouldn't make strange with him and cry. Irene wanted the day he returned to be perfect.

Mama had already bought them a brand new house on Mitten Street. It had three bedrooms and a full basement. She was planning to surprise them with the keys as soon as Roland returned home. Jake and a few of his friends had loaded all of Irene and Roland's furniture and all the household items they had stored away as well, into a truck that Jake had borrowed from a friend and moved it all into their new house. Mama and Donna had left Cassie with Mom and Dad and gone over to put the dishes away. They'd even done the grocery shopping and filled the cupboards and the new fridge with food. Mama wanted everything to be in place for them the day Roland arrived. She was planning to keep Cassie with her at her house, the first night so the two of them could become reacquainted. Mama knew Irene was nervous and excited both at the same time and she wanted to help her as much as she possibly could. She'd had to let her in on the surprise, because she'd needed some details about what kind of house they wanted. She had also allowed Irene to do a little decorating as well.

twelve

ARRIVING HOME

Roland had been nervously fidgeting most of the way home on the bus. The guys had teased him relentlessly; he was the only one in their group who was coming home to a wife and baby. He was excited about seeing both of them, but he was also frightened. He'd witnessed some terrible things while he was away and he knew he wasn't the same man now, as he'd been when he'd left. He loved Irene dearly and hoped she would still love him, even if he had changed a little. She has to understand, he thought I need her now more than ever. He wanted desperately to be a family and he couldn't wait to see his baby girl, Cassandra Elsie Petersen, Cassie. "Wow," he almost said aloud then quickly looked around to make certain he hadn't, he couldn't believe he was finally going to meet her. There were times overseas when he'd been fighting or shivering in the trenches, or the time he'd been lost in the forest, when he'd been terrified he would never get the chance to meet her or see Irene again. It was almost as though it had been that very thought that had kept him going. He'd watched some of his friends die right in front of him and others who were hurt so badly they wished they'd died. Words could not begin to describe the terror and helplessness he'd felt over there. He shook his head; he needed to put all that behind him now, he was finally home. He thought with a smile the nightmare is over.

The bus pulled up in front of the station and as it did, Roland spotted Irene with Cassie in her arms. He felt a surge of excitement; she looked exactly the same as she had when he'd left, she was beautiful. He noticed little Cassie, she waving at the bus excitedly, he felt a surge of pride watching them. The rest of the guys stood aside to let him get off the bus first. Roland nodded his thanks to them as he made his way down the isle, then bounded down the stairs and broke into a run, straight towards Irene. When he reached her, he picked her up and swung her around, he hugged her and kissed her. Cassie started laughing and to Irene's surprise said, "Da Da." Roland's heart melted, he took little Cassie in his arms and hugged her; she kept giggling and shouting, "DaDa, DaDa!" They laughed at her, and then Roland held her out, at arms length so he could take a good look at her. Her little face looked just like Irene's she had the same turquoise blue eyes but instead of Irene's dark hair, hers was fine, curly and blonde, he thought she was beautiful. He hugged her to his chest, saying softly, "My little girl!" Irene was just beaming; she had her arm around his waist.

Mom and Dad emerged from the crowd with Melissa beside them, it had been so hard for them to stay back, but they felt they owed it to Roland to let him see Irene and Cassie first. Roland hugged them and kissed Melissa on the end of her nose, just as he used to. She smiled a smile so wide she thought her face would split, but she couldn't stop it, she was so incredibly happy. Just as they were gathering and getting ready to leave for home, Mama stepped into view, Donna was by her side and Jake was behind her. She gave Roland a big hug and told him, "I'm so glad you're home, safe and sound, Irene was lost without you." Donna gave him a hug as well. Jake shook his hand and told him, "I'm glad you're home, safe." The whole group of them started walking home to Mom and Dad's. Roland only had one bag, so there wasn't much to carry. Dad carried it for him though, so he could carry Cassie, who was thrilled with her "DaDa," she hadn't made strange at all, much to everyone's surprise.

Mom had made a wonderful "welcome home" picnic lunch with the help of Melissa and everyone ate it outside in the yard. It was a good thing the weather was warm, because the house wasn't large enough to hold all of them comfortably.

Roland was different, more mature or something, neither Mom nor Dad could quite put their finger on it. When Gramps overheard their discussion and their concern, he told them, "Try not to worry so much, I know how Roland feels; I've been there myself, a long time ago." He explained, "Roland has seen things, over there that no man should ever see and it's going to take him a while to sort things out, and to put all of those images out of his mind." Gramps added, a sober expression clouding his features, "It took me almost two years to do that myself. I remember having nightmares some nights and believe it or not, every once in a while I still do." He told them after a moment, "I've already spoken to Irene about what she should expect, I told her not to be too hard on him and to try and understand." He explained, "Irene told me she just wanted him home, she said she'd expected he might be different, because he'd been forced to do things over there that were completely out of character for him. She said she could tell that from some of the letters he'd written over the two years he's been gone." He added, "She said she'd do her best to make a happy home for him to recover in. She was sure little Cassie would help with that too." Mom and Dad looked at Gramps with such appreciation in their eyes. They both thanked him and Mom told him, "We're so lucky to have you; we can always count on you to help, when we need it the most, thank you."

When lunch was finished and the cake, Mom and Melissa had made and decorated for Roland, had been eaten. Mama told Roland, smiling slyly, "I have a gift to give to the two of you." She handed him the keys to the new house she'd bought for them on Mitten St. Roland was puzzled at first but Mama explained, "Since I inherited some money from Otto's brother, I wanted to share some of it with you, I bought you a house and I had Jake and his friends move all your things into it." She said, "Irene has known about it of course, because I needed her input to know just what kind of house you wanted." She looked at Irene and said, smiling, "There will be a few surprises for you too in the house." Then went on to tell Roland, "Irene told me you always wanted a bungalow in that area, so I bought the nicest one I could find," she added, "I hope you like it". Roland was speechless; he couldn't believe she'd done that. He looked at Irene, who was beaming with pride, and smiled. She said, "Wait till you see what we've done with the place, I decorated a little and of course I did up the nursery for Cassie. The crib and playpen were already in the room and Gramps delivered a gorgeous matching dresser, which he made to match the crib. He said he had left over wood." They all knew he didn't but they knew he wanted to help make their first home special. Mama told them, "I'm going to look after Cassie tonight, so you and Irene can have time to yourselves, since it's been two whole years since you've seen each other. You'll also need to get used to your new house." Roland had tears in his eyes, he hugged Mama and said, "Thank you, thank you so very much". Mama just smiled and finally told them, "Scoot! Go see your new home." The two of them kissed Cassie goodbye, said their goodbye's to everyone else, and started walking hand in hand towards their new home.

They kept looking at each other on the way, they laughed as they tripped a couple of times, they were so busy smiling at each other to watch where they were going. Roland slipped his arm around her waist as they walked; it took about fifteen minutes to walk there from Mom and Dad's place. When Irene pointed out the house, as they rounded the corner onto Mitten St., Roland thought he was dreaming; this house was everything he'd described to Irene a couple of years earlier. He looked down at her amazed, "You remembered." He said, "Even the colour," which he noticed was yellow; exactly what he'd said he wanted. He noticed the white trim on the windows and doors. This house was perfect, it was exactly the house he had described to Irene one day when they'd been talking and sharing their dreams with each other, in their apartment, a few days after they'd been married.

When they reached the front door, Roland opened it and then he stepped back, scooped her up in his arms, and carried her across the threshold. He'd no sooner shut the door when he started kissing her and practically tearing her clothes off her. He finally gave up and just pushed up her skirt and slid her underwear down. He just couldn't wait any longer; he had to have her. Irene was tense and a little unsure though and when he sensed her apprehension, he spoke softly into her hair at the side of her cheek saying, "Its okay." He kept telling her, "I love you," until she calmed down and answered him with, "I love you too and I missed you so much." The last thing in the world he wanted was to hurt her. He had to remember it had been two long years since they'd been together. Irene kissed him passionately; she sensed the fear in him. She told him again, "I love you." That was all it took, they made love right there on the floor in the entryway of their new home. They were both so quick; it wasn't like any other time they'd been together. This time it was as though they were fulfilling a need not simply a desire. When they got up from the floor, they were laughing and joking about how some things never change. The next time they actually made it to the bed and this time they took the time to undress before making love right on top of the bedspread, they still didn't find the time to get into bed. The urgency was still there, they simply couldn't get enough of each other. Afterward, as Irene was getting out robes from the closet for them to wear and handed one to Roland, he joked about the next time, he hoped they'd make it into the bed.

They started exploring their new home. Irene showed him the nursery she'd decorated for Cassie; it was across the hall from their room. He was impressed with the job she'd done and with the furniture that Gramps had made. She'd written and described all of it in detail, in her letters but Roland thought Gramps had really outdone himself, the crib and matching dresser were really something. He saw the playpen standing up against the wall and noticed it was constructed to fold up in the middle and the mattress folded as well, making it fully portable. Irene informed him, pointing at the playpen, "Mom made that mattress for the bottom of it, you know." He nodded, smiling in reply. She showed him the beautiful quilt Melissa made for the crib, and at the same time explaining, "I used the same colours that are in the quilt to decorate the room." He told her, smiling, "It looks gorgeous." She exclaimed, "Mama even found a rocker to match everything. Look!" Roland was smiling at her excitement over the nursery.

Their own bedroom looked almost the same as the one they'd had in the apartment over the butcher shop, only it was considerably larger. The third bedroom was empty. They walked down the hall past the bath with the pink and black tiles, and pink sink, toilet and tub, to the L shaped living room and dining room. Roland noticed the living room contained all the furniture they'd originally purchased together; he smiled when he noticed Irene had added a few touches of colour in the drapes and cushions and she'd purchased lamps. He told her, draping his arm around her shoulders, "Wow, you've really been busy, it looks spectacular!" He even joked, "Hey, we'll have light all over the room now not just the bit of light from the tiny pole lamp, like we did before." The dining room was empty, except for some bookshelves. When they reached the kitchen, he marvelled at the new fridge and stove. Irene told him, "Mama bought them too." They decided to make a pot of coffee; they kissed while they looked around discovering all the things Mama had bought and placed neatly in the fridge and cupboards. She'd even bought some milk for Cassie. They figured they had lots of time to explore the basement, while they waited for their coffee to percolate. Irene told him as they descended the stairs, "I haven't been down here yet, either." She squealed in delight as she reached the bottom of the stairs and saw the brand new washer; it was one of those new automatic ones. She noticed the manual on top of it and let out a loud sigh of relief, holding it up, she said, "I'd be totally lost if Mama hadn't left this. I've only ever used a wringer washer, I've heard of an automatic, I've even seen them in the stores, but I never imagined I'd own one, at least not yet anyway." Upon closer inspection, they noticed Mama had a note on the washer, it said, "An automatic dryer will be delivered next week," and she signed it, "Mama, XXOO." Irene and Roland just gaped at each other; they could not believe Mama had done all this for them. They knew for sure now, it was her father's fault, that she'd never seemed to be interested before, he probably hadn't allowed her to be. Since his death, Mama was a completely different person. She was fun to be around and she truly was a caring and giving mother and grandmother. Irene was telling Roland all about this on their way back up the stairs to the kitchen.

They poured their coffee into cups and sat at the kitchen table, marvelling at how they could see their backyard, from there. Mama had hired a handyman to put up the fence, so Cassie would have a safe place to play; she'd had him make a sandbox as well. She also had a patio poured and the grass was seeded. They could already see little green shoots sticking out of the ground. The front of the house already had grass, it was thin, but it was there. Mama had said she was going to buy Cassie a swing set, as soon as the grass grew so it wouldn't be in the mud.

Roland was watching Irene looking out at the backyard, he smiled and told her, "You have no idea how much I missed you."

She asked him, "How does it feel being home?" He replied, with a look of wonder on his face, "It's hard to imagine I'll actually be sleeping in a comfortable bed at night and have you beside me. I've been dreaming of this day." His face grew serious as he told her, "I'll have to get used to not having to be ready to jump up and fight every time I hear a noise." He told her some of the things he could never tell her in his letters. He hadn't wanted her to worry. Suddenly he stopped; he could see the pained look on her face and the tears running unchecked down her cheeks. She reached out and hugged him, when she pulled away and reached for his hand, he could feel his own tears wet on his face. Irene whispered, "Its okay, you're home now, safe." She quietly asked, "Why didn't you ever tell me?" Roland replied, "I didn't want you to worry." He said, "You had enough to worry about raising Cassie, all alone." Irene thought, I really didn't do all that much, Mom, Dad, Mama, Donna and Melissa pretty much did all the work, I didn't do very much at all, unless I could count going to work and playing with Cassie when I got home in the evenings. She didn't think it was a good idea to tell him that though. It was better to let him think that she was just a little hard done by.

Roland asked her, "Did you tell the lawyers that you won't need to work anymore yet?" Irene looked shocked. She questioned, with a slightly angry tone to her voice, "Why would I have done that?" Roland looked at her puzzled, as if possibly she didn't understand what he'd asked. He said, drawing his brows together, puzzled, "You don't have to work anymore, I'll be working and I want you to be home when I get home and to be a full time mother to Cassie." Irene tried to control her simmering temper, she was seething inside. She almost hissed at him when she asked him, "Just how do you intend to go to medical school and work too? I plan to continue working so we can afford to live comfortably while you're studying." He backed down a bit, he thought he probably broached that subject just a little too soon but he hated the thought of her working, he was the man of the house and he was the one who was supposed to bring in the money, not her. He decided not to pursue the matter, just now. When he did speak again, he simply said, "I'm sorry, I only want you to be happy and I want to see you as much as possible. I thought if you were at home that would be better for all of us." When he saw her mood begin to brighten a little, he said, "Let's talk about happier things, there's so much I don't know about the last two years of your life and I want to know everything. Start by telling me all about Cassie, okay?" Irene thought, I thought he wanted to know all about me, but she decided to ignore it and tell him all about the cute things Cassie did and some of the not so cute things too. They laughed and talked for hours.

Roland had been watching her face as she spoke for the last few minutes and felt the stirrings in his gut; he had to have her again only this time, he wanted to have her, slowly. He reached over and untied the sash on her robe. It fell open exposing one full breast, he held it in his hand and played with the nipple until it was hard and ripe, he loved how her breathing was becoming ragged and her blue eyes were softening. He bent his head and took her breast in his mouth while his hand slid down her belly until he felt the tangle of hair. She moved ever so slightly and he could feel her hot breath on his neck. Her breathing was becoming faster. He moved his mouth over to her other breast, the nipple was already erect and he kissed it as she kissed his neck and face. Suddenly, he pushed the chair back and pulled her up to a standing position, he moved the coffee cups over to the counter as quickly as he could. Irene watched him and as she did she thought her legs wouldn't hold her, they felt like jelly, he was the same handsome man she'd fallen in love with and she continued to watch him as he finished putting the coffee dishes on the counter. He turned and crossed the short distance back to her as he looked at her, their eyes met and locked, his were dark with longing and she could see his desire.

She reached up, brought his face down to hers, and kissed him deeply. She kissed and caressed him pouring out all the pent up feelings that had been buried for so long until he couldn't stand it any longer. He gently pushed her back towards the table and lifted her up on top of it. Roland simply couldn't wait any longer he had to have her, now, he thrust into her and at the same time as she cried out in pleasure, he exploded in ecstasy. He was resting on top of her afterwards unable to move and at the same time trying not to hurt her with his weight. She recovered and started to giggle, she said, "Oh my God, the kitchen table." They both started into fits of laughter. He kissed her once more, then stood and picked her up; he walked down the hall to their room. Once the two of them were snuggled in bed, they lay in each other's arms and fell asleep.

Irene was the first to awake and was shocked when she looked at the alarm clock on the bedside table; they'd slept right through the night. She watched Roland sleeping and smiled to herself. She raised herself up on her elbow, and watched as he slept. She stayed like that for quite some time; it was so wonderful to have him home. Then she had an idea and decided to be mischievous, she lifted the covers and snuck under them. She began lightly kissing his neck working her way down with gentle kisses until he was fully aroused. Before he realized what was happening and where he was, he'd released. Irene was surprised, but at the same time that was exactly what she'd hoped for, he had done that to her so many times before he went away, but he would never let her do it to him. He'd told her that it wasn't something wives did. Irene hadn't been so sure of that though and always wanted to know what it was like, now she knew. Roland jolted, awake but managed to stop himself just as the name "Anna," escaped from his lips. He partially sat up, horrified at what he's said, but thankfully, she hadn't heard him; she was still under the covers. He was so ashamed of himself, he thought of how he hadn't able to remain faithful to her during the time he'd been away. He thought, trying to make excuses to himself for the guilt he felt, it was just that Anna helped me forget, even though it was only for a little a while, things over there that were so unbearable. I never had feelings for her; I only needed the escape she provided, he thought. Anna used to wake him this way, whenever he'd slept with her. He was so glad Irene hadn't heard him say her name. He never wanted her to know about Anna, she would never understand and she'd be so hurt and he knew he could never allow that to happen. He pulled her up and told her, "You shouldn't do that." He said, "I still don't think wives should do things like that." She shrugged and said, "I could tell you enjoyed it and I always wanted to know what it would feel like to do it." He asked her, "Well, did you like it?" She looked at him shyly and said, "Well, not really all that much, I only wanted to make you happy." He smiled and held her close, and said, "I am happy; you don't need to do that or anything else." He knew she loved him. He sighed, he couldn't bring himself to be mad at her, after all what she did felt fantastic, he'd just have to be careful not to say Anna's name, in case she ever decided to do that again.

Irene made breakfast for the two of them and afterwards, they walked hand in hand to Mama's to collect Cassie. They couldn't wait to begin their lives as a real family.

Mama was thrilled to see them, as was Cassie. She jumped up and down, holding onto the couch in Mama's living room, saying, "Mama, Mama," to Irene and holding out the hand that wasn't busy holding on to the couch, she could walk by herself, but she couldn't handle jumping yet. Cassie caught sight of Roland and stopped jumping, she turned her head slightly to the side and looked at him intently, and then to their surprise. smiled and said, "DaDa". Roland was so surprised he smiled saying, "Hello sweetie," and Cassie surprised them all when she toddled right to him. Irene couldn't believe it. Mama said, "You two look like you might just burst with happiness." Roland talked to Cassie and played with her until she started to struggle and then he had no choice but to put her down. He went over to Mama and told her, "You have no idea how grateful I am for everything you've done for us, I just can't thank you enough." She looked down shyly and said, "It's not necessary to thank me, it's thanks enough for me to see you home safe and sound, and to see you and Irene together and happy again". She said, "Now let's collect Cassie's things, so you two can take her to your new home and she can sleep in her new bedroom tonight." Then she turned to Irene and asked, "Do you want me to come to your place tomorrow morning and look after Cassie there, so she can be at home?" Roland glanced at Irene, she only looked away and told Mama, "That would be wonderful, would eight thirty be too early?" Mama answered, "You know me I'm up with the birds and I do hope you'll let me continue to look after her, it gives me a purpose in life." Irene thought to herself, yes, thank you, that was the perfect excuse and she knew that Roland had heard it. She'd use it the next time he asked her to stop working. She couldn't believe how easy Mama had just made it for her. She could keep saying it was over concern for her poor Mama, that she continued to work and of course, she would add that she really didn't mind so much anyway because she liked her job. Surely, Roland wouldn't want to hurt her Mama, especially now that he felt he owed her so much, she had to restrain herself from jumping up and down, she was so happy.

The next day the two of them were getting ready for work with little Cassie toddling around them. Roland thought she was just so cute. She was making Irene mad though the way she was pulling things out of the drawers and Irene was continually doing her best to get things back in place. Finally, she gave up, set up the playpen in the living room, and plunked Cassie in it. Cassie was not the least bit happy about that and let out a whooping big scream that had Roland in fits of laughter. Irene tried putting one toy after another in with her, but Cassie was firing them out as fast as Irene could put them in and hollering at the same time.   Roland, still laughing, glanced out the bedroom window and noticed Mama coming up the walk.   He hollered to Irene, above Cassie's wails, "Let your mother in," just as she rang the doorbell. When Irene opened the door Mama smiled at Cassie, her little face was red as a beet and she was screaming. Mama said, "Oh my, someone has a nasty temper," and scooped her up in her arms.   Cassie stopped crying immediately.   Irene told her all about this mornings events. Mama laughed, and said, "I pick up after her constantly, when she's at my house."   Irene had never thought about it much, she'd never had to deal with Cassie totally on her own before.   She thought she'd have to get used to this stage in Cassie's little life though.   Roland came out of the bedroom all dressed for work in his dress pants and shirt and wearing a tie, they were a little large on him; he had lost a bit of weight overseas.   He claimed it was because the food was so terrible most of the time and the rest of the time, they simply hadn't had time to eat, because it had been too dangerous.

Roland was going back to work at the Oil Company they'd agreed to take him back as soon as his service was over.   He'd been told to come on in on the first Monday after he returned. He had to admit he was excited to see everyone again, and he loved working in the lab, so he was looking forward to the work as well.   He noticed how lovely Irene looked all dressed up for work. He still wished she wasn't working, but he understood that for now it did give Mama a purpose in life as she called it, since the poor woman felt she didn't have one, except to be a grandma and look after Cassie.   Donna was busy with her friends, when she wasn't studying and Jake had moved out, so Mama had to find her place again.   She needed to start meeting people; he thought the woman has no friends.   She had neighbours but no real friends anymore; Otto had never allowed her to have any friends at the house, and of course, she'd never been allowed to go out anywhere, so Elinor eventually lost touch with all of them.

Otto always told her that friends were nothing but a waste of time. Roland thought, that man had a real mean streak in him and vowed he would never be anything like him. Irene noticed Roland had grown quiet and rather intense, she said to him, "A penny for your thoughts." Roland jolted and smiled at her. He said, after a moment, "I was thinking about how I haven't been to work at the Oil Company for two whole years." She asked, "Are you nervous?" He said, "A little, just because I'm not sure what will have changed and if I'll know what to do when I get there." Irene smiled and told him, "Don't worry, I'm sure they'll help you." She reminded him, "They always did like you and they appreciated the work you did as well." Roland brightened a little at that memory. He kissed Irene and collected the lunch she'd made for him, this morning. He kissed Cassie goodbye and headed out the door, saying, "See you later."

Irene was getting her own lunch ready when she said, "Thanks," to Mama. Mama asked with a puzzled look on her face, "For what?" Irene said, "I know you helped me yesterday. You know how much I want to keep working." Mama said, "Irene, I really meant what I said, I didn't say that to help you keep working at all, I really do feel that looking after Cassie gives me a purpose." She told her, "I feel so lost, I didn't have much of a life when Father was alive, but at least I was able to keep busy, with the cleaning, the laundry and making meals." Irene blurted out, without thinking, "And dodging Father's fists." The words were no sooner out of her mouth, when she regretted having said them. She watched as Mama's whole demeanour changed; it was as if she didn't have the strength to stand. Irene ran to her, took Cassie, and placed her in the playpen and miraculously the child didn't scream. She quickly took Mama's arm and sat her down on the couch, telling her, "Mama, I'm so sorry I said that." Mama looked sad but admitted, "You're right, that was a big part of my life. I was always trying my best to make sure nothing upset him. I know that I failed you kids and I'm trying

my best to be a good grandmother, because it's too late now
to be a good mother, you kids are all grown up now, except
Donna and she's not interested in spending much time with me
anymore. She's busy with her friends." Irene told her, "You're a
really good mother," even though she really didn't feel that way
and she knew Jake and Donna didn't either, but she had to try
to make her feel better, after all, she was doing her very best to
make up for it now. Cassie started babbling and laughing at her
toys in the playpen, which made Mama and Irene smile. Mama
got off the couch, went over to the playpen, and told Cassie,
"You make everything better," and brushed Cassie's cheek with
her fingers. Irene smiled at Mama, and jumped up off the couch,
as she noticed the time. She picked up her lunch and went to
the front closet for her purse and coat. She ran over and kissed
Cassie's little forehead, gave Mama a kiss on the cheek and ran
out the door saying, "Bye see you at four thirty, love you." She
blew them a kiss, closed the door and ran up the street. Thank
goodness, the bus was just on the next block; Irene was worried
she'd have missed it. She could have walked to work; but that
extra fifteen minutes she'd spent with Mama would make her
late, if she did. She hopped on the bus and dropped her coin in
the slot, she sat on the seat directly across from the driver, she
was only going to be riding a few stops.

Mama lifted Cassie from the playpen and asked her, "Do you
want to go out to the park? Grandma will put you on the baby
swing." Cassie squealed with delight she knew exactly what that
was. Mama smiled to herself as she put Cassie's hat and sweater
on. She pushed her down the street in the new stroller she'd
bought for Irene. Mama thought to herself, life's perfect as she
looked down at Cassie and smiled.

thirteen

CHANGE OF MIND

Roland was thoroughly enjoying being back at work. He'd forgotten how much he loved this job. The guys were great; they'd given him a welcome back party in the lunchroom during the lunch break. They even had a cake that one of the office girls had made and decorated, her name was Sharon; she was a junior secretary, she'd recently graduated from high school and Roland had made a point to thank her personally. When he did, she'd surprised him, by saying, "I remember you from school." He looked puzzled as he tried to place her, but she laughed when she noticed the look on his face and said, smiling, "Don't worry you wouldn't remember me, I was only a junior when you were a senior." She paused a second and added, "You were always too busy with that Irene girl to notice anyone else, anyways." Then in the same breath, before Roland could even think of a response, she asked, "What ever happened to her anyway? I never liked her very much, she was so selfish." Roland was taken aback, he thought, should I tell her or not, but in the end he decided he'd better tell her and said, flatly, looking her in the eye, "She's my wife, I married her two years ago." Sharon turned several shades of red and quickly said, as she started backing away, "I have to get back to my desk." She turned and almost ran out of the lunchroom. Roland thought that was

123

more than a little strange, he'd been under the impression in high school that all the girls had liked Irene, but decided with a shrug that Sharon was quite a bit younger and she most likely hadn't even known Irene.

Later, Roland's boss, Mr. Marsden, sent his secretary to the lab to collect him and bring him to his office. When Roland arrived, Mr. Marsden stood and shook his hand. He told him, "Welcome back! You were certainly missed while you were absent." Roland thought, absent, as if I had a choice. Mr. Marsden went on to say, "I know that the US Army pays for their veterans schooling if they attend school within a certain period of time after an Honourable Discharge. I admit I don't know all the details, however, the Company is willing to pay anything the Army doesn't cover if you're still interested in becoming a Chemical Engineer." Roland was so surprised he nearly fell off his chair. Mr. Marsden must have noticed because he chuckled and asked, "Are you a little surprised?" Roland said, "I most certainly am, I had no idea." Mr. Marsden's expression turned serious and he asked, "What exactly are your plans?" Roland told him, thoughtfully, "I had been thinking of becoming a Chemical Engineer before I was drafted, I had originally wanted to become a doctor, but I changed my mind, once I started working in the Lab." He went on to say, "I really enjoy working in the lab." Mr. Marsden told him, smiling, "I'm glad to hear it and you may continue working as much as you can handle while you attend school, however it's likely you'll only be able to during school breaks and during the summers." He said, "You just might have to go to school in Detroit, since that's the closest American University that offers the Engineering course. I'm not sure of that yet, but I'll have someone check. I think the US Army will only pay their portion if you attend an American University." Roland said, nodding, "I believe you're right, I remember reading something to that effect in the information booklet the Army supplied me with when I was discharged." Mr. Marsden stood saying, "The Company will make all the arrangements," he added, "You've made the right decision; the Lab is just the start, once you have your Degree in hand, you'll really be going places." He shook Roland's hand again and Roland left his office.

When he got back to the lab all the guys wanted to know what happened. When he told them, they congratulated him, he was the only one of all of them that had actually finished high school and since he was good at his job and smart as well, they'd all figured it was only a matter of time before the Company offered him something better. They were thrilled for him though. "What an offer, paying for school," they said, almost in unison, "Wow." One of the guys added, "Your wife is really going to be happy." That statement brought Roland back down to earth. He knew how much Irene wanted him to become a doctor; she talked about it all the time. All of a sudden, he felt guilty; he'd made the decision to become an Engineer without even so much as telling her about it. He knew she wasn't going to like that one bit.

When Roland arrived home, Irene was at the sink peeling potatoes. Cassie was in her playpen playing with her blocks. When she looked up and saw him, she smiled and said, excitedly, "Da da," and held her little arms up to him. Roland's heart melted, as he reached down and picked her up. She immediately pulled his pen out of his shirt pocket and stuck it in her mouth. He walked over and kissed Irene. She'd been watching the exchange between him and Cassie, smiling, she said, "Boy, it didn't take her long to know how to get to you." Roland said, chuckling, "No kidding, she's a smart little thing," and asked, "What's for supper?" She replied, "Mama put a roast in the oven and now all I have to do is make the potatoes." She said, motioning with her elbow toward the bowl on the counter, "Mama had even made a salad." Then added, shaking her head, "I told her not to go to all that trouble, but she insisted she needed something to do while Cassie was napping. She even made cupcakes." Irene regretted saying that word right away, because Cassie started getting excited. Cassie knew that word and she wanted one. She said to Roland, laughing, "We need to distract her, until she forgets about the C-U-P-C-A-K-E-S," she spelled it out so Cassie wouldn't hear it again. "I want her to eat some supper first." Roland chuckled and took her into the bedroom with him; he wanted to change his clothes. Cassie proceeded to pull everything out of the bottom drawers of the dresser while he changed. It took him a while to pick it all up. He was throwing her up in the air and catching her as she squealed and giggled with delight, when Irene came into the bedroom to tell them dinner was ready. She marvelled at how easily he played with her. She still had difficulty playing; it was something she could only do for a short time, she seemed to lack the patience for it, she much preferred if someone else played with her. She liked to dress her up and take her places, but she still didn't like the day-to-day work of being a mother and that included playing because to her that was work.

Once dinner was finished and the cupcakes devoured, which Cassie thoroughly enjoyed, Roland cleaned up the kitchen while Irene plunked Cassie into the bathtub. She was covered with icing and bits of cupcakes; it was even in her hair. Cassie splashed and laughed throughout her bath, she loved it, and she even loved getting her hair washed. By the time, Irene got her into her pyjamas and ready for bed, Cassie could hardly keep her little eyes open. She brought her out to Roland, who was sitting on the couch in the living room reading the paper; he'd already finished washing the dishes. Roland kissed and hugged Cassie while saying, "Goodnight sweetheart," and Irene carried her to her room and put her to bed. She swore Cassie was asleep before she even made it out of the room. Irene trudged out to the living room and slumped on the couch beside Roland. He asked, frowning, "Is she already asleep?" Irene said, "She is, she was falling asleep on the way into her room." She laughed and added, "I know the feeling; she has so much energy she tires herself out and us too." Roland laughed and agreed, "Yup she sure does", and smiled, he was so proud of his little girl. He looked at Irene and asked, "Are you tired." She said, looking at him, "I just need to catch my breath. That bath tired me out too. I also had a particularly busy day at the office." Roland frowned and reminded her, "You really don't have to work you know. I'm sure things will be just fine if you want to stay home and look after Cassie." Irene gave him a look that he didn't care for, so he decided to drop the subject altogether. Then all of a sudden she blurted out, defiantly, "Just because I have a busy day doesn't mean that I don't love what I do and I have no intentions of quitting," she went on to say, "What would Mama do and how would we support ourselves when you go to medical school." Roland decided not to say anything about the Engineering Degree he wanted, since he wasn't sure of the details yet or if he could even get into the course. He would wait to hear from his boss, before he said anything to her. He replied evenly, "Hey, I'm not asking you to quit, I just wanted you to know that you could if you wanted to."

It was a full week before Mr. Marsden called Roland into his office again. He shook his hand and told him, "Have a seat," and sat down in the chair beside him. He said, happily, "I checked with the US Army and found out that they will only pay for your school if you attend a school in the US, which we kind of figured anyways." He clapped Roland on the shoulder and continued, "I had my secretary check and the University of Detroit has room in their Engineering program for you, and all the prerequisite courses you will need to be eligible for the program are offered there as well." Roland was thrilled and told his boss, "Thank God, I can't wait to get started." Mr. Marsden asked him, "Can we sign you up, then?" Roland smiled and asked, "When do I start?" He told him, "Well there are a few things you should know, I know we can get you into the second Semester, if you work especially hard, you can make up for missing the first Semester and start with the full program in September." He smiled and without missing a beat, asked Roland, "So, are you up for the challenge of completing two Semesters in one?" Roland looked thoughtful for a moment and said, "I'll do my best." Mr. Marsden asked, once more, "So does that mean we can we sign you up?" Roland's smile grew a little wider as he said, "You bet you can!" He informed him, "I'll work as hard as I can. I have a family to support and I want to get this Degree and start earning money so my wife won't have to work if she doesn't want to." Mr. Marsden raised an eyebrow and said, apologetically, "I haven't told you about the pay and the benefits yet, have I?" He continued, without waiting for a reply, "Since the Army is paying the schooling for your Degree; the Company is prepared to continue paying you your salary, including annual rises throughout your schooling, provided you keep passing, that is." He went on to tell him, "Your wife can quit and be a full time mother and wife anytime she wants now." Roland was so happy it was hard for him to contain himself and appear professional. Mr. Marsden noticed his excitement and told him, laughing, "You can yell and jump for joy if you want to." He said, laughing, and clapping him on the back, "You look like you're going to burst." Roland laughed.

He went home that evening and once Cassie was tucked into bed, after her bath, he told Irene, "I have something to tell you." Irene asked, smiling, "Does it have anything to do with the fact that you seem extremely happy tonight?" She said, "You're usually happy, but I noticed tonight was a little different." Roland laughed and told her, "It most certainly is making me happy. The most fantastic thing happened at work today." He explained the offer his boss made him. Irene sat there with a blank look on her face. Once Roland had finished explaining everything including his taking two whole semesters in just one and the fact that they were going to pay him, he asked her, excitedly "So what do you think?" Irene was so shocked by what he'd said that she was having difficulty absorbing it all. When

Roland said he was going to be a Chemical Engineer and work at the Oil Company, because they were going to pay for his school, tons of things ran through her mind. Things like the dreams she had of the prestige of being a doctor's wife, evaporating before it ever became a reality, having to quit a job that she loved and his saying that she could now be a full time mother, "Yuk," she was thinking, "Who wants to be that". Irene heard Roland ask her, "Honey, did you hear me? I asked you what you think." Irene decided quickly to pretend she was happy about it, and told him sweetly while conjuring up a smile, "If this is going to make you happy, then it'll make me happy too." Roland took her in his arms and hugged her. He said, excitedly, "Mr. Marsden told me that this was just the beginning for me. He said I would go a long way in the Company." This thought suddenly brightened Irene's dark mood, she desperately wanted to be a "somebody" and maybe she still could. She thought just maybe it's possible that being an Engineer's wife won't be so bad after all, especially if Roland could get promotions and move up in the Company. She also thought, brightening even more, if he's away in Detroit, I can work and he wouldn't even have to know about it. Surely Mama wouldn't say anything and Mom and Dad didn't come over all that often these days and Melissa was busy with her boyfriend, so she wouldn't have to worry about her too much either. She finally relaxed, and gave Roland a passionate kiss and held him close and for the first time tonight, she said, "Congratulations honey," and truly meant it. Roland breathed a sigh of relief and kissed her in return. He smiled slyly, picked her up and carried her to the bedroom, where they made slow passionate love in celebration of his impending success. When they finally fell asleep in each other's arms, they were both completely spent.

fourteen

ALONE AGAIN

Time passed quickly, fall turned into winter and they had a wonderful Christmas they even celebrated New Years Eve together. Then in the first week of January, Roland had to leave to return to school. He kissed Irene and Cassie goodbye and hurried off to catch the bus. He was beginning to feel as if he was never going to be able to be a part of his own family. He thought with a sigh I'll fix that as soon as I finish this Chemical Engineering program and get my Degree; I'll be able to be a real husband and father then, not only a long distance, and mostly absent, one. He wondered if Irene could wait that long, he could tell that she was tired of being alone.

Irene was happy in her day-to-day life since Roland left, she missed him, but she enjoyed working and having Mama look after Cassie. Mama was even staying a little longer these days, cooking meals and helping to clean up the dishes. She even settled Cassie down at night so Irene could rest.

Mama bought a bed for their spare room with a matching chest of drawers and a night table. Irene suggested to her one evening, "You should use the spare room sometimes when you're too tired to go home." She added, frowning, "I don't like you walking home alone in the dark anyway, so on the days you want to stay late and help me with dinner and Cassie, please use it." Mama had only replied, "We'll see," but she did start to sleep in it a few nights a week. Irene loved it when she did, she didn't like being alone in the house. It had been different when Roland was in the Army, because she'd never been completely alone, first she had lived with Mom and Dad and then after Father's death, she'd moved in with Mama. She found it a bit frightening to be alone in her own house. Even in their first apartment, the Butcher and his wife lived downstairs on the other side of the shop. She hadn't known them well, she'd only delivered the envelope containing the rent on the first of every month and most of the time she'd had to slip it into the mail slot, because they went to bed so early, but at least she'd known they were there. Irene thought, as long as Mama's here to look after the details, like most of the cooking and the cleaning, as well as looking after Cassie and I only have to go to work, which I love, I'll be extremely happy. She felt a little guilty being as happy as she was though because as much as she missed Roland, she was afraid that when he came home to stay, after he finished school, she'd have to quit her job and stay at home and she dreaded the thought.

Things couldn't have been better for Irene, or so she thought, until one day in early February, she felt sick to her stomach when she got out of bed in the morning. It didn't last long, so she didn't say anything to Mama and she actually forgot all about it as the day progressed. The next day it happened again, Irene's mind was racing when she realized the last time she'd felt this way, she'd been pregnant with Cassie. She thought, closing her eyes in silent prayer, please God, no I can't be pregnant. She knew she had no choice; she had to find out for sure and called to make an appointment with her doctor. When she did make the call, she was upset to hear that her doctor had left Sarnia and moved to Toronto. The receptionist after telling her this bit of news, added cheerfully, "Dr. Grogan will be happy to see you, though, he's taken over the practise." Irene agreed, after all, she thought what choice did she have, she wanted an answer as soon as possible.

She saw Dr. Grogan the following day on her lunch break, and as sceptical about him as she was she had to admit he impressed her. He was so nice, a little younger than her old doctor was, but he was gentle and asked her lots questions. He convinced her that the concern he displayed was sincere. He told her exactly what she was expecting him to though, he said, "Drop off a urine sample in the morning on your way to work," he added, as she got up to leave, "It must be taken first thing in the morning." Irene nodded and asked, "If I bring it in tomorrow, when can I expect to hear the results?" He thought a moment and told her, "It may take a day or two, but I'll call you to come in for another appointment once your results are in." She returned to work and tried her best to put it out of her mind.

She dropped off the required sample the next morning and walked across the street to the office. She was busy all day and had practically forgotten all about it, until she returned home and Mama with a worried expression, told her, "Your doctor's office called, they want you to call them as soon as you can." Irene wondered why they'd called her home, she was positive she'd given them the number at the office. Mama asked, with a worried frown, "Are you sick?" Irene sighed and replied, "I had been feeling a little under the weather when I made the appointment but I'm better now." She said, shrugging, "They probably just called to let me know my tests were all normal." Mama seemed to accept that, because she didn't ask anything else and Irene didn't feel like talking about "what if's" right now. She would rather wait until she knew for sure, then if she was pregnant she'd tell her then.

The next day she called as soon as she got to the office and when the doctor's nurse came on the line, she told her the doctor would like to see her and asked if she could come in on her lunch break today.

Irene rushed over as fast as she could on her lunch hour she was extremely anxious about the results of her test and hoped as she waited for the doctor that he wouldn't tell her she was pregnant. She didn't have to sit in the waiting room long, before Dr. Grogan came out of his office and called her name. She sat down in the chair across from him and silently prayed he would tell her that she'd had some weird flu bug, anything would be better than being pregnant. Dr. Grogan opened the file he had sitting in front of him on his desk, as soon as he sat down. A smile appeared on his face and Irene thought, oh no, I know what he's going to say. She waited wringing her hands while he finished reading the file, he finally looked up at her and still smiling told her, "Congratulations, you're expecting!" He said, "I thought as much from the initial examination I gave you on your last visit, however, until the urine test confirmed my findings, I hadn't wanted to say so." He said, emphatically, "I believe you're three months along that means the baby should be due sometime in August." Irene didn't really care about that just now, she was wondering how she was going to handle two kids, Lord knows, she thought, I have enough trouble with one. Dr. Grogan noticed the deep frown on her face and concerned, asked her, "Do you not want to be pregnant?" Irene quickly snapped out of her nagging thoughts and told him with a forced smile, "Oh no, of course I do, I was just thinking about Roland being away at school and that I'll have to wait until he comes home again to tell him the good news." She kept up the fake smile, said, "Thank you," as warmly as she could muster, and asked, "Shall I see the nurse on my way out to make my next appointment." He answered smiling as well, "Yes, in one month from now. I'll see you then." He added, as she opened the door to leave, "Remember, if you have any problems or concerns in the meantime, call my nurse and she'll fit you in."

That afternoon when she arrived home after kissing and hugging Cassie, she asked, "Mama, are you in a hurry to go home tonight?" Mama noticed that she appeared troubled and said, "I don't have anything pressing to go home to tonight. Why?" Irene was relieved, "I was hoping you would say that, I really need to talk with you, but I'll wait until after we put Cassie to bed." Mama turned back to the sink, she knew Irene had been more than a little distracted lately. She thought as she finished washing the vegetables, now I'll finally find out what's been troubling her.

Once Cassie was settled in her bed, Mama and Irene sat at the kitchen table with a pot of tea between them. Irene told her about the new baby she was expecting and Mama was thrilled. She had just opened her mouth to say so, when the look on her face changed abruptly from sheer happiness to solemn concern as she noticed the pained look on Irene's face and instantly knew that Irene wasn't happy about it at all. Mama told her as she took her hands in hers, "Don't you worry, sweetheart, I'll be here for you, I can tell you find it difficult to look after children." Mama said trying to lift her spirits, "We can't all be wonderful with kids, but things will be just fine, because I love children and I'll always be right here to help you for as long as you need me." Irene smiled at her; she knew she could count on her. She gave her a hug and kissed her on the cheek, and said, "I'm so lucky, to have a mother like you." Mama blushed and told her, "Scoot off to bed, I'll tidy up and I'll make you a sandwich for your lunch tomorrow from tonight's leftovers, Okay?" Irene looked at Mama, her eyes were full of appreciation and said, "What would I do without you, it's more than okay." Mama smiled and told her, "I don't know, but I plan on being around for you, so you aren't going to find out any time soon, at least not if I can help it." They both chuckled at that and Irene went down the hall to bed, feeling happy for the first time in days.

Roland was home for spring break a few weeks later and was thrilled with the news. He loved kids and still wanted as many as they could possibly have. Irene told him, "Maybe this time we'll have a boy," but to her surprise he said, "A boy would be nice, but so would another girl." She looked at him with surprise registering on her face and he replied, "Hey, I really don't care whether it's a boy or a girl. Cassie has taught me that a little girl is pretty darn special. I have to admit that a few years ago I never would have thought I'd enjoy having little girls, all I could think of was having lots of boys, but Cassie has taught me so much; she's such a precious little thing. I wouldn't mind if I had nine girls, instead of nine boys." Irene swallowed, trying not to show her dismay, she was thinking, not if I can help it, mister, but answered with a little laugh, in an effort to cover her dismay over his wanting so many children, "What are you trying to do, kill me?" Roland thought that was rather funny. She, unbeknownst to him, wasn't amused in the least and decided it might be best to change the subject, altogether. She asked him, "How are your studies coming along?" He raised an eyebrow and said, "Well, I'm almost caught up, not coming home on the weekends has made a huge difference." He continued, "I'm almost ready to write the exams for the first semester, and I've already started working on the second semester." Irene hugged him, "I'm so very proud of you. I miss you but I know it's all for the best." She was thinking if he could do two semesters in one it would mean he would be away a little less time in total.

Roland asked, "Do you think working might be too much while you're pregnant?" Irene said, a little indignantly, "I worked with Cassie and both of us were fine, besides I'd go crazy and so would Mama if I didn't work." She quickly added, "I miss you too much, honey, I need the distraction." Roland nodded, but said, "When I finally get this degree I want you to stay home and look after the kids and the house, do we have a deal?" He was smiling at her, she smiled back and hugged him so he wouldn't see her face, she was afraid her expression might give away how she really felt. "Of course, darling," she said. She only agreed because she felt she really didn't have a choice, what would people think once he was working full time. She knew she would need to stay home then. She hated the thought of having to look after two kids all by herself; she thought, I'd go truly mad, thank goodness for Mama.

August arrived fast; Irene was so tired this time. She wondered if it was because Roland was home from school and working and she wasn't. She was at home picking up toys, washing, and cooking. Mama was only visiting now instead of being there daily. She'd said that she thought they needed some alone time to bond as a family. Irene would have preferred her to be there, though and consoled herself with the thought that she did say she would be back full time, in September, when Roland went back to school. Irene sighed, Mama was busy with Donna these days, and buying her clothes and helping her set up her new apartment. Donna was finished school and working for a doctor; she was a medical secretary now. Irene smiled as she thought of Mama saying that she was proud of her girls, "You two both have very important jobs," she'd said to her and Donna, one day last week when both Donna and Mama had popped in for a visit after shopping.

Irene was getting Cassie's lunch ready one afternoon, a few days later, when her water broke with a gush, all over the kitchen floor. Cassie, whom Irene had been trying her best to potty train, was sitting at the kitchen table waiting for her sandwich. When she saw the mess on the floor she struggled down from her chair and put her little hands on her hips and said, with all the authority she could muster, "Mommy, bad! Use the potty," and she stormed out of the kitchen.

Irene called Roland at work and in an effort to sound calmer than she felt, told him, "Don't panic but I think it's time, I need to go to the hospital." He answered, with a calmness in his voice that he didn't feel, "Just sit down; I'll be there as fast as I can." Irene had barely sat down after cleaning up the mess on the kitchen floor when Roland ran in the door. He'd made it home in less than fifteen minutes. He asked breathlessly running to her side, "Are you okay?" He reached for the phone, he called Mama first, to come and look after Cassie, but when she wasn't home, he had to call Mom. She said she'd be there right away. He then called a cab to take them to the hospital and hurried into their bedroom to collect Irene's, already packed and ready, suitcase. Irene seemed to be in a bit more distress now and he asked her nervously, once again, "Are you sure you're okay?" She said with an effort, after waiting for a contraction to subside, "I'm having contractions much closer together now, how long will the cab be?" She was frightened of having the baby at home. She'd been having terrifying dreams about that, lately. Roland looked out the window and replied, "Don't worry; it's already at the curb." He helped her down the sidewalk and into the cab. Irene had expected to be hours in labour, this time as well, but was shocked to find that things were moving along very quickly. She was no sooner prepped and put into a bed then Dr. Grogan told her, "You're nine centimetres dilated; we'll be taking you to the delivery room right away." Just then, the nurses started to push her bed out into the hall, and then proceeded to push her, down the hall towards the delivery room. To her astonishment, as she lay staring at the ceiling trying to ease the pain as another contraction ripped through her body, she heard Roland being asked, "Would you like to join us?" He was thrilled; he'd never expected that, either. Dr. Grogan noticed his shock and Irene's as well and said, "I think it's important to give husbands a choice." He explained as he walked beside Irene's bed as it was being transported down the hall, "This is a fairly new program the hospitals are trying and I hope they will continue with it."

Roland pulled on a gown and mask as quickly as he could, and walked into the delivery room, proud as can be. He held Irene's hand and was the first to see their new little girl. They looked at their new baby and back at each other and decided at the same time that out of all the names they'd narrowed the list down to, for girls, they wanted to call her Jean, Jean Alma Petersen. She had a soft, fine, light brown hair and eyelashes. Roland looked her over quickly; he counted ten toes and ten fingers and let out a huge sigh of relief. Irene was watching him laughing, she asked, "Were you really expecting her not to be perfect, she had to be, just look at her parents." They laughed at that.

Once the doctor was finished with Irene's stitches, he left them alone, they held hands and smiled at each other, they were so happy. They were waiting anxiously for little Jean to be brought back in, one of the nurses from the Nursery had taken her away to clean her up. When a nurse finally returned with Jean and placed her in Irene's arms, they had tears in their eyes looking at their newest member of their family. "She's so perfect," Roland said and taking her in his arms, he added, "She's so small." He looked into Jean's little face and told her, "Hi sweetie, your name is Jean Alma Petersen, your birthday is August 22, 1947, and next year you'll have a cake and presents." Irene shook her head and laughed. He became serious again, "I wish I could've been there for Cassie's birth. I never want to miss the birth of any more of our children." Irene was touched; she could see he really meant it. She said, sighing, "I hope you don't either, it was really special having you beside me this time. I hope the hospital realizes just what it means to the mothers, to have their husbands with them and that they continue allowing them to be there."

Everyone came to visit the next day, they brought flowers and baby clothes. Mama said, "Since she's a girl she can wear some of Cassie's old clothes." Irene said, frowning slightly, "I don't mind as long as no one uses the ones that are stained or worn, I want her to wear only the clean, newer looking things." Mama promised for all of them and with a smile, she said, "We wouldn't do that." She knew how important it was to Irene that her children look perfect. She had to admit, though, she wished she could convince her that kids were happier when they were allowed to be kids. She tried to tell her that they weren't supposed to be trophies. Kids get dirty, that's part of being a kid, and she had tried so many times to tell her that. Irene seemed to think that was disgusting though. Mama thought, I'll keep trying to convince her and whenever they're with me they'll be allowed to get as dirty as they want. She wished she'd had some pictures of Irene playing when she was small she wasn't always so clean either.

Roland went back to school in September and was finally beginning his Degree program. His professors had been quite impressed at how quickly he'd mastered his studies in the previous six months. Meanwhile, back at home Irene returned to work just six weeks after giving birth to Jean. Mama was there everyday and most nights again. After a few weeks of being back to work, Irene gradually cut back to four days a week instead of five, although only because Mama insisted. She now worked Monday to Thursday.

She was getting used to handling both kids by herself on the three days Mama wasn't there. Mama said she couldn't come over everyday anymore. Irene would have to be happy with the four days a week. Irene had trouble comprehending just why Mama had said those things, she didn't know it at the time, but Mama would have loved nothing more than to be there everyday, but she was making an effort to help Irene realize that she needed to be there herself for her children and that they needed her. She was hoping Irene would become a better mother by spending more time with them. Mama really didn't have anything to do on the days she wasn't at Irene's, but she'd told Irene she had housework and laundry to do and that these things were constantly getting behind. She'd said also that she was thinking of volunteering at the hospital. She'd told her, "I need to make friends; my life is too lonely at times." Irene thought that was a good idea, she only hoped Mama wouldn't give up babysitting altogether, she desperately needed her; she knew she wasn't cut out to be a full time mother.

Christmas seemed to arrive quickly that year; Irene had been so busy she hadn't even noticed how fast time was flying by. Roland was going to be coming home for two whole weeks. Irene sighed at the thought, she knew Mama wouldn't want to come over; she always wanted to leave them alone whenever Roland came home. Mama had told her she thought that they needed time as a family. Irene wasn't sure how Roland would react to the noise and confusion of Cassie banging things and singing her songs and the baby crying but most of all Irene didn't know how she would handle it, herself and was thinking "Lord help me!"

The day Roland arrived home, he was happier than she'd ever remembered seeing him. She thought smiling, I should have been able guess his reaction, he absolutely loves it. He just fell into place in the family as if he'd never been away at all. He seemed to know instinctively what to do for each of the girls. Cassie was always climbing up on his knee and asking him to read a book or play with her. She even liked to sit on his knee while he held Jean. She liked to watch him talk to the baby and she loved to watch him feed her, her bottle, which to Irene's delight, he did all the time. He really enjoyed doing it and always asked Irene if she minded. Dismayed, Irene thought, he should be the mother, I don't seem to fit the part, and I certainly don't enjoy it, I really have to work at it. She felt so inadequate as she watched him, thinking, it all comes so natural to him, I wish it did for me.

They had another wonderful Christmas; everyone spoiled the girls with presents, much to Cassie's delight, since she loved opening gifts. They all got together, both families, even Jake spent the day with them. It was wonderful, but over far too fast, they thought.

Roland had to go back to school; most times, he had to admit although only to himself, that he really didn't want to go. He wanted to get his Degree, so he could make sure he would always be able to look after his family, but he didn't want to leave them all the time. He would have been just fine to simply have less and just be a happy family, but he knew Irene wouldn't like that. She placed far too much importance on the children's clothing and things she thought they needed and he thought shaking his head, all those things cost money. Therefore, he knew he needed to get this Degree, so he would have the income necessary to take care of her as well as the girls.

Irene went back to work and Mama looked after the kids four days a week once again. In the summer Roland came home, only this time he said nothing about Irene quitting her job. She'd cut down one more day, so she only worked Monday to Wednesday now and their life as a family ran a lot smoother.

Mama had started volunteering at the hospital and had made friends of all ages, Irene was quite happy for her. Mama and her new friends played cards some evenings and met for dinner at each other's homes. She was really enjoying herself. She still maintained that she liked to look after the girls, but Irene had noticed she was looking tired quite often lately and asked her, "Is sitting becoming too much for you?" Mama replied, sadly, "I really love doing it, but I'm finding I'm getting tired sooner than I used to." She asked Irene, "After the summer, do you think you could ask your boss if you could only work two days a week?" Irene was crushed, she really didn't want to. She thought of asking Mom but she knew her arthritis was severe enough that she wouldn't able to manage the kids for a whole day, so she was left with no alternative. Mama was the only grandma that was able, physically, to baby sit. She had to cut down to only two days; she now only worked on Mondays and Wednesdays. Mama seemed to be so much happier and much less tired with this new babysitting schedule. The kids were getting bigger and with two of them now, it was harder for Mama to handle, Irene certainly understood that.

Just before Christmas that year, Donna was over visiting

and helping Irene wrap the kids Christmas presents. They were laughing and talking and all of a sudden, out of the blue it seemed, the conversation turned serious. Roland hadn't really been paying attention, but he suddenly noticed something was different, their usual banter had taken a hushed serious tone and he'd become curious enough to start listening. He walked over to the hallway where he could hear a little better, he didn't want to interrupt them, but he did want to make sure things were all right. He overheard them talking about what Donna had witnessed the day Father died. Roland wondered what was going on, frowning he stepped closer and all of a sudden, he heard Donna say, "I know Mama killed Father." He was so shocked he couldn't move and even more so, when he heard Irene say, "You must never tell anyone what you saw. Mama was only trying to protect you and herself." Irene said, "I don't blame her one bit and Donna, you shouldn't either, Father most likely would have killed the two of you if she hadn't done what she did." She added, "Heaven only knows why she didn't do it sooner. Most of us probably would have if we had to live through the things she had to." Roland couldn't believe what he was hearing. He thought, and this woman is looking after my children. He didn't like the fact that Irene sided with her either. He did know how much the poor woman suffered at the hands of that man and Irene, Donna and Jake as well. He returned to the living room, sat down, and thought about the whole situation. He decided it was probably easy for him, coming from such a kind and caring family, to find fault, but still he told himself, my God, this is murder they're talking about, if that really is what happened. He'd been quite shaken by what he'd heard and knew he was going to have a hard time with it.

After Christmas, Irene and Roland were enjoying a little time to themselves after they'd put the kids to bed. They'd watched some television and had even made love. They were seated on the couch enjoying a martini, when Roland took Irene's hand in his and as gently as he could, said, "I really don't want you to work anymore, and I think all this babysitting is much too hard on Mama." He added, "I don't think it's so good for the kids either, they should know their own mother better, than their grandmother, don't you think?" Irene thought about it for quite some time before she begrudgingly agreed. She told him, "You're right, of course, but I love my job and the bit of social life it gives me." Roland said, thoughtfully, "I understand, but I don't see any reason why you couldn't keep up the social aspect of it. Why don't you ask Mom to baby sit during lunch and go out with the girls from work once in a while, then. You could also have them over here in the evenings if you want to, Melissa or Donna would probably help look after the girls." She thought about that for a few minutes and finally told him, "I think you're probably right, it is time for me to stay home." Roland breathed a sigh of relief as he reached for her and hugged her.

He went back to school once again and Irene quit her job. Mama still visited and they took the kids to the park or they had lunches together at either Irene's house or occasionally at Mama's. Sometimes they even went to Mom's, but when they did that, Mama and Irene brought lunch and cleaned up afterward. Mom's arthritis seemed to be getting worse these days and it was becoming harder for her to do even the simplest things now. Mama offered to help her with cleaning and shopping. Mom had smiled and thanked her and admitted that she could use the help sometimes. She said that Dad helped as much as he could, but she also said he was working more and more hours now, because he was worried about having enough money to pay for Melissa's wedding. She'd said that they were sure the boy she's been seeing, Howard, was going to ask her to marry him soon and they wanted to be able to give her a nice wedding.

On Easter weekend, Roland managed to come home again. Irene and Cassie were making a cake and Jean was in the playpen playing with her toys. Cassie asked, "Would Daddy like this chocolate cake or would he like a white one." Irene told her, "Chocolate is Daddy's favourite." She asked, after thinking a minute, "Can Jean have some too?" Irene laughed and said, "Yes, of course she can." Cassie said, with a slight frown on her face, "Jean makes a mess and I don't want you to get mad, Mommy." Irene feeling slightly guilty, replied, "I won't get mad, I promise". Cassie seemed to accept that, and said, "Okay Mommy, can I put the icing on, now?" Irene smiled hoping she would forget by the time the cake was ready to be frosted. She was thinking that Cassie is the one who makes the bigger mess when she helps in the kitchen. She answered her saying, "We still have to wait for the cake to bake and then it has to cool first, okay? Watching Cassie's expressions, she knew she understood, she added, "Then we can put the frosting on it."

Roland arrived home just as Cassie was finishing with the icing on the cake, the kitchen was a disaster icing was everywhere. Cassie yelled, "Daddy, Daddy," and that started Jean yelling too except she said, "Da da." Roland looked around at the mess and then over at Irene and started to laugh. As he picked up Cassie, he said over her squeals, "Don't worry honey, I'll help you clean up." He kissed and hugged Cassie then put her down and picked up Jean. As Irene wiped up the mess, she told him, "Just be with the kids, I can clean up." She said loudly, to make sure she'd be heard over the noise, "Dinner's almost ready." She'd made a stew and only needed to put the biscuits in the oven. Roland said, "Mmmmm that sounds good." He had Jean saying "Mmmmm," and then Cassie chimed in as well. Wow what a racket, Irene thought, but Roland seemed to love it.

He sneaked up on Irene and kissed her on the back of the neck. He asked jokingly, "Already got a date tonight?" Irene couldn't help but smile. She said, "I hope so I wanted to talk to you later tonight." He looked at her seriously; she laughed and said, "No, no I just want to talk." He said, kissing her neck again, "Hopefully among other things," then went to check on the kids.

She kissed him as he passed by, and then checked the biscuits in the oven. She was smiling as she yelled, "Dinner's ready."

Cassie came running into the kitchen and Roland danced in behind her carrying Jean, he was humming and swaying back and forth, she loved the swaying motion and was giggling. He was telling Cassie, "Hey, slow down little girl." Cassie was laughing but she kept running right through the kitchen, into the dining room and around into the living room. Roland put Jean into her highchair and hid behind the kitchen wall. As Cassie came barrelling into the kitchen again he scooped her up and tickled her, both Cassie and Jean were laughing and hollering by then. He placed her in her booster chair at the table and said to both of the girls, "Okay, shush, we need to be good now and eat our supper." Both girls quieted down, immediately. Irene wished they listened as well to her, she thought it's as if he has some sort of magic power over them.

Roland was examining the little booster chair he had plopped Cassie into, he commented, "I guess Gramps made Cassie this little chair once Jean was ready for the highchair, right?" Irene nodded. It was a little chair with short wide legs that fit perfectly onto the seat of the regular chairs at the table. Cassie loved it because when she sat in it she could reach the table properly to eat, instead of having to kneel on a chair. Cassie piped up, "I'm a big girl now." Irene smiled and told Roland, "Gramps said two high chairs would be too much in our little kitchen. He said he made this little chair so it could stay on one of the regular chairs that went with the table and that way it took up no extra floor space at all." She added, "We can even take it with us when we go to our parents places for dinner, I love it!"

Once they had the kids bathed and settled down in their beds, Irene and Roland made their way to the living room and plunked down on the couch. They were tired; it had been a long day. Irene stated in exhaustion, "The girls were up extra early this morning and only had a short nap this afternoon, I'm beat."

Roland yawned, put his arm around Irene, and joked, "I could've gone to bed with them, I'm so tired." Irene nodded, "I could've too." He turned to her asking, "You wanted to talk to me?" Irene said, smiling, "Yes, I did, but I may be too tired now." She thought her little attempt at humour might put him in a better frame of mind, for what she wanted to ask him. She wasn't sure how to bring up the subject, but since she couldn't think of a better way, she decided to tell him what was on her mind, as best she could. "Roland," she started, and paused gathering her thoughts before continuing, "I want to know if you will come to the doctor with me I need you to sign an approval form so I can be fitted with a diaphragm, I tried to get one by myself but they need you to sign as well."

Roland looked at her, frowning, he didn't say anything for what seemed to be a long time, then said, in a serious tone, "Irene, a diaphragm is a device to prevent you from becoming pregnant, is it not?" He waited for her confirming nod, and then asked, "I thought you wanted more children." She said, "I do, but I'm just not ready yet." Roland replied, "You're asking for something I can't do, the Church, is firmly against birth control of any kind, you know that." Irene felt the sudden anger surfacing and swallowed hard, before saying, "Well is the church going to help me look after them all?" Roland looked very serious and replied, angrily, "Irene I will not have you talk like that about the Church. You're a Catholic yourself now and I expect you to respect the laws of the Church." Irene rolled her eyes and said, "Honey, I just don't think I'm able to look after anymore children right now. I will be once Jean's a little bit older." Roland just said to her, sadly, "Well, if you don't think we should have anymore right now, then we will just have to abstain from having sex, until you think you can handle the possibility of becoming pregnant again." Irene was shocked, she said, "Surely you don't mean that." He said, looking at her, "I don't want to do that either, but I don't know of any other way to be sure that you won't get pregnant."

Irene stood and walked out of the living room, she went down the hall and into the bathroom. She sat on the edge of the tub and cried for a long time. She didn't want to live a life of celibacy; she loved Roland and missed him when he was at school. She couldn't wait most times for him to return home so they could be close again, not that sex was so terribly important, but it was one of the ways they shared themselves with each other. Irene didn't want to lose that part of their relationship.

That night when they went to bed, instead of making love Roland just gave her a quick peck on the cheek, rolled over, and went to sleep. Irene, as silently as she could manage, cried herself to sleep. The next morning when she awoke Roland wasn't in bed beside her. She got out of bed and crossed the bedroom floor, knotting the belt on her robe on her way to the hall. She could smell coffee and she could hear the kids. Cassie was talking and Jean was making her usual gurgling sounds and laughing.

Roland looked at her as she walked into the kitchen and said, "I hope you slept well." He knew she hadn't. He'd heard her crying last night and had wanted so badly to take her in his arms, but he didn't because he didn't trust himself not to make love to her. He wanted her to be happy and if she didn't want any more children yet, then it was up to him to make sure she didn't have any. He looked at her face it was all puffy from crying and from too little sleep. He said, "It doesn't look like you feel well today, why don't you go back to bed and sleep for a couple of hours? I can take care of the kids." Irene turned and went back down the hall. She stopped in the bathroom and looked in the mirror. She was a mess, she saw her puffy eyes and red face, even her colour was pale, she actually did look sick. She was afraid Roland probably knew the truth, though, she'd had such trouble trying not to make too much noise last night, but she hadn't been able to stop crying and she was sure he'd heard her. She thought now you've done it, how are you going to fix this? She washed her face and went back to bed to think about it. She decided she had no choice but to tell the doctor Roland was too busy with school and studying to come with her to the appointment. Hopefully, she thought, they'll let me take the form home and then I can sign Roland's name myself, who's going to know. She would have to remember to ask the doctor though, if the diaphragm was the best option, he could offer her.

The next night Roland did hold her and they did make love, which put Irene at ease. She told him afterward, "I don't want to stop making love." Roland said, kissing her neck as he held her, "I don't want to either, I love you too much." He said, after a few moments, "If we have more children, we'll just have to get you some help until the kids get to a more manageable age." Irene nodded her agreement, but was thinking; I'm not going to have any more, not if I can help it.

Roland returned to school the following week. They had made love almost every night while he was home. She was so glad they'd decided that both of them didn't want to stay away from each other. She didn't know what she would do if she couldn't feel that closeness with him and she knew that he felt the same way.

That same week she managed to get an appointment with Dr. Grogan. She asked him, "Could you please recommend the best method of birth control?" He thought a moment and said, "I would recommend a diaphragm coupled with spermicidal foam." Irene asked, "Is this the best method there is?" Dr. Grogan replied, "As far as I'm concerned it is." Irene smiled and ventured, "That's good then, when could you fit me with one?" He told her, "Just make an appointment; however, I will need your husband's approval." Irene said feigning disappointment and sighing heavily, "Oh no, he's away at school and he wanted me to have one before he came home the next time." Dr. Grogan shook his head and said, "I'm sorry but I can't do it without his approval." Irene decided to tell him, "He's coming home this weekend but just for Saturday and Sunday." She quickly added sounding regretful, "Oh, but your office is closed on weekends." She gave him her best sad look, Dr. Grogan thought for a moment, then told her, "I guess I could make an exception and give you the form to take home, just have him sign it and bring it with you when you come in for your appointment." Irene could have skipped out of his office she was on cloud nine. She was ecstatic, she finally had control, herself, over whether she would have another child or not. She practised signing his name until she could hardly tell the difference between his and her forged version of his signature. She finally felt confident enough and signed the form, then tucked it into her purse. She had already made the appointment for Monday to have the diaphragm fitted.

Roland came home for the summer and Irene would sneak into the bathroom to insert the diaphragm every time she thought there was even the slightest possibility they would make love. Sometimes it was awkward, because they were still pretty spontaneous and she wondered if Roland ever wondered what was going on, when each time she'd feign having to pee and would run to the bathroom. One night she almost fainted when he said, "You smell funny smell down there." She thought it must be the spermicidal foam and decided not to use it anymore. She didn't need him becoming suspicious. All summer long, she was able to insert her diaphragm before they made love, without him questioning her. On the night, before he was to return to school she'd forgotten to lock the bathroom door and he'd walked in on her while she was inserting it. He looked at her and asked, "What are you doing?" He didn't look too happy about what he saw so she had to think fast, she knew he hadn't actually seen the diaphragm itself so she told him, "I'm just checking to make sure I don't have my period." He made a face and looked at her strangely but he left and went into the bedroom. Irene's heart was pounding, how had she forgotten to lock the door? When she entered the bedroom, he asked her with a smirk, "Is everything okay?" She smiled, a little embarrassed by what he'd witnessed but replied, "Yes, fine." He took her in his arms, kissed her, and then laid her on the bed. He opened her robe and began kissing her, he knew exactly how to drive her crazy, and several times she tried in vain to pull him on top of her. They both knew they were going to miss each other when he returned to school tomorrow and tried their best to forge memories of each other, before he left. They continued driving each other crazy with kisses and gentle touches and when he finally did enter her, they quickly found their rhythm and before long exploded in ecstasy together. They lay in each other's arms for a long time afterward. He murmured into her hair, "I don't want to leave you again," and she answered, "And I don't want you to." She told him, sighing, "It's only for one more year." Roland had done so well in school that if he kept it up he would graduate by next Christmas. He was taking extra classes as often as the school would allow him to, which meant he would graduate a whole semester before he normally would have and because in the beginning he had taken two semesters in one, that meant he would actually graduate a whole year earlier. This knowledge was the only thing enabling both of them to feel better, because they knew that eventually this forced separation would finally come to an end. They knew they belonged together.

Roland went back to school again and this time Irene cried for the first three nights in a row. Cassie was looking at her funny during breakfast on the morning of the fourth day of Roland's absence and said, "Mommy your face looks funny." Irene managed a weak smile and asked, "What do you mean?" Cassie said, "It's all red and messy." Irene told her, sighing, "Mommy's sad, I miss Daddy." Cassie asked, "Is Daddy coming home soon?" She told her gently, "Daddy's going to school so he will always have a good job and he can look after you and Jean and Mommy too." Cassie seemed to think about that for a minute and then said, "But he will come home soon, right?" Irene assured her,

"Yes he will when he can."

Jean was getting bigger by the day it seemed, she'd recently started pulling herself up to a standing position using the furniture for support. Irene was sure she was going to walk any day now. Jean watched everything Cassie did and tried so hard to do the same things herself.

One October morning Irene woke up sick to her stomach. It had only been about a month since Roland had left for school. He was due to come home for Thanksgiving in just one week. Mama came over to help with the girls, since she wasn't feeling well but Irene came out of the bedroom early in the afternoon feeling a lot better. Mama eyed her and asked, "You feel better already?" Irene replied, slightly bewildered, "Yeah, it must have been something I ate." Mama wasn't sure about that. She told Irene, "It sounds a little like morning sickness to me." Irene's eyes opened wide, she was horrified, she thought, it can't be, I used the diaphragm every single time. The next morning she was sick again. She was busy feeling sorry for herself, thinking, I can't be pregnant, I don't want to be pregnant she broke down and cried, but after deciding that crying and wishful thinking wouldn't help her situation, she called the doctor's office and made an appointment with Dr. Grogan. Just to be sure, she told herself, but with the morning sickness continuing, she already knew. She took a urine sample with her this time; she'd been down this road before and knew the drill. She figured he would ask her for one anyway and if she had it with her, she hoped she could save time and get confirmation of her pregnancy sooner.

Irene crossed her fingers on her next visit, she already knew the answer but she hoped she was wrong, just the same. She really didn't want to have any more kids. That wasn't to be, though, Dr. Grogan walked into the office, whistling. Irene was sitting in the chair across from his desk, and as he sat down behind it, he smiled and said, "Congratulations, baby number three is due to arrive in May, it seems, you're about two months along, now." Irene thought sarcastically well why not, I have kid's birthdays in March and August and now we'll have one in May too. She asked carefully trying not to reveal her true feelings about this pregnancy, "How is it possible that I became pregnant when I was using my diaphragm?" She cringed when she heard the slight edge in her voice. Luckily, though, he seemed not to notice and asked, "Have you been using the foam as well?" She admitted, with a sigh, "No, not every time." Dr. Grogan shook his head and told her, "I thought I made it clear that nothing is foolproof, although I do recall telling you, if you wanted to reduce the risk, you were to use them together." Irene blushed; she did remember him saying that. He reminded her again, "Remember, no method is foolproof; some women get pregnant no matter what method they use." My God, why do I have to be one of them, Irene thought as she did her best to smile, through her tightly clenched teeth.

Roland was coming home that weekend, only for two days, but that would have to do. Irene thought she would tell him right away and then they could tell Cassie together, Irene knew he'd love that. Cassie would be so excited. Jean was still too young to care, she thought, but you never know, she just might understand.

Roland came home and created a whirlwind of kisses and then taking each of the kids in turn, he started throwing them up in the air and catching them, as they squealed and hollered in delight. He seemed to be having every bit as much fun as they were. When Irene noticed him carrying both of them at the same time into the kitchen, where she was making dinner, she casually mentioned, "How in the world are you going to manage to do that with three kids?" Roland stopped dead in his tracks and looked at her his mouth falling open, in surprise. Cassie was yelling, "Come on Daddy, let's go." He asked, excitedly, "Are you expecting?" When she smiled and nodded, he let out a whooping "Yippee!" Cassie and Jean immediately started imitating him, even though they had no idea why. The noise was deafening. Roland put the girls down, came over to her, and kissed her gently, he asked, "How are you feeling?" She said, "Fine right now, but I was a little sick in the mornings at first, but now it's not quite as bad." He looked down at the girls and back at Irene; he whispered, "Should we tell them now?" "Go ahead," Irene replied, "I'm dying to see their reaction." He looked down at them again and proudly announced, "Mommy and Daddy have something to tell you." Both girls turned their little faces up and looked up at them, smiling expectantly. Roland asked, "How would you like to have a new baby in our house?" Cassie started jumping up and down as soon the news registered in her head. Jean crawled over to the highchair and pulled herself up and starting jumping too, she was saying, "Baby, baby." Cassie suddenly asked, "Will it be a girl or a boy baby?" Roland and Irene laughed and told her, "We'll all have to wait until the baby is born and then we'll know whether it's a little girl or boy." Little Jean was trying hard to talk but in her excitement all she was managing to get out was "baby" she had been trying to speak in sentences lately, she listened to Cassie and tried hard to imitate her. It was so cute. Roland couldn't believe it. He was just thrilled to bits. He said in awe, "I'm going to be a father again. I'll have to figure out a way to carry them all at once I guess, won't I," he said laughing. Cassie said, "We could all get on your back just like when we play horsy." Roland reached out and tickled her, as she whooped with laughter.

Thanksgiving dinner this year was at Mama's house; Mom, Dad and Melissa were invited, too. Donna and Jake were there as well. Irene and Roland told them all about the expected baby. Everyone was so excited and happy for them. Mama could see the look in Irene's eyes though, she knew her daughter well enough to know that she was not too happy about it, even though she was smiling brightly. Mama knew it was a forced smile and she made a mental note to have a talk with her. She thought maybe she'd make plans to go over and take the kids to the park with Irene and they could talk while the children played.

Mama came over on Wednesday; she knew Irene was always in a foul mood the day after Roland left, so she waited the extra day before coming over to talk to her. While the kids played at the park, she and Irene sat on the grass and talked while they watched them. Mama told her, "Don't worry so much about things; I'll be there for you to help you get through the worst of it." She said, "You know you'll probably find things easier this time, though. Cassie's at the age where she'll want to help you with the baby; she can rock the carriage and fetch things for you. You'll see she'll be a quite a little helper." Irene said, looking forlorn, "I know that, Mama, but I'm just not sure I can manage three kids and that's what's bothering me the most. I feel like I'm less of a woman sometimes, because I can't seem to handle the things that come naturally to most women." She said, "I love to go to work, but that isn't acceptable for a woman who's married, much less a woman who has children. Everyone looks down on mothers who work outside their homes, especially if they don't have to work, but work because they enjoy it and want to." She wished aloud, "Women should have the same rights and opportunities as men, and be able to work if and when they want to; life is so unfair, when you're a woman." Mama patted her hand and tried her best to console her, saying, "This time will be easier and I have a feeling you'll be pleasantly surprised." Irene smiled at her; she knew she was trying her best to lift her spirits and make her feel better.

fifteen

THIS ONE
MAKES THREE

I rene and Roland were in Irene's hospital room waiting
for the nurse to bring in their new baby girl. Roland was
asking, "What do you think we should we name her?" Irene
thoughtfully replied, "Well, I was sort of favouring Maureen."
Roland laughed, "That's exactly what I was thinking." Irene said,
laughing, "Great minds think alike" and before she could finish
Roland came back with, "And fools seldom differ." She laughed
so hard she thought her stitches would burst. "My second
choice would have been Lesley," Roland said, when she stopped
laughing, then added, "Why don't we name her Maureen Lesley."
Irene smiled and replied, after a moments thought, "Yeah, I like
it." When the nurse brought the baby in Roland was the first to
hold her, he looked into her little face and said, "Hello Maureen."
The nurse who was on her way out the door, turned and said
with a smile, "That's such a pretty name."

The whole family visited that day, taking turns of course,
because the nurses were being particularly vigilant and would
only let a few of them in the room at a time. Roland and Irene
had to answer the question, posed by their families. Who is this
one named after? They told them in unison, "No one, we just
liked those two names." Everyone seemed to be satisfied with

155

that. They all brought the usual gifts of baby clothes and flowers and nightgowns for Irene. When all the family had left, Roland kissed Irene and produced a small gold box tied with a lovely white satin ribbon. Irene looked up into his face, surprised; she softened when she glimpsed the love in his eyes. "I have a special gift for you," he said, in a soft voice that was almost a whisper. He handed her the small box, saying, "This represents our three children." Irene was so surprised, when she opened it; she looked at the beautiful ring with three large diamonds in a raised setting across a gold band and exclaimed, "Oh, Roland, its beautiful." A slight frown spread across her face, and she asked, "How is this possible? Can we afford it? He smiled and said, "The Company gave me a raise in pay a few months ago and I kept it a secret so I could save the difference and buy you this ring, do you like it?" He said, "I remembered you pointed it out in a store window, one evening when we were walking downtown together, after we had dinner at our favourite restaurant, remember?" Irene had tears in her eyes as she nodded and told him, "Yes, I remember," she paused and added, looking up at him, "You're the most amazing man, not many husbands would remember something like that." Roland replied, "The things you want are important to me." He paused a second looking at her tenderly, and added, "I love you." She smiled and told him, "I love you, so much." She fell asleep almost as soon as Roland left for home; she wore a smile on her face as she slept.

Shortly after they were home, together again, Roland had to return to school to write his exams. He'd been studying every night as soon as he'd gotten home from the hospital. Mama had come over everyday to look after Cassie and Jean, so he had plenty of time to study; sometimes he went to the library where it was quiet if the kids were a little too loud at home. He felt he was ready to write the exam, he still needed to review a few things but he planned to do that on the bus ride back to school.

Irene seemed to be very tired after this baby and Roland was worried about her, he really didn't want to leave her, but Mama assured him, saying, "I'll take good care of her, you just go and do what you have to do and good luck on your exams."

Donna had a week's holidays, from work, and she was going to be helping with the kids too. Dr. Grogan had prescribed bed rest for Irene for a week after she went home, he said she'd lost quite a bit of blood during this birth and he wanted her to have time to regain her strength. He'd given her a prescription as well. Mama was making sure she ate well, got her rest, and took her pills. The kids were allowed in to see her for short periods only. Baby Maureen would sometimes sleep beside her in the bed or in the little bassinette beside the bed and Mama would check on both of them regularly.

Roland returned after writing his exams and was glad to see that Irene had recovered and was herself again. She found it tiring chasing after Cassie and Jean, as well as the constant care she had to provide for newly born Maureen, but she told him, "I'm glad to finally be allowed out of bed, I was so bored that week." She rushed on, "I've welcomed the busy days, and I have to admit I am extremely tired at the end of the day, even with Mama's help, but it's so much better than just laying in bed all day." Roland told her, happily, "I'm home for the next six weeks, so I can help now. Unfortunately I have to go back after that if I want to graduate this December." Irene said, "I completely understand, but I have to admit, I'm looking forward to the day when we can have a normal family life, with you only working five days during the week and being home evenings and weekends." Roland replied, "So am I." He took her in his arms, kissed her tenderly and said, "That's why I'm working so hard to get this Degree, as fast as I possibly can." He kissed her again and they cuddled on the couch in the living room. Cassie and Jean were already in bed and Maureen was sleeping, as well. She wasn't due to be fed for another two hours and they hoped she'd sleep for a while longer and give Irene some much-needed rest. Roland was the first to hear her restless cries; he went into their bedroom and lifted her out of the bassinette. She stopped crying immediately and seemed to be looking right at him. His heart melted, this baby was just as beautiful as the others had been, and he thanked God that all his children were so perfect. Maureen had lots of black hair and a button nose, she had dark eyes that the doctor said would probably change colour later. She was so little, Roland always seemed to forget how small newborns were. He changed her diaper and brought her out to the living room. He handed her to Irene who was sitting on the couch and went off to the kitchen to warm up the bottle.

Irene talked to Maureen and cuddled her, she seemed to be content until all of a sudden she must have really felt hungry or she suddenly realized that no one was feeding her and she started to cry, actually more like scream and extremely loud for such a little girl. Roland rushed in with the bottle asking Irene, "Do you mind if I feed her?" Irene gave the screaming baby over to him, smiling, "Be my guest," she said. Roland sat down on the couch with Maureen in his arms and as soon as he put the bottle in her mouth, she stopped screaming and started suckling as if she was starving. They both laughed and Roland said raising an eyebrow, "This little one seems to have a temper." "Yes," Irene said, "I've been noticing that, too, she wants what she wants, when she wants it."

After Roland had fed and burped her, she fell asleep almost immediately and the two of them fell into bed, exhausted. They were asleep within minutes with Maureen in the bassinette beside their bed. They knew she'd wake them up in about four hours, when she would be hungry again.

Summer was flying by; Irene was amazed how she and Roland were able to handle the three kids. He was simply amazing, she thought; it was as though nothing fazed him. He loved kids and it showed, the only problem was that he expected a little too much of them. Irene was having trouble getting one particularly disturbing scene out of her mind. Little Cassie was doing her wooden puzzle before dinner one day and Roland was getting upset that she wasn't getting it right, he kept showing her and she still wasn't able to do it. Irene spoke to him softly so the kids wouldn't hear, "Roland, she's just little, she'll learn eventually." He shook his head in frustration, as he said, "I've shown her how to do it enough times. I'm beginning to think she may not be too bright and that concerns me." Irene was stunned, but sensing his anger she told him as gently as she could, "She's only four, honey, she's doing just fine for her age. The doctor sees nothing wrong with her development. He said she's in the normal range." At that, Roland bristled and replied, "I expect better than just normal from my kids." Irene didn't like what he'd said at all, she worried about it, and she didn't want the kids to feel they weren't good enough.

Roland went back to school and once again Mama helped Irene, she was pretty much living with them now, she only went home one night a week, two at best. Mama was proud of Irene; she was doing so much better this time. She was handling all three kids amazingly well and Mama thought that she was finally learning to be a mother. She was feeding Maureen one afternoon while Irene was sitting on the floor with Cassie and Jean doing puzzles, Jean was doing an easy shape sorter, but Cassie was doing her wooden puzzle, all of a sudden, Cassie started to cry and Irene becoming concerned, asked, "What's the matter?" Cassie sobbed, "I can't finish my puzzle. I need help." Irene sat on the floor and held her, saying, "Don't cry, honey I'm right here, all you have to do is tell me you need help and I'll help you." Cassie asked, through her tears, "Will you get mad at me like Daddy does?" Mama and Irene exchanged a look that said without words, we need to talk about this later. Irene pulled Cassie into her arms and soothed her, "I'll never get mad at you because you need help with something." She kissed the top of her head and Cassie stopped crying.

Later that night after the kids were all tucked into bed, Mama and Irene were having tea in the kitchen when Mama asked, "What was that episode with Cassie this afternoon, all about? Cassie was saying that her Daddy got mad at her because she couldn't do her puzzle." Irene told her, "Yes, I heard Roland do that once not long before he left." She said, "I spoke to him about it," but admitted, "It worries me though, because I didn't care for his response." She sighed and told Mama, "He said he was concerned because he didn't think she was very smart." Mama looked shocked and then her expression changed to one of pity and she said, "If he really feels that way then I feel sorry for you and for the kids. Children don't need that kind of pressure from a parent, especially at such a young age. She hasn't even started school yet, she'll learn everything she needs to know in due time." Irene assured her, "He's so good with the kids and they love being with him. I've been wondering if he really meant what he said to sound like that or if he was just genuinely concerned. He's so clever himself, maybe he thinks everyone should be able to grasp things as quickly as he can. I'm going to talk to him next time he comes home. I can't imagine that he'll ever be hard on the kids as far as their learning abilities go." She added almost as an after thought, "At least I hope not."

Roland returned home for Christmas on Christmas Eve, he had been cramming for an exam that his professor had allowed him take before the Christmas Holidays; he knew Roland had a family. He told him he could take it early if he wanted and then he could have Christmas without having to worry about studying. Roland was more that happy to get it finished before Christmas. He was really looking forward to seeing his family again; he'd missed them so much. He had pictures of Irene and his little girls everywhere in the dorm room, the other guys teased him about it constantly.

When Roland walked in the door his sudden appearance started Cassie and Jean squealing and hollering with delight, even little Maureen who was sitting in her Jolly Jumper was smiling and making excited noises, just because she saw her sisters doing it. Irene was in the kitchen getting the salad ready for dinner, she already had a roast in the oven that smelled heavenly. She and the girls had made a special chocolate cake for dessert, earlier and it was sitting on the counter, it read in large uneven lettering, "Welcome Home Daddy." She heard all the ruckus coming from the living room and suddenly had an idea, she pretended she didn't know Roland was home and walked out into the living room, saying, "My goodness what's all the noise about," she'd said it in such a way that the girls knew she was kidding. They started screaming in unison, "Daddy's home, Mommy, Daddy's home!" She smiled and asked, "Are you sure?" She and Roland started laughing at the girls' response; they both had such funny looks on their faces. Maureen all of a sudden started yelling and laughing. They thought it was funny how all the kids reacted.

Roland spent time with each of the children. When Irene called them for dinner, he was surprised to see another booster chair in one of the chairs at the table, identical to the one Cassie used. He asked the girls, with a smile, "Whose is this?" Jean proudly announced, "It's mine, Daddy, Gramps made it for me, it's just like Cassie's." Roland turned to Irene, she said, "Jean thinks highchairs are for babies and she says she's a big girl now, so Gramps made her a chair, so she wouldn't have to use the highchair." Irene told him, "I put a rolled up towel behind Maureen and now she sits in the highchair, she really likes it. I give her a Gerber biscuit and she's quite happy to sit there while the girls and I eat. It's so much easier than holding on to her while I try to cut the kids meat and eat my dinner at the same time." She laughed, "I used to feel like I needed an extra pair of arms."

Roland raced back and picked up Maureen, who had just started to scream, since everyone had left the living room and she was now having trouble seeing everyone. He whispered into her hair as he carried her, "Oh don't worry, you're going to be with us." He placed her in the highchair and Irene tucked the towel behind her.   Once they gave her the Gerber biscuit to munch on, she was quite happy.   Roland smiled, he told the kids, as he looked at each one of them, "This is great having all my little girls at the table at once."   Cassie and Jean beamed.   It was obvious how much they missed their Daddy.   They had asked constantly while he was away, when he was coming home. Irene talked to them about him, all the time; she wanted them to know how much he missed them as well.   Roland was very grateful that she did.

After the kids were in bed for the night, they settled on the couch to catch up with each other once again, it seemed to them that was all they ever did; they never seemed to be together when major things happened in their lives.   They were always recounting for each other all the details of their lives that they seemed to live separately, for the most part.   Irene was always telling him about things the kids had done and he was always telling her about things at school.   Roland sighed wishing he could be there to witness the things the girls did first hand, he felt they were growing up without him.   Irene told him all about the toys she'd bought to put under the tree.   He was feeling somewhat sad about that.   Irene stopped talking and looked at him.   She asked him, "What's wrong?"   He said sadly, "I feel like I'm missing all the important things that are happening in your life and the kids as well. I also hate the fact that you have to do everything by yourself."   He seemed as if he was far away after he said that.   She gently said, "Hey, did you forget that what you're doing is for all of us?"   Then she reminded him, "After you're finished school and you start working again, you can do all this stuff" and added laughing, "I might even help you, if you ask me nicely."   He was jolted back to the present, after realizing what she'd just said.   He looked up at her and caught the big smile on her face; he pulled her into a huge embrace, held her there and started tickling her.   She screeched and tried to get away, she'd always been so ticklish and Roland knew just where all those ticklish spots were. They started cuddling and Irene asked, "Would you like to talk a bit about the kids?" He pulled away so he could look at her face and asked, "Is something wrong with them?" Irene assured him nothing was, but she said, "I have some concerns about something you said the last time you were home." Roland looked puzzled and asked her, "What did I say, that's been bothering you so much." She reminded him, "You said Cassie wasn't too smart." He flushed and admitted, "I've been thinking about that myself, a lot, and I'm so sorry I said that. I really don't expect anything special from her." That statement made Irene bristle. She sat up straighter and asked him, "Just what do you expect from your children?" He answered by saying, "I only want what's best for them but I also want them to take learning seriously and to concentrate on improving the things that they aren't good at or have trouble doing," he went on to say, "I expect you to help in that regard." Irene said in return, "Roland, they're only little children that kind of stuff can wait until they go to school. Right now, they should enjoy just being children and having fun playing. I'll help them with things they need to know. I've been teaching Cassie to write her own name and Jean has been learning to do her puzzles. Cassie can even recognize simple words now. So please don't be too hard on them or expect too much." Roland promised her, "I'll try my best not to, Okay?" Irene smiled at him and hugged him.

Roland was looking at the Christmas tree, it was really quite tall, and he asked her, "How in the world did you drag that in here?" She smiled and said, "Gramps did it for me; he even brought your ladder up from the basement to put the star on top and he did all the lights, for us. The kids and I decorated the rest," she laughed, "That's why the bottom of the tree is so full of ornaments." They both laughed at that. It really did look like it was almost bare everywhere else, it really wasn't it was just because the bottom part of the tree where the kids could reach was so full of icicles and ornaments that it made it look that way. Roland asked, "Did the kids have fun doing it?" Irene told him all about it, saying, "You wouldn't believe how much they thought they were helping and they couldn't wait for you to see it." Roland had tears glistening in his eyes, trying to regain his composure he said, "Christmas is my favourite time of year, I can't wait to do the tree together once I'm finished school." Irene looked at the time, "We better hurry up and get the kids toys assembled and under the tree for them." Roland asked as he got off the couch, "We have stockings to fill too, don't we?" Irene said, "Yes we do, so let's get busy." She hopped off the couch as well and went to the linen closet to get the stocking stuffers. She sent Roland to the back of the basement to get the toys, from "Santa". The kids never played in that part of the basement, so she could easily hide things there and not worry about them finding anything. Irene had told them only to play in the front part, because there were too many things they could get hurt with in the back, she had explained to them that Daddy kept his tools back there and he'd be very upset if they played there. That was all it took, they never even opened the door to that part of the basement again. They didn't like to do anything that might make their Daddy cross with them.

Christmas was wonderful the kids were so excited. Cassie marvelled at how Santa brought her just what she wanted. Jean was delighted with her new doll and doll crib, Maureen got presents from Santa too, even though she was too young to know about Christmas yet. Roland said, "I'm sure Cassie and Jean will get her excited next year."

Mom, Dad, Gramps and Melissa all brought gifts as did Mama, Jake and Donna. Irene looked around the living room with her hands on her hips, she said, "My goodness, these kids are spoiled, they have so many gifts." The kids beamed their smiles were so bright they loved presents. Even little Maureen liked tearing the paper off. She wanted to open all the presents.

Dinner was terrific, Irene and Mama worked together in the kitchen making the gravy and yams and Mom made the salads. Melissa mashed the potatoes and Donna set the table, once the men had moved all the larger toys to the basement and set up card tables in a row in the dining room. The tables extended right out into the living room, the family was growing so rapidly that they now needed an extra table so they could all sit together. Donna had bought beautiful centerpieces from the florist and she was placing them on the tables, they looked spectacular. Mama had bought Irene a beautiful set of dishes. She had given it to her a few days early, so they would have time to wash them before they used them today. When they sat down at the table Mom exclaimed, "We all worked so well together, today, and the table looks gorgeous." Cassie told everyone, "I helped too; I folded the napkins for Aunt Donna." Everyone smiled and told her, "You did such a good job, they're folded perfectly." Cassie smiled proudly.

Roland went back to school again the day after Christmas. Irene found herself very depressed this time. She never liked having him gone, but this particular time she felt that his stay at home had not been long enough. It was tough explaining to the kids why their Daddy was never there. Cassie was really starting to ask a lot of questions. Mama came over and noticed Irene's melancholy mood. She suggested, "Let's go shopping tomorrow when the stores reopen, there will be some fantastic sales on, what do you think?" She never gave Irene time to answer, she told her, "I'll be back first thing in the morning to help you with the kids, I'll bring Donna she'll love to baby sit while we're gone. Donna loves being with the kids."

That seemed to give Irene something to look forward to. Mama thought on the way home, that she would get her some knitting or something for her to do to help her pass the time, and maybe some new clothes. She knew how much Irene loved clothes. Irene always worked so hard at maintaining her figure so she could wear the latest fashions.

Irene kept herself busy with the kids and she went for coffee with the neighbours, they all took turns having each other over. She was also knitting to help pass the time. She had started making jackets for all the girls. They were going to be heavy weight wool, so they would be warm in the early spring and the kids could wear them on warmer days in the winter as well. She already had Cassie's finished it was dark turquoise with a picture of a skater on the back and a smaller skater on the front, complete with a zipper up the front. Irene was quite proud of how it turned out. She was working on Jean's now; it was bright red, Jean's favourite colour. It was the same style as Cassie's. Irene figured it would be easier to make them all from the same pattern, just different sizes and pictures. Jean's would have ballerina's on it and Maureen's was going to be soft pink and have little baby lambs on it, in white. Cassie and Jean checked her progress almost daily. Cassie wanted to wear hers around the house. Irene had to hide it so it wouldn't get dirty. She did most of her knitting after she got the kids into bed in the evening; she had a lot less distractions then.

Roland was able to make it home for another two days at Easter. This time Irene and the girls met him at the bus station. It was a rather mild day and the girls were wearing the new sweaters Irene had knit, they looked adorable. Roland got off the bus and turned away from where they were standing waiting and started walking to the taxi stand, when Cassie and Jean starting yelling, "Daddy!" Roland turned around and when he realized that, they were his kids his face lit up. He ran over to them, he scooped up both girls, hugged and kissed them and hurried over to the stroller where Maureen was. He quickly kissed her and said, "Hi kiddo." He put the kids down and hugged Irene tightly. He said, happily, "This was a total surprise; I wasn't expecting you to be here." Irene said, "It's such a nice day, I thought the kids would enjoy the walk and especially meeting you at the bus stop." He said, "I'm glad you did, I really appreciate it." He put his suitcase on the back of the stroller and took Cassie and Jean by the hand and off they went. Cassie said, "Daddy, do you like our sweaters? Mommy made them." Roland turned to Irene, "Did you really make them?" Irene proudly nodded and said, "I did." He told her after inspecting them a little closer, "Wow, they're really nice, you're really something. I never knew you were so talented." She smiled and countered, smirking, "I have a few talents tucked away, some are hidden pretty deep though." He chuckled and they walked home talking and laughing with the kids.

Easter came and went but this time instead of spending the holiday with the whole family Irene and Roland opted for a quiet day with just their own little family. The rest of their family understood, everyone knew what precious little time they had to be a family on their own. The only thing the grandparents missed was seeing the kids with their Easter baskets, Irene and Roland promised to take pictures for them.

Spring was easier for Irene to handle, the kids loved to go outside and the park was right at the end of the street, an easy walk for the girls, Maureen rode in the stroller. Irene was so looking forward to the day when Maureen would be as easy to take places as Cassie and Jean. She loved babies, but it sure would be nice when she didn't have to cart around diapers and bottles anymore. She was finished having kids, she just wanted to enjoy these three. She hoped Roland would agree to birth control now. This time she wanted something that would work. The last time she'd had to keep it a secret from him and since she couldn't use the spermicidal foam, it didn't work anyway. Her friends told her about a new method and she wanted to ask the doctor about it. She sighed thinking she really wanted Roland to agree this time.

Summer weather came early, by the time Roland's semester ended at the end of April the weather was already hot and humid.

The kids were running through the sprinkler every day. The day Roland came home Irene and the girls met him at the bus again. All three of them were so excited, even Maureen who was saying, "Daddy." Cassie and Jean had painstakingly taught her to say Mommy and Daddy. They were having difficulty teaching her to say their names though. Maureen called Cassie, "Cee" and Jean was "Een." The girls were extremely patient with her though, they kept repeating what they wanted her to say and if Maureen was in the mood she would try to say it back, if she wasn't she would press her little lips tightly together in defiance, it was quite comical to watch.

This time when Roland got off the bus he knew exactly where they were standing waiting for him, he'd been looking out for them all the way down the street so when the bus rolled to a stop he'd already found them. He bounded off the bus and looked at the kids and started waving and running. Irene let the kids run up to him. Maureen couldn't keep up with her sisters; her little legs were too short. Cassie and Jean reached him in no time, Roland picked them up, one at a time this time and then he noticed Maureen running as fast as she could, he had to smile, she was actually saying, "Daddy, me, Daddy, me." Cassie told him, "Daddy, she wants her turn." Roland laughed as he scooped her up, and kissed and hugged her too. When he set her down, she wanted right back up again. He looked at Jean and Cassie and they said almost at the same time, with exaggerated sighs, "You better not put her down or we'll have to listen to her crying all the way home." Roland laughed and told them, "I guess I'll just have to hold on to her then, won't I." They walked home, talking and laughing, Irene was so happy to have him home. She knew it would be a short summer vacation, because he would need to start his final Semester early if he planned to be completely finished by Christmas. She was just thankful for the time they would have.

Once they had the kids in bed, they sat on the front porch

and talked for a long time, the night was warm and gorgeous, the windows were open so they could hear the kids it they cried. The neighbours waved and some came over to chat, but mostly they were alone and enjoyed talking and simply being together. Irene said, as she looked up at the stars, "I can't wait for the day when you'll be home every night." He was gazing up at the stars too and lazily replied, "Neither can I, I have just one more Semester." He looked serious, and added, "I hope I can keep my marks up. I have to in order to graduate with honours." Irene frowned and told him, "Don't worry so much, even if you don't get honours, you'll still be a Chemical Engineer." She said, "Who's going to ask you if they can see your marks, anyway? They only care that you have your Degree." Roland sighed, "I know that, but getting honours is important to me." She knew that only too well, she remembered he was never happy in high school either unless he was at the top of the class. She sure wasn't driven that way. She was happy just to do what she pleased. She hoped Roland would be successful as an Engineer, she knew they made very good money, from what he'd told her so far and she knew he could also advance rapidly in the Company. She just didn't quite understand how all that worked. She would have to ask him once he was finished school and was actually back at work.

Irene, Roland and the kids had the most wonderful summer and they'd had so much fun, Irene didn't want it to end. Roland bought the kids a paddling pool and they played in it everyday after lunch. Irene enjoyed sitting on the patio with Roland drinking lemonade and watching them play. Cassie and Jean were such little mothers with Maureen; they took excellent care of her. Irene was finally feeling like she could relax occasionally.

Roland wasn't able to come home again until Thanksgiving, in mid October. He could only manage three days which included the bus ride and that took the better part of a day, so it didn't leave much time for them to be together as a family. Once again, they celebrated the Holiday with only their own little family, so they could have a little more time with each other. They put the kids to bed at night and immediately went to bed themselves so they could make love. They missed each other so much. They joked about it sometimes to lighten their mood but they agreed that it was becoming increasingly harder to be apart. They talked about it a while and figured that maybe the reason it was harder now was because they knew that very shortly, they wouldn't have to be apart anymore and just knowing that was exciting them and making it all the more difficult to wait.

Roland came home early that Christmas; he was actually home a week before Christmas. He had asked Irene to wait to shop for the girls this year, because he wanted to come with her. This was the first year he would be able to shop with her. She happily agreed. She had arranged for Melissa to stay with the kids while they shopped. When Roland and Irene were ready to go, Melissa told them, "Take your time, go for lunch or dinner if you want, I have lots of time." She said, "I'll baby sit everyday this week if you need me to. The Accountant I work for closed the office for Christmas and he won't be opening again until the day after New Years. So I'm officially on holidays." She went on to say, "Howard's working, so I'll be more than happy to spend my time with the girls." Roland laughed and told her, "A simple yes would've sufficed." She punched him in the arm. He said, rubbing his arm and pretending to be hurt, "You always were a chatterbox and a rough neck too!" He laughed and Irene said, shaking her head, "You'd better be quiet before she gets mad at you and leaves. Then you won't be able to come shopping after all because you'll have to baby sit while I go," and she tugged at his arm trying to pull him out the door.

Christmas wasn't such a good day for Irene she was sick to her stomach when she got up. Roland thought it might be the martini she'd had with him the night before. She wasn't so sure, she wasn't used to drinking, but this didn't seem to be from the drink. She relaxed in the morning and by midday, she felt fine.

They were spending Christmas at Mama's this year. They had "Santa" at their own house in the morning and even though Irene wasn't feeling well, she managed to sit on the couch and watch the girls open their presents. Roland was such a sweetheart, she thought looking at him lovingly. He got the kids cleaned up and gave them breakfast; he even dressed them in their little Christmas outfits and took them to Church all by himself. Irene usually went with him, but she didn't trust herself not to be sick to her stomach in Church.

They didn't say anything to anyone at Mama's because Irene was feeling so much better by the time they arrived at her house for dinner. Mom and Dad arrived shortly after and they all opened their gifts from each other and then sat down to an exceptionally delicious dinner. Mama had always been an excellent cook. She said when everyone complimented her on the dinner, "It comes with a lot of practise." She continued, "I cooked everyday for years, I'd never eaten in a restaurant until I went with you kids a few days after Father's funeral." Jake had wanted to cheer them up a little so he'd taken them to a wonderful French restaurant; he had thought that Mama deserved the outing. Irene and Donna had discussed how Jake had told them he felt that night and they both came to the same conclusion that he may not have thought Mama deserved that treat at all, if he'd known what she'd done. Although she recalled, Donna had told her, you never know, he hated Father for what he put her through, so who knows how he would have felt. Irene told herself, once again, closing her eyes momentarily that she had to quit thinking about that. She looked up and smiled at everyone, they were all having such a good time. She forced herself to stop thinking about it and put it out of her mind completely as she stood and helped clear the table to get things ready for dessert.

sixteen

ANOTHER
GRADUATION

During the times Roland was home from School he'd met with his boss, Mr. Marsden, on several occasions. He'd attended important meetings and when Irene asked him about them, he never said much, except, "It's mostly business and I still have a lot to learn. I'll be able to tell you everything soon; nothing has really been decided, just yet. I know I'll be expected to attend all the meetings from now on, so I'll hear first hand of any decisions they make that concern us." He always seemed to be smiling these days though and she asked him several times, "Why the big smiles?" He would only say, each time she asked, "You're going to be so happy, you'll see." No matter how hard she tried, he wouldn't say anything else so she finally gave up asking him.

Roland went back to school the second week of January, only this time Irene went with him. Both of their families were coming up on the Saturday for the ceremony too. Irene had asked Brenda if she would watch the kids for her. She and Harold didn't have any children of their own yet and said they'd be thrilled to watch them for a few days. Irene only hoped the kids would behave for them.

She bought a gorgeous gown for the ceremony and dance.

172

This time, since it was a University Graduation not high school, they wore their gowns to the Ceremony, which was part of the dinner. The dance was held immediately after; there were no breaks or running home to change this time. All of the graduates invited their families and close friends. She was so excited, for Roland. They knew she was pregnant again and planned to tell everyone after the ceremony at dinner. Roland thought that it would be a wonderful surprise for everybody and Irene agreed. She dreaded that she was going to have to go through diapers and middle of the night feedings again, though and told herself, at least this time Roland will be home to help me with the kids and Mama will be there if I need her, as well.

The ceremony was beautiful and of course, as Irene had expected, Roland was on the Dean's list, he'd graduated with honours. When the Dean gave Roland his Degree, he announced, "I have never before in all my many years at this University, seen such a hardworking student." He told everyone, smiling proudly, "This man finished his degree in less time than any of the Faculty has ever seen a student accomplish this before." He turned to Roland and said, "Congratulations," as he shook his hand once more. Roland being a little shy and not used to all this attention, lowered his head, tucked his Degree certificate under his arm and walked down the stairs and back to their table without once raising his head. He proudly showed his family his Engineering Degree and Mom and Dad had tears of pride in their eyes. Gramps kept clearing his throat; he was so proud he couldn't even speak. They all hugged and congratulated Roland and shook his hand repeatedly. Irene kissed and hugged him; she felt like jumping with joy that he was finally finished school.

During dinner, Roland told the family he had a couple of announcements to make. Irene's head shot up in surprise. She whispered in his ear, "What's the other one? I thought we only had one." She was smiling because she thought that in his excitement he had made a mistake. He said to her, "You'll see." Irene's smile disappeared as a bewildered expression settled over her features.

Roland stood up and began, "First we want to tell everyone that we are expecting our fourth child and we've been told this baby should arrive in July. I'd also like to tell all of you, including my lovely wife," and he smiled down at Irene, "I've been promoted at the Company, thanks to my Chemical Engineering Degree," which he waved in the air. "They've promoted me to Supervisor of the new Lab." Irene stood up, saying, "Oh, honey, is this what you've been smiling about the past little while?" and she kissed his cheek. He replied excitedly, "Yes and the fact that I'll now be making more than double what I was making before, because I'll be heading up the new Lab in Regina, Saskatchewan." Irene almost fell back into her seat it took all her strength to simply stand. She lowered herself slowly into her chair, stunned; her face fell, as did everyone else's at the table. Roland looked around in dismay and said, "Hey you guys, I thought you'd be happy for me." Irene bit her bottom lip to stop from crying and said as calmly as she could muster, "Roland, I don't want to leave our home and our families." Roland looked around sadly and Dad piped up and said, "Congratulations son, I know you worked hard for this. You're now an Executive at the Company and if you want to keep advancing in that Company, we understand, you can't turn down important promotions like this one, when they offer them to you." Roland was relieved that at least Dad understood.

Mama had been watching Irene, she was worried, she knew Irene didn't do well after she had a baby, she needed full time help and if they moved all the way out there, how was she going to help her. She understood Roland had worked extremely hard for this and this opportunity was fantastic for their little family. She sighed, thinking Irene is a grown woman; she will adjust, and prayed she was right. It seemed to her that Roland would be making enough money; they could hire some help for Irene, if she needed it. She would have to remember to mention this to Irene, hopefully that would help her to feel a little better.

The dance was wonderful. Irene was trying hard but she had to admit she wasn't enjoying it as she'd hoped she would; she wasn't sure how she felt about everything Roland had said. She wished he'd told her sooner, he certainly had the opportunity to do so and that angered her. She was going to talk to him about it. Suddenly she was plagued with the thought, how could he do that to me, gritting her teeth, she thought he probably expected me to be happy about it, doesn't he know how much I love Sarnia and being close to our friends and our families? Just then, someone from one of Roland's classes came up and congratulated her on his success, and that brought her back to reality, she forced herself to smile and thanked the man, she hadn't been listening at first and hadn't caught his name.

Later, while they were dancing a slow dance together, Roland said, "I'm sorry, I guess I should've told you first and then told the rest of the family but I wanted to surprise you. I thought you'd be happy about us making so much money and finally being able to afford to do anything we want, without Mama's help." He held her tighter and pleaded, "Please don't be mad at me, I only wanted you to be happy. You know how much I love to surprise you." Irene sighed, he really was sorry and she couldn't stand to see him sad on his special night. She brightened a little thinking, he will be making so much more money, how had that fact slipped my mind. She forgave him saying, "Its okay, I love you and if it makes you happy, I'll be happy." While they danced, she mused about the fact that they would soon have a lot more money and imagined what she could do with it. She also wondered how important a position, this new promotion of his was, would he be an important Executive, she wondered, which would in turn make her a respected executive's wife? She mused I could volunteer. She was aware that people of stature volunteered for something or other, and she thought she would like to try it; and she could shop, she realized suddenly. Oh just the thought of having beautiful clothes and being able to buy the kids cute clothes was so exciting. Mama was the one who always paid when she shopped now, she would be able to pay for things herself soon. She just needed to stop having babies so she'd have more time. Suddenly a thought came to her and she smiled to herself, maybe she could get someone to help her with the kids, she knew she could get Roland to agree to that, after all he was taking her away from her family and all the support she had here and now they were going to have four children. She knew she could make him feel guilty enough to hire her some help.

By the time the dance was over and they were heading back to the Dorm, she had completely gotten over the shock of the whole thing. She asked him, "When do we have to be in Regina?" Roland said, "All the details weren't available at the last meeting I attended." He added, "They told me they would know more soon, hopefully, by the time I go back to work." He thought a minute and said, "I wish I knew too, it would make it easier for us to plan with the new baby coming and all." She said, "It'll be okay as long as we don't have to be separated anymore." Roland swallowed he didn't have the heart to tell her that they still would have to be, just until he was settled in his new position, it would probably only be for a few weeks, he thought. He knew she wouldn't be happy about it, though. The Company was going to be sending him out to Regina next month, to set up the new lab and get him started. He needed to hire a secretary as well. They were giving him free reign there and he was somewhat excited about it, he had never hired anyone before. He knew he would have to get used to it, he was going to be responsible for the hiring and firing, if necessary, of all the staff at the new Lab. He hoped he was up for the challenge. He looked over at Irene he knew he would have to tell her about it soon, but not tonight, he thought as he reached for her, to hold her.

seventeen

THE NEW POSITION

Roland was seated on the plane on the way to Regina, Saskatchewan, just saying the name of the place made him realize how far away it was. He'd never flown before and was in awe as he looked out the window. In the Army, they'd put them on a boat to cross the ocean, which was a horrible experience and told himself, one I will never repeat. The flight itself was exciting; his stomach was in knots though and he wasn't sure if it was from the flight, the new position or both. He knew he was nervous about this new job; it was going to be like starting all over again. He decided to use the time on the plane to catch up on some reading he needed to finish before he started work in the morning and pulled the papers out of his briefcase. His thoughts wandered back to Irene and how angry she'd been when he told her that he would have to come out to Regina alone for the first couple of months. She was so angry she hadn't spoken to him for days after. Thank goodness, Mama had intervened or he'd still be in the proverbial doghouse. He loved her, but he knew she could be very self absorbed at times. All she'd ever talked about since he'd told her about the transfer was what was she going to do all by herself out there. He didn't think she'd ever given a single thought to the fact that he would

177

be alone out here, too, especially now, he had no one, only his co-workers and he hadn't even met them yet. She had both their families there for her. He wished she could be a little more understanding sometimes.

The captain announced they would be landing at the Regina Airport in approximately thirty minutes. Roland finished his drink and tucked his papers away in his briefcase. He watched out the window, as the plane made it's decent into the City, and marvelled at the amount of snow on the ground. Sarnia had had leaves beginning to grow on the trees, when he'd left. This place was still snow covered and the trees looked bare and dead. Oh boy, he thought with a heavy sigh, Irene isn't going to like this place much, she hates the winter at home and this place looks like it might be really cold and desolate in winter. This is already the beginning of April there shouldn't be this much snow, should there, he wondered, maybe this is just an exceptional year, he decided that must be the case and put it out of his mind as he enjoyed the aircrafts' decent and arrival at the airport.

When he got off the plane he was met by a gentleman he'd heard about but had never actually met, Mr. Ayre, he was the head of the plant here in Regina. Roland was surprised at how young he was and he was astounded that this man would actually meet him, himself, instead of sending someone else. Mr. Ayre came right up to him and smiling widely, said, "Welcome to the beautiful City of Regina." He shook his hand and told him, "I was pleased to hear you'd accepted this position." He also told Roland, "By the way, I want to let you know upfront, I believe in an open door style of management, meaning that you can always come in and talk, about anything that's bothering you."

Roland and Mr. Ayre proceeded to the baggage claim area where Mr. Ayre informed him, "I had my secretary make reservations at the Regina Inn, that'll be your home for the next twelve weeks." He also said, "And I've taken the liberty of making dinner reservations for this evening. I hope that's alright with you?" Roland answered, "Of course, I would be pleased to have dinner with you, Mr. Ayre." Mr. Ayre looked at him, shook his head and said, "One of the first things we need to clear up and immediately is I want you to dispense with the Mr. and just call me Don. We'll have a better relationship if we're on a first name basis." He stated, "We're a very informal office here in Regina." Roland liked that idea. He smiled at Don and asked, "Will anyone else be joining us for dinner?" Don said chuckling, "I was going to surprise you, but yes, I've invited a few other people you'll be working with." Roland was pleased and told him, "I like the idea of meeting people first, before I start working with them." Don told him, nodding, "I do too, that's exactly why I arranged for this dinner, I've always thought, if people can be put at ease on their first day on the job that things usually go much smoother." He went on to say, "We run a different ship from the one in Sarnia, they're much more regimental, where we pride ourselves on being more relaxed here," and he added with a wink, "We have a lot more fun here, too."

Back in his hotel room, Roland was thinking about his encounter with Don and decided he really liked the man. He thought looking out the window; I just might like this place, despite all the snow. He walked across the room and started unpacking his suitcase and hanging up his clothes. He had ample closet space and the bureau of drawers was really quite large. He would have plenty of room for Irene to put her things away too when she came down in a few weeks to look for a house. He looked around nodding and thinking, she would definitely approve of this hotel. The room was large it had an oversized bed, the large bureau of drawers that he'd just put his clothes into and a huge bathroom containing a soaker tub with claw feet, two sinks and a huge mirror running behind them and another mirror covering the whole wall adjacent to the tub. Leaded french doors lead out to the sitting area, which consisted

of a couch and two wing chairs, one had a matching footrest and
a lamp behind it, perfect for reading, he thought. There were end
tables with lamps on either side of the large couch and a large
square coffee table in the centre. Behind the sitting area was a
bar complete with a fridge and an assortment of glasses. There
were new bottles of whiskey, rum and vodka lining the shelf
above the counter and there was a note. Roland curious reached
over to pick it up, it read, "I didn't know what drinks you'd
prefer, there's several varieties in the fridge, if anything is missing
or you would like something else, please call room service, the
Company will pick up the tab for anything you need or want."
The note was signed, "Don Ayre." Roland couldn't believe it; he
opened the fridge and at first glance noticed there were bottles
of pop of all kinds, Coke, Club soda, Ginger Ale and an array of
juices. There was even a bottle of milk. Roland closed the fridge
and opened the cupboard doors below the bar; he found a whole
selection of snack foods, including crackers, chips and cheezies.
He opened the fridge again and this time looked a little closer,
he noticed cheeses of all sorts in the drawers and an assortment
of dips on the shelves. He'd closed the fridge and turned around
to return to the sitting area when he heard a knock on the door.
He quickly glanced at his watch, thinking Don is really early;
he crossed the floor to the door. When he opened it a bellhop
greeted him cheerfully, "Good afternoon sir, I wanted to bring
this up promptly; it was just delivered to the front desk." He
handed Roland a huge fruit basket filled with all sorts of fruit
and goodies. He turned to leave and as he did, Roland tried to
give him a tip. He shook his head saying, "No thank you sir, I
have already been compensated by the gentleman who told me to
bring it up to you." Roland looked dumbfounded. The bellhop
told him, "That's how the Oil Company does things." He said,
"All tips are paid by the company and us bell boys aren't allowed
to accept tips from the guests who are living here and working
for the Company." Roland told him, looking surprised, "Thanks

for the heads up, no one filled me on that bit of information."
The bellhop left asking, "Will you be requiring a wake up call in
the morning, sir?" Roland thought a second and told him, "Yes,
six thirty will be fine, thanks" and smiled. .

Roland arrived downstairs at the hotel's dining room at
precisely the correct time; he wanted to make a good impression.
To his surprise, Don was already standing at the entrance waiting
for him. Roland frowned and checked his watch, he asked, "Am
I late?" Don said "No, not to worry, I just didn't want you to feel
uncomfortable not knowing where to sit." He led the way to a
table full of men and women in a private section towards the
back of the restaurant. It seemed the company had reserved this
private room and there were thirty-four people already seated
at the table. Don made the introductions and Roland tried
his best to remember their names. One girl he thought looked
familiar, but he couldn't place her with any certainty. When
Don introduced her though, the second he said, "This is Sharon,"
Roland instantly remembered her, he thought, she was the girl
who possessed the distinct dislike for Irene. She said, "Hello,"
and shyly told everyone, "Roland and I met when we were still
in Sarnia." Roland smiled at her. She was the only familiar face
in the whole room; he wasn't sure how she'd respond to him,
since their last conversation, a couple of years ago, hadn't gone
well. He thought, regardless of that situation, a familiar face
is still a welcome site. All the people he met at dinner were
exceptionally nice and very welcoming. Roland received many
offers to join things like the bowling league and curling league.
They explained that he'd need something to do during his time
off. One of the guys announced with little prompting, "It's kind
of cold in the winter to be outside too much." They all laughed at
that. Roland asked, "Just when does spring usually arrive here?"
Someone yelled out, "We had snow in June last year." Roland
looked shocked and they laughed, and the guy beside him told
him, "The weather is for the most part unpredictable, but when

summer finally gets here it's usually pretty hot." Most of the guys were not from Regina, either, most seemed to be from Ontario, as well, some of them had been here for several years though. Only a couple of them had been transferred here within the last year. A few of the secretaries from the secretarial pool were there as well and Don said, "It would be a good idea to get to them know too." He said, after dinner, "Before I forget I'd like to talk to you about an excellent candidate for your private secretary, remind me about it tomorrow, will you?" Roland replied, "No problem, I'm looking forward to the meeting in the morning."

The dinner was over early and people started heading out, as they left the restaurant, Don asked him, "Are you comfortable in the hotel?" Roland thought, is he kidding, but instead answered, "For sure, it's more than comfortable." Don told him, "I'll be making arrangements for your wife, Irene, to visit as well." Roland couldn't wait for that to happen. He hadn't even been there one full day and he was already missing her. She would have enjoyed the evening and he knew she'd love this hotel.

The next day there were meetings and more introductions, mostly people he needed to meet with in order to get the Lab up and running the way he wanted. He had to hire a few people as well. Don talked to him about his secretary; "I'm suggesting that you try Sharon. I thought the two of you would get along well, since she's from Sarnia too." He told him, raising an eyebrow, "She told me that you two even went to the same high school." Roland was a little apprehensive but he agreed to try it. He did ask, "What recourse will I have in the event she doesn't work out?" Don assured him, "If you're not completely satisfied with Sharon's work, please discuss it with me immediately and I'll have her moved to another department and you may hire whom ever you wish." Roland was happy with that answer. He was quite surprised though when he returned to his office and she was already sitting at the secretarial station outside his private office. She smiled at him and told him, "I was told to start immediately." He shook her hand, saying, "Welcome to the Lab," and asked her, "Would you make some calls to confirm my appointments, for tomorrow with the contractors?" He also said, "Check on ads for hiring staff for the Lab, as well." He knew she probably knew more about running this place than he did right now. He planned to glean as much knowledge from her and everyone else in the place as he could manage; he knew he was going to need all the help he could get.

Sharon loved helping him, she had always liked Roland, she'd had a crush on him in high school, but he'd never noticed her. She told herself, under her breath, "I'm going to do everything in my power to make sure that doesn't happen now." She watched him walking into his office and smiled, thinking he still has that fantastic body. Once he closed his door, she got to work, she was determined to do a terrific job, she wanted to ensure that she would become indispensable to him.

Roland learned quickly and the Lab was up and running and fully staffed in just three weeks. Don came by Roland's office to congratulate him on doing such a fine job. He asked him, "Have you got time for lunch today?" Roland responded with "I sure do, just name the time and place." Don laughed at that.

They went to a wonderful steak house in the downtown area. Roland was impressed the place was terrific and the food was out of this world. Close to the end of the meal, Don asked, "How's Sharon working out?" Roland told him, "Just super; she seems to anticipate what I need to get done and usually has things started without my even asking and she's quick and efficient, as well." Don simply smiled; he said, nodding, "My own secretary trained her. She was a junior when she first came out here; since she's been trained she's just been waiting for a new Executive to be transferred out here, so she could be his private secretary." Roland was impressed, he thought one of these days he'd have to ask her what brought her all the way out here. He figured he'd wait for her birthday or some other occasion and take her out for lunch, then he'd be able to learn a little more about her.

Don told Roland, "We've made arrangements for Irene to join you." He asked, "Will that be okay with you?" Roland smiled and said, "Yes, for sure." Don said, smiling wide, "Yeah, I thought so. We'll be flying her over, at the end of the week." Roland said, "Thanks, has anyone told her yet?" Don replied, "Yes, I had my secretary telephone her to let her know about the tickets this morning." Roland asked, "How'd she react? She's always been terrified of flying." Don said, with a surprised look, "Don't worry she didn't mention anything like that to my secretary. She'll be here this Friday." Roland worried about her flying, especially with her being pregnant and all, he thought I'll ask her about it when I call her tonight. Don interrupted his thoughts telling him, with a smile, "By the way take some extra time to be with her when she arrives, you don't have to be at the Lab all the time you know, you have to learn to delegate some of the work."

Irene arrived and Roland met her at the airport he'd arrived way too early but he was excited about seeing her again and couldn't wait. She looked radiant when she emerged from the plane. He watched her walk down the stairs, she was searching for him, looking frantically through the small crowd of people congregated at the entrance to the gate that she and the others who'd gotten off the plane with her, would be entering. When her eyes finally rested on him, she smiled and he watched the tension ease from her features. He hurried to get closer so he could take her in his arms as soon as she stepped off the stairs leading down from the plane. She laughed and they kissed passionately when he was finally able to reach her. He asked, "How was your flight?" She said, "It was frightful but I wanted to see you so badly I had to swallow my fear and put up with it." She added, "I read my book or looked at magazines most of the time, to keep myself occupied and I chose an isle seat so that I wouldn't have to look out the window." Roland asked, with concern in his voice, "Is it okay for you to fly when you're pregnant?" Irene said, "Yes I told you on the phone it was, I asked Dr. Grogan and he said since I'm past the first trimester its fine." All the way back to the hotel, they talked about the kids and Roland's new job and he told her of all the wonderful people he wanted her to meet someday.

Irene was so excited when she saw the hotel, she said, "Wow, they put you in a really nice place." He told her, "Wait until you see the suite, you're going to love it!" Her eyes widened and she said, "Suite" he laughed and told her, "Come on I'll show you." She protested his haste, saying, "Hey, wait a minute, what about my bags?" Roland smiled and whispered to her, "The bell boy will bring them up." She whispered back, "My goodness, you really have come up in the world." He laughed at that and took her hand, they boarded the elevator and as soon as the doors closed, he pulled her to him and kissed her. She felt so good, he told her slyly, "I can't wait to get you alone." Irene couldn't wait to finally be alone with him either.

The elevator stopped on the top floor and he crossed the hall and opened the door. Irene was noticing the lush carpeting in the hallway and the big solid wood doors of the rooms. When Roland opened the door, she stood there gaping, and slowly entered the suite, as she did, her eyes grew as large as saucers, she couldn't believe the place. She managed to say, "This place is really beautiful." He gave her the grand tour and they ended up in the bedroom. He couldn't stand it anymore, as he looked at her, passion filled his eyes and he pulled her near him and began undressing her. She was unbuttoning his shirt at the same time as he was unfastening her skirt. Finally, since they were having such trouble with each other's buttons on their clothes, Roland just yanked up her skirt and slid down her underwear, he left the garter belt and stockings on, since they would be too much trouble to remove. He slid down his own trousers and shorts. He lay her down on the bed gently and entered her as he kissed her again. The two of them were so hungry for each other it

didn't take long for both of them to explode with pleasure and
just as they did, they heard a knock at the door. Irene jumped
up and ran to the bathroom as Roland quickly pulled up his
shorts and trousers and sorted himself out. He brushed his hair
back with the palm of his hand on his way to the door. The
bellhop had Irene's bags; he set them on the floor just inside
the room and left quickly. Roland was sure he knew what was
going on and had to chuckle to himself, the bellhops all knew
how long he'd been at this hotel alone; you couldn't hide much
from them. Irene peeked out the bathroom door and they both
laughed but immediately flew back into each other's arms. This
time they took the time to undress each other before making
love again. Once they were spent, they lay side by side and
talked about how much they'd missed each other. Irene wanted
to know if he'd found any suitable places for them to live, yet.
"I've had a Real Estate agent looking into things." He told her,
"The Agent has some properties for us to see this week. We still
have to phone him to make the final arrangements." Irene was
curious and wanted to know, "What kind of prices are homes
here?" Roland gave her some examples and she was surprised
at how little the asking prices were compared to Sarnia. He
said, watching her reaction, "I know they're a lot cheaper here,
I figured it was because Regina isn't a very big city and it's in
the middle of the Prairies, not quite as desirable as Southern
Ontario, I thought, anyways." Irene agreed with him, she said,
"I read about Regina at the library, I wanted to know a little bit
about it before I came. Roland was impressed, and asked, "Did
you like what you read?" She answered, "It seemed okay, I only
read about the history of it and things like that."

They looked at homes most evenings after Roland was finished
at work. Even though Don had told him to take time off, he felt
guilty and in the end only took a few days off instead of the
several days, Don had suggested he take. Irene spent most of
her days shopping and walking around the downtown area, she

said, when he asked her what she did each day, "I'm just getting acquainted with my new home." This statement made Roland extremely happy, he didn't care how much she spent, as long as she was okay with living here and it seemed she was beginning to like the idea.

They finally found a home after viewing at least six each time they went out with the Real Estate agent, which was every evening while she was there. They submitted an offer on it the day before she was scheduled to fly home. The builder accepted the offer and the Real Estate agent took them back one more time to view the house, just to refresh their memories. The home was spectacular; it was a two storey with four bedrooms and two bathrooms. The area was brand new and consequently there was mud everywhere.

Roland knew that the kids would be a handful in the mud and he wondered if Irene had considered the extra work, she'd have to do just to keep things clean in the house, until the grass grew enough to get rid of the mud. She seemed to be more interested in the fact that the Real Estate agent had said that the home was in a very exclusive area of the City. Irene seemed to be mesmerized by that and Roland found it quite amusing since she came from the same "just having enough to get by" upbringing as he had. Oh well, he thought to himself, let her have her fantasies, she's certainly entitled to them. He knew he had previously and still was putting her through some pretty tough times. She'd had to handle the kids pretty much on her own for the past few years. He knew even once they were together here, the Company would be sending him back and forth to Sarnia and sometimes to Toronto for training sessions and meetings. He hadn't discussed that with her yet, he kept putting it off, she always seemed to be so hopeful that they were finally, going to be together as a family and never have to be separated again. He knew now that that simply wasn't possible especially if he wanted to advance in the Company.

eighteen

A FAMILY
AT LAST

Irene arrived in Regina, kids in tow, at the beginning of June 1952. The weather was chilly but the sun was shining brilliantly. She was glad she'd remembered sweaters for the children. She glanced down at them; they looked so cute in their little dresses and patent shoes. Maureen was wearing her orthopaedic shoes; she had a problem with her hips that the paediatrician thought could be corrected with these special shoes. Maureen cried every time the other girls got pretty new shoes and she wasn't able to. She hated putting on those "ugly tie-up things," as she called them. Irene felt sorry for her; she hated the awful shoes as well and wondered why they couldn't make them a little more stylish. The doctor had, told her that he thought it would be best, if she wore them for a few years. He had explained to Maureen that she would be able to wear pretty shoes when she was a little older and she had cried. To make matters worse, Cassie and Jean teased her continually, as they had off and on during the flight. Irene had to scold them several times.

Maureen was the first to spot Roland and started yelling, "Daddy," loudly, trying to make sure he saw them. Irene was a little embarrassed, and told her, "Shush!" She explained, sternly,

188

"There are other passengers getting off this plane, with us, and they don't want to listen to that." She let out a quick breath in disgust and held her head high, wondering, my goodness, what must everyone think; my children are acting like hooligans. She insisted that her children behave, but when they were as excited, as they were today, they were extremely hard to control and she knew she was fighting a losing battle. She managed to make them walk slowly down the stairs, so they wouldn't trip and land on their heads, as she'd told them, in an effort to frighten them into taking their time. Once they reached the bottom, she lost control of them completely, they were full of energy at the sight of their Daddy, and simply couldn't contain themselves. They left her side and ran to Roland, yelling and laughing. Irene looked around at the other passengers and noticed they were smiling at the children's noisy reunion with their father. She relaxed and decided to just let them be, this time. They hadn't seen their Daddy for such a long time and they were very excited.

The whole family would be staying in the hotel until their furniture arrived from Sarnia. It wouldn't be too long since the movers had promised it would be here by the end of the week. Irene and Roland were shocked at how quickly their home in Sarnia had sold. It was only on the market three days and a young couple had made a very respectable offer. It closed the day after the movers finished loading up their belongings onto the truck. Everyone, her friends and both their families had helped her pack and watch the children, in the few weeks before the movers arrived. They'd had tears in their eyes as they worked, everyone wondering the same thing, just when they were ever going to see each other again. Irene grew teary-eyed thinking about it and decided to put it out of her mind.

She hugged and kissed Roland once he finished hugging and kissing the kids. Her mind wandered back, she knew they would arrange to go back to Sarnia on vacations and she was sure that Mom and Dad would make the trip out here as well. They had said they'd never seen the prairies and would like to. Even Mama said she would fly out to see them, too, as soon as they were settled. She found it soothing just thinking about seeing them all again

When they reached the hotel, the kids marvelled at the size of the building and then they couldn't believe the suite of rooms. They ran from one room to another exclaiming, "Wow" over and over. The Company had reserved the adjoining room, so the children would have a comfortable place to sleep, that wouldn't interfere with Roland and Irene's enjoyment of their own suite. Roland had to admit, they'd done everything they possibly could to ensure that his family would be comfortable. He wondered if all the other Oil Companies did the same thing for their employees when they were transferred.

Once the kids had rested a bit in their room, they went downstairs to the dining room for dinner. Cassie, always the little mother, told her sisters, "It will be very fancy and you will have to behave like little ladies." Cassie had become quite the expert on things since she'd started school. Irene and Roland smiled at each other when they overheard her instructions to her sisters. Maureen shook her head, said defiantly, "I'm not going to listen to you, I'm going to listen to Daddy," marched over, and took his hand. She just couldn't get enough of him. Irene thought of all the children, Maureen seemed to be the one who missed him the most. She had found her crying many times and when she'd asked her what was wrong, she often would ask when her Daddy was coming home. Irene always felt sorry for her. She was the youngest and the other two girls were a little hard on her, sometimes three really was a crowd, it seemed. They teased her a lot. She would do almost anything they told her to do, she was so trusting and her sisters sometimes took advantage of that. They were able to pull the same stunts repeatedly with her. Maureen always said, that she thought they would be nicer this time, whenever Irene questioned her about why she let them fool her again. Poor little thing she's so gullible, Irene thought. She had mentioned the older girls' behaviour to Roland and he had promised, now that he'd be around to observe things first hand, he would certainly put a stop to any of their teasing or unfairness directed towards their little sister.

The moving van was on time, on moving day. Irene and Roland had hired a baby sitter to watch the girls at the hotel. She was the daughter of one of the fellows Roland worked with. She was quite good with the kids and they took an instant liking to her. She was taking them to the Café down the street for lunch, and told them, "They even serve peanut butter and jelly sandwiches!" While the kids were hollering, "Yeah", she whispered to Irene, "I also planned a trip to the park, if that's okay with you?" Irene smiled at her and said, "That's fine." The kids were excited they'd never had a baby sitter who wasn't family, except for Brenda and Harold and they saw them so often they practically were family, they even called them Auntie Brenda and Uncle Harold.

Roland had picked up the keys to their new house the day before and just as they emerged from the taxi in front of the house, the moving van pulled up behind them. As they hurried into the house, Irene was once again in awe and whispered to Roland, "I can't believe that this house is really ours". He smiled, "Well you better get used to it, because I think we'll be here for quite awhile." The two of them exchanged smiles and just as Roland was about to kiss her, one of the men from the moving truck, knocked on the open door and hollered, "You mind if I look around? I need to know where things are, so we can unload the truck in an orderly fashion." Roland yelled back, "No problem, come on in," as he and Irene hurried to the door. They followed him, as he walked around the house, answering any questions he asked and telling him where they wanted certain things. Once the rubber mats were placed over the hardwood floors and up the stairs, for protection against damage, the men began bringing the furniture and boxes in.

Irene was excited, she knew she'd have a lot of work ahead of her just keeping it clean, until the grass grew and obliterated the mud, but she thought this house would surely be worth the extra work, she loved it. The hardwood floors gleamed; the kitchen had shiny white metal cabinets with a grey counter top with chrome edging to match the handles on the cupboard doors. The floor was grey, red and white tile; there was a huge window over the sink that overlooked the backyard. Irene imagined the kids playing in a sandbox and swinging on a swing set. Of course, they didn't have those yet, but she and Roland had discussed these additions when they'd bought the house. They wanted to make the yard a wonderful place for the kids to play. They'd even discussed the idea of a vegetable garden at the far end of the yard; there certainly was plenty of room for one. Irene suddenly snapped back to reality as she looked at the mud, and thought with a sigh, I wonder how long it will take the grass to grow. She walked to the large living room off the grand entrance and wondered if others would see it the way she did, Irene thought it was truly grand; it had so much room and a closet for coats that was plenty big enough for all their coats and jackets. The dining room was formal and separate from the living room. All the rooms on the main floor could be accessed from the central hall, except the small den, which was tucked in off the kitchen near the back door, a quiet place for Roland to do some reading or get some paperwork done when he brought it home with him. The basement steps were off the landing at the back door entrance. The basement was something Roland was looking forward to finishing, himself, he'd mentioned to her that he thought it would be fun; he'd always wanted to tackle finishing a basement by himself. Irene was glad he wanted to finish it; she thought it would be a great place for the kids to play, when the weather wasn't nice enough for them to be outdoors. The staircase to the second floor was just visible from the front door; it was covered in hardwood as well. Irene thought frowning; the kids will have to wear rubber-bottomed slippers, because in only socks, that will be far too slippery. There were four bedrooms upstairs and two bathrooms, one at each end of the hall. Irene was thrilled with this; there would be one for the children and one for her and Roland.

She looked out the living room window at the street, they already had some neighbours, and she could see some of the women watching, from their front windows, as the movers unloaded the truck. She hoped her furniture was what it should be for such an upscale neighbourhood. She'd never given so much as a thought to those kinds of things before, she'd been so happy just to have a house. She thought, now that Roland was an important person in the Company and since she lived in such an upscale neighbourhood, she might have to be more in tune with her surroundings and make sure the furnishings they owned were suitable for such a beautiful house. She wouldn't want to make the wrong impression on people here.

Roland noticed her frowning; she was lost in thought, and asked, "What are you thinking about?" At the sound of his voice, she started. He laughed, "You were really far away, what's got you so jumpy?" She thought for a second and answered, "I was just thinking of how many people already live on this street and I was hoping some of them would have children the same ages as the girls." Roland said, "The few times I came out to check on the house, I did notice some children playing, but of course I don't know which homes they live in. They looked to be similar ages to Cassie and Jean though." Irene replied with a sigh, "That would be so wonderful." She didn't want Roland to know she was thinking about maybe not having good enough furniture for the neighbourhood. He didn't like it when she "put on heirs" as he called it. He said so many times he didn't care how much money he made, he just wanted to be a regular family, not anyone uppity or special. He'd told her, after they bought the house; he really hoped she wasn't going to become a snob now that they were going to live in this neighbourhood. She recalled laughing and telling him he knew her better than that. She would have to be careful if she wanted to make a good impression here, because she knew Roland wouldn't agree with replacing too many things. She would have to see what she could do without him becoming suspicious of her motives.

The movers left late in the afternoon and she and Roland worked non-stop long into the evening so they would all be able to move into their home, the next day.

The kids were so excited, on the way in the cab; they were asking, "Can we pick out our own rooms?" Irene told them, shaking her head, "Your furniture is already in your rooms." Once they arrived and were standing in the entryway of their house, she said, "Go and see if you can find your own rooms upstairs." They giggled and chattered excitedly all the way up the stairs. Jean was the first to return to the main floor she was smiling as she announced, "I love my new room." She looked out the front window, in the living room while Irene was unpacking a box of Royal Doulton figurines; she wanted to know, "Are there any kids my age around here?" She was five years old now and would be going to school next year. She stated, as if it was a matter of fact, "I will need to have friends to walk to school with." Roland and Irene just looked at each other, amazed then Irene said, "Can you believe it, she's right, where did the time go?" Maureen piped up, "I want to go to school too." Roland told her, "You'll go when you're old enough, for now you can help Mommy with the new baby just as soon as we bring it home from the hospital." He looked at Irene, "That's only a month or so away." Maureen seemed to be excited about that. The kids went with Irene to their rooms to put the things away that they had packed in suitcases, for their stay in the hotel.

Roland worked everyday at the office and Irene worked at keeping the house clean and the kids clothes clean. She was so sick of mud. Roland tried to help and said, "The grass should be grown by the end of the summer." He went on to say, "Next year will be much better." He'd put up stakes and string around the seeded areas, but the kids still ended up on them, whenever the ball went astray or they walked too close to the edge of the sidewalk and slipped into the mud. He'd listened to Irene complaining every day since they moved in. Finally, he said to her, "Look, I can't do anything to make the grass grow faster." She was in tears most of the time and he really didn't know what he was going to do if this kept up.

One day he came home and found her lying on the couch, she was trying so hard not to cry. He could see that her water had broken and she was in labour. He ran over to her and asked, "Why didn't you call me at the office?" She said, "I did and the girl said you were in a meeting and would call me back as soon as you could." Roland looked puzzled for a second, he hadn't had any meetings that afternoon, and then snapped back to the present when he heard Irene groan, and asked, "Do you need an ambulance or do you think you'll be okay if we take a cab?" She started to cry, "I don't know for sure, the contractions are pretty close together now and they're really intense." She groaned and doubled over with another one. Roland was panicking he called an ambulance and ran across the street to Ann's house. They'd met Ann when she'd brought over a cake on the day they moved in to the house. She'd noticed Irene was pregnant and had offered to sit with the kids if Irene should need it. Roland banged on the door and told her as quickly as he could what was happening she came over right away to take the kids over to her place and told Irene, before she left, "Don't worry about anything; I'll take good care of them." Irene tried to say thank you, but another contraction hit her just as she opened her mouth. Ann quickly ushered the kids out the door, she didn't want them to be afraid of what was happening to their mother.

The ambulance arrived within minutes and Irene made it to the hospital just in time. She gave birth to another little girl.

Roland was all smiles when the nurse told him, he loved babies. Irene cuddled Dawn; she was such a tiny, sweet little thing. She had light blond hair and because she was so tiny and Irene hadn't been in labour long she was almost perfect. She wasn't wrinkled or red, like most full term babies, she was just perfect. Irene handed her over to Roland, who couldn't wait to hold her. He kissed her little forehead saying, "You're beautiful, just like your Mommy and your sisters." He told her, "Your name is Dawn Marie Petersen and your Birthday's July 14th and next year you'll have a cake and presents on your birthday." Irene watched the two of them and smiled. She didn't like the thought of going through diapers and middle of the night feedings again, but she had to admit this baby was adorable, she knew the kids would love her.

Roland made the calls to his family and hers, as well as all their friends. Mama announced, as soon as Roland told her. "I'll get on the next plane so I'll be there to help when Irene gets out of the hospital and I'll look after the girls now so they won't have to go to the lady across the street." When Roland got off the phone with her, he felt a little guilty for thinking that he'd rather the kids just stayed with Ann. He still couldn't get that conversation he'd overheard between Irene and Donna, out of his head. He couldn't believe that Mama had killed Otto but judging from what he'd overheard, it seemed she had. He didn't want her around his kids too often, but he knew he couldn't tell Irene that or he'd have to tell her why and she'd very be hurt. He wasn't sure if she believed that her mother killed her father anyways, and he couldn't talk to her about it, because she wasn't even aware that he'd overheard that conversation. He thought if he asked her about it now she'd wonder why he hadn't said anything at the time. No, he thought, shaking his head, it's definitely too late to talk to her about it now.

Irene came home from the hospital six days after she went in. Mama was waiting for her at home along with the girls who were anxious to see her and the new baby. Cassie wanted to know, "Did you really call her Don, that's a boy's name, Mom," she said in disgust. Irene chuckled and told her, "Not if you spell it D-A-W-N, then it's a girl's name." Cassie wasn't so sure. Jean and Maureen didn't care what her name was they just wanted to hold "it". Roland gently took Dawn from Irene and once the girls were seated on the couch, he gave each of them a turn holding her. They were proud as could be when it was their turn to hold her. Mama commented on her complexion, she said, "She's so fair and she's so little. She added, "She looks like a beautiful little doll."

Irene was so glad Mama was there, Dawn cried so much, she was a colicky baby and they had learned from the doctor that it could last for up to six months. Irene couldn't stand the constant crying. She'd always thought that there was nothing more annoying than the sound of a baby crying. She made the mistake of telling Roland that one day when she was frustrated with it and he'd scolded her for it, he said, disgustedly, "How can you even say that, poor little Dawn's in pain, I'm sure she'd rather not hurt, but she can't help it if she does." Irene felt guilty after that and really did try to help her, but it didn't matter what she did, Dawn continued to cry. The girls were becoming increasingly upset by it they thought she was sick. Mama explained to them, "Sometimes babies just are this way and she will grow out of it, we just have to wait."

It lasted for almost three months then it seemed like all of a sudden the crying stopped and Dawn was quiet and happy. Irene enjoyed holding her and talking to her now. She smiled and made little gurgling sounds. Even the girls liked to be around her now they would make funny faces at her and make her laugh. Irene felt such relief she could actually relax now. She still didn't like all the work involved with looking after four children, but what choice did she have. Roland seemed to be happier when he came home from work, now too. Finally, things were settling down and they were becoming more of a normal family, in a

funny sort of way because even though Mama insisted that Irene
do most of the work involved in looking after the children, Irene
still relied heavily on her. Mama knew Irene would have to get
used to it though because she couldn't stay with her forever.

One week to the day after Dawn stopped crying, Mama
announced, "I've made arrangements to return home tomorrow."
Irene was shocked she hadn't expected her to leave so soon. She
started to cry, saying, "Mama, please don't go, I need you, I can't
manage on my own."   Mama shook her head and said, as gently
as she could, "You're a family, you, Roland and the girls, you need
to be on your own and you are perfectly capable of looking after
your children, all by yourself. You did just fine before this baby
and now that she's so good, you'll do it again." She smiled at Irene
and told her, "I never told you this before but I'm very proud of
you, you're a good mother." Irene shed a few more tears, but in
the end, she understood that Mama had her own life to get back
to. She'd made some good friends over the years since Father had
passed away. Mama was happy now and Irene was happy for her,
and yes, she thought I probably can handle my children on my
own; it's just so much easier when Mama's here, though.

nineteen

FALLING APART

Irene was having a particularly bad day; the older girls had been in the mud in the flowerbeds and had tracked it all over the hardwood floors. Maureen had pulled all the toys from the shelves and had them strewn throughout the bedrooms and hallway upstairs. Dawn, a toddler now, had apparently awoken early from her nap and quiet as a little mouse, had painted her crib almost completely with poop from her diaper. The upstairs reeked. Irene wouldn't have known so soon if Maureen hadn't come downstairs holding her nose and telling her, "Mommy, upstairs is stinky." Irene wondered what she was talking about; it smelled fine when she'd put Dawn down for her nap about an hour ago. She was finishing mopping up the muddy mess Cassie and Jean had made and told Maureen, "I'll be up to see in a minute." She put the mop and pail away and headed up the stairs, when she was only half way up the stairs she could smell what Maureen was talking about. As she continued on, she noticed that it seemed to be stronger in the hall just outside Dawn's room. Reluctantly she pushed open the door; she gagged the smell was nauseating. Little Dawn was standing up holding onto the rails jumping up and down excitedly when she saw her. Irene couldn't believe her eyes, poop was everywhere, all over Dawn and all over the crib as well, even the wall the crib was standing against was covered. Irene felt like screaming.

Roland came in the door later that day, his usual happy self, but once he hung up his coat and looked around the corner and he spotted Irene sitting on the couch with her hands over her face, his mood sobered. He immediately ran to her concerned, asking, "What's the matter." She was sobbing so hard her whole body was shaking. She proceeded to tell him what "HIS" children had done. She yelled, through her tears, "I've had enough!" Roland was taken aback, he asked, "Where are the girls, now?" Irene hissed, "I sent them to the basement to play." He asked, "What about Dawn?" Irene bellowed, "After I bathed her, I set up the playpen downstairs and told Cassie and Jean to watch her, I had no choice, I had to clean up the mess in the bedroom."

Roland sighed and tried his best to calm her down, he said, finally, "I'll take care of the girls tonight; I can see that you're very tired and upset." He turned away from her and headed downstairs to see his girls. They came running to him as soon as they saw him, even Dawn had her little arms stretched out to be picked up. They told him sadly, "Mommy says we were very bad today," and they told him tearfully about all the bad things they'd done. Roland felt sorry for them. He thought, what's wrong with her, they were only being children. Cassie said, "Mommy said we were very bad and she spanked us really hard and said we had to stay down here and play. She even spanked Maureen and she didn't do anything." It was then that Roland noticed the red welt on Maureen's little leg as she reached for her blanket, the one she carried with her whenever she felt sad or tired. Roland thought with a sigh as he hugged Maureen, what am I going to do. Irene can't seem to cope. He looked at his girls sad faces again and decided at that moment that he'd look into getting a part time Nanny.

Roland made the supper that night and after the kids finished eating, he bathed them and put them to bed. Irene lay on the couch; she said when he walked in the room, exhausted, "I have a terrible headache." She was cross and she was taking it out on him. She told him through clenched teeth, "I never wanted to have this many kids; it's too hard on me to look after them all." Roland tried to console her by telling her, "You just had a bad day, most of the time you tell me the girls are really good." Irene just rolled her eyes and said, "Most of the time isn't often enough for my liking."

When Roland came home from work a few days later, he told Irene "I have a few things I want to talk to you about, after dinner." She looked at him thinking; he probably just wants to lecture me again about how lucky I am to have these beautiful children of his, he has no idea just what brats these so-called "beautiful children" of his can be.

Roland had thought of almost nothing else these past few days, except how awful she'd looked when he came home that day. The kids were unhappy these days and he had to admit that he wasn't happy anymore either. He thought about happier times when she used to ask how his day was; now all she did was complain about her day. They had no sex life anymore; she always said she was too tired. He wondered it she was just afraid she might get pregnant again. He was a devout Catholic and he didn't want to use birth control methods, other than the rhythm method they'd always used. He truly hoped things would improve once she had a little help.

When the kids were tucked in bed and they were alone in the living room that evening, Roland told her, "I looked into getting you a Nanny to help out a few days a week." Irene turned her head and looked at him she was stunned. She finally spoke and asked him almost venomously, "What made you change your mind?" She'd been upset with the fact that he had always just brushed off her feelings about having trouble dealing with the kids. Roland's heart sank when he heard the tone in her voice. He said patiently, "I can see the toll this situation is taking on our family and our relationship, as well". She looked at him with narrowed eyes and said dryly, "You're getting me a Nanny, so I will be more rested at night, so that you can try to make more babies with me, is that what you are trying to say?" She was so resentful, Roland wasn't sure if he should even attempt to tell her how he felt, but he tried anyway, he looked down at the floor and said, "I love you and I would do anything I can to make you happy." She seemed to soften a bit and he took her hand in his. He snuggled her in his arms, trying his best to console her. Some of the things she'd said to him had really hurt, but he decided he wouldn't even try to tell her how he felt about that. He thought sadly, she most likely doesn't care all that much right now anyway; she only seems to care about how she feels lately.

The Nanny starting coming over on Monday, Tuesday and Thursday, Irene was thrilled. She got her nails done and did some reading on Monday. Tuesday she had an appointment at the hairdresser, she was going to make a standing appointment for every week at the same time now that she didn't have to worry about the kids. She was elated she wouldn't have to wash and do her own hair anymore, she felt so privileged. Thursday she shopped and met up with some of her new friends that she'd recently met in the neighbourhood. They invited her over for coffee and of course, they were all jealous that she had so much freedom now that she had a nanny, which made her feel wonderful. She met another woman from up the street who also had a Nanny; Irene instantly took a liking to her. They agreed to get together occasionally on the days their Nannies looked after their children. Irene had so much time to do what she wanted now, she felt like a different person.

Roland liked the change he saw in her. They had started to have a sex life again which Irene had agreed to as long as he would withdraw and not ejaculate inside her. She'd heard from one of her new friends that this would work to prevent her from getting pregnant again. She'd told him that four kids were plenty and he'd reluctantly agreed. Even though he wanted more children, he could see that she clearly didn't, besides, he was enjoying having his wife back.

Irene had just settled herself on the couch one day with a book, when the doorbell rang. She had kissed the kids goodbye a few minutes ago, Nanny was taking them to the Zoo for the day and was wondering who could it be, then thought maybe Nanny has forgotten something. As she walked across the living room, she thought, I hope it's not anyone else I don't feel like entertaining anyone today, I want to relax. She'd been looking forward to a lazy restful day. She opened the door, expecting to see Nanny or one of her friends and was pleasantly surprised, there on her porch, stood an extremely good-looking man, he smiled a most captivating smile and introduced himself. He said his name was John, something, and he was asking her if he could show her some of his newest brushes and kitchen gadgets. Irene was embarrassed and had to ask him to please repeat what he'd said. She pretended she was distracted and told him she had not been expecting anyone. She thought to herself, I was distracted all right, but only because he's so damned good looking, I can't take my eyes off him. He said his name again, she still didn't catch the last name, but this time she did understand that he was from Fuller Brush. The other girls on the street had talked about him; this was the first time he'd called at her door, though. He asked again, "May I come in and show you my line of products?" She blushed and stepped aside so he could enter. His arm brushed her breast ever so slightly as he walked by and her breath caught at the contact, she was embarrassed but also shocked by the electricity it sent through her. She told herself don't be silly, you're a married woman. John sat on the couch and showed her all the kitchen gadgets and brushes in his bag. Of course, she bought a few items and made sure she bought something out of the catalogue that he didn't have with him, so he would have to come back. She tried her best to keep him there as long as possible. He seemed to be very interested in where her kids were. He asked, "Do they all go to school?" She told him, "No no, I have a Nanny," and proceeded to tell him which days the Nanny took the kids out." John said, with a wink, "I'll have to be sure to call on those days then won't I." He quickly added, "I love children, but they can interfere with your being able to concentrate on my catalogue and my products." He winked at her again. She knew she should have looked away when he made that kind of gesture but instead she smiled. He ran his finger down her cheek and she felt the electricity again and never even attempted to stop him. He left promising, "I'll return next week with your order, I'll also bring some other items that you might be interested in seeing." Irene found herself looking forward to his return next week. All day she kept telling herself she was being silly. She promised herself, if he touches my cheek that way again I'll tell him that it's inappropriate and to stop.

As the week passed, she discovered she was really looking forward to seeing John again. Roland had asked about him, but only questions about what he sold. Irene had answered, "Mostly kitchen stuff." Roland's reply was, "What man would want to do that?" Irene thought to herself, a very handsome one and immediately cautioned herself not to think that way.

Thursday finally arrived and when Nanny took the kids out, Irene was all nerves. She told herself not to be so silly he was only a salesman and making her feel good was probably part of his job. He was more than likely just a harmless flirt. He rang the doorbell and before she opened the door she quickly checked her appearance in the hall mirror, she'd worn a lovely sweater set in a soft rose colour and a dark skirt that showed off her figure and her legs. She had even applied a little lip colour. When she opened the door, he didn't even ask this time if he could come in, he just barged right in, went straight to the living room, sat down on the couch and put down his things. Irene followed, watching him. His aftershave was almost hypnotic; she was in awe, he was even better looking than she'd remembered. He started opening the bags he brought with him and he showed her, her order. He looked up at her and his eyes roamed over her briefly and he smiled a slow sexy smile. He motioned for her to sit beside him and said, "You need to look things over, to make sure they're exactly what you ordered." She sat beside him and bent over slightly, reaching for one of the items but at the same time, he bent to pick up his briefcase and they accidentally bumped foreheads in the process. She jumped back surprised; he looked up at her, and lightly touched her arm asking, "Did I hurt you?" He said with his face only inches from hers and his voice full of concern, "I'm so sorry." He moved her hair and inspected her forehead to be sure there was no mark, she sat very still looking up at him, their eyes met, he smelled so wonderful she thought, as he lowered his mouth to hers. She knew she shouldn't do this; her mind was screaming, no, but the rest of her was telling her, yes. She felt helpless as she let him kiss her, it felt so good, she kissed him back and felt the heat rise inside her, she actually felt dizzy. She'd felt so unattractive lately. Roland was absorbed with work and usually tired when he came home each evening, he just didn't pay as much attention to her anymore he was great with the kids, but not her. Suddenly she felt his hand on the back of her neck and his kiss deepened, making her feel like jelly. She began to feel guilty and pulled away. He looked at her for a few seconds and she noticed the longing in his eyes, but he looked away quickly and carried on showing her different things in the catalogue. She felt a little uncomfortable sitting beside him now, but he kept presenting items and talking about the products as if nothing at all happened, and she soon relaxed. She gave him another order and he left saying he would be back as soon as the order was in.

Irene thought as she was closing the door, after he left, what am I doing, I never should have ordered anything. I should not let him come back in this house ever again. She stewed about it most of the day, berating herself for being so stupid. She kept asking herself, am I really the kind of woman who needs to have constant attention from a man. She decided, tonight once the kids are all tucked in bed I'm going to snuggle up with Roland and get him interested in making love. She hoped that would satisfy her need for male attention. She thought about Roland and suddenly realized he'd never been as distant with her as he'd been lately. She knew most of it was her fault and she also knew she needed to make amends; she still loved him deeply.

John was due to come out to the house with her order today, it was Thursday, and he'd always stopped by on Thursdays, so far. Irene told herself, aloud, "I'm going to pay for my order and then I'm going tell him not to stop at my house anymore." She didn't trust herself where he was concerned. She decided to sit down on the couch and wait; as she waited, she thought of all her attempts to be with Roland, last week and had concluded that he simply wasn't interested in her any longer. She recalled painfully, how he'd reacted when she tried to snuggle with him, he'd kissed her nose and told her he had some reading to do and went off into the den and shut the door. She'd picked up her knitting and waited, when he finally he came out of the den; he'd only rubbed his eyes saying he was exhausted. They'd gone to bed and he'd gone right to sleep after giving her a quick kiss on the cheek. A few nights later, they had made love, but she thought he seemed different somehow, he didn't spend time arousing her as he used to. He kissed her, but everything seemed to be rushed, as if he wanted to get it over with quickly. She lay awake that night wondering if he just didn't think she was attractive anymore. She'd lost all the weight with the last baby too, just as she had with the others, she didn't think she looked so bad. She'd kept herself up most of that night wondering what she could do.

Morning turned into afternoon and Irene wondered if something had happened to John, he was usually here in the morning. She made herself a sandwich and after she ate it, she picked up her book and began reading. John never did show up, she thought with a shrug, that's probably a good thing, maybe he sensed that I was going to tell him not to come over anymore, he seems to be good at sensing things. She thought of his kiss and part of her wanted to do it again. She told herself, aloud, "No, you don't!" Just then, Nanny brought the children home and Irene went to the door to greet them.

Roland was spending more time at the office than he knew was necessary. Sharon was always coming up with reasons for him to read something. Sometimes she would come around beside him and lean into him making sure she touched him while she showed him some report and asked him for clarification. One time she had even brushed her breasts across his arm. Today she was wearing a thin silk blouse; he could have sworn she'd been wearing a jacket over it earlier. He was having trouble taking his eyes off it; he could see her nipples through the thin material. She said she needed to show him some papers and get his signature on some of them. She closed the office door and came around to his side of the desk as she showed him the papers she leaned into him. He could feel the weight of her breast on his arm and the erect nipple against his skin. He turned to look up at her, her face was inches from his, and he reached up and pulled her mouth to his. She kissed him back passionately; suddenly he realized what he was doing and where he was. He pulled away with a jerk, but she said, soothingly, "Don't worry, I locked the door." She kissed him again with even more passion and Roland found her impossible to resist. He pulled her down into his lap and returned her kisses with a passion that had been pent up inside him for so long, he moved his hand over her breast as she undid her blouse; he could feel himself getting closer to the point of no return. She opened her blouse and undid her bra; Roland noticed it fastened in the front. She moved the thin material to the side and Roland couldn't help himself, she was now sitting up straight on his lap and her breasts were just inches from his face, he took each nipple in his mouth, one at a time and just when he was pulling away to kiss her mouth again; she reached out and took his hand and slid it under her skirt. He realized with a thrill of excitement that she was wearing nothing under it, as he touched her he found he was having difficulty controlling his desire. Suddenly he started thinking about Irene and as he was about to tell Sharon he couldn't do this, she rose from his lap and lay back on his desk. Her blouse was still wide open exposing her gorgeous full breasts, he watched as she pulled her skirt up over her hips and at that moment, he lost all control. He leaned over and kissed her hard and at the same undid his trousers and entered her. He could still remember that first time as if it was yesterday. She was so skilled at exciting him with little kisses and sexy looks that constantly drove him mad. She never once made any demands on him, she seemed to be quite happy to go to lunch together occasionally and make love in his office, after hours. Sometimes they went to her apartment instead of going to lunch and made love there. They would leave at separate times and meet there, so no one would suspect.

Roland felt guilty about his affair but he was tired of listening to Irene and needed an escape. She still complained about "his" kids, they were always "his" when they were bad and "theirs" when they behaved. She never took any interest in his life anymore; she'd even told him that his "work stuff," as she called it, bored her. She only ever talked about herself and the things she wanted, either for herself or for "her" house. He sometimes wondered if she'd married him because she thought he could supply her with all the things she wanted.

A couple of weeks later, on a day when Nanny had the kids, Irene had been sitting in the living room absorbed in her book, when the doorbell rang. When she answered it, she was speechless; she was so surprised to see John, standing there. He told her, "I'm very sorry I missed coming for a couple of weeks, I do have your order with me, though." He told her sorrowfully, "My Mother suddenly took ill and I had to take time off to take care of her." Irene asked, "Is she all right now?" He lowered his eyes and replied, "I had to put her in a nursing home, the stroke paralysed her and I just couldn't be there all the time. I need to work to make enough money to be sure she's taken care of properly." Irene felt terrible for him. She opened the door wider and told him, "Have a seat in the living room." She added, "I'll be right back, I just have to run upstairs and get my cheque book."

She was upstairs in her bedroom rummaging through her purse looking for a pen, she'd found her chequebook, but she needed something to write with. She looked up sensing someone was watching her and gasped when she saw him standing at the entrance to her bedroom. She wasn't sure what to say or do. He walked over to her and took her face in his hands. He said lazily, as he gazed at her, "I missed you so very much." She swallowed, this close to him, she knew she was going to have difficulty resisting him. Just as she opened her mouth to tell him, he covered her mouth with his. She felt his tongue inside her mouth and felt her knees weaken. He must have noticed because he picked her up and carried her to the bed. He was so smooth she hardly noticed her clothes coming off. He was kissing and caressing her, she hadn't felt this good for a long time. He quickly undressed and lay on top of her. He felt so good; his body was firm and muscled. When he entered her, she was more than ready for him; all her thoughts of Roland had somehow been forgotten. When they finished making love, she felt a little shy and was embarrassed. He simply got up and started dressing; he seemed to make a point of not looking at her. She dressed quickly, grabbed her pen and chequebook, and started walking out of the room. He reached out, took her arm, and pulled her back. He said, "I meant what I said, I really did miss you." She told him, "I missed you too." As soon as the words were out of her mouth, she regretted them. John kept visiting once a week and she kept buying Fuller Brush products, so no one would suspect what was really going on. She found him irresistible and didn't want to give him up, she loved the feeling of being beautiful again and that's exactly how he made her feel, it was such a wonderful feeling, she thought.

Irene was concerned about Roland working so hard. She'd invited his boss over for dinner one evening. She thought these things were expected of her, from time to time. She'd tried to get Roland on the phone to let him know, but she wasn't able to reach him, his secretary just kept telling her he was in a meeting. When he finally arrived home that evening, she told him, "I've been frantically trying to reach you all day. She added, "Hurry, you have just enough time to change, Don and his wife Arlette will be here any minute for dinner."

Roland hugged each of the kids and kissed them goodnight, on his way to their bedroom to change. Irene had put them to bed; she'd already fed them their dinner earlier. She never liked the children at her so-called dinner parties. He heard the doorbell ring and swallowed his fear, he was worried that she might refer to the fact that Don was working him too hard, keeping him late almost every evening. He wasn't sure how he was going to handle it if she did. He knew it was his own fault; he should have ended it with Sharon a long time ago. He didn't have feelings for her anyway; she was nothing but a pleasant distraction, someone who never made him feel bad. She always told him how clever he was and she was actually interested in the topics he chose to talk about. She was interesting and easy to converse with as well. She was well read and talked about things she'd read in the newspaper and books she'd recently read, she never spoke to him about shopping or clothes, like Irene did all the time. He'd wrestled with himself to break it off with her, for quite some time now; he'd just never done it. She was always so eager to please him, so much so, that once he was with her, he never wanted to leave.

Dinner was superb; as usual, Irene was an excellent cook. She really enjoyed that one chore. She was serving the cake and coffee, when she said to Don, with a sly smile, "You've been keeping Roland quite late these days." Don's happy expression changed to one of puzzlement but he recovered and said, "Well sometimes it is necessary." Then he glanced over at Roland and Roland blushed. Irene thought, what's going on here. She let them change the subject and pretended she hadn't noticed the looks the two men had exchanged or Roland's slight blush of embarrassment. She was going to try to learn a little more before she confronted him, she thought. She straightened a little in her chair, she couldn't believe that Roland would cheat on her; she thought it must be something else; he couldn't possibly be having an affair. It didn't matter that she was having one herself, she just couldn't believe that he would do that to her.

Don and Roland talked about the courses and meetings Roland was to attend in Toronto. Irene knew he was going to have to go; she was surprised that he hadn't before now. Don said he'd wanted Irene and him to have time as a family before they rushed him off on a trip. Roland would be gone for about two months, he thought.

Irene sighed, she hadn't been listening too closely, she'd been too wrapped up in her own thoughts. She had heard that Roland would be off on a business trip soon though and thought; at least I have Nanny to help me. She hated having the kids all on her own. They were cute and she thought she really did love them; but they were just so much work, a bit of a pain if she was going to be truthful. She could never tell anyone that, though. She smiled to herself thinking that she needed to be a lady and a lady didn't do that, they just had others look after their brats for them. She would have to look into having Nanny come out five days a week. It couldn't cost that much more, she thought. She knew she could get Roland to agree. Her thoughts turned to John, she was so glad she had that little distraction, once a week, especially now that she thought Roland might have one of his own. She thought with a smile, if he really is having an affair, I might be able to use that bit of knowledge to my advantage.

twenty

FACING
THE TRUTH

Irene accompanied Roland to the airport and took the kids along with her. She'd kept Cassie and Jean home from school today so they could come with her, they wanted to say goodbye to their Daddy, too. They were very quiet on the taxi ride home and Irene worried about them; she knew they were going to miss him terribly. Two whole months when you were as young as the children were was a very long time. She tried to think of a way to explain their Daddy's absence to them, in a way they would understand. The why was simple she told them he had to work and go to meetings, that they understood, but the length of time he would be gone was something else. She thought of telling them how many sleeps it would be before he returned home but that seemed like an eternity, even to her. She finally settled on how many times they would go to Mass, at Church, that number didn't seem quite so outrageous. Maureen looked thoughtful for a few minutes after her explanation and then asked, "How many times will we say our sleeping prayer?" When she noticed her Mom frowning, she said, "You know, the one that says now I lay me down to sleep?" Irene thought this kid thinks of everything but decided to simply tell her, "That's a good question, I'll think about it and let you know." Maureen

213

seemed to be satisfied with that, for the time being, all though, you never knew with her she could very well remember sometime in the near future and ask when she was going to let her know. Irene had to smile at this rather different child she could be so serious at times for her age.

Cassie who'd also been thinking, suggested, "Let's make a ribbon time chain." Irene asked, "What's that?" Jean and Maureen were listening intently; they both thought their big sister knew everything. Cassie explained, "My teacher, Mrs. Metz, taught us how to make them, she said we would all make one of our own at the end of November to help us count down the days until Christmas." She asked, "Mommy, why can't we make one to count down the days until Daddy comes home?" She added, her voice raising an octave, "It's easy we just have to make a chain out of ribbon, each loop of ribbon is one day." Irene thought that's a lot of loops, maybe the kids will forget about it, by the time we get home.

The kids didn't forget and that evening they made the chain, Irene found some ribbon leftover from Christmas, she only had bits and pieces of all different colours, but the kids didn't care. She decided that they could each make a chain and take turns cutting a loop off each night. One chain would have been too long, so they made three of them each consisting of twenty days and hung them on the kitchen wall near the table.

The days passed ever so slowly, Irene had such trouble on the days she had to deal with the kids on her own, and she was cross with them often. She just didn't seem to have the patience she should have. Each day as one of the kids took their turn cutting a loop from one of the chains; they complained that there were still too many loops left to be cut off. Sometimes they cried that their Daddy was never coming home because it was going to take way too long for there to be no more loops left on the chain. Irene felt sorry for them, but she was going through her own hell right now and was far too preoccupied to be of much help to the children.

She wasn't sure she could face Roland when he did come home. She'd been experiencing, what she though might be morning sickness again and she was terrified that this baby might not even be his. She'd been carrying on with John for far too long now and they'd never taken any precautions. It just seemed that every time he came over she was always going to tell him that she couldn't see him anymore and then they would somehow end up in bed before she got the chance. She thought with a sigh, he was just so damned good-looking she couldn't help herself, it seemed, and it didn't hurt either, that he was wonderful in bed. Roland used to be like that she thought but lately when they did make love, which was rare; it was always over so quickly. Roland was always tired and usually went right to sleep after kissing her goodnight, leaving her to lay there feeling undesirable. He didn't even notice when she changed her hairstyle or had it coloured. She bought silky see-through nighties, she even tried wearing the nightie she'd worn on their honeymoon and he hadn't even noticed. She couldn't help feeling that he just didn't find her attractive anymore. She remembered the looks that were exchanged between Roland and Don when she'd mentioned that Don had been keeping him late, so often. She knew there must be something going on. She never said anything to him though because the very next morning the morning sickness had started and Roland had told her he was leaving the next week for Sarnia. She didn't want him to leave knowing she suspected him of having an affair. What if she was wrong, she knew she'd have to find out for sure, first.

She thought about it for days and suddenly had an idea, and said aloud, "I'm going to invite Sharon over for lunch on a day when Nanny has the kids." Irene figured that if Sharon isn't the one, she might know who is. She would just have to be careful about how she asked her; she might have to trick her into telling her, just in case she felt any strange loyalties towards Roland.

Irene saw the doctor later that week. She took the required morning sample with her, and succumbed to the examination and as she expected was told to make another appointment for the following week. Irene thought to herself, he already knows I'm pregnant. She knew because judging from her previous experiences with the other four children, her doctor had told her he would have his nurse call her, on the occasions he wasn't sure, but the times he already knew, but just wanted the test results for confirmation, he'd always said to make another appointment.

Irene worried for the next few days until the doctor's office called and the receptionist asked, "Could you come in tomorrow? There's been a cancellation at ten o'clock if can you make it then. This way you won't have to wait until next week." Irene was thankful, she thought even if she was pregnant it would be better knowing than not knowing and driving herself crazy with worry for a whole week. She replied, eagerly, "Yes, I'll be there, thank you."

She arrived at the doctor's office and sat nervously in the waiting room, she'd already chewed off all her nails over the past few days, she looked down at her hands and thought, they look terrible. She vowed no matter what the outcome today, she would have to start taking better care of herself, or when Roland did return he wouldn't like what he saw. She'd started to gain weight, as well, over the last few weeks since he'd been gone, she was lonely without him and had turned to food for comfort, John just wasn't filling the void anymore.

Dr. Seamore called her into his office and as she sat down in the chair across from his desk, she told herself repeatedly, remember if he says, I'm pregnant, smile, if not look disappointed. She was so nervous she hoped he wouldn't notice. He seemed to be taking a long time looking at her chart. She was getting anxious. All of a sudden, he said, "I'm sorry, I guess I should tell you that you definitely are pregnant, congratulations, however I have a few concerns. The results of the blood tests we ran on your last visit indicate that you are very low in iron and I would like to take your blood pressure again today as well, it seemed a little high the last time." Irene followed him into the examining room that adjoined his office. He told her, "Hop up on the examining table; I want to take your blood pressure." He asked her, as he removed the cuff, "Is anything bothering you, lately?" She thought to herself, I have four kids now and you're telling me I'm about to have a fifth, and I don't even know who the hell the father is, what do you think! Instead, she smiled weakly and trying her best to sound sincere, said, "I'm just having a tough time without my husband, these days." She explained, "He's out of town on business and I'm always nervous staying alone with the children, when he's away." The doctor frowned and said, "Over the next few months we'll watch you fairly closely." He told her, "Make an appointment for two weeks from now instead of the usual one month period?" He wrote her a prescription for a medication that would help calm her nerves a little and wrote the name of the iron supplement he wanted her to take as well. She thanked him and as she left his office, she forced a smile and said, "I'll see you in two weeks." She made the appointment with the nurse and left.

All the way home on the bus she fretted about who the father might be. Dr. Seamore thought she was about three months along, so that means it could be either of them, then suddenly thought, who would know anyway, the kids I have now, really are his and none of them look anything like either of us or even each other for that matter. They'd thought that Cassie had looked like Irene when she was born, but she didn't anymore and her other children didn't look like either of them either, at least not now. She thought Maureen sort of resembles Roland, but not that much. By the time she reached her stop, she'd relaxed a bit. She thought, Roland will be home in another four weeks, then another thought hit her, she knew she had to break off her relationship with John before he found out she was pregnant. She knew things would be better that way anyway, she didn't need him getting any ideas.

She called Roland at his hotel that evening to let him know about the baby, as usual, he was thrilled. He asked her, "Do you want your mother to come out this time as well?" She was surprised to hear him ask that, she'd had the distinct feeling that he hadn't liked it the last time she'd come out to help. She wasn't sure just why though, she'd asked him after her mother left and he'd told her not to be so silly. He'd said she had an active imagination sometimes. She thought to herself at the time, no I don't, but had let it go. She replied, saying only, "I don't know just yet, I may not need her this time."

The next week the whole family was feeling better, it seemed. The kid's chains were getting shorter and they were finally down to only one. They knew it was finally getting closer to the day Daddy would come home.

Irene called Roland's office and invited Sharon over for lunch on Friday, but she said she had to work and Irene couldn't imagine what she was doing since Roland wasn't there. Sharon seemed to understand Irene's hesitation and explained, "I've been helping out the other secretaries while Roland is away." Irene asked, "Would you be free on Saturday then?" Irene was thrilled when Sharon replied, "As a matter of fact I am and I'd be delighted to come."

Irene had taken care of John, he'd shown up at his usual time and tried to barrel his way, into her home, when she stopped him by holding her hand firmly against his chest and telling him she wanted to talk to him. He'd stopped in the entrance a little shocked and looked at her. She told him flat out, before she lost her nerve, "I don't want to see you anymore, please leave." He'd tried to put his arms around her but she'd stepped back and with a stern face and voice, she said once more, "I want you to leave right now and don't ever come back." She would always remember the stunned look on his face, she wasn't sure but she thought she saw a glimpse of what looked like pain in his eyes as he turned abruptly and left. Irene suspected he was fooling around with other women, as well; she wasn't stupid enough to think she was the only one. She really didn't have any feelings for him anyway. He'd just been a pleasant distraction for her. It was unfortunate that things happened the way they did. She thought no one would ever know who fathered this child, including her, and she didn't think it would matter anyway.

Saturday approached quickly and Irene had to admit she was a little nervous about it. She had the Nanny come out an extra day so she wouldn't have the kids underfoot. Nanny was going to be taking the kids to the park and downtown to see a Disney movie, she was even taking them to a restaurant for lunch. Nanny is such a blessing, Irene thought.

She busied herself making little sandwiches and stirring the soup she'd made. The smell of the cinnamon buns she'd baked earlier was making her hungry, she'd been too nervous to eat breakfast this morning. She put the coffee on, and as she looked around making sure everything was just so, she smiled, she was especially pleased with the way she'd set the dining room table. She thought the flowers, napkins and tablecloth were perfect. She'd purchased them in a light cream colour and they showed off the dark cherry wood table beautifully. The bouquet of pink and yellow lilies sprinkled with baby's breath added both colour and fragrance. She wanted to be certain Sharon noticed her beautiful home but she didn't want it to be too obvious that she was trying to impress her.

Sharon arrived on time at exactly noon; Irene was impressed with her punctuality. She opened the door and noticed the business suit she was wearing. Irene had on a simple winter white skirt and sweater set and her black patent pumps with a pair of silk stockings, everything she wore was "designer label" of course, but she'd chosen her outfit carefully today, she hadn't wanted to seem too dressed up for a simple lunch in the afternoon. She'd glanced in the mirror in the entryway on her way to the door and was pleased with her look, she thought she portrayed "a well to do" housewife. Sharon looked like the secretary she was in her simple navy suit and light pink blouse. Irene greeted her warmly, kissing her on the cheek, saying, "Please come in and make yourself at home." She led her straight to the dining room. Sharon was admiring Irene and Roland's home and she exclaimed, "Your home is really quite lovely." Irene replied, smiling, "Oh thank you, have a seat here in the dining room and I'll bring lunch in." Sharon surprised her by asking, "Can I help you with lunch?" Irene smiled again and shrugging, told her, "Sure, you can bring in the sandwiches, while I serve the soup." Once they had the sandwiches and soup on the table, Irene poured coffee into her silver coffee pot and carried it to the dining room as well where she placed it on the silver tray with the sugar and cream. She asked Sharon, "Is coffee okay?" Sharon replied, "Oh yes, I drink it by the gallon at the office, I rarely drink tea." Irene laughed, "Me either, only when my mother comes to visit." They both laughed when Sharon said, "I do exactly the same thing when I'm with my mother."

Irene and Sharon got along so well, they had so much in common. Irene discovered they had even gone to the same high school in Sarnia. Lunch lasted almost two hours; they chatted about anything and everything, it was such a comfortable feeling Irene thought, to find someone with as much in common, as they had. She almost forgot to ask her about Roland. Finally, she said, looking down as the table, "Sharon, I hope you don't mind if I bring up a rather sensitive subject." Sharon looked concerned, but said, without looking directly at her, "What's on your mind?" Irene paused a second and then blurted out, "I think Roland is having an affair." The look on Sharon's face told all. Irene was shocked, after getting to know her, and liking her as much as she did, she would never have guessed that she could be the one Roland was involved with, but the guilty look she wore on her face and her failure to be able to meet Irene's gaze, told all. Irene suddenly felt silly, she'd wanted Sharon to tell her who it was, but now that she knew it was her, she felt foolish and she had to fight to keep the rage she felt rising in her throat, under control.

Sharon lifted her eyes and the two of them stared at each other. Sharon got up quickly and turned to leave but Irene stood in her way, and told her, seething, "You sit right back down." Sharon nervously sat down again and started to cry. Irene almost screamed at her, "Why on earth, would you even want to have an affair with a married man?" She added, "Especially one that's such a devout Catholic." Irene regretted that last part as soon as the words were out of her mouth. Sharon could read her thoughts because the expression on her face changed a little. Irene said haughtily, rolling her eyes, "Yes I know if he was such a devout Catholic why would he have an affair." She added, "I hope you know that he'll never file for a divorce because of it though." Sharon told Irene, sobbing, "I never had any intentions of taking Roland away from you, things just happened and somehow everything got out of control. I've had a crush on him since high school, but he was always too busy with you to notice me." Irene listened without speaking when Sharon said; "I thought you used to be so self absorbed back then." Through her continued sobs, she said, "After getting to know you over lunch, I'm really sorry I ever got involved with him, if I hadn't maybe we could have been friends." She went on quickly, "I don't know anyone here, except co-workers who all grew up here and already have their own circle of friends."

Irene looked at Sharon, who was sobbing uncontrollably now. Irene sighed and took her hands in hers telling her, "I have no idea why I'm consoling you at a time like this, but I really do like you and I understand how lonely it can be to move to a strange city and not know anyone and have no family around. I can forgive you, if you promise to stop seeing my husband right away. And yes, I would like to have you as my friend too." Irene watched Sharon, who was so obviously sorry for what she'd done, and thought, who am I to condemn you when I did exactly the same thing, except what I did was a little less wrong, since John wasn't married. Irene said, when Sharon was still crying and unable to speak, "I'm willing to forgive you and be friends, that is if you want to." Sharon leaned over and hugged Irene, she said over and over again, "Thank you, thank you." She confided, "You have no idea how guilty I've been feeling for the last little while, ever since I saw you downtown, one day, you, Roland and all your little girls. I had to duck into a shop, I was crying so hard. I didn't want Roland or you to see me. In the beginning, I wanted to get back at you for always keeping Roland so busy at school and keeping him from noticing me, then after a while, I realized how stupid that reasoning was, you didn't even know I existed and neither did Roland. I'm so sorry." Irene held her and let her cry for a while, then finally said, "Okay, that's all we're ever going to say about this subject, so no more crying." She asked Sharon, smiling mischievously, "Would you like a little something in your coffee?" Sharon smiled, through her tears, and said, "That sounds good." Irene got up and went to find some liquor; she came back with a coffee flavoured one that she particularly liked. She poured generous amounts in both their cups.

By the time Nanny came home with the children, Sharon and Irene had already cleaned up the lunch dishes and were chatting over another coffee and liquor in the living room. Sharon smiled at the children. Cassie asked her, politely, "Who are you?" Sharon told her, "I'm your Daddy's secretary at work, my name is Sharon." Jean and Maureen both stepped up and told her their names; Dawn just hung on to Nanny's leg and shyly peaked out at her. Both Irene and Sharon had to laugh at her. Finally, when she thought no one was looking she came a little closer. Sharon said, "Hello, Dawn, I'm Sharon." Dawn looked at her and finally she said, softly, "Hi." She turned quickly and ran upstairs, when she returned; she had her newest doll with her.

She walked up to Sharon and placed the doll in her lap, "This is my baby," she said. The ice was broken and Sharon and Dawn sat side by side throughout the evening, even at dinner, which Irene insisted she stay for.

When Sharon finally left for home, it was almost midnight. She'd called a cab and when it arrived, she hugged Irene and told her, "I'm so glad we sorted things out, now I hope we can be good friends." Irene hugged her too, and said, "I am too, come on over tomorrow too if you like, we can cook together and just have fun." Sharon said, "I'd love that." Irene added, "You could stay the night too, if you want." Sharon said, "I'd love to but I have to get home to feed my cat." Irene smiled, looking around pretending to see if any of her kids heard, and said, "Shush, don't say that too loud, the kids have been wanting a cat for ages. I was going to get one and surprise them, but now with another baby on the way, I think I'll wait." They both laughed at that. The taxi pulled up in the driveway and Sharon scooted out the door promising to return tomorrow.

Irene mused as she turned out the lights and went upstairs to bed, who would have thought that this woman could have an affair with my husband and once she admitted it, I would forgive her and become her friend. She thought shaking her head and smiling, life could certainly be strange at times. She liked Sharon though and surprisingly enough she completely understood her. She knew one day she would probably tell her new best friend about the affair she'd had and that that affair was the reason she understood her so well. Irene had the feeling they were going to become very good friends.

On the taxi ride back to her apartment, Sharon thought about all that happened that day, she was so glad she'd accepted Irene's invitation for lunch. She'd been going to call her and tell her she couldn't come, because she didn't think she could have pretended that nothing was going on, but after meeting and getting to know her, she felt so guilty for what she'd done with

Roland. Irene was so understanding, she couldn't believe it, and she really liked her. She smiled; she knew they were going to have a long and wonderful friendship. She needed to tell Roland that it was over, she knew that it wouldn't bother him much, she knew he loved Irene, he always had. Funny thing was that now she did too. She smiled settling back into the seat, thinking things have a way of turning out right sometimes.

twenty-one

BABY
NUMBER FIVE

I rene, felt as if she was getting larger by the minute. Dawn had told her, just the other day, "Mommy, you're so fat." She'd almost cried; she knew that little Dawn hadn't meant any harm and besides she thought, it's true. She felt different somehow with this pregnancy, and wondered if just maybe this baby was a boy. She didn't remember being quite as large with the other four or feeling this way. She had Nanny helping her out, five days a week now because she was having difficulty getting up and down the stairs, her legs were almost always swollen, and her blood pressure was elevated, despite the medication, the doctor gave her and her own efforts to reduce the salt in her diet. Her Iron was okay again though, thanks to the tablets she was taking. Roland worried about her constantly, she felt it was unnecessarily so, sometimes, though.

He'd been home every evening after work ever since he returned from Sarnia, which was almost five months now. She knew he wondered if she and Sharon had talked about his affair with her. He behaved like a different man now. He seemed to want to do anything he could to make life easier for her. She was amazed when he'd insisted on driving her to the hairdresser once a week, since she wasn't able to take the bus right now;

he'd even said he'd take her twice a week if she wanted. Irene thought, that's a complete turn around for him, because he used to complain, there was no reason I couldn't do my hair myself like other women did. He used to say I was very spoiled, now he's the one doing the spoiling. She thought with a smile, he'd even suggested they shop for new furniture for the living room and dining room. Irene had been shocked, not even a year ago, when she'd asked him to come and look at some furniture with her, he'd said, rather tersely, "The couch and chairs are hardly worn at all and will be fine for a few more years yet." He also said, at the time, "I think the dining room furniture looks great, you always use a tablecloth anyway, so who'll ever know there are stains and scratches on it." She'd been so mad; she hated having things that didn't look fresh and new. Now that the doctor had ordered Irene to rest more, she had plenty of time to think about things, she decided she liked the "new" Roland. She really enjoyed all the pampering and spoiling, she thought, with a smile, I could get used to this. She decided not to confront him about his affair; she'd only use that if she absolutely had to, it was so much better to keep him wondering, she thought smiling.

Time passed rather quickly for Irene, she was surprised, she had originally thought it would drag by slowly, since she wasn't able to do much, her legs were still sore and swollen, Dr. Seamore, said she had phlebitis. She wasn't sure exactly what that was, but he'd said something about blood clots and he didn't want her moving around too much.

Sharon visited her a few times a week and when she did, they enjoyed themselves so much. They especially enjoyed watching Roland; he never seemed to be able to relax when they were together. They'd discussed that it was a little mean of them, but they'd agreed mischievously, it was fun just the same. Nanny kept the kids busy, when they weren't in school. She was a Godsend and Irene was truly grateful for her.

Roland had to attend a meeting in Calgary just a few days

before her due date. He hated to leave her, but she insisted, "You worry too much, I'll be just fine." He was leaving on Monday and would be back on Wednesday. She knew if he didn't attend the meeting he could be passed over for the next promotion, he'd already been promoted a few times since they moved to Regina several years ago.

His boss, Don, had been talking about Roland being transferred to Toronto one day if he kept up the good work. Don talked quite a bit about the promotions and bonuses Roland could earn, sometimes she was bored at the dinner parties listening to nothing but Don and Roland talking about promotions and raises. It seemed all the people from the refinery only talked about work, it seemed to her that none of them were interested in anything else. The men either bowled or curled, depending on the season and the women talked about their children and little else, they didn't seem to have any interests outside of their families, except maybe their insatiable collections of recipes. They hosted recipe swaps that Irene had attended from time to time, since she also loved to cook, but the women's company itself was so boring that eventually she'd stopped going to the swaps altogether.

September 9, 1958 unbeknownst to them, was going to be a day they would never forget. Irene kissed Roland goodbye before he left for the Airport, the kids had said their goodbye's before they'd left for school. Nanny was going to be picking them up after school; Irene was to do nothing but rest, according to her doctor. She sat on the couch and watched the taxi back down the driveway and waved good-bye to Roland, she continued to watch until it disappeared from view.

She decided shortly after that she was bored and decided to get a load of clothes done, so the kids would have enough underwear to last the week. Since she couldn't get out these days, except for her doctor appointments, supplies of things like underwear and socks were getting frightfully low. She thought and said aloud, I might have to ask Nanny to pick some up the next time she goes shopping. I'll have to give her the money and tell her to go to the children's store I shop at though, that way I'll know for certain that she purchases quality items. She sighed, Nanny was just too frugal sometimes, Irene could see it in the way she dressed herself, when she came to watch the kids. Irene thought with a shake of her head that she could exercise a little more style in her wardrobe. She suddenly said aloud, "My goodness, I really do have too much time on my hands, if I'm sitting here worrying about Nanny's clothes," and she laughed at herself.

She sorted the clothes in the laundry hamper and took the first load to the basement. She had to sit on a chair after getting them in the machine. She thought, my God, I'm really not very strong, I guess it must be the result of not being able to do much lately. I'll regain my strength once this baby is born and I get back on my feet again. She managed to get the laundry almost completed. On the last load when she heard the dryer stop she trudged down the stairs to get the clothes out of the dryer, before they would have a chance to become too wrinkled. When she reached the bottom of the stairs, she felt unbelievably weak and her back was bothering her a great deal. She decided, taking a deep breath to ease the pain, the laundry's going to have to wait and began making her way over to the closest chair in the Rec room. She felt a stabbing pain in her abdomen, she held on to the back of the chair as she felt another and all of a sudden, she felt a gush. She thought to herself, no, not now. She thought her water broke. She turned to walk towards the stairs, so she could telephone someone for help when she noticed the bright red spots on the floor. She felt another stabbing pain and felt herself falling as everything went black.

Sharon was late getting off work that day, she'd tried to call Irene to let her know she'd be a little late, but there was no answer each time she tried. She thought, with a shrug, she probably just couldn't get to the phone quick enough. She knew Irene's doctor had prescribed complete rest, which gave her an idea. She thought I'll just stop off at the Dominion store and pick up a few things to make supper for her and the kids. It was right at the corner where she had to transfer buses anyway. She figured it would only take a few minutes. She finished her shopping and luckily enough the bus was coming down the street as soon as she arrived back at the bus stop. She was proud of herself for timing that perfectly. She'd known she had only twenty minutes to shop and get back to the bus stop to catch that bus and she'd made it just in time.

When she reached Irene's she knocked at the front door and when there was no answer, she tried to open it but found it was locked. She decided to try the back door, she was in luck, it was open and as she entered, she noticed the milk bottles were still between the doors where the milkman had left them. She thought, that's funny, Irene must have forgotten them. She picked up the milk and went up the stairs that led to the kitchen, she called Irene's name but when she didn't hear her answer she put the milk in the fridge and set the bag of groceries on the counter and went upstairs to look for her. On her way back down the stairs again, she thought, that's strange, Irene's not supposed to be going anywhere. She'd checked all through the bedrooms and the bathrooms. She checked the main floor, now she thought the only place left is the basement, if I find her down there I'm going to scold her, she's supposed to be resting. When Sharon descended the stairs and turned the corner into the main part of the basement, she noticed the laundry room door was open, and then she noticed Irene, she was on the floor in the Rec room. Sharon screamed when she saw the blood. She bent down to look at Irene and noticed she wasn't moving; she panicked and started crying, she patted her face lightly and called her name in an effort to revive her. Irene stirred slightly and her eyelids fluttered. Sharon told her frantically, "I'm going to phone an ambulance, I'll be right back." She raced up the stairs to the hall table and quickly dialled the operator and told her it was an emergency, she gave the details the operator asked for and ran back down the stairs to sit with Irene until help arrived. She looked chalk white and Sharon had never been so scared in her life. Within minutes, she heard the siren and the ambulance attendants were at the door, she let them in, explaining that her friend was pregnant, and showed them where she was, she said, "I never attempted to move her, I was afraid to."

Sharon quickly wrote a note for Nanny and hurried into the ambulance with Irene. They were at the hospital when Sharon phoned Don Ayre and told him what had happened. He said, "I'll get in touch with Roland and make the travel arrangements as quickly as possible, I hope I can get him out on a plane tonight." Sharon sat in the waiting room and berated herself, she thought I shouldn't have stopped at the store; I would have been there sooner if I hadn't.

Roland arrived at the hospital about midnight and was surprised to see Sharon sitting there, in the waiting room. She filled him in on what happened as he sat on the chair beside her, he was leaning over with his head in his hands. He blamed himself, he said, "I was so worried about losing my place for the next promotion, I didn't even consider how dangerous it was for Irene to be left alone." He let out a breath, and said, "God, I hope she'll forgive me." Sharon sympathized telling him, "It's not your fault, the last time I spoke to her about it she completely understood your having to go to Calgary, she thought it was fine, she said it was only for two days anyway."

Dr. Seamore came out to talk to them. It was already two in the morning, he said, "Irene lost a lot of blood, but is resting comfortably now and the baby is doing fine." After explaining all that had happened he finally, said, "Congratulations you have girl number five." Roland smiled at that but his frown returned quickly when he asked, "Will Irene be okay?" Dr. Seamore assured him, saying, "She should be fine, we're giving her blood right now, she will need to stay in the hospital for the next ten days or so to rest, but after that you can take her home. She'll need help with the children and housework for a little while, as well." Roland told him, nodding his understanding, "I already have a Nanny and I can certainly get a cleaning lady to do the housework. And on the weekends I'll do it myself." Dr. Seamore seemed satisfied with that. He nodded and said, "You can see Irene as soon as they bring her down to her room." He added, before he left, "And the baby will be in the viewing room of the nursery as soon as they finish cleaning her up."

Roland made all the necessary calls to the family to tell them of the new arrival. Mama said, when he called her, "I'll come out if you need me." Roland told her, "You don't have to this time we have a Nanny and I'm going to hire a housekeeper, as well. You're certainly welcome to come out if you like, but it isn't necessary this time, since Irene will have lots of help." She surprised him when she answered, "Okay I might come out later then once Irene is feeling a little better." Everyone he'd called was relieved to hear that both Mom and baby were okay. Roland had decided to spare them the details; Irene could fill them in on those later. He wasn't sure if she was going to remember much, from what Sharon had described to him had happened.

Roland tiptoed into Irene's room; he didn't want to wake her if she was asleep. She had been asleep, but awoke with a start when he walked in. He ran to her bedside telling her, "Don't worry it's only me." She asked, "What happened?" He said, "We have another little girl, she is doing fine and you need to rest." She smiled up at him and whispered, "I don't remember," and promptly fell asleep again. He quietly left the room after kissing her forehead and went home.

Their neighbour, Ann, was looking after the kids; she had taken them to her place when it was time for Nanny to leave for the day. She was a wonderful woman; she always seemed to be there when they needed her. He couldn't for the life of him, understand why Irene didn't like her.

The next morning as soon as Nanny arrived he sent her over to Ann's to pick up the kids and called a cab to take him to the hospital. On the way, he decided it's time I bought a car. He couldn't understand why he hadn't before. Irene had always wanted one. He'd always figured they didn't need one, but he was beginning to think it just might be a good idea, now. He thought I'll buy one for myself now and when Irene learns to drive, I'll buy another one for her. He smiled to himself, thinking it would certainly make grocery shopping easier.

He walked into Irene's room and kissed her. He said, "I haven't even seen our newest addition yet." Irene said, "I probably have, but I don't remember." They both laughed at that, they called the nurse's station and asked if someone could bring the baby in. The nurse said she'd have one of the nursery nurses bring her down. She said Irene couldn't have the baby in her room while she was alone, just yet because the doctor said she might not be strong enough yet.

Irene looked at Roland after he explained what the nurse had said on the phone and said, "I guess you're just going to have to stay here with me, if I want to see my daughter." He smiled at her and just then, the nurse appeared with a little pink bundle. She handed her to Roland; he was in awe at the sight of her. Irene watched him and laughed, she said, "I would have thought you'd be used to this by now." He said, "I never get used to the feeling of holding a brand new baby." Irene asked, "Can I hold her too?" Roland carefully passed her over to her. He sat on the edge of the bed and told her, "Tell me if the baby is getting to be too much for you." Irene nodded, "I will." They looked down at her smiling, she was a perfect little thing, she had dark black hair and lots of it, and she had blue eyes as well. Irene said, "We never came to a decision on a name." Roland looked thoughtful and said, "I think we'd narrowed it down to Penny or Susan, right?" Irene answered, "Yes, that's true, I remember we did decide on the middle name, though, it's going to be Diane." Roland cocked his head to the side a little as if in deep thought and said, "Well, let's try them out." He said looking at the baby and smiling, "What do you think of Susan Diane Petersen," the baby just laid appearing to be looking right at him. He continued with, "What do you think of Penny Diane Petersen," and the baby started to cry. Roland and Irene couldn't believe it, they laughed at her. Roland took the baby and said, "Well then, I guess your name's going to be Susan," and they both said at the same time, "I guess that's settled then." He cuddled her and said to her, "Well little Susan Diane Petersen, your Birthday is September 10, 1958, and you have four big sisters, who can't wait to meet you. Next year they'll probably want to have a big birthday party for you with cake and presents." Irene said, smiling, "That speech sounds familiar, have you said it before?" She smiled at him warmly, thinking of how much she loved him.

When she came home from the hospital this time, she wasn't able to climb the stairs by herself, Roland helped her down in the morning and she mostly lay on the couch or sat and did some knitting or sometimes she held the baby, but she wasn't allowed to do much else. She read to the kids each night before they went to bed.

When it came time for Roland to go back to work, the Nanny and the housekeeper took over. They were so efficient; she didn't have to do anything. She wasn't sure if she really liked that this time. She'd always dreamed of life like this, but I guess, she told herself, I might enjoy it more if I was able to get off the couch once in a while, not just to go to the bathroom and even then, I need help. She decided it was nice to have some help, but there were things she would prefer to do by herself. She would only need a Nanny two or three days a week, eventually, but she was going to ask Roland if she could keep the housekeeper, but maybe just once a week for the heavier cleaning, such as washing the floors and cleaning the bathrooms. Right now, she was doing the cooking as well and that was a job Irene loved and looked forward to taking over again.

Once Irene was on her feet again, life returned to normal. Nanny would come over and take the kids after school, she looked after Susan on a daily basis, for which Irene was grateful. She had trouble looking at Susan without wondering about who her father really was. She sometimes saw a strong resemblance to John, which shocked and worried her. Roland thought with her dark hair and blue eyes she looked like her, but there was something different about her and Irene had difficulty feeling close to her because of it.

She felt guilty for blaming an innocent baby for making her have feelings of inadequacy as a mother and subsequently a wife. Irene was also having difficulty resuming sexual relations with Roland, he wasn't pressuring her or anything, but she was so afraid of having another baby, she didn't want, that she simply couldn't bring herself to get close to him. She told him she was still sore, which he seemed to accept, but she knew eventually, as time went on he no longer would. She was going to try to talk him into some kind of birth control. They must have some new methods by now, she thought. However, that evening when she spoke to him about it, he was still just as adamant on the subject as he'd been before. She told him, pouting, "You're stuck in the olden days!" He got mad and went upstairs to bed without even telling her. She was so busy stewing about what he'd said; she hadn't even noticed he'd left. When she turned to talk to him again, he wasn't there; she waited for him to come back and when he didn't she went searching for him. She found him snoring in bed, not just on the bed, but actually in his pyjamas and in bed. She was furious, never in all their married life had he gone to bed without her, when he was home at least not without telling her anyway. She got herself ready for bed and laid down beside him, she turned away from him and cried herself to sleep.

twenty-two

ROUGH TIMES

The kids were growing like weeds; Susan was already celebrating her third Birthday. Summer was over and the older kids had already been in school for the past few days.

Roland was home today since it was Saturday and was busy helping the girls blow up balloons for the party tomorrow. They were inviting a few of the little three year olds on the street and a few slightly older kids as well. Cassie, Jean, Maureen and Dawn all had little Susan so worked up and excited about her party; she was running around in circles. Irene and Roland wondered if she really even knew what a Birthday party was, but they knew if the older kids had their way, she was certainly going to learn. They were telling her about the cake and her presents and toys. Susan was jumping up and down and yelling, "Yeah, yeah," and singing, "Happy Birthday to me." Finally, Irene who wasn't in the best of moods, had had enough and hollered at them, "Quiet down! Now!" Roland walked into the kitchen shaking his head, "They're just kids, go easy on them," he said. She glared at him, "You should talk! You're hard on them yourself whenever they bring home their report cards, it's terrible, so don't you tell me I am!" She continued angrily, "Cassie gets sick to her stomach, every time report card day rolls around and you think, I'm hard on them! I only have trouble dealing with their excessive noise!" Roland lowered his head, turned and went back out to the living room.

He told the kids quietly, "You have more than enough balloons now, so go and get your homework done, none of you will have time to do it tomorrow with the party." Maureen said proudly, "I already did mine, Daddy." He answered her crossly, "Then go and read something. Go!" Irene heard the exchange and hurried into the living room to try to help Maureen deal with her Dad's gruff response to her. She made it just in time to witness the dejected look on her face as she turned and took off for the stairs and raced up them. She asked Roland gingerly, "What was that all about?" He said gritting his teeth, "I thought they should to do their homework, we both know they won't want to do it tomorrow." She said, "That's fine, but Maureen finished her's on Friday when she came home from school. She told me so proudly she was going to get it done early because she wanted to make Daddy happy." Roland looked somewhat sheepish, but didn't say anything else. He picked up his paper and pretended to read, trying to hide the guilt he felt. He thought Irene makes me so angry; I just wanted to be alone, without the kids for a short time, so I could calm myself down; you'd think that was a crime the way she carries on.

Later after dinner, the kids asked, "Can we wrap Susan's presents, Mom?" Irene told them, "Of course, I'll read her a story to keep her busy, but try not to take too long, you know she won't sit still for very long." They rushed off to find the tape and paper. When they finished they stashed the gifts in the linen closet upstairs. Irene had finished reading Susan her story and was bathing her, when they burst in and announced, "We're done!" Irene smiled at them, "Get ready for your baths then." She scooped Susan up in a towel and took her to her room to put her pyjamas on. Roland suddenly appeared, saying, "I'll take care of dressing Susan for bed, while you tend to the older girls." Cassie, Jean and Maureen as well, were getting to the age where they were embarrassed for him to see them in the bathtub but at least I can still help with Dawn and of course Susan, he thought. He dressed Susan in her pyjamas and kissed her goodnight. He carried her to the bathroom door, snuggling and tickling her and said, "We're ready, Mom," to Irene and she gave her a kiss goodnight and he tucked her into bed. Dawn was out of the bath by the time he came out into the hall, so he helped get her settled into bed as well. She shared a room with Susan so that made it a little easier to get both of them settled. He blew them a kiss as he closed the door on his way out. He returned downstairs to the living room to wait for the other three to be finished.

He sat there, in his favourite chair deciding how he was going to broach the subject, of Irene taking care of the kids herself and finally letting Nanny go. The older kids were easy to care for now, in fact they even helped with the younger ones. He was sure Irene didn't need Nanny's help anymore. He also thought they could cut back on the cleaning lady and instead of having her once a week cut back to once every two weeks. His co-workers had been shocked when he'd let it slip about having both a Nanny and a cleaning lady. They'd said, practically in unison, "Wow, you must be making way more than the rest of us." He'd been so embarrassed, the truth was he wasn't making that much more and it was time Irene learned to live within their means. He thought rolling his eyes; I could keep both the Nanny and the cleaning if she didn't shop quite so much. She spends like there's no tomorrow. The kids had to be dressed in the latest styles and she had to have up to the minute fashions, Heaven knows why, he thought she doesn't even go out that much; she mostly stayed at home, except for a few things she was involved in. He felt a twinge of guilt over not being able to recall exactly what those things were or what she actually did, but he knew she didn't need such expensive clothes for them, whatever they were.

The kids came downstairs to kiss him goodnight and Irene

asked him, "What's got you in such deep thought?" He said, "Once you get the kids into bed, we'll talk." She glanced back at him as she told the kids, "Come on lets get up to bed, tomorrow's a busy day. We have to get up for church and have brunch when we get home and then," she paused and they joined in, "We'll have the party." She smiled and chased them upstairs.

Roland could hear the kids saying their prayers, when he heard the final words, I pray the Lord my Soul to keep, of the, "Now I Lay Me Down To Sleep" prayer that Irene had taught each of them to say when they were little; he knew she would be on her way downstairs shortly. He went over again in his mind exactly what he wanted to say to her. He prayed she wouldn't be too upset, she was so hard to live with when she was.

Irene came back downstairs and sat down in her chair across from his. They hadn't sat together on the couch for what seemed like an eternity. They didn't even go to bed at the same time most nights anymore. Roland was always saying he was tired or if she mentioned she was; he would tell her to go on up to bed. He always seemed to have an excuse why he couldn't join her. Either he wanted to watch something on TV or he'd say he had some things to catch up on for work. They never made love anymore, which suited her just fine, most of the time, because she didn't want any more kids. She was still trying to loose the weight she'd gained from her last pregnancy, and she couldn't seem to do it this time. Sometimes though, she had to admit she missed the closeness, she thought about how they used to be, so happy together, and it suddenly brought tears to her eyes. She reached down mindlessly and picked up her knitting. She snapped out of her thoughts, when she heard Roland ask, impatiently, "Did you forget, I wanted to talk to you?" She sighed and answered, "I can knit and listen too." He breathed out a breath heavily and barked at her, "Will you please stop." He continued crankily, "I went over our books today and I can't see us going on this way, we need to make some sort of compromise.

It seems spending is getting out of hand." She looked up at him, "You mean my spending, right?" He said, "Well, you could shop less." He quickly added, "I was thinking we could cut out the Nanny entirely and only have the cleaning lady once every two weeks and that would save us quite a bit." She looked serious as she thought about what he said and surprised him when she said, "If I agree to those things then you won't make me give up my shopping?" Roland reluctantly agreed, then brightened at the thought that she won't have time to shop, when she has to look after the kids all by herself. She'll have to clean the house on the week the cleaning lady isn't going to be here as well. He looked across at her, he was about to say something to that effect, but changed his mind, thinking there's no use starting an argument, so he said, only, "Well I guess that's settled, then. I'll call Nanny tomorrow and let her know." He added, "I'll help you as much as I can with the kids and the house." She nodded and replied, evenly, "I know you will."

He got up from his lazy boy after a few minutes and asked her, "Want to sit on the couch with me?" She gaped at him, unsure if she'd heard him correctly. He said, "Hey, surely you haven't forgotten how to snuggle." She replied, sarcastically, "It's been so long maybe I have." They both chuckled at that, Roland put on some music, and they danced around the living room. Irene felt like a young girl again, swirling around in his arms. They hadn't danced for ages. When they went to bed that night they made love for the first time in a long time. Irene worried the next morning, if she might be pregnant; she knew the timing had to be close.

She discovered thankfully, over the next few weeks, that she wasn't pregnant and she certainly didn't have to worry about that happening in the near future. They never seemed to find the time or the energy to be close again. They were both always so tired. Roland was taking some courses, so he had studying as well as work and Irene found looking after five kids extremely tiring. She'd reverted to the "his "kids again whenever they misbehaved. Roland was fed up hearing it. He couldn't even remember hearing her refer to them as "ours" anymore.

She was always in a bad mood, it seemed, and he felt very sorry for the kids. He knew he wasn't easy on them either; he couldn't stand it when they didn't get good grades. He'd always gotten excellent grades himself and expected nothing less from his children. That was something Irene didn't agree with. She'd said, one evening when they were discussing it, "I didn't get fantastic grades, my report cards were mostly C's and the odd B." She asked him, "Do you think I'm stupid?" He'd almost slipped and said yes, she could read it in his eyes; she threw the dinner she'd just finished making in the sink and hissed at him, "Since I'm too stupid, you can make your own damn dinner," and ran upstairs and slammed the bedroom door. She didn't come down again at all that night. He had to order from that new Gene's fried chicken place and call a taxi to pick it up. He didn't want to leave the kids alone, they might talk to their mother and he knew she wasn't in any mood tonight to deal with them. After he fed them, he struggled to get them into bed by himself. He told them, "Mommy doesn't feel well." The older ones were hard to fool, they just looked at him funny, but they knew better than to say anything and quietly went to bed when they were told to.

As time went on Irene and Roland grew farther apart. The girls noticed there wasn't as much laughing or even simple conversation at home anymore. Cassie was getting older and was more interested in boys, Jean was coming up behind pretty fast, Roland thought. He couldn't imagine his little girls dating, he thought I remember how I used to think, I don't want any boys thinking that way about any of my daughters. Oh well, he thought dismissively, I still have plenty time before I have to worry about that sort of thing, my girls aren't old enough to date just yet.

twenty-three

A CLOSE CALL

As years passed, Roland and Irene made amends. They didn't have much choice. They had a family to take care of. The girls were getting older now, Cassie was almost 17, Jean was 15, Maureen 13, Dawn 10, and Susan was turning 4 in September. Roland wondered one afternoon, how in the world am I ever going to pay for college for all of them. He thought warily, Irene's now expecting number six, as well.

Irene pretty much stayed home these days; she was busy with the girls and was now expecting another baby in November. She was sitting at the kitchen table enjoying a cup of coffee, waiting for Roland and thinking of how this mess started. She recalled, shaking her head, she had been experiencing severe abdominal pain for quite sometime before she'd gotten pregnant; her gynaecologist had booked her for surgery; she'd even been admitted to the hospital her hysterectomy scheduled for the following morning. She'd gone through the pre-surgery examination and was sitting in her hospital room, saying goodbye to Roland, for the night, when the doctor came in. She recalled Roland had said a flippant, "Hello," and then noticed the serious look on the doctor's face; he'd asked, frowning, "Is there a problem?" The doctor looked from one to the other and back at Irene and said, "Irene you're pregnant." He then asked, "Do you

241

want to continue with the surgery?" Irene was about to say yes, when Roland recovering from the initial shock of the news, all of a sudden said, a little too loudly, "No, we can't." Irene looked at him wildly, she was shocked at what he's said. The doctor frowned and explained, "It is possible that she will lose this baby anyway; or if she tries to carry it to term," he continued solemnly, "There is a strong possibility that both of them could die." Irene inhaled sharply, sheer shock, then fear gripping her; she didn't like the possibility that she could die as well. Roland gaped at the doctor, with his mouth hanging open. The doctor realizing the shock he'd just instilled in them and sensing the tension between them, left the room but on his way out, he said, "I'll let you discuss it." Then added, "I will require a decision this evening though, you can have me paged once you've decided or if you have any questions."

When the doctor left, Roland, pleaded with Irene, "Please, we're Catholics, we can't kill this baby." Irene, through her tears quietly said, "Do you want to risk my life for the sake of the Church?" Roland said, "Of course not, but I can't abort our baby either." Irene became very quiet. She looked defeated. She said, quietly, "Go tell the doctor, you've decided that we're going home." Roland took her hand, "I'll be praying, I have faith, I think that will make everything turnout alright." Irene glared at him snatching her hand out of his grasp. She couldn't believe he cared more about his precious church than he did about her. What would his kids do without a mother, she wondered, did he even think about that? They didn't even know this baby yet, she was only a few weeks pregnant, how much could it possibly matter, if they didn't have it, they already had five children. She shook her head thinking the doctor said I could lose it anyway. She suddenly felt shame for thinking the way she did but not only did she not want another baby she didn't want to die. What I want should matter, she thought, but sadly, she knew it didn't. Roland would be the one to make the decision and she would just have to go along with it. She wondered if she would ever be able to forgive him for this.

She got out of bed and started pulling on her clothes, as Roland left the room to have the doctor paged. He walked down the hall with his head down and to his surprise; he actually bumped into him at the nurses' station. He told him quickly of their decision and briefly explained the reasons why they'd decided in favour of not aborting the pregnancy. The doctor only said, "I would like to see her in my office later in the week." He gave Roland a card and told him, "Make an appointment with my nurse," but as Roland was walking away, he called after him, saying, "I wish you would reconsider, this could be very dangerous for your wife." That statement brought Roland to an abrupt halt, he took a deep breath and continued walking towards Irene's room, he knew no matter what the doctor said he couldn't abort the baby, the Church was against it.

The ride home was silent and strained. Roland felt guilty for insisting Irene go through with this pregnancy, what if she did die, he kept thinking. He knew he wouldn't be able to live with that, hell he thought I'm going to have trouble living with the possibility of it. I'll have to pay a visit to the church and ask Father Hogan for advice; maybe I'll feel better after I talk to him. He stole a glance at Irene and wiping at the beads of perspiration that were forming on his forehead with the back of his hand, said a silent prayer that she'd be okay.

Irene was quiet the whole ride home and said she didn't feel well and went upstairs to their room as soon as she walked in the door when they arrived home. Roland had the pleasure of telling the girls the news. Cassie and Jean were excited, they both loved babies. In fact, all three of the older girls loved little babies. They all babysat for the neighbours, Roland was quite proud of them because all their neighbours who had small children only wanted his kids to baby sit for them, they were all so good with little ones. Maureen was looking after some of the neighbour's children right now. She wouldn't be home until suppertime. Roland would have to tell her as soon as she arrived, so she wouldn't feel left out. Dawn thought it would be fun to have a baby in the house, but Susan just said, pouting, "I don't want any babies." They had to smile at her reaction. Cassie and Jean tried to talk her into it, but she still insisted she didn't want any. She asked suddenly, "Is Mommy going to be sick all day?" Cassie told her, "She might be," and added, "I'll look after you though, so don't worry about it." Susan seemed to be happy with that for now.

Roland called Father Hogan and made an appointment to see him the next day after work. Irene was just coming down the stairs as he hung up the phone. She asked him, without a shred of emotion in her voice, "Is something wrong? You don't make a habit of seeing Father." Roland swallowed and told her, "I need to talk to someone about this situation." Irene clenched her teeth and said, "That's what marriage is all about we're supposed to talk to each other and work things out between the two of us ourselves. Father has never been married, so how the hell would he know what we're feeling. He doesn't care if I live or die and apparently neither do you." Roland flinched and looked at the floor; he didn't have a clue what to say to that and he couldn't force himself to meet her gaze. He felt horrible forcing her to do this, when she clearly didn't want to do it. He could feel the doubt creeping into his consciousness and wondered how he would feel if someone else made decisions for him, even decisions concerning risking his life. He sighed heavily; he knew he needed some advice.

When Roland arrived home the next evening, he was late. The girls and Irene were already at the table eating dinner. She glared at him and said, "You could have called," she paused a moment, then added, "I decided that everyone shouldn't have to have a cold dinner just because you didn't have the decency to call." Roland was upset; Irene was berating him in front of the children. He forced himself to smile and reminded her, "I had an appointment with Father Hogan, remember?" She looked at him with pure rage evident in her eyes and asked, "And what did Father decide my fate should be?" Roland said nothing; he left the kitchen quickly and headed upstairs. On his way he called over his shoulder, "I'm going to change," trying to act normal and hoping the kids wouldn't be too confused with the heated exchange they'd just witnessed.

Once dinner was finished, Roland and Irene retreated to the living room to talk. The girls did the dishes and Jean gave Susan a bath. Roland tried to talk to Irene about the appointment with Father. He began, "Father reminded me to have faith in God's plan for us. He said he could not condone abortion, even if both lives are at risk. He said we should pray and have faith in God." Irene just couldn't handle listening to anymore she got up and left the room. She headed upstairs to their bedroom. She was having great difficulty controlling her emotions; she almost didn't make it to her room before she broke down in fits of crying. She cried violent sobs and tried her best to be quiet, so she wouldn't frighten the children, but she couldn't she was too upset.

Jean told Susan when she heard her mother's muffled sobs, "Stay here, I'll be back in a minute to help you get into your pyjamas." She flew down the stairs to get her Dad. She told him, "Mom is crying, really hard." Roland told her, "Don't worry, she's just very emotional right now with being pregnant and all." He ran upstairs and when he opened their bedroom door he found her on the bed, face down. She was trying her best to muffle the sounds of her crying. He knew she didn't want to frighten the kids. Roland felt sorry for her, took her in his arms, and comforted her; he stroked her hair, saying, "I'm sure things are going to be okay." She held onto him and cried until she'd cried herself out. She was exhausted when she finally stopped.

Roland laid her down on the bed, told her he'd be back in a minute and went out to tell Cassie, Jean, Maureen and Dawn that Mom still wasn't feeling well and that he was going to stay with her. He told them, "Don't stay up too long," and reminded them, "You have school in the morning." They asked him, "Is Mom okay?" He replied, forcing a smile, "Yes, she'll be fine in a day or so." He headed back upstairs hoping and praying he was right. Irene was still lying on the bed, just where he'd left her, her breathing still hadn't returned to normal. He helped her get out of her clothes and into her nightgown. He put her to bed, got into his own pyjamas, and snuggled her beside him until he heard her breathing even out and she was asleep. It didn't take him long to fall asleep himself once he knew she was sound asleep.

Morning came quickly, Irene awoke and found herself still wrapped in Roland's arms, and she lifted her head slightly to see the clock on the nightstand. She gently nudged him saying, "You'll be late for work." Roland kissed the back of her neck and said, "I'm not going to work today; I want to stay home and take care of you. I'm going to arrange for Ann to take Susan for the day." He also told her, looking down at her, "I want us to have some time together, alone." He dressed and went downstairs to check on the girls, they were almost ready to leave for school.

When he left the room, Irene sat up. She was suddenly feeling hungry. She thought that was a good thing, maybe she would be able to drag herself out of bed and down to the kitchen for something to eat. She headed for the bathroom to brush her teeth and splash some water on her face. She looked at her reflection in the mirror and couldn't believe how horrible she looked. She soaked a face cloth in cold water and held it to her face to take the swelling down, when that didn't work, she tried cold cream; it didn't work either. She finally gave up, tied her robe tightly around her waist, and headed down the stairs.

The kids took one look at her and offered to stay home with her today. Roland shook his head and told them, "No, I'm going to stay home and take care of Mom today. Now, you better get to school, gather your books and lunches and get moving or you'll all be late for your first class." The three older girls and Dawn went out the door, after one by one kissing their mother on the cheek and telling her, "We hope you feel better." Susan just hugged her and asked, "Can I stay in bed with you today?" Irene smiled at her and said, "Wouldn't you like to play with the kids at Aunty Ann's?" Susan said, "Yeah, I like them." Roland told her, "That's good, because you're going to spend the whole day there today." Susan clapped her hands together and asked, "Can I bring my doll?" He told her, "Run upstairs and get it then and bring your blanket too." When Susan ran out of the kitchen to get her things, Roland told Irene, "I'm only going to take her across the street and I'm coming right back to make your breakfast." He poured her a cup of the coffee that he'd started when he first came downstairs, it had just finished perking. He set out the sugar and cream and ran out of the kitchen to get Susan saying, to Irene, "Don't do a thing; I'll be back in a minute." When she heard the front door close, she sat with her coffee thinking; I might as well try to be happy. I know I can't do anything to change the circumstances anyway and the girls don't deserve to have such a miserable mother, as I know I've been lately.

Irene finally got used to the idea of having another baby and it turned out that there really weren't any problems with her pregnancy. They had regular appointments with the specialist Dr. Cubbin and on each visit so far, he'd found everything to be normal. He said, "I hope the delivery won't be too much for you but if it turns out to be, I'll do an emergency caesarean section." Irene said thoughtfully, "I've heard of that, but I'm afraid I don't know what all it entails." When the doctor explained it to her, she looked horrified. Roland was worried but he was trying hard not to let his concern show. On the way home he told her cheerfully, "You probably don't have to worry, you most likely won't have any trouble during the delivery, remember Dr. Cubbin said that he would perform the caesarean only in the event that you couldn't deliver normally." Irene looked at Roland and shook her head, she said, "I know but I'm frightened just the same." Roland took her hand and held it for the rest of the ride home.

Time seemed to fly by. Irene was watching the snowfall as she was sitting in her favourite chair in the living room, it was piling up quite quickly in the driveway; Roland was going to have to shovel it when he got home from work, if one of the kids didn't get to it first, she thought.

The older girls were involved in activities after school most afternoons, either volleyball or some other sport. Dawn was upstairs doing her homework and Susan was sitting at the kitchen table colouring. The house was quiet. Irene sat there enjoying the view she had of the falling snow, when all of a sudden she felt a sharp pain in her lower abdomen. She settled back in the chair and put her feet up, thinking it might have been from the pressure caused by her sitting up so straight. It was November and the baby was almost due, she was uncomfortable doing most everything now. She couldn't wait to get this over with, Dr. Cubbin had said he didn't think there should be any problems now; she'd had a fairly typical pregnancy. Even she had to admit it had been an easy one, so far except for the emotional roller coaster in the beginning. She felt good, however, this past month she'd been rather uncomfortable, but she knew that was to be expected since it was getting closer to her due date and she was huge. It was difficult now for her to get around. She felt another stab of pain; a ripple of fear ran down her spine as she tried shifting around in her chair, in the hope it would help. The pain kept getting stronger and she was becoming increasingly more frightened. She was home alone with only her two youngest children, she didn't want to frighten them, but she was frightened herself. She turned and noticed Jean coming up the drive, she thought, thank God and waited to hear the door close before hollering, "Jean, come here, quickly!" When Jean arrived at her side, breathless, Irene didn't even give her a chance to open her mouth. Instead, she moaned with another pain and asked her raggedly, "Please, call an ambulance, I think the baby's coming." She put a hand on the huge mound her abdomen had become. Jean raced to the table and picked up the phone, she dialled 911 and gave them the particulars as she watched in alarm as her mother tried hard not to scream in pain. She ran back to her Mom's side and told her, "The ambulance should be here in a few minutes." She asked her, "Mom, should I get the suitcase you have packed upstairs?" Irene gripped with another stabbing pain was only able to nod in response. She stopped on the first stair and asked, "Do you have everything packed in it, is there anything else I should put in it for you?" Irene finally able to speak, told her breathlessly, "Everything's already in it, thanks though." She was becoming increasingly more uncomfortable, the pains were coming closer together and she felt like screaming. She held her lips together tightly; she didn't want to frighten Jean anymore than she already had.

The doorbell rang and Jean ran to let the ambulance attendants in, they were very efficient, they had Irene strapped to the stretcher and on the way out the door in no time. One of the men grabbed the suitcase from Jean and told her, "Your Mom asked me to tell you to take good care of your little sisters," and added when he saw the worried look on her face, "Your Mom will be just fine." Once Irene was inside the ambulance, she started crying, the pains were so intense and she was feeling the need to push. The attendant told her, "Take deep breaths and don't push." She couldn't help herself, she cried and told them, "I can't stop, I have to push." She felt the warm gush and immediately thought her water broke, but she felt strange and then felt herself slipping into darkness and suddenly there was no pain. She could hear the attendants, but she couldn't make out what they were saying before she slipped, entirely into the darkness.

Roland rushed to the hospital as soon as Jean told him what

had happened, when he arrived home. He'd been just about to shovel the drive when Jean came running out of the house wearing only her slippers on her feet, yelling to him, "Mom went to the hospital in an ambulance." He said, "Okay, I'm going to the hospital right now," as he frantically opened the garage door and climbed into the car. He was so afraid there would be complications with the delivery.

He parked at the first spot he saw and sprinted into the emergency department. The nurse told him where she'd been taken and he hurried into the elevator. When he reached the nurses station on the fifth floor and told them who he was, they asked him to have a seat and they'd try to get some information for him. He couldn't just sit there, he starting pacing back and forth, trying to calm his nerves.

The nurse finally came over to him and told him, "Your wife was taken to surgery shortly after she was admitted." Roland felt like someone had punched him, he asked her, "Do you know if she's going to be okay?" She said, "I don't know, I only know that she'd lost a lot of blood and was unconscious when she arrived." She quickly added when she saw the colour drain from his face, "The doctor on call is one of the best gynaecologists the hospital employs and he's doing the surgery." She showed him to the waiting room and told him, "We will all just have to wait." She offered him some coffee and told him to have a seat. She promised to keep him informed.

Roland waited for what seemed like an eternity. He called the girls and did his best to reassure them, so they wouldn't be worried. He'd tried his very best, but he knew he hadn't sounded all that convincing, when he'd told them that she would be fine. He decided to only tell them that sometimes babies could take quite a while, so not to get worried if he didn't call back for a while. When he hung up, he thought he'd done the right thing; he didn't want to tell them that she was in surgery. He wasn't there to console them and he wasn't sure if they could handle that kind of news on their own, they were still pretty young.

Roland had just gotten up to get his umpteenth cup of coffee when a doctor appeared through the swinging doors. He almost dropped his coffee when he heard the doctor call, "Mr. Petersen." There were a few others in the waiting room and Roland had never met the doctor that was on call. He spoke up a little too loudly and said, "Yes I'm here." The doctor came over to him and shook his hand and introduced himself, "Hi, I'm Dr. Kneely," he said and lead him into a private room off the waiting area and closed the door. He asked Roland, "Please, will you have a seat?" Roland sat down; he swallowed hard and asked, "Is she okay?" Dr. Kneely told him, "For now she's holding her own, she lost a lot of blood." He reached out, laid a hand on Roland's arm to comfort him, and gently said, "If she makes it through the next couple of days, she should be okay, it was touch and go throughout her surgery." He said, looking very tired, "We lost her more than once." Roland started shaking; the doctor kept his hand on his arm and told him, "You can stay in this room as long as you need to." He felt sorry for him and told him, "Irene will be in recovery for quite a while and then we'll be moving her to intensive care." He opened the door and just as he was about to leave, he turned to Roland and said, half smiling, "You might like to know, you have a daughter, she's healthy, she weighed in at just over 10 lbs. ask one of the nurses at the nursery to let you see her." He looked at Roland and before he left said, sympathetically, "I'll do everything I can for your wife."

Roland watched the door for a long time after Dr. Kneely left. He couldn't believe what had happened; she'd been just fine when he left for work that morning. Dr. Cubbin had said he was surprised at how well the whole pregnancy went. What the hell happened he wondered, shaking his head, he hoped he wouldn't lose her. He prayed asking, "If Irene could just live, I'll be the best husband I can be." He pleaded with God, "Please, I don't want to be punished for my sins like this."

Eventually he left the room in a daze, he walked down to the nurse's station, and asked them, "Where's the Nursery?" One of the nurses felt sorry for him and walked him down to the third floor, she said, "I'm leaving on my break and I don't mind showing you where it is." Roland asked her, "Do you know if I can see Irene, my wife?" She told him, "After you've seen your new daughter come back up to the surgical floor and I'll find out for you." When they arrived at the nursery, there were only two nurses on duty; the others had gone on breaks. They told him, "Have a seat and we'll bring the baby to the viewing room as soon as we can." He must have sat there for fifteen minutes when all of a sudden a nurse appeared and said, "Mr. Petersen", Roland jumped. He apologized and told her, "I'm sorry, I seem to be off in my own little world." She smiled and told him, "Come to the window, your little girl is in the fourth crib from the right." Roland was stunned by how perfect she was. The nurse could see the look of awe on his face; she came back out and told him, "C-section babies are almost perfect since they don't have to go through the stress of being born." Roland nodded unable to take his eyes off her. She was pink and bright, her little eyes were open and she seemed to be looking right at him. He knew babies couldn't see when they were first born, but he could have sworn this one could.

Roland sat by Irene's bedside for almost a solid week, she came around occasionally, but only for a few moments at a time, she mostly just slept. The first couple of nights were rough, she was in intensive care and Roland was not allowed in, he could only stand at the window and watch helplessly as she fought to live. She was being well looked after, but he wanted to sit beside her and talk to her, just in case she could hear him. He wanted to tell her how sorry he was that she was going through this, he wanted her to know he was with her.

The older kids cried a lot, he'd had no choice but to tell them what was happening. They agreed they would not tell

Dawn or Susan, but it was very hard on them trying to pretend that Mommy was coming home as soon as the doctor said she could. That was what they'd agreed to tell the two younger ones. Roland spent all his time at the hospital, even on the first few nights when he wasn't allowed into the room in intensive care; he'd still stood outside in the hall and watched her through the window. Irene had been in her own room for about a week now, she still slept most of the time, she was still too weak to stay awake for long periods of time. Roland was pleased to see some colour returning to her skin, she'd looked ghostly white up until this morning. He couldn't believe his eyes when he arrived and saw she was awake and sitting up slightly in bed. She was still very tired, she said and she couldn't stay awake very long and fell asleep shortly after he'd arrived. He sat there smiling watching her sleep, he felt happier now than he'd felt for days. He wanted to be there every time she woke up, which was becoming much more frequent.

Dr. Seamore and Dr. Cubbin came in to visit a couple times a day. They were finally smiling now; Roland had been so worried, because they'd always worn such sober expressions up until today. Dr. Seamore told Irene, when she awoke with a start at the feel of the cold stethoscope on her chest, "You gave us quite a fright, we were very concerned about you for a while, and we're very pleased to see that now you're on the road to recovery." He asked her, "Have you seen your new daughter, yet?" Irene said, "No, I haven't" and she asked with excitement in her voice, "Could someone bring her in so I can see her?" Roland asked the doctor, "Is she strong enough to hold the baby?" Dr. Cubbin just laughed and said, "Well, that baby is a big one, but she can probably manage if you sit on the bed and help her." He looked at Irene and smiled. While Dr. Cubbin finished examining her, Roland went to the nurses' station to ask if someone could bring the baby to Irene's room. Just as the doctor was leaving the room, the nurse appeared with a little pink bundle. She brought her over for Irene to see. Irene asked, "Can I hold her?" The nurse looked unsure. Roland smiled and told her, "Dr. Cubbin just left and he said she could if I sit on the bed and help her." The nurse waited until Roland had settled beside Irene and gently handed the baby over to Irene. Roland told her, "Don't worry, this baby is number six, so I'm quite used to handling babies." Her eyes widened and she said, "Wow, you must be an expert by now. Is it okay with you then if I leave her here and come back in a little while?" Roland assured her, "Oh for sure, we'll be just fine."

Irene held the baby with Roland's help but when he sensed she was tiring he gently took her from her arms. Irene didn't fall asleep this time she just sat back against her pillows and said, "She's perfect." Then added with wide eyes, "But huge!" Roland laughed and said, "She is the biggest one we've had, isn't she." He suddenly said, "We have to name her, Cassie and Jean want to call her Brooke, they heard the name on a television show and they both loved it." Irene said, thoughtfully, "I kind of like that name too, don't you?" He thought about it and said, "Yeah, I do it's different. She needs a second name though, what should we do for that one?" Irene thought for a moment and asked him, "What about Sharon, after my best friend and your old secretary?" He bristled, at the thought, but decided it was only a second name; they wouldn't use it except on legal documents. He told her, forcing a smile, "Yes, why not." She smiled and said, "Then I guess we've made it official." Roland looked into their new daughter's little face and told her, "Your name is Brooke Sharon Petersen and your birthday is November 8, 1962." Irene laughed and said, "Aren't you going to tell her that next year she'll have a cake and presents and a party." He laughed, "I guess I'm a little rusty, I must be out of practise." She said, "Don't get any ideas; this is definitely the last one." He said, laughing, "No worries there, Dr. Cubbin says that as soon as you are strong enough for the surgery he'll be doing your hysterectomy." Irene rolled her eyes and said, "I'm not looking forward to that. This incision is so sore, I wish he would have put in a zipper or buttons or something, so I won't have to have another one." They laughed and she sank into her pillows.

The nurse appeared for little Brooke and in the time it took Roland to hand her to the nurse and turn back to her, Irene was sound asleep again. The nurse enquired, "Was she awake the whole time the baby was in the room?" Roland said, smiling "Yup, she was." The nurse replied, "That's the longest she has been awake yet." Roland nodded smiling and answered, "For sure."

Roland went home that evening feeling like a new man, he could finally relax, knowing Irene was going to be okay. He hadn't been to work for almost two weeks and was planning to go the next day for a little while. His boss had told him to take as much time as he needed, he could see that Roland was upset and he was worried about him as well as Irene. Roland had kept everyone at the office up to date on how she was doing and now that she was finally out of the woods and getting stronger, he couldn't wait to tell everyone the news.

He told the kids the good news and told them that pretty soon she'd be able to come home. The kids cheered and Roland smiled, he didn't think he'd ever been happier. He decided it was time to make good on his promise. He was going to make sure that his family said the Rosary together, to thank the Lord that their family was still together. He'd promised God when he'd first learned that Irene could be in danger that the whole family would pray together, if he would only spare her and the baby. He knew his prayer had been answered; it was time now to do his part. He was sure the girls and Irene would love to join him saying the Rosary every evening.

twenty-four

TRANSFERRED

Irene and Brooke had been home from the hospital for almost a month now. Brooke was the happiest baby they'd ever seen. Irene wondered if it just might have something to do with the fact that the other girls were always holding her or rocking her in her bassinette. The child was almost never on her own. Irene was on the mend and was feeling exceptionally well. Her hysterectomy was scheduled for just eight weeks from now. Roland had arranged to take his holidays beginning on the day she was to be released from the hospital. He knew the older girls would be very helpful. They'd practically become experts at handling Brooke and Susan and with four of them, usually at least one was available at any given time. The problem was they had school during the day, so he'd need to be with Irene and the baby and of course Susan, during the day, he figured the older girls could take turns helping him in the evening with dinner and taking care of the younger ones. That way they could all get their homework done.

Roland came home from work in the early afternoon on his first day back to work since Irene came home from the hospital. He looked very serious and told Irene, "We need to talk." He looked upset, Irene put Brooke down in her little chair beside the couch and immediately sat down, Roland sat beside her, he

256

began telling her, "Don called me into his office this morning and told me that the company requested that I transfer to Toronto, to head up the Logistics department. I didn't want to make that decision without talking to you first."

Irene was surprised, she tried hard not to let on though, but she couldn't believe it, he usually made all the decisions himself and told her about them later. She asked, "What about the girls and school?" Roland replied, "We wouldn't move until after the school year is over, probably not until August." Irene thought about that and asked him, "Will you have to go out on your own for a couple of months like the last time?" Roland smiled, and answered, "No, this time we'll all go together, I'll start in this new position once we're moved into our new house." Irene was silent. Roland looked at her and ventured, "Do you want to move or just stay put, here?" She took her time answering, "Wouldn't it hurt your career if you refused this promotion?" Then she quickly added, with excitement seeping into her voice, "We'd be closer to our families if we did move. Think about it, we could actually drive to Sarnia from Toronto, so we could see them more often. Our families could also come out to see us; it would be so much easier and less expensive for them." She continued, suddenly sounding very excited, "We'll have to make sure we have enough room for them, though." She looked at Roland, smiled and said, "We're going to have to find a house with a lot of bedrooms, we'll need room for all our kids and room for visitors as well." They laughed and Roland asked, "So does that mean you're okay with it then?" Irene nodded and said, "Yes, I guess I am." She asked, "When do you do you think we should tell the kids?" He answered quickly, "Tonight after we finish the Rosary, I'd like to get it over with." Irene thought, well that could be a problem; she knew how much the kids hated to say the Rosary every night and were usually in foul moods after it. They constantly told her, it interfered with their homework and they complained it hampered the time they had to spend with their friends. Cassie complained constantly about it and one night she'd even told Roland, "I wasn't the one who promised God I'd say it anyway. You did! And I don't want to say it anymore." She remembered Roland had actually slapped her across the face for saying that. She'd told her later that same night, "I hate Dad for hitting me!" Irene had tried to console her, telling her, "Dad was just upset," but even she knew that was a feeble excuse. Irene didn't think Roland's hitting her was the solution, but Roland hadn't wanted to talk about it. Irene decided that he must have felt bad and that was the reason he refused to discuss it.

She hoped the kids would be receptive to the move but the more she thought about it, she was sure they wouldn't be. All of them had made good friends and were involved in activities both in and out of school. Cassie had her singing lessons, Jean had her dancing, Maureen had baton, Dawn was taking piano and even Susan had started tap dancing lessons. It was a shame that they would have to move, but Irene told herself, Roland's position in the company was far too important for him to turn down this promotion; it may hurt his career if he does. She sighed, thinking; she and the kids would just have to make new friends in Toronto.

Dinner was the usual, pleasant exchange of each other's days. They didn't allow any fighting or teasing among the kids at the table. They discouraged it all the time, but at the dinner table it was expressly forbidden, if any one of the kids, with the exception of the really little ones, violated that particular rule they were sent to bed without supper or snacks. Roland always thought children learned rather quickly if they knew there would be uncomfortable consequences for their actions. Irene had more that once questioned him as to where he learned these things from, since his own parents were so gentle. Roland said shaking his head, "You only think that way because you joined the family once I was grown up, Melissa wasn't yet, but she was a girl, so Dad wasn't hard on her. Dad was very strict with me, though."

Irene reminded him, "You have girls, so maybe you shouldn't be so hard them either." He just shot her a look that let her know, in no uncertain terms, that he wasn't interested in pursuing the matter any further, so she'd let it drop.

Maureen and Dawn did the dishes while Jean and Cassie gave Susan and Brooke their baths and got them ready for bed. Roland and Irene sat in the living room waiting for the girls to finish so they could begin their nightly ritual of saying the Rosary. Cassie and Jean were whispering upstairs about not wanting to say it, the two of them were always trying one excuse or another to try to get out of it. Maureen sometimes cried when her friends came to the door and her Dad told them she couldn't come out for a while yet. She hated this ritual just as much as her sisters did.

Once the Rosary was finally finished and everyone had blessed themselves with the sign of the cross, the kids jumped up and started for the stairs. Roland told them, "I want you to sit down again; I have something I want to tell you." He told them, "I have been promoted to the logistics department, in the Company." Cassie interrupted, saying, "That's wonderful, Dad." and she and the others stood up to leave the room. Roland said, "Just a minute I haven't told you the rest yet." They sat down again and Roland began telling them, "This new position I will be undertaking is in Toronto." Cassie and Jean breathed, "No!" at the same time. Roland looked at Maureen, she was already beginning to cry, she said, "That's too far away, I won't be able to see my friends." Dawn said, shrugging, "I'll miss my friends here too," then she brightened and said, "But I'll make new ones in Toronto and then I can write letters to my friends here." Cassie who seemed riveted by shock was only half listening to Dawn. She didn't want to dampen her little sister's spirits and was trying her best to keep from breaking down in front of her. Finally, when she couldn't hold herself together a single second longer, she ran from the room and up the stairs, she slammed her bedroom door shut and threw herself on the bed and cried into her pillow.   She had a new boyfriend, that Mom and Dad knew nothing about, and she really thought she loved him. She decided sobbing; I'm going to run away from home. She knew she still had plenty of time to figure out the details since they weren't supposed to be moving until the summer and it was only December right now, four days before Christmas. Cassie thought, some Christmas this is going to be. Just then she heard her door open, she turned to look and relaxed a little when she saw it was Jean. Jean ran to her and hugged her, she knew how Cassie felt about Terry, she'd told her about him a couple of weeks ago and had made her swear not to tell anyone.

Jean didn't have a boyfriend at the moment; she had dates, when her Dad allowed her to go out, which was mostly just to the school dances, but there was no one she really cared that much about. She told Cassie, "I'm willing to give it a try, and see what Toronto's like." Cassie shook her head and stopped crying enough to divulge, "I'm not going and they can't make me." Jean looked shocked; her eyes were huge with concern when she said, "You can't stay here by yourself!" Cassie breathed a ragged sigh and said, "I still need to figure everything out, but I know for sure I'm not going to go to Toronto." Jean told her, with tears slipping down her cheeks, "I'll miss you if you don't, please think about it," and she hugged her again. Maureen came into the room just then; she said, "I don't want to go either." Cassie and Jean looked at her, and Jean told her, "You're too young not to." Then she said, "Don't worry, Maureen we'll have each other, it'll be like an adventure." They sat on Cassie's bed crying and talking about how they all felt. Cassie told Maureen, "You can't tell anyone, but I'm not going," she told her again, "Please don't tell a single soul. Swear?" Maureen told her tearfully, "I swear." The three older girls were very close and Jean and Maureen said in unison, "I can't imagine life without you, Cassie." They looked at each other and smiled through their tears at that. Cassie told them,

"I can't imagine being without you two either." They started to cry all over again. Just then, Irene came in. She looked at the girls and shook her head, she said, "You know you girls should support your father on this, he's just trying to do what's best for this family." She added in abhorrence, "Stop behaving like babies!" With that, she whirled around and left the room closing the door firmly behind her. Cassie whispered, "I wish there was a way we could stay together here and let them go to Toronto by themselves." Maureen and Jean smiled at that suggestion but they all knew it simply wasn't possible.

Time seemed to be passing far too quickly; Christmas had been unusually quiet, with the girls rather subdued over the impending move. January zipped by uneventful and February had been extremely cold so far. Irene was absorbed in her thoughts as she was packing her suitcase for the hospital; she was to be admitted to the hospital, tomorrow afternoon. The surgery was scheduled for the day after tomorrow. Brooke was down for her nap and Susan was watching Sesame Street on TV. Irene was nervous about her impending surgery; she hoped it wouldn't be too painful afterwards. She also hoped for a speedy recovery. She had to admit even after six kids, she was still afraid of anything having to do with hospitals. She consoled herself with the idea, that at least this time she was definitely not pregnant. She shuddered thinking about the last time she'd been admitted to the hospital, to have this very same surgery. She tried to cheer herself up with the idea of never having any more kids for sure after this. She told herself, aloud, "I've paid my dues, I've had enough kids." She loved her kids, in her own way, but she still thought they could be real brats at times and would much rather have stopped at just one or two instead of the half a dozen she ended up with.

Just as she finished packing her things and closed the clasps on the suitcase, she could hear Brooke making little noises in her crib. Irene smiled, Brooke rarely cried when she woke up, she just laid there and watched the little animals on the mobile that was attached to her crib and made little gurgling noises. She was the best baby. Irene tiptoed into the room and watched her; she was all excited watching the mobile. Suddenly, Brooke stopped moving and turned her head as if she sensed someone there; she started moving her little arms and legs excitedly again when she spotted her Mom. Irene smiled and walked over and lifted her up and as she lay her down on the change table to change her diaper, Brooke smiled back at her, Irene was thrilled, she leaned over kissing her and talking to her and Brooke kept smiling and making little noises. Irene was sorry she was going to have to go now. She loved this stage, when they started to smile and make little noises it was so sweet.

Jean came into the room; she'd just come home from school and said, happily, "Hi, want me to look after Brooke while you make supper?" She couldn't believe it when her Mom told her, "Brooke was smiling." She took over from Irene, and finished changing Brooke's diaper and was talking to her, when all of a sudden Brooke smiled at her too. Jean was so excited, she told Brook, laughing, "Just you wait until your other sisters hear about this." She lifted her up and said, "Mom I'm going to keep her with me for a while, is that okay?" Irene told her, "That's fine, but she's going to be hungry soon." Jean called back, "That's okay I'll feed her."

Irene left the room after she tidied up, thinking, it's nice having these older kids, they're so helpful, they've made my life so much easier after having Brooke and even after Susan. She went downstairs to check on Susan and to start dinner. Roland would be home in just over an hour and she hadn't started anything yet. She thought I might make a ham and scalloped potatoes. She peeked into the living room, Susan was still watching Sesame Street, she was singing along with Big Bird, so Irene continued into the kitchen to get dinner ready.

She was standing at the kitchen sink, peeling potatoes when

she heard Cassie and her friend Bonnie laughing downstairs. Irene thought, she must've come home while I was upstairs with Jean and Brooke. She walked over to the stairs and was just about to call out to Cassie and let her know that dinner would be in about an hour or so, but just as she reached the stairs, she stopped; she couldn't believe what she was hearing. Cassie was telling Bonnie, "I'm not planning to go to Toronto with my family at all." She went on, much to Irene's astonishment and said, "Bonnie when I told Terry, he said he would help me. He even said maybe we could get married." Bonnie reminded her, "You'll need your parents' permission to get married." Cassie replied, "Well, he said that maybe if I was pregnant, I might not need their permission or if I did they might be more agreeable then. He said they wouldn't want to shame their families." Irene stood there in utter shock. She couldn't believe what she'd just heard. She moved back to the sink, picked up a potato, and mechanically started peeling it. She thought, I'm going to have to talk to her as soon as possible, I can't tell Roland about this he'd have a fit. She thought, since I'm going to be away, in the hospital for the next little while, I'll have to talk to her tonight. I'm only going to tell Roland if it's absolutely necessary and even then only after I'm home again.

Cassie came upstairs to get some lemonade for herself and Bonnie. Irene tried to calm herself and forced herself to say, "Hi, when did you get home?" Cassie looked at her for a moment before replying and then asked, "Is something wrong? Your voice is shaky." Irene said, "No, I'd like to talk to you later, but I don't want your Dad to know about it, just yet." Cassie's heart leapt, she wondered if Mom had heard anything, she'd thought she was upstairs in her room packing. She didn't know she was in the kitchen or she never would have even dreamed of talking to Bonnie in the house. Cassie swallowed and tried her best to sound normal and said, "Sure whenever you want." She finished pouring the lemonade and hurried back downstairs. She told

Bonnie, in a whisper, "Oh my God, I hope my Mom didn't hear us, she wants to talk to me tonight." Bonnie told her, "You just have a guilty conscience, don't worry so much, it's probably that History test that you didn't do so well on the other day." Cassie thought about it a minute and said, "Yeah, you might be right," but she was still worried.

Irene couldn't stop thinking about what she'd overheard that afternoon. Roland noticed her nervousness and asked, "You okay?" She said, "Yes, I guess I'm a little nervous about tomorrow." He told her as he put his arm around her shoulders, "I'll be right there with you, I'm not going to the office at all tomorrow or the next day." He wanted to be there to reassure her. She said, "Thank you, that will be a wonderful help to me," and did her best to smile. She told herself Cassie was young, surely she wouldn't go through with the plans she'd overheard, she was just being dramatic, she thought.

Once the dishes were done and the little ones put to bed, they started the Rosary. As soon as they finished Irene went upstairs saying, "I want to make sure I have everything I'll need for the hospital packed in my suitcase, come with me Cassie, maybe you'll notice something I missed." Cassie replied, "Sure," all the while thinking, I hope she doesn't know. Irene ushered Cassie into her bedroom and shut the door. She told her quietly what she'd heard and asked Cassie, "Do you really plan to do that?" Cassie started to cry, she said, "I don't want to get pregnant, but I don't want to move either." Irene put her arms around her and drew her into an embrace she told her, "I know how you feel." Then she told her how she'd felt about moving out here to Regina and leaving her family and friends behind. Cassie dried her eyes and hugged her Mom, she told her, "I hope you come back home soon, I'm going to miss you." Then with wide eyes, she asked her Mom, "You didn't tell Dad, did you?" Irene said, "No, and I don't intend to. Please don't go through with it and neither one of us will have to worry about that." Cassie said, "I won't."

She left her Mom's room thinking to herself, it might already be too late, she'd missed her last period completely and the next one was due next week. She hadn't even told Bonnie about that, she was too embarrassed to admit that she and Terry had already had sex. It was something all her girlfriends talked about, but no one had actually admitted that they'd done it yet. Terry had told her that they were in love and that sex was a natural thing for them to do. Cassie knew she was not his first. He bragged about all the women he'd slept with. She'd desperately wanted to appear mature in his eyes. She loved him and wanted to show him how much, so for the past few months they'd been going to his house and using the garage to make out. He had his own little business doing bike repairs that he ran out of his parents' garage and he also had an apartment above the garage that was accessible from a little room off the workshop. That apartment is where she lost her virginity to him. He'd been delighted that he was her first. He told her, she was special, she thought about that day and how she wished he'd told he loved her. He said things like, "we're in love" or "we love each other" but he had yet to actually say the phrase, "I love you." She thought with a shrug, he probably would in time, at least she hoped so.

twenty-five

DISAPPOINTMENT GALORE

R oland and Irene watched as the last of the boxes were loaded into the moving van. They were going to be spending their final three days in Regina at the Regina Inn. They'd decided to drive to Toronto instead of flying; they were determined to try to have some sort of vacation for both themselves and the kids along the way. They were hopeful the kids would enjoy the trip; they planned to stop at any attractions along the way that they thought the kids might enjoy.

All the kids were having trouble with the move, none of them wanted to go, except of course Susan and Brooke, who were too young to care where they lived. They were all going to miss their oldest sister. Cassie had announced she was pregnant and said her and Terry were going to get married. Roland and Irene had suggested a home for unwed mothers and adoption for the baby but Cassie had been horrified at the suggestion that she should give up her baby. Not knowing what else to do they signed the permission form for her to marry. Irene thought, better that she was married than not, after all what would people think, she couldn't imagine. She thought it would be better to be far away from such a disgrace, she was glad they were moving now. Terry's parents were not too pleased with the two of them getting

266

married so young either, however Terry was already eighteen, so they had no say whatsoever and the wedding was tomorrow, so it looked like it was going to happen now, no matter what.

Roland had been so upset with Cassie when she'd announced that she was pregnant, he'd hit her harder than he'd intended, actually he hadn't meant to hit her at all, it just happened. They'd been in the kitchen when she'd told them and he just snapped and hit her across the cheek with the back of his hand. Cassie fell and on her way down, she'd hit her opposite cheek on the edge of the counter and the force with which she'd fell and struck the counter had knocked her out. Roland recalled with regret how she'd lain on the floor, motionless. Irene had screamed and when he'd turned her over, tears had been streaming down his face when he saw the damage he'd done. A huge red mark was forming on her right cheek where he struck her and the left cheek had a gruesome look to it. Roland was afraid he'd broken her cheekbone. He bent to pick her up and noticed the blood on the floor, he was truly frightened. He took her out to the car and Irene grabbed a towel and yelled upstairs to Jean, "We'll be back in a few hours." She followed Roland out to the car. Cassie was awake now and crying. She said groggily, "I have a headache and my cheeks hurt too." Irene looked over at Roland, he was shaking; she asked him, "Are you able to drive?" He didn't answer he just put the car in gear and drove in silence.

When they reached the hospital, he led Cassie into the Emergency department, she was holding the towel against her face, and most of the bleeding had stopped now. He told the nurse what had happened. She sympathized with him saying, "You must feel terrible. It wasn't your fault that she fell into the counter." She shook her finger at Cassie and took her down the hall to an examination room. The doctor examined her and stitched her cheek and as he worked, he said to Roland, "She has a few contusions and this laceration, which I'm stitching now, but otherwise she's fine." Once he finished, he walked Cassie and

Roland back out to the waiting area and on the way remarked, "At least there were no broken bones. The cut and the bruises will heal in time," he added, "Bring her back in ten days to have the stitches removed". He turned to Cassie, "Remember take only aspirin for your headache and as I told you before, the baby seems fine." He took Roland aside, and said, "Be careful, it's okay to punish your kids but sometimes it's better to walk away for a few minutes, to give yourself time to settle down before you react. That way you won't run the risk of hurting them too badly." Roland nodded, and said, "Thanks for your time and for the advice." He looked across the room at Cassie and went on to say, "I feel bad about hitting her anyway, but I certainly never meant to hit her so hard." The doctor just nodded his understanding and shook his hand then hurried off down the hall.

Cassie was sitting where they left her holding the bloodied towel. Roland took her arm and led her out to the car where Irene was waiting for them. She had wanted to wait in the car, she thought it was so embarrassing that they had come to the hospital at all; they probably wouldn't have if Cassie hadn't been bleeding so much. She was always afraid of what people would think. She asked Cassie, "Are you okay?" Cassie replied with a quick, "Yes" averting her eyes and seating herself in the back seat of the car. Irene looked at her and felt sick, her face was swelling now and it looked painful, she said, "As soon as we get home I'll make you a couple of ice packs, one for each side of your face. Cassie had looked out the window and cried most the way home. He shivered at the memory of what had transpired that evening as he and Irene pulled up to the hotel.

They arrived at the church a half hour before the ceremony was to begin. There weren't going to be any guests, just Bonnie, Cassie's best friend and Allan, Terry's best friend. Bonnie wasn't eighteen yet and therefore wasn't old enough to stand up with them at the ceremony, so Father Hogan said he would have the organ lady, Mrs. Smilskie, do the honours. Terry's best friend was eighteen, which made him old enough to be best man. Cassie really didn't care who did what, she just wanted the wedding to be over with quickly, she hated being anywhere near her Dad, now. The bruises had almost healed and there was just a small read mark on her left cheek now, she wasn't sure if it would always be there. When the doctor had removed the stitches, he'd remarked that it would most likely fade.

Terry had surprised her when she'd told him what happened, instead of holding her and comforting her as she had imagined he would; he'd said, "You probably deserved it." It hurt a great deal to hear him say that. She wasn't so sure she even wanted to go through with this wedding, but she didn't know what else to do. She'd tried to talk to her mother about it, but she'd told her, "Don't be so silly, you're just getting nervous." She'd said, "It's called "cold feet" and most brides feel that way." Her Mom also told her, "You're damaged goods, no other man will want you for his wife now that you're no longer a virgin, so you'd better marry this man, he's your only hope." Cassie had felt so awful; she never tried to talk to her Mom about it again. She looked at Terry now and wondered if he would change once they were married and the baby was born. She wished she could turn back the clock, she didn't want to get married anymore and she didn't want to have this baby either. She knew if it were possible now she would just like to go to Toronto with her family. She didn't want to stay here without them. She was so frightened, tears were pooling in her eyes. Terry looked at her strangely. Father Hogan smiled at her; he thought they were tears of happiness.

The wedding pictures were taken quickly, there was no photographer, only their parents snapping pictures and then everyone got into their cars. They were all going to the Executive Steak and Seafood House, downtown, for the wedding dinner and to celebrate the union of "Mr. and Mrs. La Farge." Roland had made the reservations and he was paying for it. Terry's parents had offered to help with the bill, but he had politely refused their offer. He thought since it was his daughter, he should be the one footing the bill. It was the least he could do for her. Her dress hadn't even been an expensive one; she'd bought a simple cream coloured suit. She hadn't wanted many accessories to go with it either; it was only at Irene's insistence that she allowed them to buy her matching shoes and a handbag. Irene had also bought her a gorgeous necklace and bracelet with matching earrings. They were made of clusters of pearls with diamond chips in between them. Roland had to admit she looked stunning when he walked her down the aisle.

He had to bite his tongue when Father asked if anyone knew any reason why these two should not be joined, Roland wanted to holler out, "She's just a child, she can't get married," but he knew he couldn't. Cassie wanted to do this, so he thought he better shut up and go along with it; he knew he had certainly caused her enough pain and grief already.

These poor kids aren't even going on a honeymoon, he thought. They could barely afford to pay rent for the apartment Terry's parents were allowing them to rent, above their garage. The rent was going to be so little; Roland asked them, "Why are you even charging it?" Terry's parents looked a little forlorn and his mother said, "We wanted to try and teach Terry to be responsible, I'm afraid we've spoiled him terribly over the years." They looked around at all Roland's children and added, "We were never able to have any other children, Terry is all we have and we gave him everything he wanted. We didn't think anything of it at the time, but lately we've been noticing that he's not very responsible or mature either and we've been determined to do our best to help him grow up." Roland's fears increased tenfold, he wished he hadn't spoken with them, he was sure now that Cassie wasn't equipped to handle this situation, she'd always led such a sheltered life, up until now, that is.

Irene, Roland and Jean arrived back at the hotel rather late that night. They had sent Maureen and Dawn back earlier along with Susan and Brooke, both of whom had been falling asleep. Maureen had volunteered to take them back and Dawn had asked if she could go too. Jean wanted to stay until everyone else left. She'd wanted to stay with Cassie as long as she possibly could. The two of them had been especially close. Maureen was fairly close to them as well, but she couldn't bear the thought of saying goodbye so she'd chosen to do it with the help of the little ones. That way, she later explained, it was easier because she had to get it over with quickly, since the little ones were restless and tired and she had to get them back to the hotel and into bed. Irene and Roland had said very little on the ride home and Jean had said nothing; she'd only stared out the window. She was crushed that Cassie was not going to be going with them. She didn't like Terry and she certainly didn't trust him to take care of Cassie. She sighed; there was nothing she could do about it.

They left very early in the morning the next day; the only ones who had gotten any sleep were the little ones. The rest of them had had great difficulty. Roland and Irene tossed and turned most of the night and Jean and Maureen, talked most of the night, whispering so they wouldn't disturb anyone else.

They'd been on the road only a few hours and the drive was getting tiring already. Brook was sick to her stomach and threw up all over the front seat. They had nothing to clean it up with so they'd been left with no choice but to ride in the stench until Roland could find a place that sold something he could use to wash it off. Just after it happened, Roland had pulled off the road in a gravel driveway leading up to a farm. He used a bottle of 7UP from the cooler they always carried with them in the car whenever they ventured out on a long trip. They'd filled it with pop, before they left and it was the only bottle of 7Up they had, the other bottles were all Coke and he'd been afraid that the Coke would stain the light coloured seats in the car. He used the 7UP to wash off as much as he could. They'd used Kleenex to clean up Brooke and the little car seat she was sitting in but they really needed a hose to clean the car seat off properly. The little steering wheel on the front of the baby car seat was a mess, the whole thing was. They had no choice but to keep going even with the overwhelming smell. It put everyone in a foul mood. Irene said to Roland, without even thinking, "This is the worst vacation we've ever had, I wish we would've just flown and spent some time exploring Toronto instead of being cooped up in the car like this." Roland exploded, he yelled, "You were in full agreement with this car trip; it's not my fault this kid got sick." Irene tried to calm him down, she said, "I didn't mean that it was your fault, calm down, I was just thinking out loud, I'm sorry." Unfortunately, it didn't help Roland's mood much.

They drove for over two hours before they finally found a gas station. The attendant gave Roland a bucket of water and a few rags and Roland got to work cleaning the car while everyone else walked around and stretched their cramped legs. When he was satisfied that it was clean, he bought a car freshener to hang on the rear view mirror to make sure the smell wouldn't be overwhelming anymore. He asked the attendant, "Is there a hose I can use to clean out the bucket and to clean off the car seat?" The attendant told him smiling, "Yes, there's one at the side of the building, help yourself." It didn't take long to get the little seat clean again. Roland dried it off with clean rags and put it back in the car hooking the metal hangers over the back of the bench seat between him and Irene.

He stretched and asked Irene, "How's Brooke doing now?" Irene said, shrugging, "It must have just been something she ate because she seems fine now." Roland looked at his watch, it was already three thirty in the afternoon, and asked, "Do you think maybe we should call it a day, just to be sure she's okay?" He motioned to a motel across the street and from Irene's point of view; she noticed the motel had a little playground and even a swimming pool. She looked up at him nodding and smiled, saying, "The kids will love it and I think you and I need a bit of a break too." He smiled at her and nodded too.

The next few days were thankfully, uneventful. Jean and Maureen never smiled much, which bothered Roland. Dawn, Susan and Brooke had a good time in the places they stopped at along the way which were mostly things like Kiddie Land and parks with swings and teeter-totters. Roland tried hard to find things that Jean and Maureen would like. He even stopped for the night at a motel in Sault Ste. Marie that had a shopping centre across the street from it. He was certain they'd love it they always loved to shop. He gave them each some money and told them, "Buy whatever you like. Here's the spare key for the motel room, in case you're back before us." He smiled at them and said, "Take your time and have fun."

He and Irene took the younger ones to a park and to A&W for dinner. They loved the Root Beer served in little mugs and the burgers and fries. Jean and Maureen went to a fish and chip place in the shopping centre. Neither one of them could find anything they wanted to buy. The only thing they'd each purchased were writing paper sets. Jean's had little puppies on it and Maureen's had flowers. They decided they were going to spend their time in the car, writing to their friends. The fish and chips were good, but neither of them had much of an appetite and they couldn't finish. They paid the waitress and headed back to the motel. On the walk back, Jean asked Maureen, "What do you think Mom and Dad are going to say about neither one us, spending much money?" Maureen replied, "I think they know how sad we are and I think they'll understand that we just aren't in the mood for shopping." "Yeah, you're probably right," Jean said with a sigh.

Roland and Irene were sitting in lawn chairs outside the room with the door wide open so they could keep an eye on Susan and Brooke who were watching TV. Dawn was sitting on the sidewalk beside them playing with her doll. Roland saw them approaching, he said to Irene, frowning, "They only have one small bag each, I wonder what they did all this time?" He smiled and said to the girls, once they were nearer, "Those little bags must have some pretty expensive stuff in them." Maureen and Jean shook their heads and Jean said, "We couldn't find anything we wanted, except these," and they showed their parents the stationary sets and told them, "We had fish and chips for dinner in the mall," and they held out the change to their Dad. Roland looked at the change and was amazed they'd spent hardly anything. He didn't take it back, instead he told them, "Keep it you might see something you want somewhere else." Both girls shrugged and went into the motel room and began writing letters to their friends. A little while later, they came out and asked, "Do you have any stamps?" Roland told them, "No, we don't, but I'm sure we can find a post office tomorrow."

Roland and Irene felt bad for both of the girls. Roland wondered to himself, just how Cassie was doing. He didn't particularly like Terry, but he didn't voice any of his concerns, he didn't want to worry Irene but he wondered if he'd done the right thing, moving the kids. He even wondered if Irene had really wanted to move, she'd made some good friends in Regina, maybe she didn't want to go back out East either. He decided he'd have to get used to involving her more in the decisions that affected them. He was only kidding himself when he told himself he did, because he knew he really didn't. He'd tell her that they were going to make a decision together and then pretend to be interested in her concerns, and then do what he wanted to anyway. He thought I've been more than a little selfish. It had also been selfish of him to make the whole family live up to a promise that he'd made to God. He'd thought a lot, about what Cassie had said, he knew she'd been right, when she told him she never made any promise and she didn't want to keep the one he'd made. He knew now it hadn't been right for him to expect her to or the rest of the kids to, either. He wasn't sure if he'd ever even asked Irene, he figured he probably did and she'd most likely said it was okay, just because she didn't want to upset him. He needed to make some changes in his behaviour. The more he thought about his behaviour the more he realized he'd been a real ass.

They finally made it to Toronto and with all the stops they'd made it took them a week. They checked into the Holiday Inn, which was the closest motel they could find to their new home.

Irene and Roland had flown out to Toronto a few months earlier and purchased a beautiful home, it was a four level back split with a double car garage, on a quaint tree lined street. The builder had managed to build around the trees and the effect was breathtaking. All the homes on the street were brick and they all had double car garages. The neighbourhood was in a mid to upper class area in Agincourt in the Metropolitan area of Toronto. There were schools and shopping close by. The home hadn't been finished when they'd purchased it but the builder had assured them it would be ready when they needed it. Roland asked the kids, "Once you take a break from the car and have unpacked your things, would you like to take a ride out to see our new house, it's not far?" Dawn and Susan answered excitedly, "Yeah!" They couldn't wait to see it, Maureen and Jean simply replied, "All right." Once they found their rooms in the Motel, Jean and Maureen went to theirs and shut the door, they had a room adjoining Roland and Irene's and the other three had the adjoining room on the other side, which left Irene and Roland's room sandwiched in the middle. The Company spared no expense, as always, to make sure they were completely comfortable. They were going to be staying here until the moving van arrived with their furniture, which would only be a few days from now.

Roland drove them out to the house and true to his word; the builder had the house finished, at least from what they could see from the street. Roland parked the car and they climbed up onto the front porch so they could peer in the windows. The carpet was down and the place looked lovely. Irene noticed the light fixture she'd selected hanging in the dining room. It looked fantastic. She was beginning to feel rather excited the place was really lovely. The brick on the outside was similar in colour to reclaimed brick, with the reds and blacks and greys, but had a little more detail in the brick. It had a white front door with oval shaped glass in the centre of it and side lights on either side. Irene looked through one of the sidelights, she loved the look of the flooring she'd chosen for the entryway, she could see clear back to the stairs; the door was open in the hallway, so she could almost see up to the bedroom level. The carpeted staircase with its oak banister was gorgeous. She was taking in everything she loved about her house and didn't even realize the rest of the family was no longer on the porch with her. She jumped when a man came up behind her and asked, "Are you interested in buying a home?" As she turned to face him, she said, "This is the home we bought." The salesman said, wide eyed, when he recognized her, "Oh, Mrs. Petersen, my apologies I didn't recognize you. Would like to see inside? It was just finished the other day and it looks great." She said, "My family is just in the yard somewhere and I want to let them know they can go in the house as well." He said, as he opened the door, "Don't worry, I'll get them, you go ahead."

Irene stepped into her new home and gasped, it looked even lovelier once she was inside then it had from the window. She took off her shoes and walked on the thick, soft broadloom she'd selected for the living room, it felt so luxurious; she continued through the dining room and then crossed the central hall and entered the kitchen. It was unbelievable; she couldn't wait to cook in it. It was huge with solid oak cabinets; the style was a Hollywood design, with a huge eating area. This house is fantastic, she kept thinking. She continued upstairs to the bedroom level, there were four good-sized bedrooms with a large bath and huge master bedroom with ensuite bath and double closets. Irene marvelled at the workmanship. The baseboards and doors were mahogany coloured, stained oak as were the banister and railings. The bathroom fixtures were the latest colours, the main bathroom was a light shade of yellow and in the master bedroom bone. Irene descended the stairs to the entry level again and continued down to the family room level, this level consisted of a huge family room with a wood burning fireplace, a wet bar and sliding glass doors leading out to the back yard and an extra bedroom, a bath with a huge stand up shower and gorgeous turquoise coloured fixtures. The laundry room was on this level as well, it had lovely oak cabinets and a ceramic countertop just like the kitchen had. Irene descended down to the final level where the children's playroom was, it had thick carpeting in the area where they would put a couch and TV and tile flooring in the rest of the space. There was a small powder room in the corner; they'd thought it would save the kids from having to run upstairs.

Irene could hear the kids running through the house as she reached the top of the stairs where the family room was located. She called out to them, "I hope you removed your shoes before going through the house." They yelled, "We did already." The pounding of little and not so little feet continued. Roland asked Irene, once he found her, "Have you been through the whole house, already?" She nodded and smiled, "Yes I have." He asked smiling in return, "Is everything okay?" She replied, "Oh, better than that." She took his arm and proceeded to drag him all through the house. He loved watching her she was like a kid with a new toy. He could tell she loved the house. He had to admit he did too. Now that they could see all the colours they'd chosen, installed, he was quite impressed it looked great.

They spent the next few days after the moving van left, arranging and rearranging furniture. Finally, when they thought they had it right, Irene said, "We might need some new things, there just doesn't seem to be enough furniture in this place."

Roland agreed he told her, "You were right we didn't have this many rooms in the last house. I don't have to be at work for another few days why don't we go shopping for the furniture we need." She said, "That would be great," and she gave him a big hug and kiss. It only took them 3 days of shopping to find everything they wanted.

Once all the new furniture had been delivered and the drapery people had finished hanging the drapes and blinds she'd ordered, they started to feel like the house was becoming a home. They were still having trouble getting used to where things were, but they all loved the house just the same.

Roland was starting work on Monday and the girls were starting school. Jean and Maureen still didn't smile much, they said they loved the house and they liked the room they shared, but they didn't like Toronto. They said they preferred Regina because that's where their friends were and both their parents knew first hand, about those feelings, since they had also experienced them, when they had moved to Regina, years earlier.

Dawn and Susan loved their new school; they discovered they had classmates that lived around the corner from them. They rushed home each day and quickly changed from their school clothes to play clothes and ran outside to play with them.

Irene met the woman next door and really liked her. She had four boys, all quite a bit younger than her girls, in fact, the woman herself, was a few years younger than Irene was, but they got along famously. Her name was Mary and her husband was Anthony, Tony for short, he owned several hair salons in the City. Consequently, Mary's hair was quite lovely. She said Tony did it for her every morning before he left for work. Irene thought to herself, how wonderful. Tony was Italian and loved to cook, he invited them over for dinner quite often. He'd say as he prepared one of his delectable dishes, "I always wanted to be a chef, but I couldn't afford the tuition," he laughed and continued, "I barely scraped up enough money for hairdressing school." They all laughed at that, he was a very successful businessman in the City. He owned over twenty salons.

Roland was becoming increasingly frustrated at work he despised his new job. In Regina, he'd been able to walk around the plant and talk to people; he'd always loved that aspect of his old job. In Toronto, there was no plant just the executive offices and he was cooped up all day in his own office. The Company frowned upon his socializing with his coworkers because the work he was did, dealt with highly sensitive information, as his boss described it, and consequently he felt isolated most of the time. His boss told him, when he'd found him talking to some co-workers in the cafeteria one day, "Once you've achieved the position you have, Roland, you don't need to associate with people beneath you, as you had to in Regina." Roland was horrified, on his way home that night, he thought, what the hell have I gotten myself into. He confided to Irene, "I hate what I'm doing." Irene could see how upset he was and asked him, "Are you saying you want to go back to Regina?" Roland replied, "I can't the company is downsizing and that plant will be laying off workers and closing entirely over the next few years, however there are opportunities in Calgary or Edmonton, would you mind living in one of those cities?" Irene knew she was going to hate herself later for agreeing but said, "If that would make things better for you, I don't mind. I would hate to have to leave my house and our neighbours, but I do understand why you want to leave." She added when she noticed a look of relief cross his face, "We'll find another house we like just as much as this one."

Jean met a boy she liked at school and brought him home after school everyday with her, his name was Gord and he lived in the same area. Irene thought he was a nice kid and he was especially good with the little kids, as well. He and Jean took Susan and Brooke for long walks and over to the park quite often. Irene liked him he seemed perfect for Jean.

Maureen stayed over at her friend Carol's place quite a bit.

Irene wondered why she never brought the girl home, very often.
She'd asked her a few times but Maureen just brushed off her
comment saying impatiently, "Because Carol has to look after
her little brother, her Mom's a nurse and she works shifts at the
hospital." Maureen hoped her Mom wouldn't ask too many more
questions, because she'd met a boy, actually a man, and she didn't
want to tell her Mom just yet, she knew she wouldn't approve.
Tom, was almost twenty-two, she realized that he was probably
a little too old for her but she liked him just the same. He had
his own car and he was super nice to her. He did pressure her to
have sex though and since Maureen had never done that before
and wasn't sure if she even wanted to, she was afraid when she
was alone with him. She managed to keep him happy, though,
without actually doing "it" as she and Carol called sex. Carol
said, "It's nothing to be afraid of, Mark and I have been doing
it for a couple of months now and it's really kind of fun." She
told her, "It only hurts the first time and even then it didn't hurt
me for long." She advised Maureen, "Just close your eyes and
hold your breath the first time. That's what I did, and it wasn't
so bad." Maureen thought about it and decided maybe she'd try,
but she would have to talk to Tom beforehand, because if it did
hurt too much she wanted to be sure that he would stop.

A few days later, they were alone in his car parked at the far
end of the park near his house. It was dark and he was kissing
her and fondling her breasts, she'd been allowing him do that for
a little while now and in fact she actually liked it. He started his
usual descent with his hands and reached inside her jeans; he
caressed and explored for a few minutes, and then he picked up
her hand and put it on the bulge in his pants. She was shocked
she'd never felt anything like that before, it was big and she was
really becoming quite frightened now. She stopped kissing him
and asked, "Tom, I need to know, if we do "it" and it hurts me too
much would you stop?" He answered, while kissing her neck,
"Of course I would. But I'll go slowly and I won't hurt you." She

kissed him again and as he returned her kiss, he tugged her jeans down and laid her down on the back seat. He undid his own jeans and pulled them down enough for him to be able to get himself inside her. He started out slow, asking often, "Am I hurting you?" She replied, "No," each time thinking, this doesn't hurt at all, but just as she finished that thought he pushed harder and she let out a cry. He started to pull back and she relaxed a bit, thinking, he won't hurt me, but he suddenly changed his mind and said, "It'll only hurt for a second and then you'll start to like it." He didn't give her a chance to respond. He pushed into her and she screamed but he just kept pushing and then he started to move faster and harder. She started to cry and shortly after she heard him groan and the movement inside her slowed and stopped. It finally didn't hurt anymore. She was still crying, when he moved off her, he looked at her, frowning, and told her, "Don't be such a baby!" He said, rolling his eyes, "It can't be hurting now, so stop crying." She told him, pouting, "You said you'd stop if I asked you to and you didn't, why not?" He told her in a tone of voice that insinuated he was speaking to a child, "It only hurts the first time after that it won't. I only wanted to help you so you could enjoy having sex too. I did you a favour, because now you have the first time behind you and you can start enjoying it, next time." She sat up and pulled up her jeans. She was thinking maybe he was right; that maybe she was acting like a baby. She wanted to be older and more mature because he was; she hoped she hadn't made him think she was an immature idiot. She told him, "The next time will be better," and smiled up at him. He kissed her nose and said, "That's my girl."

That night when she and her sister were in their beds, she whispered telling her what she had done. Jean asked her, in a serious tone, "Did Tom use a condom?" Maureen thought a moment and told her, "I don't even know what that is, so I don't know." Jean told her smiling, "It's okay, don't be embarrassed, how could you know," and she proceeded to explain it to her.

Maureen replied after thinking for a second, "I don't think he did then, because I never saw him put anything on." Jean said, "Then he probably didn't." She confessed, "Gord and I have done it too, but he insisted on wearing a condom, he said he didn't want me to get pregnant." Maureen told herself, the next time they would have to use one, she told Jean, "Since it was my first time I probably don't have anything to worry about. Right?" Jean thought about it and said, "Yeah, probably not." They both went to sleep shortly after, but before Maureen fell asleep, she thought about how stupid she'd been with Tom and that she'd make sure that it didn't happen again.

The next night when she saw Tom she asked him, "Do you have a condom with you?" He looked surprised and asked her, "How do you know about those?" Feeling like an authority on the subject after her little talk with Jean the night before, she said, "I talked it over with my older sister." His jaw dropped, in awe and he asked, "Wow, you can talk to your sister about stuff like that? Aren't you afraid she'll tell your parents?" Maureen smiled and quickly replied, "My God no, we've always been able to tell each other anything, we would never breach our trust in each other, besides she told me that she and her boyfriend Gord were doing it too." Tom just laughed and pulled her into his arms saying, "I don't believe it." This time when they made love, it didn't hurt and she was very relieved and she had to admit, she'd actually liked it that time. When she told Tom how she felt, he said, "Good, but now you need to learn to relax, so you can have an orgasm." Maureen wasn't sure what to say to that. Tom noticed the puzzled look on her face and asked her, with an amused smile, "Do you even know what that is?" She felt so naïve and looking down at her hands in her lap, shook her head in answer, too embarrassed to meet his gaze. He said, "Would you let me show you?" Unsure, she asked him, "What are you going to do?" He said, "You'll see, just relax and trust me." He started kissing her and gently massaging her through her panties and when he sensed she was becoming aroused, he gently slipped them down, he'd already dispensed with her jeans, earlier. He was applying pressure in just the right places, she started feeling limp and all of a sudden, she felt like she was going to explode, she felt a rush of sensation that made her cry out and raise her hips to him. He couldn't help himself; he quickly dispensed with his own clothes and entered her. She cried out in pleasure as they climaxed together. He thought to himself, wow. He eased off her and asked her with a sly smile, "Did you enjoy it this time?" She answered breathlessly, "Yes, I did," and she meant it. It had been fantastic and she'd never felt anything like that before. Suddenly, she gasped and turned to him, wide eyed and said, "We didn't use a condom either time tonight." He shrugged and said, "I forgot, I got so excited I didn't even think about it." She confessed, "I didn't either, but I don't want to get pregnant, so we have to use one next time." Tom smiled to himself; he thought she was wonderful. He needed to make sure she would always be his. He wanted her to get pregnant so she'd stay with him. He was quite pleased with himself that he'd thought to tell her a few weeks ago that she couldn't possibly love him if she wouldn't have sex with him. It had worked so well and she enjoyed it now too, so he figured he'd done her a favour. He pondered; I've always been good at showing girls what fun sex can be. He thought with a smile I'll have to teach her a few more things, since she learns so quickly.

As time passed, Roland was becoming increasingly more depressed; he felt cooped up and trapped in his new position at work. He missed the walks he used to take around the refinery in Regina and the chats with the guys in the departments he looked after. That afternoon during the ride home on the subway and the bus ride that followed, he thought about his life since they'd arrived in Toronto. He knew he'd eventually have to confess exactly how he felt about things to his boss, the opportunity simply hadn't presented itself yet. He also knew it wasn't just the new position that was getting him down. His behaviour when Cassie told him she was pregnant still haunted him. He knew he'd been wrong to strike her, he also knew he should never have agreed with Irene and allowed her to marry. He could have lived just fine with the so-called shame; he knew he'd enjoy having a grandchild. Irene made him so angry at times; she felt she was too good to have a daughter who got into "trouble" as she called it. She was always more worried about what other people would think, than the welfare of her own children and subsequently her grandchild. He'd let her have her way too many times. He thought about the time Maureen was sick and she had the ladies over for bridge. She wouldn't do anything for poor Maureen, because, as she put it, what would the ladies think. When he'd come home from curling, he couldn't believe she hadn't even called the doctor and Maureen was really in a bad way, she couldn't even lift her head off the pillow. What had really gotten him upset was that Jean had been the one to tell him. Irene had been busy cleaning up after her bridge party and he recalled she'd been humming as she tidied. He hadn't said anything to her he just got Maureen ready as best he could without hurting her further and took her to the hospital. She'd been kept overnight for observation and as things turned out she'd twisted her neck falling off the trampoline at school. The doctor had told him that she'd be fine in week or so, but Irene had no way of knowing that she hadn't been more seriously hurt. When they'd spoken about it the next day, she'd dismissed his concern, insisting she knew Maureen hadn't done any real damage. He remembered her saying, "Mothers just know these things," but he hadn't been so sure.

He was very disappointed in Maureen herself these days; she was hanging around with a boy, actually a man, who was way too old for her. He feared she would end up the same way as Cassie. Irene was always complaining about Jean bringing home Gord and sitting in the family room everyday after school, she'd never minded in the beginning, but now she claimed it was getting tiresome. She complained about Maureen never being home, Roland thought, she doesn't even think about the fact that maybe Maureen doesn't stay home much because she's tired of hearing her complain constantly, he distinctly remembered her saying to him, "I don't think I can please Mom no matter what I do, she's never happy." Roland had told her at the time, "That's not true," however he was beginning to think that maybe she'd been right. Irene also complained that the younger ones made too many demands on her. She'd say, "Your kids are too much of a handful for me to handle on my own." She of course wanted a cleaning lady, so she could devout more time to shopping and going out with her friends. She told him many times, "I think I paid my dues, long ago bringing up all your kids!" She constantly complained she was too busy with "his" kids to meet new people. Roland felt stressed just thinking about her; he reminded himself that he always felt keyed up these days and decided not to blame everything on her. He didn't like feeling this way and he knew he had to do something before it drove him crazy.

twenty-six

COMING APART
AT THE SEAMS

R oland felt he'd put up with things he didn't like, both at work and at home for far too long now. He'd talked to Irene again one evening about how he felt; only this time he'd been surprised when she simply said, "I don't want to move again." She'd looked at him her eyes hard and cold, and continued, "I'm just starting to make new friends and I also found some of my old friends, you know the ones whose husbands had been transferred out of Regina before you were." She pouted, "I'm finally getting to the point where I might be able to be happy, and I don't want you to ruin everything for me by making me move, again." He'd tried to tell her, "Irene, I'm not happy," but as usual she only cared about herself and never even listened to anything he had to say. She even answered his concerns with, "Oh for Heaven sake, just give things time, they'll turn out okay," and brushed off everything else he said as if it wasn't important. He was slowly realizing that any concern she had shown for him in the past had been nothing but a charade.

The next day he got off the bus at the subway station and walked down the stairs to the platform, to wait for the train, it wasn't actually underground at this point, but slightly below

286

street level. He waited and as he did, he tried to make sense of everything that was bothering him. He decided he was going to talk to his boss and let him know how he felt about this new position of his. He thought he'd given it more than a fair chance and he still hated it. As he got off the subway at St. Clair station and walked up the steps and out onto the street, he made his decision, he was going to have his secretary, Lisa, schedule a meeting with his boss, Mr. Sparks, as soon as possible.

Roland had no sooner gotten involved with the days activities, than Lisa buzzed him on the intercom. She said, "Mr. Sparks is able to see you now, if you're free." Roland instructed her, "Let him know I'm on my way," as he hurried past her struggling into his jacket. He walked briskly down the hall to the elevators, straightening his tie as he waited for the doors to open. He rode up to the eleventh floor, Mr. Sparks' office was the only executive office on this floor. He did share the floor with a large secretarial pool and with their assistance; he ran the entire Toronto executive office. He also oversaw all the refineries right across Canada, although, overall, they were a relatively small part of the worldwide organization.

Roland approached Mr. Spark's secretary, she smiled and told him, "Please, go right in, Mr. Sparks is waiting for you." Roland nodded his acknowledgement and felt a twinge of nerves as he pushed open the large oak door.   Mr. Sparks came out from behind his desk, smiling as soon as he saw Roland. He shook his hand and led him to a corner of his oversized office. The corner contained some comfortable upholstered chairs with a large coffee table between them. Roland looked around and thought this place makes my own office look like a closet. He told Roland, "Have a seat, I like to use this area, instead of the desk, for casual meetings such as this. It feels so much more informal." He leaned over in Roland's direction, once they were seated and added, "And the chairs are much more comfortable." Roland smiled and once the niceties had been exchanged, Mr.

Sparks grew serious and asked, "What can I do for you, today?"
Roland explained how he felt about his new position, making
sure Mr. Sparks knew he was very grateful for the opportunity
the position afforded, however, he told him, "I was much happier
running the refinery in Regina and not being bound to a desk."
Mr. Sparks had listened attentively, without interrupting. When
Roland finished he sat quietly for what seemed like ages, which
Roland knew was probably only seconds, he was so nervous,
waiting for his reply. Mr. Sparks finally said, "I appreciate how
candid you've been with me," and added, "I know how difficult it
can be to do things well, when you don't like what you're doing."
He shared with Roland, "We're planning to close some of the
refineries across Canada and Regina is going to be one of them."
Roland wasn't surprised, he'd already heard about the closures,
but Mr. Sparks did say, "Between you, me and the gatepost, I
know the fellow who runs the refinery in Calgary will be retiring
this year. I'd like to recommend you as his successor. How
would you feel about a move to Calgary? He didn't even give
Roland time to reply before he added, "There's going to be an
opening in Edmonton to run that refinery as well and you'll be
eligible for that promotion as well when it becomes available in a
year or two, provided you're accepted for the position in Calgary."
He watched Roland's face register surprise then asked smiling,
"Will you need time to think about this move, before I give my
recommendation to the board?" Roland shook his head and
told him, "I've thought about it long enough already." They both
chuckled at that remark. Roland asked, "When will you know for
sure?" Mr. sparks replied, nodding, "I'm quite sure you possess
the qualifications and experience necessary for the position and
I'm also quite sure that no one else is in line for it, so I suspect
board approval will be nothing more that a formality, however
hang in there for a few more days. I'll get back to you by the
end of the week." Roland was smiling, saying, "Thank you," as he
walked to the door. Mr. Sparks walked along with him looking

thoughtful and replied, looking serious, "No problem, I've always believed people excel far quicker doing something they like to do." He shook Roland's hand as he said, "You'll be hearing from me, soon." Roland breathed a sigh of relief, once he was inside the elevator, on the way back to his own office; he felt a little lighter, as if a huge weight had been lifted from his shoulders.

He'd liked Mr. Sparks, he found him to be very sincere. Roland recalled how he listened and actually cared not only about what he said, but he also cared about how he felt. He could tell from the way he never once interrupted him, like so many others in high positions, Roland remembered only too well, who liked the sound of their own voices.

As Roland rounded the corner and was approaching his Secretary Lisa's desk, Lisa looked up; she said, "You have an urgent message from Mr. Ayre, in Regina. He said it was extremely important he speak with you as soon as possible." Roland said, frowning, "Get him on the line, please," as he opened the door and entered his office. He closed his door and removed his jacket wondering, what could possibly be so important in Regina. He'd just sat down at his desk when Lisa buzzed, "Mr. Ayre's on line one." He picked up the phone and was about to ask how he was doing, when Don blurted out, "Roland, I'm calling you from the hospital, it's Cassie, she's been admitted." Roland was stunned, he felt his mouth go dry and asked, "What happened?" Don said, "Her husband; Terry beat her up pretty badly." Roland felt the air in his lungs whoosh out of him, and suddenly felt weak; he hung his head and asked in a sad voice, "How is she?" Don said, "She looks bad, Roland I haven't spoken with the doctor yet, though." Roland asked him, "How did you even know that she was in the hospital, did she call you?" Don told him, "Yes, she did. Cassie told me she'd called her mother a few days ago, and she said her mother told her, she had to grow up and learn to deal with her own husband. Cassie admitted that it was before Terry had actually hit her, but she said she told her Mom she was frightened of him and wanted to come home." Roland sighed, "Thanks Don. Is she in good enough shape to travel?" Don replied, "I'll have to check with the doctor and get back to you." Roland told him, "As soon as she's able to travel, get her a plane ticket to Toronto, I'll send you the money." Don said, "Don't worry buddy, I'll take care of her, she'll be on a plane just as soon as her doctor allows it." Roland thanked him again, hung up the phone, and sat there motionless, staring blankly. He wondered why Irene hadn't discussed this with him, heck; she hadn't even had the decency to tell him about it. Cassie was his daughter too and he deserved to be told about everything that concerned her, especially something like this. He resolved that he was going to talk to Irene tonight. He thought, feeling the anger rising inside him, I've had enough of this nonsense. Just then his intercom buzzed and Lisa was telling him, "Mr. Ayre's on line one, again." Roland grabbed the phone, "Don?" he asked. Don answered with, "Cassie will be discharged from the hospital on Friday. I've made reservations for a flight leaving Regina at noon that same day, I'm going to pick her up at the hospital, the doctor told me he'd sign the discharge papers and I could pick her up at ten thirty, I'll take her straight out to the airport. You'll have to take her to a doctor out there to have her stitches removed. " He added almost as an afterthought, "By the way, Cassie gave me her key, so I'm going to pack up her things at her apartment for her and get her some travelling clothes." He added, "Cassie says Terry's not there; she says he told her, after he beat her up that he was leaving for Michigan, to stay on his brother's farm." Roland offered, "Be careful, Don, you never know." Don assured him, "Yeah, I don't trust that guy either, I'm taking a friend with me, just in case." Roland told him, "That's a good idea; you can never be too safe." He said, "Thanks again, I don't know how I can ever repay you." Don replied, "Hey that's what friends are for," and hung up.

That evening after dinner, he told Irene, "I need to talk to you." She looked at him strangely and sneered in answer, "Not now, your kids are around." Roland ignored her reply, and said, more as a statement than a question, "Jean and Maureen can you look after your sisters," and without waiting for a reply, he ushered Irene upstairs to their bedroom.

She perched on the chair in their room looking annoyed, as if he'd done something wrong. Roland told her what had happened to Cassie. Irene shook her head and muttered, "What did that silly girl do now?" Roland grabbed her by the shoulders and started to shake her, he suddenly realized what he was doing and let go and asked her, "What the hell's the matter with you? She called you days ago and told you she was frightened, you didn't even have the decency to tell me." Irene sighed heavily and said flippantly, with a wave of her hand, "I don't tell you everything that goes on around here, you're always working and I'm quite used to handling the kids on my own, thank you." Roland replied venomously, "You're right I am working a lot, because you never stop spending!" Irene told him, "Don't you dare blame me; I've needed to do something to make myself feel better all these years." She thought for a minute and feeling she needed something to shock him into being nice to her again, she blurted out, "I know about your affair with Sharon and it's been bothering me all these years." Roland looked at her with contempt, he simply said, "I figured you knew and that was a long time ago, why bring it up now?" He didn't care to hear her response, he continued, "I've made arrangements for Cassie to come home, and she'll be here early Friday evening." Irene yelled, "Roland, you can't, what will everyone think, you and I'll be ruined, we can't let everyone see out pregnant, and now recently separated, daughter." Roland walked up to her, boiling with rage; he had to work hard to control himself so he wouldn't lose his temper with her, he thought he might strangle her if she provoked him any further. When he was able, he finally said, "Would you rather her husband kills her, would that make

you feel better?"   Irene just sat there as she watched him open
the bedroom door and slam it closed again. She thought just
how did he find out Cassie had called me anyway, she shook
her head thinking, Cassie must have called him herself, after I'd
forbidden her to do so. She'd told her not to bother her Dad with
such trivial matters. She'd also told Cassie to grow up and try to
be a better wife to her husband. That little brat, she thought,
now I'll have to come up with some sort of explanation for her
behaviour, when my friends find out about her. Irene thought,
here we go again, another baby to take care of, well I'm just going
to have to put my foot down and tell Cassie I'm not going to be
the one looking after it.

Roland left the house immediately after he'd spoken with
Irene; he decided to go for a long walk, to calm down. He wished
things had turned out differently for them. Irene is such a
different person, he thought, than she was when I married her.
She's so selfish and uncaring when it involves others, even her own
children, if they get in the way of what she wants. He only hoped
she'd treat Cassie nicely and be a little more sympathetic towards
her, when she arrived; the poor girl's been through enough and
she needs her family now more that ever. He started thinking
about what Irene had said that she'd known about his affair with
Sharon. He knew she'd known, he could tell, she'd behaved so
differently after she became friends with Sharon, he wished he'd
spoken to her about it then but he hadn't wanted to admit his
own infidelity, even to himself, at the time. He supposed it was
probably his fault for the changes in her and tried to imagine
how he would have felt if he had found out that she'd had an
affair. He knew he would have been deeply hurt and thought,
shaking his head; she must have been as well. He knew he'd have
to work at getting their marriage back on track and he suspected
that it was going to take nothing short of a miracle.

He said the Rosary repeatedly for the rest of his walk, he
felt he needed to do some sort of penance for the sins he'd

committed and then, he thought just maybe things will be okay. He certainly needed to make restitution. He'd almost reached his own front walk, when he decided to smile and try his best from now on to make Irene happy and his children as well; he was going to start tonight.   He thought that maybe he should tell Irene about moving to Calgary, now might be the best time since she would be worried about saving face here in Toronto. He'd tell her that the Calgary refinery had very few people who'd started out in Toronto and that she could start over again, they all could, provided he got the position. He'd make sure she understood it wasn't final yet, but he would explain the situation exactly the way Mr. Sparks had explained it to him. He'd made him feel that it was nothing more than a formality, recommending him to the board. He'd even said there was no one else in the running for the position.   Roland was looking forward to getting back to an actual refinery again, he'd never liked being tied to a desk and that was the unfortunate reality of any of the head office positions, with the Company.

Roland had taken the car to work on Friday; the fellows at the office ribbed him about it. They joked that the buses must not be running today, when they saw him in the parking lot. He was the only one of all the executives who lived such a distance from the office and yet, didn't drive his own car to work. They'd teased him relentlessly, telling him his tires were going to rot in his own garage. Roland had laughed along with them.

Mr. Sparks was his first meeting of the day, and this morning he actually came to Roland's office. Roland was impressed; Mr. Sparks came in as soon as Lisa announced his presence. Roland could tell by the look on his face, that he'd gotten the position in Calgary. Mr. Sparks congratulated him and wished him well. He told him, "You won't actually be moving or starting out there, until closer to the end of next summer." Roland didn't care; at least there was a light at the end of this tunnel he felt he'd been trapped in for so long.   He thanked him and shook his hand before Mr. Sparks left his office. He did a lot of thinking about the new position that day, in spite of all that was happening in his personal life, he realized he was actually excited about the move. After work he stayed a little longer to tidy up a few loose ends, which really could have waited until Monday, but Roland needed to kill some time. He had to pick up Cassie at the airport. He estimated it would take about half an hour to get there and another 10 minutes to park the car so he filled the extra time reading until it was time to leave. On the drive to the airport, he thought about Irene being asleep when he'd returned from his walk on Monday night and he'd never had the chance since to tell her about his transfer to Calgary. Every night since then there'd always been something else going on either with the kids or Irene was going out somewhere. He simply hadn't had the opportunity to tell her, yet.

Roland pulled into a vacant space in the airport parking lot and put some coins in the meter. When he arrived at the gate, where Cassie's flight was to arrive, he still had about fifteen minutes to spare, the flight was a little late. Roland sat on a bench and waited. He could see out the window and would know when the plane taxied in. He didn't have to wait long, before the plane appeared on the tarmac and he walked to the window, he watched the technicians attach the stairs and open the door of the plane. He felt like a kid, he was excited to see Cassie again, he'd missed her so much and so had her sisters. She was one of the last to exit the plane. Roland at first didn't recognize her, he expected a pregnant Cassie and she wasn't even showing, in fact she looked like she'd lost quite a bit of weight and as she drew nearer he noticed she looked almost sickly, she was so pale and thin. He wondered if that was even possible at this stage of her pregnancy. Cassie walked slowly down the stairs and Roland could tell she was in pain. He rushed out to meet her and once he got close, he was appalled at the sight of her. She was wearing a scarf to try to cover the bruises and the black eye. He was sickened further when he noticed the cast on her left arm. He could see she was very thin and frail looking, even more so now that he was close. He wrapped her in his arms and held her there, fighting the tears that were welling up inside of him. She started to sob and he soothed her saying, "Don't worry you're safe now and no one is ever going to hurt you again, if I can help it." Roland released her and they walked into the building. Cassie said in a small sad voice, "I have to give the Airline instructions on where to deliver the casket." Roland's mouth fell open and was just about to ask her, what she meant, when it all clicked in his brain, the thinness of her small body, the fact that she wasn't showing at all. He looked at her and saw the raw pain in her eyes. He told her, "You just sit down here, on this bench and I'll take care of that."

He approached the airline counter and spoke to a customer service representative. She was extremely helpful; she'd dealt with situations similar to this before and knew exactly what to do and what arrangements had to be made. She asked, "Where do you live? We can ship the casket to a funeral home near your home." Roland gave her his address and she left the counter and returned a few minutes later, she told him, "It's all taken care of," and she gave him the number of Owen's Funeral Home. She said, "They'll receive the casket later today and you will have to contact them to make arrangements for the burial." Roland thanked her and returned to Cassie. He asked her, as he approached, "Do you have any luggage?" She shook her head slightly and said, "I don't, Mr. Ayre packed up my things for me, he brought me a change of clothes when he picked me up. And this," she held up a small bag, it contained her toothbrush and some toiletries and another change of clothes. She said, "The rest of my things are coming on the train." She admitted, "I don't have much though, Terry destroyed most of my clothes in his fits of rage. He seemed to like tearing up things I liked, just to be mean." She had tears in her eyes as she spoke. Roland put his arm around her shoulders and walked her to the car. She fell asleep on the ride home. Roland looked over at her and thought, you poor little girl, you've been through so much and you're still so young. He promised himself, I'll do my best to protect her from now on.

Irene looked shocked when she saw Cassie. The girls gasped at the same time and glanced at each other. Jean, Maureen and Dawn decided to pretend nothing was wrong, so they wouldn't make her feel uncomfortable; they smiled and hugged her. Irene hugged her as well and walked her over to the couch in the living room. She took the scarf off Cassie's head and noticed the stitches along her hairline as well as the bruises covering her face and the cast on her arm. She asked, "Cassie, are you hungry?" Cassie replied, "No, just thirsty." Irene asked Maureen, "Please, get her some iced tea from the fridge." Cassie shook her head and said, "I'd rather have a glass of ice water, instead." Maureen replied, "I'll be right back with it." Irene told Cassie, "If you need to talk, I'll be here for you anytime you're ready." Cassie looked at her thinking, yeah right; you say that now that everyone can hear you, but only said, "Thank you is there somewhere I can lay down?" Irene led her to the bedroom off the family room and told her, "This is your room and the bathroom is just down the hall across from the laundry room." She added, "You're at home now, so try and relax." She kissed Cassie's cheek lightly and helped her onto the bed. Irene covered her with the spare blanket at the foot of the bed. She left and closed the door.

Irene returned to the living room, looked at Roland and asked him, "Did she tell you what happened?" Roland sat down wearily and told her exactly what Cassie had told him, which wasn't much. He also told her of the little girl Cassie had lost. Irene gasped, she said, "Oh my god, where is she?" Roland explained, "I had the casket delivered to the funeral home on Sheppard Ave., the one called Owen's, the airline said it was the closest one." He added, "I'll have to call the funeral home and make arrangements for the burial." Irene asked, suddenly, "Roland, where are all Cassie's things?" Roland explained, "Don Ayre packed up what there was in the apartment and put it on the train." He said it would arrive in about a week." He also told her, "Terry destroyed most of her clothes and some of her other things as well. I'm not too clear on exactly what happened, we'll just have to wait and see if Cassie wants to tell us, when she's a little stronger."

Irene walked away; Roland could tell she was upset, so he followed her. She walked to the kitchen and sat down at the table. She started to cry and through her sobs said, "I didn't realize Cassie was in such distress, why didn't she tell me? I would have helped her." Roland looked at her and said, "Irene, she tried, you wouldn't listen." Irene held her head in her hands and softly said, "I honestly didn't know that things were that bad." Roland got up and left the kitchen, she deserved to feel badly, and he had to get away from her before she did her usual and laid the blame on someone else and in this case, it would undoubtedly be Cassie. Irene needed to realize that she was the one at fault; she was the one who could have prevented all of this, if she would have just listened to Cassie in the first place. Cassie wasn't the type of girl to cry wolf, whenever she asked for help she needed it.

He cracked open Cassie's door to check on her. She was sound asleep; as he watched her sleeping, he thought she looked so frail. He closed the door softly and went to the family room, it was just behind her bedroom, he was going to be there for her in case she awoke and needed someone. He thought shaking his head sadly, that's the least I can do for her.

Irene stopped crying and got up from the table. She decided she could do nothing more tonight; she blew her nose, then checked her reflection in the hall mirror. She yawned and went in search of Roland. When she found him in the family room, she asked him, frowning "Are you coming to bed?" He told her,

"No I'm not; I'm going to be here, close by, in case Cassie needs someone in the night." Irene told him, "Don't be absurd, she's asleep and you'll only be upstairs. Cassie's a big girl now and she can take care of herself." Roland sighed and told her, "You can go to bed without me." Irene turned on her heel and stomped off. She came back a few minutes later and announced, "I just checked on her and she's asleep, you're being silly, staying up all night, for nothing." Roland decided she didn't deserve an answer and kept reading the paper. Eventually Irene left, he knew she'd stood there glaring at him, he'd felt her stare boring into him; he could hear her going up the stairs, now. He rose from the couch and paced the room, he was very nervous about how she would treat Cassie. He got a pen and paper from the desk in the corner of the family room and wrote a note to Cassie telling her to knock on his door if she needed him in the night. He taped it to the inside of her door and went upstairs to talk to Irene. He decided he'd tell her about the transfer tonight. That way she might feel a little better about Cassie being back home.

He entered their bedroom and heard the water running in their bathroom. He walked over to the door and knocked, Irene pulled the door open looking annoyed. She was drying her face; she looked up at him and asked, "Is there was something you wanted?" He said, "I'd like to talk to you." She looked at him and said, "I hope it's not any more bad news, I can't take anymore tonight." He watched as she applied her moisturizer to her face and walked out of the bathroom. She perched on the chair and rather indifferently said, "Go ahead, I'm listening." Roland told her all about the transfer to Calgary. When she didn't respond, he said, "Irene, don't you see that this is a blessing? You won't have to worry about people talking about Cassie and us. They won't even know us in Calgary." Irene looked like she was thinking it over. She cautiously said, "I guess it might be better, but I'm still going to be hurt by all this. I'll have to make friends all over again." Roland thought, here we go again. He walked across the room and opened the door. Irene asked him, "Where are you going?" He said, "Back downstairs to make sure Cassie is okay, you can go to bed, if you want to."

When Roland reached the hall outside Cassie's bedroom, he placed his ear up against the door, when he didn't hear anything he knocked softly. When there was no answer, he opened the door a small crack and peered in. She hadn't moved an inch. He retrieved the note, closed the door, and retreated to the family room. He went to the bar next to the fireplace and poured himself a whiskey; he added a little water and made himself comfortable on the couch, thinking about how this move would once again affect his family. He hoped it wouldn't prove to be too much for all of them. He knew he would also want the promotion to Edmonton in a year's time or so. He wondered what effect that would have on them, as well. He sighed and sat back sipping his drink, silently praying things would somehow work out for all of them.

Cassie seemed to be a little better the next morning; she'd risen and showered after Irene had taped a plastic bag over her cast so she wouldn't get it wet. She stepped into the only other clothes she had with her. Irene commented when she caught sight of her, "Your clothes are too big for you." Cassie replied, sadly, "I know they are, but it doesn't matter, I don't look that great right now anyway." Roland felt sorry for her, he said, "I called the funeral home while you were in the shower, are you feeling up to going out to speak with them today?" Cassie quietly asked, "When?" Roland said, "I made a tentative appointment for eleven today." Cassie nodded and said, "That's okay, I know I have to do it soon."

After breakfast, Roland took her to the funeral home and they arranged for the baby, which Cassie had named Karen Cassandra La Farge, to be buried on Monday morning at nine. Roland had great difficulty fighting back his tears; as he watched her select, a small headstone with a little white angel perched on the side. She spelled out the baby's name to make sure the engraving would be correct. The director asked, "Are you happy with the casket, you can select another one if you like." Cassie just said, "No, I'm okay with this one." She turned to her Dad and told him, "Mr. Ayre bought it for me; he said he wanted to help me and he really did, Dad."

Roland and Cassie left the funeral home and Roland drove straight down Sheppard Ave. to Agincourt Mall, where he told Cassie, "You need to pick out something suitable for the burial service." Cassie found a black skirt and jacket and a purple blouse to go under it. Roland bought her a coat as well, he said, "It might be chilly that day," and as they were leaving, he reminded her, "Since your boxes haven't arrived yet you'll need some shoes, too." Cassie looked at him and told him, "I hadn't even thought of that, thanks." She had so much on her mind lately, she'd forgotten all about not having her things yet. Roland asked her, "Do you need anything else?" after he bought her a pair of black pumps and handbag. She said, "No, Dad, but thanks and thanks for all the things you bought me, today. Once they were back in the car, Roland handed her some money, when she started to object, he said, "Take it, you never know when you might need something." He also told her, "And please don't hesitate to let me know if you need more. Cassie looked over at him and said, "Thanks, you really are wonderful, Dad." Roland wasn't so sure of that, he thought he left a lot of room for improvement in that department. He looked at her and stated, "I wish."

Roland drove Cassie and the girls out to the cemetery on Monday morning, all the girls wanted to be there for Cassie. Irene had simply said, "I'm not feeling well," and stayed behind. Cassie had just taken her hand before they left and told her, "I hope you feel better soon." Roland looked disgusted; as he glanced over at Irene, he knew she felt fine. She'd told him the night before that she didn't want to go because she was worried about being seen by someone she knew and she didn't want to have to explain. Roland had tried to tell her that Cassie needed her family. Irene had said, "There is nothing I can do anyway and I'll be here when she gets home, in case she needs to talk."

The priest thankfully kept the funeral mass short and when the girls climbed back into the car, they were all in tears. Roland was having trouble not breaking down, himself. He would have loved to have had that little girl for his granddaughter; he was looking forward to having many grandchildren, one day. He wished things could have been different for Cassie; she seemed so grownup and strangely haunted these days but he thought with regret, she'd certainly had a tough few months.

He pulled up in front of a quaint little restaurant on Yonge Street, in the heart of the City. Susan asked, "Are we going to eat here?" Roland smiled at her reflection in the rear view mirror. He told her, "I'm going to treat everyone to brunch." Susan asked, frowning, "What's that?" Roland smiled and told her, "It's kind of a cross between breakfast and lunch." Susan smiled and took Cassie's hand as they left the car. Cassie smiled down at her and said, "Are you going to look after me." Susan said, solemnly, "I missed you when you weren't here and I want you to know how much I love you." Cassie looked at her and gave her the biggest hug. All the others joined in. Finally, Roland laughed and told them, "Hey, we're blocking the sidewalk lets hurry up and get into the restaurant, I'm starving." They hadn't eaten much this morning; none of them had felt very hungry then. He wanted them to eat something now, especially Cassie. He jokingly commented to her on the way into the restaurant, "Don't worry I'll cut your meat." She smiled at him and shook her head.

When they arrived home, Irene looked up at them, from the couch in the living room. She'd been reading to Brooke. She asked, "How's everyone doing?" Susan told her all about the delicious food they'd eaten at the fancy restaurant downtown. Irene had to smile Susan was so excited. Irene thought that maybe they needed to take the kids out occasionally. They never really did that, at least not to any fancy places. The last time that she could remember was in the hotel, before they'd left Regina and Cassie's wedding dinner, before that. Susan went on and on. Finally, when Irene could get a word in, she asked, "Cassie, how are you doing?" Susan fell silent; she knew that her sister was feeling bad, she was too. She would have liked to see Cassie's baby, but she died and Susan didn't understand why and no one had told her. Dad had only said, "It happens sometimes," when she'd asked.

Roland found he was putting a lot of effort into work these days and not hating it quite as much. He thought about why that might be and the only answer he could come up with was that he knew he wouldn't be here for too much longer. The move was now scheduled for the beginning of August. The only thing that was aggravating him lately was that the kids didn't want to move again. The younger girls really didn't seem to mind that much, although they'd said they would miss their friends, but Jean and Maureen were adamant that this time they weren't going to go.

Maureen was acting strange these days. He wanted to talk to her, but she seemed to be avoiding him, lately. Irene had said the same thing. She said, "Maureen is always sneaking off to Carol's house." Maureen commented to Jean one day, "I don't like to be at home anymore, things have changed too much and now with the move coming up, I just want to find a way to stay here, with Tom." Irene had expressed her fears, more than once to Roland, that she could see another Cassie coming up, but Roland had dismissed that idea, he told Irene, "Maureen wouldn't do that, not since she knows how awful things turned out for Cassie."

One evening when Maureen came home from a date with Tom, Roland was waiting up for her. He startled her as she came down the hall from the front door. She said regaining her composure, "Hi Dad, I'm going up to bed." Roland grabbed her

arm as she went by. He said, "I'd really like to talk to you first."
He let her arm go, when he saw the tears on her face. He gently
took her by the shoulders and turned her to face him. She cried
harder. He led her to the couch in the living room and told her,
"Sit down." He crossed the room and closed the French doors
so they wouldn't disturb anyone; everyone was sleeping, since it
was already after midnight. Roland returned to the couch and
sat down beside her. He began, "I'm not going to scold you for
coming home past your curfew." She was only a few minutes
late, so he told her, "I'll let it go this time." He noticed she didn't
seem relieved and wondered what could possibly be so wrong;
she looked devastated, he decided to venture asking her, "Is there
anything wrong?" She lifted her head and he could see the tears
running down her cheeks and dripping into her lap, she was
crying so hard. He felt the fear rise up in his chest and asked her
again only this time he said, "What's wrong, Maureen?" She hung
her head and told him, "I had a doctor appointment yesterday
and he told me that I'm pregnant." Roland sat there stunned.
He didn't say anything for what seemed like a long time. He was
trying not to react and make the same mistake with her as he
had with Cassie; he closed his eyes and said a silent prayer before
speaking, when he spoke to her he simply said, "Maureen, you
need to let me think about this situation for a little while. I'll
also need to discuss it with your Mother." Maureen replied sadly,
"I already told her Dad, she told me to pack my things and leave."
Roland was even more stunned; he closed his eyes again only
this time he was trying to hold back his tears. He told Maureen,
"Go to bed, I'll talk to you again tomorrow."

Roland sat there riveted to the couch; he had no idea what
to do. He couldn't believe Irene hadn't told him about Maureen.
She'd just kicked the kid out of the house, how the hell could
she have done that, he wondered. He stood up and stalked over
to the French doors, he was going to wake her and find out for
himself why she hadn't told him, he was seething inside; she

had no right not to tell him things, especially when they were as important as this. Just as he reached for the doorknob, the door opened. Roland pulled his hand back, startled, he'd been in such deep thought he hadn't heard a thing. His gaze settled upon Irene, she'd opened the door but wasn't sure if she wanted to enter, she stood there wide eyed, watching him. She didn't think she had ever seen him look quite so angry. He said with a clenched jaw, "Good, I was just coming upstairs to talk to you."

Irene walked into the living room gingerly; she skirted around him and sat down on the chair adjacent to the couch. Roland shut the door and turned to face her, he watched her as he crossed the room and sat on the couch. He asked her as calmly as he could muster, "Why the hell didn't you tell me about Maureen?" Irene shook her head and waved her hand in dismissal at his concern, and said, "Oh that, is that what this is all about? How did you find out, anyway?" He answered, his eyes forming slits," I waited up for Maureen and spoke to her when she arrived home, I was going to scold her for being late, but she was already crying when she came in the door, so I asked her what was wrong." He said, shaking his head, "The particulars don't matter, you didn't answer my question, why didn't you tell me?" Irene looked at him, anger rising in her face and told him, "I'm sick of your leniency with our kids, these days; you know how I feel about having another baby in this house." She continued, "Maureen is far too young to look after a baby by herself and I'm certainly not going to do it for her." Roland's expression turned to contempt when she continued, "I can't believe how irresponsible that girl is." She didn't look at Roland's face or even notice that he was now standing. All of a sudden, his voice boomed, "You are the worst mother I have ever seen!" When she looked at him, she spat back, "Well at least I've been here, not out somewhere trying to get ahead in a career or cheating on you like you did to me, with Sharon." Roland lost it and slapped her across the face. She screamed and ran from the room.

The kids were in the upstairs hallway, they were calling down asking, "Is everything okay?" Jean said, "We heard a scream." Roland thought oh my God, that's just what I need. He heard Irene's voice as she said calmly, "Go back to bed, everything's fine, I just slipped and almost fell. I guess I let out a scream when it happened." She told them again when they hadn't made any effort to move, "I'm okay, get back to bed" and she chuckled a little and told them, "I guess I'm just clumsy," to reassure them. The kids giggled a bit and went back to bed. Irene came back into the living room; she told Roland through clenched teeth, "If you ever strike me again I'll make sure your children find out about it." Roland told her, sincerely, "I'm sorry for hitting you," he said, "I just lost it. I couldn't believe you threw Maureen out of the house without even talking to me about it first." Irene looked at him for a few seconds through eyes drawn into slits, finally she said, "You will not undermine my decision, Maureen has to go, if she's going to have that baby. She can go to the children's aid for help and after she has the baby and has given it up for adoption, she can return home, if she chooses to." Irene turned to leave and then promptly turned around again, she said, "I told her that she had the option of going to a home for unwed mothers if she preferred that, and I told her that as long as she gives the baby up, when it's born, she can come home again." She added, "Just so you know, Maureen refused." She looked at Roland and asked, "Have I made myself clear enough? Maureen is out or else." Roland looked at her defeated, he finally said, "Fine." She said, "Just so we're clear, I won't only tell them that you struck me I'll also tell them you cheated on me. Feeling defeated, he walked past her saying nothing else and continued up the stairs.

Maureen spoke to Tom about the conversation she'd had with her mother. She told him what she said she must do and told him sadly that her father had sided with her mother. "They both made themselves perfectly clear," she said, "I can only come home if I give the baby up for adoption as soon as it's born." She looked grief stricken and went on to say, "My Mom checked and she told me the children's aid has a mother's helper program, she told me to check it out and gave me the number to call." She looked at Tom and said, "Mom thinks that I would be paid a small allowance and she thinks my job would be to help look after the couple's children." She told Tom, "Mom also said I could go to a home for unwed mothers if I want, I think she said it was called the Rosalie House."

Tom was shocked into silence, he couldn't believe her parents were doing that to her, she was only fifteen years old. He was glad though, that they weren't thinking of charging him with statutory rape, which his own mother had warned him they could do if they decided to. He asked Maureen, "What are you going to do." Maureen started crying, she couldn't believe he'd asked her what was "she" going to do, why hadn't he said "we." She closed her eyes as she pulled herself together and said, "I'm going to go to the children's aid to see what being a mother's helper is all about. I think I might like to do that."

Tom was relieved. He wasn't quite sure how he was going to convince her to give up the baby for adoption; he knew she really wanted to keep it. He also knew he didn't want to lose her in the process. He reminded her, "You know that I'm adopted and all of my brothers and sisters are too and we're all quite happy." He said, "You have to think of adoption as giving a baby to people who really want a child but can't have children of their own. It gives them a chance to have one." Maureen nodded and said, "I'll think about it." He thought for a few minutes and tried a different tack, "You'll only be sixteen when you have this baby, did you know you need to be at least eighteen in order to receive mother's allowance or any financial help from the government?" Maureen didn't know about that, she thought she'd check with the children's aid and see what her options were. She now knew she couldn't count on her parents. She'd talked it over with Cassie and Jean, they weren't much help either, they wished her well and offered to help her in any way they could, but they admitted that there was only so much they could do.

Irene's Mother was visiting at Christmas that year. Irene told Maureen, "You will have to go to a motel while your grandmother is here if you haven't already gone somewhere else by then, I don't want her to know that you're pregnant." Maureen said, "Mom, it's hardly even showing, none of my friends can even tell." Irene told her, "I can see that little tummy and if I can see it so can she and I don't want your grandmother putting two and two together." Maureen looked horrified she ran to her room crying, she'd never been alone for Christmas before. She thought my mother doesn't love me anymore, since I've disgraced our family. She'd told her during one of their conversations, "You're damaged goods, no self respecting man will ever want to have you for his wife, they want to marry virgins." Maureen thought, sadly, I'm a terrible person, I deserve this.

twenty-seven

A MUCH
SMALLER FAMILY

I rene was unpacking the last box in the kitchen, she paused
and looked around, she loved her new house. The kids were
excited about having their own rooms. They finally didn't
have to share bedrooms anymore. There were only three of them
at home now and the house had six bedrooms. Irene thought
cheerily, life is going to be so much easier, now. She wouldn't
have to cook as much, although the older girls had certainly
helped with that chore, but now that there were less kids in
the house it was going to be easy to cook for them anyway, she
wouldn't need their help.

Dawn and Susan had already made friends in the
neighbourhood; they would be going to the same school as the
girls they'd met. Brooke was playing with the little boy next
door, Kenny; they were the same age and got along famously.
They were playing at his house today, his mother, Tina, had
suggested it. She'd said it would give Irene time to unpack in
peace and Irene was grateful for it.

The phone rang and when she picked it up, she heard
Cassie's voice. Cassie was living in Winnipeg now, she'd moved
there to be close to the boy she was going out with, Irene could
never remember his name. She was working for the Post Office

308

and sharing an apartment with a girlfriend. Thankfully, Irene thought she didn't want to have to worry about her anymore. Cassie wanted to know how they liked the new house and they chatted about it for a while, then Cassie asked, "Mom, can I have Maureen's new phone number?" Irene said, "You could if I had it, but I don't." Cassie was appalled; she couldn't imagine not having your own daughter's phone number. Irene told her, "Maureen said she'd call as soon as she had a place to live. She's been staying with Tom's parents, since she had the baby. I don't have that number, either." Cassie talked to her mother for a little while longer and hung up.

Irene went back to arranging her kitchen cupboards. She was thinking of Maureen and how, thank God; she had had no choice but to give up that baby. She hadn't been eligible for any assistance since she wasn't eighteen and Tom hadn't wanted to get married right away. He wanted to wait until next year, Irene had suspected he didn't want to start their marriage with a family and she was glad because she didn't want to be a grandmother just yet, anyways, she thought she was far too young for that nonsense. She did feel a bit sorry for her, though, but she soon dismissed it, thinking, oh well, she can always have more kids she's young. She hoped Maureen would marry Tom; no other man would want her anyway, once he found out that she'd had another man's baby. She rolled her eyes thinking what a disgrace. She hoped none of her friends ever found out, what would they think; she wouldn't be able to live with the shame.

Roland walked in the side door and his sudden presence brought Irene abruptly, out of her thoughts. She asked him, "How was your day?" He answered, "Pretty good," and smiled. He kissed her cheek and said, "I'm going upstairs to change, I want to cut the grass while it's still light and fairly warm out." Irene told him, "I haven't had a chance to start dinner yet anyway." He said, "Don't rush on my account." He left the kitchen and hurried up the stairs, taking them two at a time. Irene thought, things are so much better between us these days. She attributed that to the fact that they had fewer kids in the house now. Jean had started University this past year and was taking sciences; she was even going to be living with the same couple Maureen had lived with during her pregnancy, in a suburb of Toronto. She suddenly wondered why Maureen had been in such a rush to move out of the first home she was in, but she shrugged and dismissed the thought, she really didn't care that much anyway. She thought as long as the older girls were basically okay and not living with her it didn't matter to her where they lived or what they did. She didn't dare tell Roland that, though.

She could hear Roland whistling upstairs and smiled to herself as she looked through the cupboards and the fridge assembling ingredients in her mind as she started to think about what to prepare for dinner. She finally decided on a tuna casserole and a macaroni and cheese casserole, she figured if she made both, no one would complain, if one of them didn't care for one, they'd like the other. She put water on the stove to boil for the noodles and another pot for the macaroni. Roland came downstairs and walked into the kitchen on his way to the garage, he asked, "What did you decide on for dinner?" When she told him, he replied, "Mmmmm" and went out the door and into the garage to start the lawnmower and cut the grass. She smiled thinking, he's always so easy to please when it comes to what I make for meals, he never complains about anything I make. She started humming along with the radio as she cooked.

Roland thought as he started up the lawnmower and began to cut the grass, I'm so much happier at work these days; I just wish my home life could be as happy. He had to struggle often to put the older girls out of his mind; he knew they were very disappointed in him. He recalled how Maureen had looked crushed that he hadn't helped her that day when he'd visited her, in Toronto. He'd gone back on a business trip and had asked Jean for her number, before he left. He'd asked her to promise

not to tell her mother. He'd explained that he only wanted
to make certain Maureen was okay, Jean had told him at the
time that she understood.   He recalled Maureen's face when he
showed up at the door that day; she'd looked so different. She'd
told him, quietly, "We can talk on the porch."   He'd tried to
ask her questions and just keep the conversation as light as he
could. He didn't want to be insensitive or hurt her feelings in
any way, but she'd refused to say much of anything. She'd sat
quietly answering his questions, but never elaborating and she
wouldn't contribute anything on her own. He'd even tried to
give her some money, he remembered her saying, "I don't need
any." He thought, shaking his head, I ended up leaving it on
the porch, when she wouldn't accept it. He remembered he had
asked her how she was doing. She'd looked up at him with eyes
that seemed so full of pain and softly answered, "Fine." He would
always remember her eyes, they were lifeless somehow, almost as
if she was dead inside, all the sparkle and shine that he'd loved
so much was gone. She looked like a hurt, broken doll. She'd
been just a child, having a child. He tried to hug her before he
left but she stepped back, he ended up just kissing her cheek and
saying, "Goodbye." He put the money on the porch and left. He
could see her watching him drive away, in the rear view mirror
of his rented car. She looked so small and alone. He would
never get that image of her or her lifeless eyes, out of his mind.
He'd berated himself repeatedly since, he should have told her
to call him, if she needed him. He wished he had. He thought
of Irene's threat, that day, when Maureen had told him that she
was pregnant, as he had on so many occasions since. He hadn't
then and still didn't want her to tell his children, that he'd been
unfaithful or that he'd struck her that one time. He knew she
would, if he pushed her, and he didn't think he could live with
the shame of his children knowing what he'd done.

　　Irene and Roland moved to Edmonton just one year after
they'd moved to Calgary. Roland promised Irene and the three

younger girls that it would be their last move. He'd said, "We're all going to grow old here, this time," and the girls had laughed happily. He sometimes felt like he had two families, the three older ones and the three younger ones. There wasn't that much difference in age between Maureen and Dawn, but Dawn had stayed a little girl, thank God. He thought of how Maureen had become so grown up and distant now.

They'd moved into their, new home in Edmonton, exactly one week ago and were now, all five of them, seated aboard an Air Canada flight, on their way back to Toronto for Maureen's wedding. Maureen was having Brooke as her flower girl. She was having a friend of hers, Mary-Lou as her matron of honour. Mary-Lou's husband, Adam was Tom's best man as well as one of his best friends. Jean was one of the bridesmaids and Wendy, the girl Maureen had shared an apartment with, for the past year, was her other bridesmaid. The wedding was going to be rather small with only 100 or so people in attendance. They were getting married in the Catholic Church since Tom was also Catholic. Their reception was to be held at a brand new hall, called "The Embers" it was located several miles from the church but Maureen had left the planning of her wedding a little late and it was all she'd been able find for a reasonable price. Cassie's boyfriend, Gary had volunteered to be their photographer. He was in the Services and had chosen to learn photography as his trade and was thankfully, extremely good at it.

Irene, Roland and the kids were staying at the same Holiday Inn they'd stayed at when they'd moved to Toronto a few years before. The kids thought it looked different, somehow. Irene told them, "It was brand new the first time we stayed here; it looks different because it's landscaped now. Remember, it had sidewalks but no grass or flowers or trees or anything." Dawn said, "I remember that," and Susan chimed in, "So do I," even Brooke said, "Me too." Irene said to Roland, with a smile, "Brooke was just a baby; she can't possibly remember anything about it at all." They both laughed at that.

The wedding went well. Roland and Irene had taken the whole family, including both Cassie and Jean's boyfriends and now Maureen's husband to breakfast the day after the wedding. It was the last time they would be together as a family for probably, quite a while. The happy couple took off on their honeymoon, to Niagara Falls.

Roland and Irene went on to Sarnia to visit their families. Melissa was still living in Sarnia, with her husband, Howard, and all five of her kids and Roland wanted desperately to visit them. He knew he would have to do so without Irene, since she and Melissa hadn't been on speaking terms for years. Roland often wondered what had happened between them. When he'd asked Irene she had only said, "Melissa is awful and downright mean as well," he'd tried to get her to tell him more, but she had refused to elaborate. He recalled when he asked Melissa she said, "I never liked Irene," she'd told him, "I always thought she was a selfish little twit." He thought, the two of them had made those comments years ago, would they feel differently this time, he wondered.

What Roland didn't know and Irene was trying to make damn sure he never did, was that Melissa had found out about the affair she'd had in Regina. Irene couldn't believe it at the time, Melissa's best friend Alexandria had told her about it, because John was her brother. Irene had been so flabbergasted hearing that little piece of information, when Melissa confronted her with it back then, she couldn't believe it, just my luck, she remembered thinking. She'd ended the affair anyway, long beforehand, but she still didn't want Roland to find out. She'd begged Melissa not to tell him. She'd even told her, in her defence, that Roland himself had had an affair with his secretary back then. Melissa had called her a liar but she had said she wouldn't have blamed her brother if he had cheated on her, because, she was such a witch. In the end she'd promised Irene she wouldn't tell Roland, but only because telling him would hurt him too much. She told her with venom in her voice, "You don't deserve my brother!" The two of them hadn't spoken more than just a few words to each other ever since. Irene was nervous most of the time whenever they returned to Sarnia to visit with Mom and Dad, she didn't trust Melissa to keep her promise. She thought she'd done a pretty good job of keeping Roland and Melissa apart for all these years, with the exception of a few times that had been unpreventable, but even on those few occasions she'd managed to keep them from having any real privacy to discuss anything of a serious nature. This time was going to be a challenge, though. Roland was so eager to see her again, he said, "I didn't have much time to catch up with her at the wedding, so I'm looking forward to going over to her house to visit with her." He added, "I understand that you probably don't want to come along." Irene cringed, she knew Roland would wonder, what was going on, if she suddenly changed her mind now and actually wanted to visit Melissa, so she smiled and said sweetly, "Yes, I think you should." She rolled her eyes, knowing he wasn't looking and thought I hope something comes up and he doesn't have time to visit with her. She really didn't want him to go. She was so afraid and she wasn't sure Melissa could be trusted with her secret, forever.

They had a good visit with their families. Mama was so happy to see them. Irene noticed she was beginning to look so old these days and was seriously worried about her. She'd suggested to her, "It may be time to sell the house and move into something easier for you to manage." Mama told her, firmly, "No, I'm just fine here, the boy next door cuts the grass and shovels the snow in the winter, and I have a cleaning lady that comes in once a week. I even have the meals on wheels people bring me a hot supper each night. What more could I possibly want?" Irene felt guilty about her being on her own, but she wouldn't move out to Edmonton, either, so what could she do.

She wished Donna or Jake could help Mama more, but neither one of them lived close by anymore either. Jake had moved to Waterloo and started up his own machine shop and Donna was working for a daily newspaper in Detroit. Irene really didn't keep in touch with them much anymore. She'd invited them out for Christmas a few times, but they'd always had some reason or another why they couldn't come, so she'd finally stopped asking.

Mom and Dad were always happy to see them whenever Irene and Roland visited; they took the initiative to come out west and visit occasionally, too. They had flown out to the house in Calgary and now they were talking about flying out to Edmonton for Christmas. Irene thought smiling, won't Melissa be pleased when she hears that, she almost chuckled aloud and covered her mouth, feigning excitement when Mom looked at her, she smiled wider and practically oozed when she told her, "Oh I hope you do, we'd just love to have you, the kids will be so excited." Mom said with concern, "Don't tell the kids just yet, not until everything is all settled and we know we're coming for sure. I wouldn't want to disappoint them and I haven't bought the plane tickets yet." Irene promised she wouldn't. Mom looked troubled and asked, "I want to know if you would welcome Melissa as well, in the event she may be able to visit?" Irene tried her best not to look as shocked as she felt. Trying to keep her voice as even as possible, she smiled and said, "Of course, anytime."

twenty-eight

THE
UNEXPECTED

I rene was cooking supper, she was making spaghetti and had just finished making the sauce when the phone rang as she picked it up she almost dropped it in the sauce. She managed to finally get it to her ear and say, "Hello," but almost dropped it again when she heard Donna's voice on the line; she started to ask her, excitedly, "How are you?" However, before she could get all the words out Donna interrupted her, "Irene, its Mama." Irene froze, and asked, reluctantly, "What's wrong, is she okay?" She was petrified of the answer. She knew how frail Mama was becoming she could hear it in her voice each time she called her, which she did every week without fail. Donna started to sob and Irene knew something was terribly wrong. She panicked and started to cry as well as she waited for Donna to speak again. When she did, she told Irene, "Mama died last night." Irene felt as if she'd had the wind knocked out of her, she had to wait a second until she could breathe again, and then asked, "Why didn't you tell me last night?" Donna replied, "I didn't know myself until this morning, Mama's neighbour, Clara Mason, found her." Donna said through her tears, "Clara called the ambulance, but it was already too late." Donna was breathing in short ragged breaths, "Clara explained to me, she'd

316

had to go through, Mama's phone book to find my number. She said she had called me, because I lived the closest." Irene asked her quietly, "Where's Mama now?" Donna answered, "Still at the hospital, they called and asked me which funeral home we would like to use, I didn't know." She waited for Irene's answer, "Just tell them to use the closest one to the hospital." Donna said, "I'm going to leave for Sarnia right away, how long will it take for you to get there?" Irene said, "I'll be out on the next available flight." She reminded Donna, "Call Jake." Donna said, "We should all stay in Mama's house." Irene said, "Maybe but we might find it too hard, if we do we'll move to a hotel, instead."

When Irene hung up the phone, she immediately called Roland, at the office. He told her how sorry he was and said, "I'll have my secretary make your travel arrangements. Would you like me to come with you?" She thought for a moment and softly answered, "Maybe you should stay here, so the kids will have someone to talk to, they'll have lots of questions." Roland agreed with her, but worried about her making the trip alone.

Irene was on a flight the next day. She had to change planes in Toronto, but she still managed to arrive in Sarnia in time to help with the funeral arrangements. When she walked into the funeral home, Jake and Donna were already there. Irene was suddenly struck with the reality that Mama was really gone. Things had been so busy, with packing, explaining Grandma's death, to the kids and shopping for a suitable outfit, in black, she hadn't allowed herself time to think. Now standing in this awful place, she felt, cold and numb as the realization that Mama, who'd always been there for her, was now gone, forever. She thought about never being able to see her or speak with her again.

Jake and Donna noticed her standing at the back of the room and Jake got up and led her to a chair. He said, "I know it's hard, I can't believe she's gone either." The director spoke in a sympathetic tone; he said, gently, "Now that you are all present, would you follow me, please." He lead them to a room filled with caskets and explained the differences between them. Jake quickly chose one he thought would be suitable and turned to ask Irene and Donna, "Are you in agreement with my decision?" They both nodded, glad that he was taking the initiative. The director then explained the service to them. Mama had not wanted to have a church service; she'd told them years ago that when she passed away, she only wanted a service at the funeral home and a burial immediately following. She'd made each of them promise they would respect her wishes, when the time came.

Donna and Irene walked out of the funeral home, on either side of Jake, holding onto each arm. "It's a good thing the door is a double one," Jake said, trying to lighten the mood, "Or we would've all gotten stuck." They laughed a little at that. He asked, "Have you eaten?" Irene and Donna both shook their heads in reply.

He took them to a nice little restaurant on the river. They talked about old times and about Mama, of course. Once they'd finished their meals and the wine Jake had ordered, to help them relax, they began talking about where they were going to stay. Irene said, "We weren't sure if we would be able to stay at Mama's." Jake agreed, saying, "Yeah, I understand that, I'm not sure I could either." He suggested "Why don't we all stay at a hotel, since the funeral won't be held until the day after tomorrow, we should go over to Mama's first thing in the morning and decide which things we want to take back home with us. We'll also need to decide which of her things we'll give to charity and which ones we'll sell and we need to find out where she kept her important papers." Irene spoke up, "I know they were in the safety deposit box at National Trust downtown. Mama told me, once all of us had moved away; she'd named National Trust as Executor of her Estate. She said that would make it easier for all of us." Jake and Donna nodded, and Jake said, "Mama was probably right, since none of us is able to stay too long." Irene had her kids and a husband and Jake and Donna had their jobs to get back to.

They checked into the hotel downtown by the river across the street from the restaurant they'd had just eaten in. They agreed to meet in the lobby at eight o'clock for breakfast the next morning. The porter took the bags from the trunk of Jake's car, Irene and Donna had put their bags in his trunk, when they'd all met at the funeral home. They'd decided it would be easier if they kept all the bags together until they decided where they were going to stay that night.

Irene called Roland as soon as she was settled in her room. He told her, "The kids are all in bed." Irene asked him, "Did they ask you a lot of questions about Mama?" Roland paused and said, "They had some questions, but nothing too difficult." He said, "We prayed the Rosary together and I think that helped soothe them." Irene rolled her eyes, thinking, for sure, that's just what they needed. The kids still had bad memories, even the three youngest, of saying the Rosary every night when they lived in Regina. Brooke of course had no recollection of it, but Susan and Dawn had told her all about it. The kids associated the Rosary with the constant unhappiness and fighting that used to erupt, all the time, in their home. They remembered the older girls wanting to be with their friends or needing to get their homework done. She wondered if Roland ever really noticed just how they'd felt about it. Then wondered if it would have mattered to him anyway, he'd always done whatever he thought was right anyway, no matter how the rest of the family felt about it. She thought it was ridiculous sometimes.

The service was unbearable for Irene, she wasn't sure she could get through it, she and Donna clasped each other's hands throughout it, hoping to glean strength from each other. Mom and Dad came to pay their respects, as did Melissa and Howard. Irene barely noticed them she was so grief stricken. The prayers at the cemetery were short and Mama was laid to rest beside Father. Irene suddenly wondered if she would really want to be there, but they hadn't know what else to do, Father had purchased the two plots years ago and Mama had never said anything one way or the other to them and they could find nothing in her final instructions, which she'd painstakingly written out in detail and left in her jewellery box on her dresser with the key to her safety deposit box attached to it. They thought that since they could find nothing to tell them any different, that possibly she wanted to be buried there. Donna thought it might be that she'd wanted to assuage the guilt she felt for what she'd done all those years ago.

Donna, herself had never wanted to marry, for fear her husband would turn out to be like Father, she shuddered at the thought. Irene held her hand tighter, the slight pressure Donna felt on her hand jolted her back to the present and she realized Irene must have thought she was struggling with the prayers the minister was reciting, she wasn't, she hadn't even been listening. She began feeling guilty that she'd been so lost in her own thoughts that she hadn't even heard the prayers for her own mother.

The three of them made their way out of the cemetery and back to the car. Mama had left strict instructions that she did not want any sort of wake or get together afterward; she said she wanted only a simple funeral and burial. They'd followed her instructions to the letter; they wanted to make sure that everything was the way she'd wanted it to be.

Jake suggested they return to Mama's house and finish the chore of going through her things. He said, "We should visit National Trust, as well and retrieve the papers from the safety deposit box." Donna and Irene agreed it would be better than just sitting around thinking; at least it would keep them busy.

They finished packing up Mama's clothes, they'd each decided on a small keepsake. Irene chose the necklace she'd worn on her wedding day, Donna chose the small sapphire ring Mama used to wear whenever she got dressed to go out and Jake chose the picture on Mama's dresser, it was of the five of them, when he and his sisters were little. It was an old picture, but they were all smiling, even Father, Jake had always loved looking at it for as far back as he could remember.

They locked the house and drove to National Trust. They told the manager what had happened and he ushered them into his office. He asked them, "Would you like me to handle everything from here on, since all of you live out of town?" They gave him a key to Mama's house and a copy of the death certificate and Jake told him, "Yes, we'd appreciate that; however we'd like to get the papers from the safety deposit box before we leave." Jake explained, "I have the key, Mama left it in her jewellery box, along with her instructions for her funeral." The manager took the key and together with his key, opened the box; he placed it on the table in a small private room and as he left, he told them, sympathetically, "Please feel free to take your time."

Irene was sitting closest to the box, so she removed its contents. She frowned as she did; she was surprised by what she saw, and said to Jake and Donna, "Look! There are envelopes for each of us with our names on them." She handed each their envelope bearing their name and then opened the large brown envelope that contained a copy of her will. Irene gasped when she read it. Mama had left her estate to them, she'd expected that, but what she hadn't been prepared for was the amount of money involved. Mama had over one million dollars in her account at the trust company. This, in addition to her home and antique dishes and furniture was all to be left to the three of them. Irene's mouth fell open in shock, her eyes opened wider, as wordlessly; she pushed the papers in front of Jake and Donna so they could read them for themselves. As they read, their jaws dropped as well they looked back at Irene, who was still speechless, they couldn't believe it.

Curiosity now aroused, they decided to open their envelopes. Each of them had tears running down their faces as they each read them. Mama confessed, in each letter, what she'd done all those years ago. She wrote, "I am so sorry I took your father from you. I will do my best to explain exactly what happened on that frightful day." She told them everything, she simply wrote, "When I told him, that day that Donna and I were going to see Irene and the baby, he yelled and told me to get back in the house. When I saw him starting to climb down the ladder and saw the rage in his face, I was consumed with fear, I had never in all our years together, seen so much anger in his face, without even thinking I pushed the ladder as hard as I could. He fell to the ground and I panicked when I saw he had only knocked the wind out of himself with the fall and after a few moments, when his breath returned, he was beginning to get up again. He glared at me with even more rage than before; I didn't think about what I was doing, I was only trying my best to prevent him from reaching me. I picked up the hammer that had also fallen to the ground and hit him with it as hard as I could. I remember being terrified of what he would do to me and Donna as well. Please believe, that my only thought had been, that I had to stop him, but I killed him instead. I'm so sorry." She ended each of the letters by telling them she loved them dearly.

They were openly crying as they left the private room. The Manager noticed their distress and reassured them, "Don't worry about a thing, I have each of your phone numbers and addresses and I promise I will take care of everything for you." He continued, almost as an afterthought, "And I'll send each of you a cheque, once all property is sold and the estate is settled." He held the door open for them as they left the building and added, "Please do not hesitate to call me if you have any questions or concerns."

The three of them piled into Jake's car and drove in silence, they were still feeling the shock of reading Mama's confession. Jake parked in a parking space directly in front of their hotel; they entered and mindlessly walked to the restaurant on the far side of the lobby, across from the front doors. They chose a private table toward the back and still without speaking to each other, ordered drinks as soon as the waitress appeared at their table. Once their drinks arrived they started speaking to each other, they discussed the contents of each of their letters and discovered they were identical except for some personal comments Mama had made to each of them at the end before she'd signed them.

The decision was unanimous they decided to burn them. They agreed they didn't want to disgrace Mama's memory in any way, the poor woman had explained she'd done it out of fear, for both herself and her daughter. They also decided they would never discuss the subject again. Donna felt a strange relief, there were times she recalled, when she thought maybe, she had been seeing things that day. She now knew for sure that she actually did see what she'd thought she had. That fact didn't exactly make her feel good, but at least now she knew she wasn't crazy. Jake lit a match from the book of matches the restaurant supplied on the table and one by one held each of their letters over the ashtray and lit them on fire, they watched each one ignite, then he simply dropped them one by one into the ashtray, once they were all reduced to ashes, they ordered dinner. They ate without speaking much; each was lost in their own grief. When they finished they said good night, agreed to meet for breakfast early the next morning and immediately returned to their rooms for the night, they were emotionally exhausted.

Irene was seated on the plane, bound for home, the next day, wondering why Mama had felt she needed to confess. She wondered if in some small way it helped her to cope with what she'd done, knowing that when she died, at least her family would know the truth. She closed her eyes and thought, Mama, I understand, and I'll always love you, no matter what and I promise I'll never tell anyone, not even Roland. Fresh tears were forming in her eyes as she thought about how poor Mama must have suffered once the reality of what she'd done had set in, because Irene knew in her heart that Mama had never meant to kill him, she simply wasn't capable of such a thing.

Roland met her at the airport and the ride home was unusually quiet. He didn't want to risk being insensitive, so he decided to wait before he asked her for any details pertaining to her trip. He glanced over at her and noticed, she was sad, which he'd expected, but he saw something else, she appeared to be extremely depressed, her face was white and she hadn't said more than two words since he's picked her up. He knew it must be hard for her, she'd always been so close to her mother, he understood her silence and gave her the space she needed, he knew she'd talk to him when she was ready.

The kids had been warned by their Dad not to ask questions when their mother returned home, Roland had explained to them that she was having a difficult time dealing with her mother's death. The kids really did seem to understand and he so was glad they did, he thought they're growing up so quickly.

During the days following Irene's return, Roland simply didn't have the heart to discuss anything that would further upset her. She was having such difficulty accepting that her mother was gone. He felt sorry for her, but at the same time he thought, if she continues to struggle, I'm going to need to talk to her about getting some help, possibly counselling, he'd heard that it could be quite helpful in circumstances like this.

She seemed to be crying less the following week and was actually beginning to act and sound like her old self again, Roland was relieved to see the improvement, until the day she received the letter from National Trust and a cheque.

She was sobbing at the kitchen table, that evening when Roland walked in the door. He hurried over to her and as he took her in his arms, he noticed the envelope and letter lying on the table. As he tried to soothe her, he noticed the cheque sitting on the table beside the letter. He had to blink a few times; he couldn't believe his eyes and said aloud, "Oh my God, that's a lot of money!" He realized what he'd said but it seemed she hadn't heard him anyway. He began stroking her hair, as he held her saying, "There, there, it's going to be okay," all the while looking over her head at the cheque, he was sure he must be reading it wrong, but the more he looked, the more he knew he was correct. The cheque was for $438,049.26, he swallowed hard.

She finally lifted her head from his shoulder and sat down again; she wiped the tears from her face with a tissue and looked at him, with a shaky voice, she said, "I haven't even started any dinner yet." Roland looked at her tenderly and shook his head, he smiled and said, "We can order pizza; I want you to take a break tonight." He paused then couldn't help saying, "Irene, I knew your mother was doing okay financially, but I had no idea that she'd been that wealthy. Did you?" Then he asked, "Was her estate split evenly between the three of you?" Irene replied, mindlessly, staring at the table and nodding, "Yes, it was." Roland thought, my God, the woman never let on she had this much.

He thought of all the things she'd done for them when he'd arrived home from the services and the homes she'd bought and furnished for Donna and Jake, as well as buying his and Irene's first home and most of the furniture in it. He couldn't think of anything she'd ever purchased for herself, other than necessities, but he knew she certainly spent her money lavishly on her kids and grandkids. He thought she truly was a special person, in spite of what he'd overheard Donna and Irene say all those years ago about what she'd done to their father. He had never mentioned his overhearing that conversation to Irene, he thought maybe he should have back then, he knew it wouldn't be right to ask her now; he didn't want to tarnish her memory of her mother in anyway.

twenty-nine

LIFE GOES ON

C hristmas seemed to arrive quickly that year and as promised, Mom and Dad came out to visit. Their flight arrived early in the evening, two days before Christmas.

When they'd called to let Roland and Irene know that they'd purchased their tickets and would be coming for sure, they'd told Roland excitedly, when he answered the phone, "We have an extra special surprise in store for you, as well." Mom continued with an excitement he rarely heard from her anymore, "Melissa's going to be coming out to visit as well, she'll be coming after Christmas though and she'll only be staying for three days at your home because she's going to be visiting her best friend Alexandria. She recently moved to Edmonton after her marriage broke up. Alexandria is living with her brother, John now, out there in Edmonton." Roland listened as she continued, "Melissa's going to be staying with Alexandria for the balance of the week she'll be in Edmonton." Roland was thinking, uh oh, how am I going to tell Irene about this? Mom continued on, "Melissa wanted me to tell you that she and Alexandria might like to visit together too, she wanted me to ask you if that was okay. Melissa said Alexandria wanted to meet your kids as well." Roland answered, enthusiastically, "Of course, they're both welcome."

326

Irene almost fell over when Roland got off the phone and told her what Mom had said, especially the part about Melissa and Alexandria visiting, together. She wondered if they'd notice that Susan resembled John, she never did figure out who the father was. She hoped no one would ever notice the resemblance, if there really was one to be seen, sometimes she thought she was just imagining it because she was nervous about it. Roland looked at her strangely and asked, "Is it really so bad, it's only for a few days and she is my sister." Irene quickly replied, "No of course not, I was just thinking it's a shame she can't come for Christmas as well, but I'm sure she wants to spend it with her own children." Roland was still looking at her, he was a little bewildered and replied, "I'm sure she does." He was mulling over the sudden change in her and finally decided to just ask her, "What brought about this sudden change of heart? I thought you despised Melissa." Irene sighed and trying her best to sound sincere, simply said, "It's been a long time, and I think we should both try to get along now. I'm certainly willing; I hope she is as well." She didn't look back as she left the room or she would have seen the stunned look on Roland's face. He was truly stunned but also glad; he'd missed his little Melissa, terribly all these years.

Irene made it to the bathroom where she locked the door and turned on the water. She splashed her face with cold water repeatedly; she'd actually thought she would faint, when Roland said Melissa and Alexandria planned to visit together. Irene tried her best to calm herself, she had no idea what she was going to do, but she sure had a lot of thinking to do between now and the time Melissa arrived. She couldn't believe John was actually living here in Edmonton, she wondered just how long he had been. She suddenly remembered a time when she'd been shopping at Eatons, she'd had Susan with her that day, she remembered feeling as if someone was watching her and when she'd looked up was shocked to see a man whom she thought looked like John, but when she'd moved away from the rack of clothing in front of her, to get a better look, the man had simply vanished. She remembered the incident well, because she'd been shaken by it and eventually had to tell herself not to be so silly. She'd put the whole experience out of her mind and had almost forgotten about it, until now.

The kids were excited about Grandma and Grandpa being there for Christmas. Brooke was the only one who still believed in Santa Claus and she couldn't wait for them to discover with her, what Santa would bring for her and her Sisters.

Irene was a bundle of nerves; she was trying her best not to show it. She played things over and over again in her mind, she imagined all different scenarios and tried to think of responses that Roland would believe, but she knew if either Melissa or Alexandria told Roland about John, she wouldn't be able to deny it. She thought angrily, I'd like to know just why John told his little sister about our affair anyway, that wasn't something most people spoke freely about to their families. Irene would give anything to know exactly what he'd said, maybe he hadn't said anything more than just telling her he'd been her Fuller Brush salesman and maybe Melissa had read into things and tricked her into admitting it all those years ago. She thought, remembering the incident, why didn't I deny it, that was so idiotic of me, I couldn't have been thinking properly that day. She suddenly smiled to herself, if I have to, I'll just deny it now; I may have no choice in the matter anyway. She thought with a sigh, I'd just better make sure that whatever I say will be credible. She took a deep breath, thinking, I can do it, I've always been good at deception in fact no one knows just how good I am. She smiled thinking, that's because everyone always believes me. And thought, scowling, except Melissa, she's always been a problem, I'll just have to find a way to discredit her, if necessary.

Mom and Dad's flight was on time, when Roland picked them at the airport, he'd gone alone, since the whole family couldn't possibly fit in the car. He told the kids to make sure everything was ready for Grandma and Grandpa when he brought them home. They hurried in the door as soon as Roland parked the car in the garage, they couldn't wait to see the kids and Irene. Hugs and kisses were exchanged all around and the kids ushered them into the living room, and Irene returned to the kitchen.

Roland had been studying Irene from the kitchen door; he noticed she was miles away. He asked her, "What's got you in such deep thought?" She jumped and told him, "Oh, I was just thinking about Christmas dinner and ticking off a mental list of things I still need to get done." He walked into the room and kissed the back of her neck, she was surprised. She turned to face him and asked playfully, "What's gotten into you?" He smiled, "I'm just so pleased that you're doing your usual best, to make this the perfect Christmas for my parents." She turned, surprise registering on her face and said, "Roland, my God, I love them too and I want them to enjoy themselves. I don't want Mom to have to do anything; I noticed her arthritis was quite a bit worse when we were in Sarnia this past summer." Roland commented sadly, "Yeah I noticed that too." He brightened and said, "Don't worry between you, me and the kids; we'll keep her out of the kitchen as much as we possibly can." Irene told him, "I've already spoken to Dawn and Susan, I discussed with them my concerns about their Grandma and they completely understood. I was so pleased with the genuine concern they showed at their young ages. They both told me they'd do their best to help her." Roland looked pleased as he left the kitchen, he said, "I'm going to see if they need refills of their drinks or anything else, since dinner is still a little ways away. By the way do you need any help with dinner or do you want one of the kids to help you instead?" She said, "No, I pretty much have things in the oven. We just have to wait until it's ready. I'm going to ask Dawn to set the table for me so I can come and join you for drinks."

Christmas was wonderful; the turkey was cooked to perfection and was delicious with all the trimmings. Mom told Irene, smiling, "You're such a wonderful cook." Irene blushed, and said, "Thank you," as she picked up another card. They were playing cribbage, while the kids did the dishes. Brooke was playing with the new Barbie dolls; she received from "Santa."

Mom commented, looking towards the window, "I hope Melissa's flight won't be late, but it probably will because of all this snow, and look it's still coming down!" They'd had a major snowfall the night before and it wasn't supposed to get any better over the next 24 hours. Roland told her, "We'll have to check tomorrow about an hour before we expect to leave for the airport. We'll make a quick call to the airline and enquire about the expected time of arrival, they'll let us know if the flight's on time or if they're expecting a delay."

Irene thought, wouldn't it be wonderful if it were cancelled altogether or with any luck crashed. She shook her head at the thought of the latter, she really didn't want that to happen, but she didn't want her to visit either. She knew the chances of either scenario actually happening were slim, anyways. Melissa would be here, whether she liked it or not, she might arrive a little later than expected, due to the snow, but undoubtedly she would arrive and Irene knew she'd just have to deal with it.

Susan and Dawn came out of the kitchen and announced, "All the dishes are finally done." They made sighing sounds and flopped on the couch as if they were utterly exhausted. They had a dishwasher, but Irene didn't want the pots and serving dishes to go in it, she was afraid they would be ruined, so of course the girls had to wash those particular items by hand. They joked about it; they even imitated her when they knew she wasn't near enough to hear. "Remember; don't put those in the dishwasher!" They'd say wagging a finger and imitating her. Even the older girls joined in when they came to visit. It had been a long standing joke, Mom washing the dishes by hand even though she had a dishwasher, but they all knew she was afraid of things getting "wrecked". Whenever she said that the girls muttered under their breath, "So what, it's about time you bought new pots and pans anyway." Then they would ask her, "Haven't you had these same ones since you and Dad were married? Weren't they a wedding gift?" Each of the kids would say, "When I get married I'm not going to have any dishes that can't be washed in the dishwasher." Irene would simply smile and say, "You say that now but you'll probably be just like me," and she'd chuckle at them and say, jokingly, "You little brats, I know you joke about it, when you think I can't hear you." They always laughed at that, they knew that their Mom knew of their long-standing joke.

Roland looked over at them sprawled on the couch and asked, "You girls want to play cards with us?" They shook their heads and both of them said the same thing, "No, we'd rather go and listen to our new records," and they headed off up the stairs, to their rooms

The next night after supper Roland called Air Canada to make sure Melissa's flight was on time and thankfully, it was. Irene asked Mom and Dad, "Do you want to go with Roland to the airport?" Dad immediately answered, "Sure, I'd like to go and keep him company." Mom said rubbing her legs, "I think I'll stay back with Irene, the cold is too hard on me." Irene gave her a sympathetic smile and said mischievously, "We'll just have to get you warmed up, somehow then, won't we." She headed for the kitchen and now curious, Mom followed her. Irene made hot chocolate and added a generous splash of Bailey's to each of their cups. Mom tasted hers and told her, "Mmm, this is really good!" Irene leaned towards her and whispered, "We can have as much as we want too, we're not going anywhere." Mom laughed and commented, "Don't you think it would be funny to see how the boys would react if the two of us were drunk when they got back here?" Irene thought that was funny too, "I can't even begin to imagine the looks on their faces if we were," she said laughing. Mom and Irene talked and drank their spiked hot chocolate until they heard the car and knew that Melissa had arrived. Irene was sorry to discover that the liquor wasn't helping at all, to calm her frayed nerves.

Roland opened the door and yelled, inside, "We're here!" Melissa was the first to enter the house. She stopped, looked around in amazement and after a few moments exclaimed, "Wow, this place is beautiful!" She elbowed Roland and told him, "I never knew you were doing this well." He laughed and teased her saying, "If you hadn't been such a stranger all this time you might've known." He was immediately sorry he'd opened his mouth. Melissa didn't say anything in reply, though; she just hugged Irene and the girls and told them, "I'm so glad to see all of you." Irene hugged her in return and motioned with her hand while saying, "Come on in," and offered, "Would you like a spiked hot chocolate, like Mom and I have?" Melissa smiled, "That sounds wonderful, thanks." They sat in the living room and talked for quite a while.

Melissa, after finishing her second hot chocolate, stood up stretching and said, "I'm exhausted from the trip, could you show me where I'll be sleeping?" Irene told her, "Of course, I'll show you." She took her upstairs and showed her the room and bathroom she'd be using and where the spare towels were kept, in case she needed more. She even made sure she had a spare blanket. She hugged her and told her, "You know, I'm glad you came." Melissa said, "Goodnight," and closed her door, she sat on the edge of the bed thinking, Irene is afraid I'll tell her dirty little secret, that's why she's treating me so nicely. She smiled to herself as she got ready for bed, it felt good to make Irene nervous for a change, after all Irene had been making her nervous since the moment she first met her, all those years ago. She knew she'd never divulge the truth about her affair to Roland; she knew he would be very hurt, if he learned his "perfect wife" had cheated on him. She knew he thought Irene was perfect, he always had. Melissa smiled a sly smile and figured there wasn't any harm in having a little fun while she was here though.   She thought, laughing to herself, I'll enjoy watching her squirm, she deserves it, she's always been such a two faced witch. Melissa couldn't figure out why her brother never saw it. She sighed, changed into her pyjamas and crawled into bed. She'd need to call Howard and the kids tomorrow morning; it was too late now with the time difference, she'd wake them if she called now. She wanted to make sure everything was okay at home and then she could really relax and have fun. She loved Roland's kids and was looking forward to seeing more of them over the next couple of days.

She was excited about seeing Alexandria again. She couldn't wait to tell Alex that it was true; her brother and Irene really did have an affair. She'd never told her before because she'd promised Irene that she wouldn't tell a soul, but if she swore Alex to secrecy she couldn't see the harm in telling her now. Alexandria had told Melissa quite a while ago about her brother, and how John had had affairs with several women, all of whom had been his customers during the time he'd worked as a salesman for the Fuller Brush Company in Regina. Melissa had asked Irene about him only because she knew that she'd had a Fuller Brush salesman named John, so she decided to tell her about the affairs John was having and in fun asked her after if she was one of these many women. She'd never dreamed it might be true, she'd only meant to tease Irene that day. She still remembered the look on Irene's face, when she'd mentioned his name and told her about him, she'd become nervous and had actually been afraid. Melissa had realized then that she was guilty and that she'd had an affair with John.   She hadn't even tried to deny it, Melissa thought, she'd just shot back at her, almost in tears with, "Roland had an affair too, you know, with his secretary from the office!" Melissa wondered now, if that might have actually been true, at the time she'd dismissed it because she thought Irene was only trying to justify her own infidelity. Melissa fell asleep wondering if Roland and Irene's marriage was as happy as everyone thought or were they simply pretending that it was.

The next morning Irene was the first one up. She quickly washed, dressed, and went downstairs to start the coffee and make breakfast for everyone. She tiptoed past everyone's bedroom doors and continued down the stairs. Once in the kitchen she started a pot of coffee and sat down at the table to think. She'd slept badly and couldn't wait for Melissa to leave. As the percolator was finishing, Irene set out the cups with the cream and sugar, she starting making pancakes for the kids and putting them in the oven to keep warm until they came downstairs. She plugged in the toaster and set the table. She decided she'd make bacon and eggs as well, once everyone was up. She sat down with a cup of coffee and was just getting involved in a story in the morning paper, when she heard someone coming down the stairs.

She laid the paper down on the table and waited to see which one of her children would appear. When Melissa casually strolled into the kitchen, Irene was startled to see her. She smiled and offered cheerily, "Good morning, you're up early. Would you like a cup of coffee?" Melissa told her, waving her back into her seat, "Don't get up, I can manage." Irene watched her pour her coffee and asked, "Did you sleep well?" Melissa said, smiling, as she walked over to the table, "I guess I was tired, I fell asleep as soon as I lay down." They sat at the table together in silence for a few minutes before Melissa asked, "Irene, could I ask you a rather personal question?" Puzzled, Irene said, "Yes," a little reluctantly. Melissa sighed and asked, quietly, "Did Roland really have an affair with his secretary?" Irene was surprised by the question, she'd braced herself expecting a different question altogether, she nodded and whispered, "Yes, but..." she paused and reminded Melissa, "Roland would be crushed if he knew his little sister knew about it." Melissa said, "Yeah, I think you're right, he thinks, I think he's perfect," she said with a smile. She paused a moment and said, "I guess I should've listened to you when you said he did." Irene just looked away and told her, "We should

change the subject; there are too many ears around this house."
Melissa smiled, and said, "Hey, can I help with breakfast?" They
could hear the kids getting up upstairs. The two of them cooked
together while they each talked about their lives and their kids.

Roland finally came downstairs, he looked at the clock and
said, stretching, "I really slept in this morning," but he laughed
and said mischievously, "I'm sure it couldn't have had anything to
do with the drinks I had before bed." He suddenly noticed Irene
and Melissa were getting along quite well and sighed happily, he
was pleased; he thought this was a long time coming. They'd
made a huge breakfast and Roland was hungry, he sat down as
Melissa put a plate full of eggs and bacon in front of him. She
was still making toast and told him, "It'll only be a few more
minutes and your toast will be ready, too." Roland commented,
as he began eating, "It's a good thing Mom and Dad's flight isn't
leaving until this afternoon it gives them more time to visit with
all of us."

The three days Melissa spent with them were actually fun,
Irene had to admit. She was still happy though, to see her with
her coat on and her packed suitcase beside her in their front
entryway. She was worn out with worry and thought; thank
goodness, I got through it. Melissa said her goodbyes giving out
hugs and kisses and thanked Irene once again before she left.
Roland was taking her over to her friend Alex's brother's place.
She was going to be staying with them for the remainder of her
vacation in Edmonton. She asked Roland, once they were in the
car, "Would you mind if I brought Alex over to see you guys and
meet the girls one evening?" Roland told her, "You know you're
welcome anytime and so is Alex." Melissa said, "Thanks, I forgot
to mention it to Irene though." Roland assured her, "She'll be
pleased to see the two of you." Melissa had to wonder about that,
but she was determined to come over with Alex anyway.

Roland mentioned Melissa had asked him if they would
mind her visiting with Alexandria, as he climbed into bed that

night. Irene said with a frustrated sigh, "I guess we won't be able
to stop her." Roland sat up and looked at her, bewildered and
said, "I thought you'd enjoy their company." Irene replied, "Oh
don't worry, of course I will, but I have to admit I'm getting tired
of having a house full." She said, sighing, "It's hard having this
many adults in the house, I have to cook quite a bit more and
plan more elaborate meals, when we have company." Roland
was satisfied with that explanation and laid down again. He
snuggled close to her saying, "Don't fuss too much, they won't
care if the dinner is simple, they just want to visit with us."
Irene just told him, quickly, "I'm tired and rolled over." Roland
felt hurt, but decided that she probably was tired. He would see
how she felt after everyone had gone back to Sarnia. She might
be more willing to make love then. It was only a few more days,
he thought as he rolled over, himself.

Roland had answered the phone on his way into the kitchen
for dinner. It was Melissa, she was asking him, "Would it be okay
if Alex and I come out to dinner tomorrow night?" Roland told
her, "No problem, we'd been wondering why you hadn't called
sooner." Melissa said, "Sorry, we've been busy catching up and
shopping." Roland laughed and arranged a time to pick them
up and hung up the phone. He sat down at the table and told
Irene what had transpired on the phone. Irene sighed heavily
and asked, "What should I make for dinner?" Roland replied,
"Anything that's easy, Melissa's not picky and if Alexandria is,
well then that's her problem." The kids thought that was funny.
Brooke asked her, enthusiastically, "Can you make spaghetti
and meatballs?" Irene smiled at her and thought about it, for
a moment, then said, nodding at her, "That's a very good idea,
thank you, we'll have spaghetti and meatballs and a salad and
I'll make a pie for dessert." She smiled at Brooke, and then asked
Roland, "Would you get me some apples from the store in the
morning?" She added, "Buy a stick of French bread as well."
Roland saluted her and answered, "Yes ma'am." The kids thought

that was funny too. Irene laughed and rolled her eyes. She asked him, "What time are they coming over, anyway?" He answered, "I told them I'd pick them up at four o'clock."

Dawn helped peel the apples for the pies and Susan was busy tearing lettuce for the salad. She'd washed it and was making sure it was in manageable bite sized pieces, just the way her Mom wanted it. She said proudly, "I'm going to add celery and tomatoes, as well." Irene was rolling pastry, she'd already made the meatballs and the sauce, and it was simmering on the stove. She was going to add the meatballs to the sauce as soon as they were cooked through, she checked them once again. She wanted them to add flavour to the sauce so she needed to make sure they were done so they'd have plenty of time to simmer gently with the sauce.

Roland walked into the kitchen, the only one who wasn't working was Brooke, she was sitting at the table making cookies, as she called them, with leftover pie dough, she was using the rolling pin from her new baking set that she'd gotten for Christmas. Irene was fluting the piecrust before putting the pies in the oven. Roland told them, "Things smell awfully good in here." Irene offered her cheek for him to kiss; he was leaving to pick up Melissa and Alexandria. He asked, "Is there anything else you need at the store?" She looked thoughtful and told him, "I think I have everything I need, thanks," then added, "I hope." He smiled at her and shook his head, she was always forgetting things and he was forever making trips to the store. He thought that was a small price to pay, she was a wonderful cook and a terrific hostess and she always made their guests feel welcome.

Roland showed up with Melissa and Alexandria around four thirty that afternoon. Irene and the kids had the table set and everything was ready for dinner. The pies were cooling on the windowsill above the kitchen sink. Everything smelled wonderful and Irene had to admit it looked pretty good too. She made her way to the door just in time to see Alexandria gasp.

Irene followed Alexandria's line of sight and realized she was looking at Susan. Irene looked panic stricken, Melissa noticed and said to Alexandria, a little too cheerily, "I told you they were gorgeous kids." Alexandria seemed to compose herself and answered, "Yes, but I still can't believe how gorgeous they are and this house is just beautiful." Alexandria handed Irene a beautiful bouquet of flowers, "For the hostess," she said. Irene passed them over to Susan telling her, "Please put these in some water." She then took their coats and said, "Thank you," to Alexandria, "The flowers are gorgeous, but you didn't have to bring anything." She added, "Please come in and make yourselves at home." She turned and asked Alexandria, "What would you like to drink?" as she mindlessly named off a few choices. She told Irene, "Please call me Alex," and said smiling, "Oh, a martini would be lovely, but only if you're making one for yourself and Melissa."

Roland came in from outside and announced, "I shovelled that walk again!" He was talking about the snow never stopping, when Irene interrupted him with, "Sorry dear, but would you mind making martini's for all of us?" He answered, "Coming right up," and hurried to the kitchen to get started, while Irene set out bowls of nuts and pretzels and put the flowers in water, Susan had put them in a vase, but had neglected to fill it with water. She couldn't help but notice Alex was staring at Susan again, Irene was growing more nervous by the second. She'd always known that Susan, resembled, Alex's brother, John but since none of her kids looked much like either of them anyway, she really hadn't worried too much about it or at least she'd tried not to worry about it. Now that this woman, Alex, was here and obviously noticed the resemblance, she knew that everything could very possibly change. It seemed the older Susan became, the stronger the resemblance became. Irene wasn't sure how Roland would react. He'd had an affair himself, but she knew that this wouldn't be so much the affair that would be the problem, although that would be bad enough, it would be the fact that she'd never told him, not even when she'd had the perfect opportunity all those years ago, but instead she'd always played the wounded party. Moreover, she had always held his affair over his head whenever they'd had any arguments she'd used it repeatedly to get what she wanted. She thought with remorse, it's quite possible that he might not forgive me if he finds out. She knew that since he was Catholic, he would most likely never divorce her though and that gave her some consolation. She also knew that if he found out he would have the perfect reason never to speak to her again. She also knew Roland believed that once a couple was married, they were married for life, no matter what happened, but she wasn't naïve enough to believe he would behave as if nothing happened, it was very possible that he might even leave her. She closed her eyes and offered a silent prayer that he'd never find out and then she'd never have to worry.

Irene noticed Susan get up and walk towards the kitchen, she said on her way out, "I'm going to help Dad bring in the drinks." Susan walked into the kitchen and asked, "Dad, can I help you?" Roland looked at her and replied, "Sure, but I thought you were playing your new game with Dawn?" Susan said, with a shrug, "We were playing, but since Melissa and Alexandria came over, I kind of feel uncomfortable." Roland looked surprised; he frowned and asked her, "Why?" Susan said shyly, "Alexandria keeps starring at me." Roland chuckled and asked her, "Do you think maybe you're imagining that?" Susan told him, "No, because Dawn saw it too! Dawn even said that when she first walked into the house she heard her gasp, when she looked at me." Roland touched her nose affectionately and told her, "Don't worry so much, your a beautiful girl and maybe Alexandria is noticing just that," he added, with a grin, "Who knows, maybe she's a little jealous because she isn't as pretty as you are." He winked at her and gave her a couple of drinks to carry. When he saw that her serious face hadn't changed, he assured her, "I'll keep an eye on things, though, just to be sure."

The two of them carried the drinks out to the living room. The conversation kept going for about an hour and Roland had to admit he did notice that Alex was looking at Susan quite a bit; the child wasn't imagining it. He thought maybe he'd ask Melissa later, if she knew what it was all about, if she'd even noticed.

Dinner was excellent as usual, every one had eaten their fill, and in some cases more than that, Roland thought as he finished his second piece of pie. He said, while rolling his eyes in a mock faint, "I'm stuffed," and offered, "Can I help tidy up?" Irene shook her head and sent him out of the kitchen with the kids following him. She said, "I have more than enough help tonight." She let the kids go off to play, while she, Melissa and Alex did the dishes.

Alex said rather quietly, "Susan is a beautiful girl." Irene braced for more, but Alex said nothing more and let the subject drop. Irene after an awkward moment asked, "What have you two got planned for tomorrow?" Alex told her, "We were thinking we might go to a show and then out to that new restaurant by the airport. Would you like to come?" Irene said, "Thanks, but maybe another time, I've some housework to catch up on and I promised to help my neighbour get ready for her annual New Years party." Irene told them, "I offered to make some appetizers and a salad as well as a few deserts and if that isn't enough, I'm also going to help with some of the decorating. From what I understand most of the neighbourhood attends this party." She continued, "It'll give Roland and I the opportunity to meet some more of our neighbours, we really like the ones we've met so far." She told them, "In the summer, I hope to host our first party; I want it to be a barbeque, so we can be out in the yard." Melissa looked out the window and said in fun, "In the mud?" as she looked outside in the backyard. Irene smiled and said, "Well, I'm hoping your brother will have the deck, off the family room, built by then." They laughed when Irene told them, "It's a little "iffy" since he works so much, he may never have the time to build it." Melissa told her in fun, "You shouldn't complain, he's a hard worker and wants to make sure his family is well looked after." Irene told her, with a smile, "Don't you worry; I do know it and I really do consider myself extremely lucky."

They took their coffee out to the living room after they finished the dishes and talked a little more. Melissa suddenly giggled and stood walking over toward Roland's chair and asked loudly, "Roland, are you ready to take us back now?" Roland had been dozing off and on and she'd startled him with her question and he jumped, telling her, "You little brat." That started Melissa laughing, she said, "Come on big brother, lets go, then you can go to bed and really sleep, when you get back." She and Alex thanked Irene for her hospitality and the wonderful dinner she'd prepared and left with Roland.

Irene let out a huge sigh as she closed the door. Susan who was in the living room overheard her and asked, "What's wrong, Mom?" Irene told her, "Oh, nothing much, I'm just tired." Susan said, "I'm glad they're gone." Irene studied her, frowning; she asked "Why?" Susan told her, "That lady, Alex was starring at me." Irene dismissed her, shaking her head and saying, "You probably just thought she was." Susan interjected, "No, Dad saw it too, I'm not imagining anything!" Irene was becoming a little nervous, she had no idea that Susan had noticed anything and she was definitely not aware she'd discussed the situation with her Dad. She changed the subject quickly, asking her, "Did you like the pies? We work pretty well as a team, don't you think?" Susan smiled and answered, "Yeah, we do, I think Alex and Melissa liked them too." Susan continued tidying up her game and Irene sat back and relaxed as best she could with everything that was playing on her mind.

The kids were upstairs when Roland returned home from taking Melissa and Alex back to Alex's brother's place. He came in the front door and noticed Irene was sitting on the couch in the living room, she hadn't bothered to turn any lights on. He said, "Hey, what are you sitting in the dark for?" She told him,

"I was looking out the front window, watching for you, it's easier to see outside when it's dark if the lights in here are off." He nodded and replied, "Yeah, I guess it is." He walked in, sat down beside her, and told her, "I had a pretty good day. Did you?" She said, "Yeah, I did, but I'm so tired, I'm glad we're not expecting anymore company overnight for a while." He laughed and then his voice grew serious and he said, "I know it's a lot of extra work for you." She replied, "I really don't mind, you know, I just need a bit of a breather in between."

They sat and talked for a while, about the kids and his work schedule, he told her, "There's a special project, I've been working on and I may need to go back to Sarnia for few days." She said, "Okay, I'll help you get things ready for your trip, when are you going?" He replied, "I'm not too sure myself, but I'll find out this week sometime, if in fact it will be necessary for me to make the trip to complete this project." He said, "By the way, Susan told me Alex was starring at her today." Irene said trying to feign laughter, "Yes, she told me the same thing, I told her it might just be her imagination." Roland said, "I'd originally told her the same thing but then I started watching Alex myself and I was rather surprised to find out Susan was right." Irene was startled by that statement, he noticed how she'd reacted, it wasn't just surprise, it was fear. Totally bewildered by her reaction, he thought, what could she possibly be afraid of. He decided since she was tired he would let it go for now. He thought he'd ask her later and if he didn't get anywhere with her he'd ask Melissa if she'd noticed and if she had, he'd ask her if she knew what it was all about.

Irene stood up from the couch, yawning and announced, "I'm tired," she turned to Roland and asked, "Are you tired too?" When he replied, "I am a little, but I have some reading to do. I brought some papers home from the office the other day and I have to get to them." She kissed his cheek, said, "Don't stay up too late," and went off to bed.

Roland began reading but found he couldn't concentrate, his mind just kept coming back to Irene's reaction, when he told her he'd also noticed Alex starring at Susan and that Susan hadn't been imagining it. He just couldn't figure out why she would be startled by that. What could be bothering her about it? He decided he was going to find out. He would start by taking Melissa out for lunch when he was in Sarnia and see if she knew anything. He didn't think he'd get anywhere asking Irene about it. He knew her well enough to know she'd only deny being afraid and dismiss the whole thing. In the event Melissa couldn't shed any light on his concerns, he thought he might have to ask Alex herself, once he returned to Edmonton.

thirty

ANOTHER DISASTER

Irene was busy washing and ironing the clothes that Roland would need for his upcoming business trip, he was going to be leaving the day after tomorrow. She was somewhat glad he was leaving this time, she needed time to think. The encounter with Alexandria had been entirely unnerving for her. She knew both Alex and Melissa thought Susan was John's child and she knew if she were to be completely honest with herself, she would have to admit she thought so too. She'd known for years now, but she'd only allowed herself to think in terms of, "she could also be Roland's" who was she kidding, she could see for herself that Susan was the spitting image of John. "I'm going to drive myself crazy," Irene said aloud and thought I must find a way to be absolutely certain. She recalled a magazine article she'd read not too long ago about a blood test that confirmed paternity, she'd have to ask her doctor about it and see if she would agree to perform the test. She thought shaking her head, I'll have to come up with a reason to tell Susan, she knew the child would ask why she needed to have a blood test and she would need to tell her something that not only she would accept but Roland as well. She would have to discuss this whole uncomfortable issue with the doctor, she knew she was going to feel totally humiliated doing that but hopefully, the doctor would be able to help her get to the bottom of this, once and for all. One way or an other she knew she needed to know before it drove her absolutely crazy.

Irene sat in the waiting room at the doctor's office, becoming more nervous by the minute. She hated to tell this woman her secret, but she felt she didn't have any choice. She was so ashamed of herself, she was sure she'd turn a thousand shades of red just telling her this embarrassing part of her past. The nurse called her name and Irene jumped, she looked around and it seemed everyone was looking at her. She had to remind herself that no one knew her secret; she smiled and said as lightly as she could muster, "Goodness you startled me," and followed the nurse down the short hallway and into the doctor's office. She'd told the receptionist when she'd originally made the appointment that she only wanted to talk, to Dr. Tonn, so consequently she was taken directly to her office and not to an examining room. Irene was grateful for the subdued lighting in the office; she would have felt so much more exposed in the bright lights of the examining room.

Dr. Tonn entered and greeted Irene warmly saying, "Hi, how are you? It's been a while." She sat down behind her desk and asked, "What can I do for you today?" Irene's first thought was to flee but instead she stammered, took a deep breath and finally said, clearly, "I have to talk to you about something very embarrassing and I need to be sure it will be kept confidential." Dr. Tonn leaned her head to the side slightly while she looked at her and told her, "Don't worry, I wouldn't dream of telling anyone anything we discuss." She noticed Irene squirming a little and added, putting down her pen, "I won't even make any notes if it will help you to relax and feel more comfortable." Irene felt a little better knowing that there would be no written record of what she was going to say and told her all the sorted details as briefly as she could. She finally said, "I need to know for sure if Roland is her father or not." Dr. Tonn just nodded and Irene asked her, "How will you determine it?" Dr. Tonn smiled and replied, "Try not to worry, it's really not a difficult test, I'll need to order a blood sample to be drawn from Susan and also one from Roland." Irene reminded her, "Your partner Dr. Laurel is Roland's doctor and he's been for many blood tests in the past so the results should be here in this office." Dr. Tonn smiled shaking her head and explained, "We'll need a sample for this particular test, so any previous tests would be of no help for this situation." Irene thought a moment and told her, "Roland was just in for his annual physical a few days ago and he still hasn't gotten the blood work done yet, he's planning to do it, either tonight or tomorrow night. I know he wants to get it done before he leaves on his business trip." She added, her voice full of hope, "Could this test be added to the usual tests, without him knowing about it?" Dr. Tonn said thoughtfully, "I could speak with Dr. Laurel, if that's okay with you, and ask him if he would call the lab and order that another vial of blood be drawn from Roland for this test. I'm going to ask if he would do this as a favour and not disclose it to Roland, but please understand this is not something we should be doing, but I'm sure Dr. Laurel will make an exception, as I have in this case. She continued, "When the lab draws blood from Susan, they will already have Roland's and then they can perform the paternity test, immediately." She assured Irene, "It can be done provided Dr. Laurel agrees and calls the lab to order the test, I will have to explain why to Dr. Laurel though. Are you okay with that?" Irene said, breathing a sigh of relief, "Yes, Okay. How should I explain to Susan why she needs a blood test?" Dr. Tonn thought about it a moment and told her, "Say that my office called and asked for it. You can tell her the last blood test we did to check for anaemia was borderline," she reminded Irene, "It actually was, remember?" Irene nodded, listening intently and the doctor continued, "We wanted to do another test, a few months later, to make sure that her blood count hadn't slipped further, it's a little earlier than I'd planned to retest, but we'll check it anyway at the same time we do the paternity test." Irene smiled a strained smile and the doctor noticing, told her, "I know it's hard but try not to worry, I'll do my best to help you." Irene stood saying, "Thank you, so much." Dr. Tonn smiled and said, "Hold on, don't leave yet, I need to give you a requisition form," and as she filled in the form, she said, "Just take her to the same lab you took her to the last time. I'll call you if there's a problem with Dr. Laurel, but I'm not expecting one, especially once he's made aware of the circumstances."

Irene breathed a huge sigh of relief as she left the office with the requisition in her hand. She got into the car and started sobbing. She couldn't believe she was finally going to find out for sure. She had no idea what she was going to do if John actually turned out to be the father.

Roland was getting ready to leave for work the next morning and Irene casually asked him, "Did you go for your blood work yet?" He stopped what he was doing and said, "I'm surprised you remembered, but yes, I did run into the lab on my way home from work, yesterday." Irene said evenly, "I was just making sure, because I knew you wanted to get it done before you left tomorrow."

She left the bedroom and walked down the stairs to get breakfast ready. Roland finished dressing and bounded down the stairs, half way down he ran into Susan who was on her way up, she was sulking. He asked her, "Why the long face?" She said with a pout, "I have to get a blood test and I hate having to do that." He smiled and told her, "Oh, that's nothing to worry about, I just had one yesterday and it was over so fast I barely noticed." She just looked at him in disbelief and continued up the stairs. When he walked into the kitchen, he said to Irene, "You didn't tell me Susan has to have a blood test done." Irene told him with a wave of her hand, "The doctor's office called and wanted her to have one since she was borderline anaemic last time, and they just want to make sure it hasn't slipped any lower, it's just routine." Roland shrugged and sat down to eat his cereal and drink his coffee. Irene breathed easier; she was making progress and she thought she was managing to avoid suspicion, as well, which was good.

The kids left for school and on their way out the door, Irene reminded Dawn, "Remember, make sure you walk home with Brooke today, you'll be babysitting her while I take Susan for her blood test, so don't forget your key." Dawn rolled her eyes and told her, impatiently, "Mom you don't need to tell me again, I know I'll be babysitting Brooke." She added, "How long will you be, anyway?" Irene told her, "We shouldn't be too long, and by the way, don't roll your eyes at me." Dawn answered, "Sorry," and managed to look apologetic.

Irene was waiting at the curb, later that day, when school let out. She was watching for Susan, just in case she'd forgotten. She sat there shaking her head thinking, when she didn't see her right away; hopefully she hasn't forgotten and gone off to one of her friends houses. She thought, Susan is such a forgetful child. Irene wanted to get this over and done with. She sat drumming her fingernails on the steering wheel and glanced at her watch, they only had half an hour to get to the lab before it closed for the day. She finally noticed Susan coming down the steps talking with her friends; she called out the car window, "Susan you need to hurry up!" Susan looked up and shook her head; she turned to her friends to say good-bye and ran over to the car. She opened the back door, threw her books on the seat, and slammed the door. She opened the front passenger door, climbed in, and slammed it too. Irene was glaring at her, and trying not to sound too harsh, said, "Please do not slam the car doors!" Susan said, crossing her arms over her chest, "I didn't mean to, but I want to go to my friend's house today, I don't want to go for a stupid blood test." Irene sighed and told her, "It'll only take a few minutes and then we'll drive over to Safeway and you can pick out the kind of bread you want to have with supper," she added "And you can even choose some ice cream for dessert." Susan brightened up a bit and the ride became a little more pleasant. Susan was a difficult child and Irene had trouble getting along with her. She couldn't quite figure out why, but she'd never felt quite the same about Susan as she did for the rest of her children.

Irene held Susan's hand during the whole ordeal of "blood letting" as Susan called it. She had to smile, they only took two vials from her arm, but to Susan, it was a "bucket full." They left the lab and Irene thought to herself, "Please let the results be what I want to hear." Susan was asking her, "What will happen if I don't have good results on my blood test?" Irene told her, "Oh, don't worry, Dr. Tonn thinks you're most likely fine." She added to make her feel better, "It's the doctor's job to make sure you're healthy." Irene hoped that she'd reassured her, Susan was only young, but she was already showing signs of being a hypochondriac and Irene didn't feel like dealing with her antics today.

A few days passed and when Irene spoke to Roland on the phone, he asked, "Did Susan's blood test come back yet?" Irene told him, trying not to let the strain show in her voice, "I haven't heard anything," she quickly added, "But your own doctor hasn't called either, so I'm pretty sure you're both okay." Roland replied, "Yeah, they do only seem to call if there's a problem." He said, changing the subject, "Oh yeah, I took Melissa out to lunch today." Irene drew in a breath and immediately covered her mouth with her hand; she hoped Roland hadn't heard her. He did though, because he asked her, "What was that for?" She paused a moment thinking then said, "I'm sewing and just picked myself with the needle." She made a few "Ow" sounds to add credibility to her story and said, "There I just put it down, now what did you say?" He repeated, "I took Melissa out to lunch." Irene asked him, as cheerily as she could manage, "Did you two have a good time?" Roland waited a little too long in answering and Irene held her breath. She was terrified Melissa might have told him something. Roland simply said, "Yes, we did have a good time, we talked for quite a while." Irene waited to see what else he would say but all of a sudden he said, "I have to go but I'll tell you all about it when I get home, love you." Irene answered without thinking, "Love you too," and hung up the phone feeling sick, she wasn't sure what to think. Her first thought was to call Melissa, but as she reached for the phone, she stopped herself, thinking if Melissa did tell Roland anything, she'd be sure to tell him as well, that I called and asked her about it. She thought she better just wait it out. She knew she wouldn't be getting much sleep for the next few days, anyways, maybe even longer, depending on what Roland had to say when he came home.

The next day, early in the afternoon, Dr. Tonn called, Irene had just arrived home from the grocery store when the phone rang. She'd hurried as fast as she could to the phone on the hall table. Dr. Tonn sounded serious; she asked Irene, as soon as she'd said, hello, "How soon can you get to my office?" Irene said breathlessly, "I could be there in about twenty minutes." Dr. Tonn told her, before hanging up, "Okay, I'll be waiting for you."

It was Wednesday and Irene knew she only worked half days on Wednesdays, which was making her even more afraid of what she would tell her. She hurried and put the items in the fridge that had to be refrigerated and left all the other groceries sitting on the kitchen table, still in the bags and ran out the door. As she drove, she was certain she would have an accident, she was having such difficulty concentrating on her driving, she was so frightened of what Dr. Tonn would say.

When she arrived at the doctor's office, she pulled into the first parking spot she saw and dashed across the sidewalk to the door. Dr. Tonn, as promised, was waiting for her; she unlocked the door to the office and let Irene in. Irene said nervously, "Thank you for seeing me, I know you're finished for the day today." Dr. Tonn didn't say anything in reply, as she led her back to her office and motioned for Irene to have a seat. She rounded her desk and sat in her chair. She opened a file and told Irene very seriously, "I have the results of the paternity test," she said, "I asked Dr. Laurel to have an extra vial of blood taken from Roland and he had obliged and called the lab." Dr. Tonn looked up at Irene and told her, "There is no easy way of telling you this." She noticed Irene's jaw drop and continued, "Roland is not Susan's father." Irene drew in a sharp breath and began shaking; Dr. Tonn came around the desk and sat on the chair beside her. She tried her best to think of something to say to make Irene feel better, but she could think of nothing, and just patted her hand in comfort. Irene asked through her sobs, "Could there be a mistake?" Dr. Tonn shook her head and said, "The results have been double checked, there's no mistake." She looked thoughtful and said again, "Roland definitely is not her father," then quickly asked, "Do you know who is?" Irene was appalled, but answered, "I've only ever been with this one man other than my husband." Dr. Tonn, noticing the shock that registered on her face simply said, "I'm sorry, I wanted to know if you knew for sure who Susan's father was, just in case because I could perform the same test on the other man as well if you weren't sure." Irene's mind was racing as she asked, "Will Susan or Roland ever have to know?" Dr. Tonn said, reassuringly, "There's no reason at the present time to tell either one of them." She added, "However, if Susan were ever to become ill it might be a different story. If she needed blood, you could help her because you are O negative and therefore a universal donor, but in the event she requires a transplant or something similar, it would be imperative for her to know about her father." She said quietly, "It's always best to know what diseases run in both a child's parents and subsequently their families." She said, "If it makes you feel better, though since she's a girl, your medical history is the most important as well as your mother's." She patted Irene's hand again and told her, "Try to come to terms with this; it's not the end of the world. Things like this happen and you'll have to try to get past it and move on."

Irene asked, without thinking, "Could this maybe be the reason I have trouble feeling the same feelings for Susan as I do for my other children?" Dr. Tonn looked at her, trying hard not to let the shock she was feeling show in her face. She averted her eyes and waited until she was sure she could speak properly and simply said, "That could be the reason, I suppose, sometimes guilt can manifest itself in ways we don't understand or are sometimes not even aware of." She wanted to shake her and tell her that this child was still hers, hadn't she looked after her all these years, she was still her mother. She wanted to scream at her, this is your fault, not Susan's, but she didn't. She simply told her, "Irene I will be here in the event you need to discuss anything further," and stood, signalling the end of their meeting, she had to get this woman out of her office before she said something she would regret. Irene rose, thanked her and left. She got into the car and drove home, she noticed she didn't really feel anything, she just felt numb, totally and completely numb.

She reached home and parked the car in the garage. She, pushed the garage remote and the door slid closed, she turned off the motor and sat there for a long time and cried; she hated herself for having that silly affair so many years ago. She thought; now I'm going have to pay the price and maybe Susan and Roland will too. Then her mind wandered and she thought, who knows what Melissa said to Roland. She thought suddenly, I'll only admit my guilt if I have no other choice.

She got out of the car and walked into the house. She decided with a shake of her head to put the whole incident out of her mind, telling herself, there's nothing I can do about it now anyway. She started humming as she put away the groceries she'd left on the kitchen table. She got out the pork chops she'd put in the fridge before she left. She was going to make them for dinner with scalloped potatoes. She knew the kids liked beans in tomato sauce with pork and thought she'd make a salad as well. She looked at the clock, it was only three o'clock, she mused aloud, "I'll make a chocolate cake for dessert, and the kids will be pleased, they love cake."

By the time all the kids were in bed that night Irene was completely calm. She'd concluded, that if Roland had found out, well so be it. He'd had an affair himself, years ago, so she expected that he of all people should understand. She went to bed feeling much better and was actually able to fall asleep quite quickly.

Irene was cleaning up the kitchen after breakfast, when Roland arrived home. She was surprised to see him so early and asked, "What time did your flight leave Toronto?" She knew he'd flown from Sarnia to Toronto and then took a non-stop flight to Edmonton. He told her, "I've been up most of the night travelling or waiting for taxies." She gave him a little push, in the direction of the stairs, telling him, "Go up and have a nap, I'll help you unpack later." Roland trudged off up the stairs, and Irene told him on the way, "At least you'll have some quiet time; it's a long time before the kids come home from school." He called back down the stairs and said, "I don't want to sleep too long or I won't be able to sleep tonight." Irene answered, "I'll wake you in a few hours." He murmured, "Thanks, make it three," and continued on upstairs to bed.

Irene sat down at the kitchen table with a cup of coffee and thought about what Roland would have to say to her, later. She wondered if Melissa had indeed told him about her affair or if she'd simply had a pleasant lunch with her brother and Roland only wanted to tell her all about it. She said aloud to herself, "I'm being silly, I'll just have to wait and find out what it is he wants to tell me." She wondered if it would really matter all that much if he knew now anyways, it wasn't as if they were ecstatically happy these days. They just might all be better off if things were out in the open, everyone except for Susan. She didn't want to tell the child that her Dad wasn't really her father. Irene gasped; she suddenly realized she'd have to tell the other girls as well. She knew she just couldn't do that, she couldn't tell them she'd cheated on their Dad. They were too young for her to tell them that their dad had cheated on her as well, years ago. The trouble was he didn't have a child from that relationship, so she knew that what she'd done would be far worse in everyone's eyes. She couldn't believe that a man could have an affair and although it wasn't considered wonderful, it certainly wasn't the end of the world but if a woman had an affair, well it was terrible and so was the woman. It should be the same for both sexes; she thought and let out a sigh. She shook her head, she knew it didn't matter what she thought, it wouldn't change anything. She was the one who was in the wrong, as far as everyone would be concerned. She would just have to do her best to make sure no one ever found out.

She tiptoed up the stairs, three hours after Roland had gone up to lie down, and eased the door open trying not to make any noise. She wanted to wake him gently, but as soon as she opened the door, he was lying on his side resting his head on his arm looking directly at her. She jumped when she saw him. He laughed and said, "What were you doing sneaking in like that?" She said with her hand on her throat, "I wanted to wake you gently; I know I hate it when I get jolted awake unexpectedly." Roland rolled over on his back and asked her, "What time is it?" She replied, "Don't worry it's still early afternoon. The kids won't be home for a couple of hours yet." Roland's eyes widened and he had a smirk on his face, he said, mischievously, "Well we have plenty of time then," and reached up and grabbed her arm and pulled her down to him. She laughed and so did he, but when they kissed and held each other their laughing ceased and their kisses became more passionate as they slowly undressed each other and made love.

They lay under the covers afterward, wondering aloud why they hardly ever made love anymore. Each seemed to be under the impression the other was upset and if that wasn't the case, there just weren't enough hours in the day. Irene turned over on her side and looked at him; she said, "Whatever the reason is it doesn't matter, I miss being close like this, the way we used to be." Roland looked into her eyes and told her, "I do too." They promised each other they'd make time for one another from now on. Roland suggested, "We should tell each other everything, even things we don't think the other wants to hear. It's better to be honest than not, don't you think so?" Irene wondered again if he knew something. She simply nodded and jumped out of bed telling him, "The kids will be home soon." She finished dressing and began to make the bed. Roland went around to the other side and starting helping her pull up the covers and place the pillows back on the bed properly. They finished and as Irene checked herself in the mirror, she said, "They should be here any minute."

They reached the bottom of the stairs, at the same moment Brooke followed by Susan burst in the side door. Brooke was complaining, and pouting, "Mom! Susan walked too fast on the way home from school and I couldn't keep up." Susan's only comment was, "You walk too slow and besides, I don't like you listening to everything my friends and I have to say." Irene looked at Roland and rolled her eyes. Susan came running around the corner and almost bumped into Roland. Her eyes lit up as she yelled, "Daddy!" Brooke came running, shouting, "Is Daddy home? Really?" Irene continued into the kitchen to start dinner leaving Roland to ask the kids about school.

Dawn came in just before dinner was ready and asked, "Mom can I go to Kathy's house to study tonight?" Irene told her, "Ask your Dad, he's in the living room with your sisters." She replied, "Okay, I didn't even know he was home."

Irene was glad to have some time to think, she was certain Roland didn't find out anything from Melissa or he would have wanted to talk to her about it, but since he wanted to make love instead, she thought he couldn't possibly known. She began thinking about what he'd said about telling each other everything though, and that statement was really nagging at her. Maybe he did know and was willing to forgive her; possibly, he just wanted her to tell him herself. She didn't have a clue and thought she'd go crazy thinking about it. She knew she would never be able to simply come out and say, Susan isn't your child, she just couldn't hurt him that way, it would tear him apart, not to mention the rest of their family as well. The other kids would be affected by it too and she knew she couldn't bear the shame if they found out.

When Roland went to back to work the next day and thought about calling Alex, he was thinking about Melissa's reaction when he'd casually mentioned that Alex had been starring at Susan throughout most of her visit when she and Melissa came for dinner. He recalled Melissa had said in an almost squeaky voice, "I hadn't noticed." At the time he'd thought, I know you well enough to recognize that voice but chose not to say anything. He wondered what she could possibly be hiding; he couldn't for the life of him figure it out. He thought she hasn't changed in all these years and a frown settled on his face as he remembered the look of shock that registered on her face, it was as if he'd slapped her or something, not just asked her a simple question. He'd been taken aback by it. Once she'd recovered sufficiently she'd only asked, "Are you sure?" He'd explained how Susan was uncomfortable and had come to ask him about it. He'd told Melissa, "I told her she was imagining it, but I started watching after that and I noticed it myself." Melissa had seemed anxious and asked, "Did Irene notice this too?" Roland recalled how when he looked at Melissa, he could see what appeared to be guilt register on her face and remembered wondering, what the heck is going on, here. She'd immediately changed the subject and talked about her kids. She'd invited him to come to dinner that night, so he could see them for himself, which he had and he'd had a wonderful time. He still wanted answers and thought maybe he should call Alexandria, but he wasn't sure if he would be making a mountain out of a molehill or not. He decided to wait a little while longer and if it was still bothering him in a few days, he'd definitely call her and talk to her, he knew it would probably be a little awkward and then thought, what if she doesn't even remember? He wondered if maybe he should just let it go, he might make a complete fool of himself if he continued. He shook his head to clear it and got to work.

thirty-one

MORE WEDDINGS

Roland and Irene were sitting in the family room watching a movie on TV when the phone rang, Irene ran to the hall table to answer it. She came back to the family room with her hand covering the phone and mouthed to Roland, "Its Jean." She listened intently and as her expression changed from one of complacency to something just short of shock, all of a sudden, said with her voice raising a notch, "Oh my God, and when are you planning that?" Roland looked up expectantly as she looked over at him and smiled, she put her hand over the phone again and told him, "Jean and Rob are getting married, this summer!" Jean lived in Toronto, not too far from Maureen and Tom and was telling her Mom that she and Rob had rented an apartment in the same building that Maureen and Tom lived in, in fact theirs was just one floor below Maureen's and the lease would start exactly one month before their wedding. Irene said, "That's really nice it will make it so much easier for us to see both of you when we come out for a visit."

Irene hated the idea of staying with the kids, but she also knew Roland would probably insist on it. He thought they could all sleep in sleeping bags on the living room floor. He told her once before when they were discussing visiting them, that they could stay with Maureen and sleep in the living room on the floor, he had added that the kids would love it. She was going to make sure they had a hotel room though, especially this time. She had a terrific excuse, she planned to tell him that they all needed to get ready for the wedding and there wouldn't be enough room or enough bathrooms in the girls' places combined. She knew Roland would understand that. She'd been so lost in her own thoughts; she hadn't heard some of what Jean was saying. She pretended they had a bad connection and asked her, "Can you repeat that, there seems to be some interference on the line." She was surprised to hear Jean say, "I'm going to be coming out for a visit next month. I need a little vacation and the dentist I work for is going to be closing the office for a week, he's going to Florida."

When Irene hung up, she told Roland about Jean's plans to have her wedding in June. They discussed it for a little while and Irene made sure he understood they would need to stay in a motel this time, which to her amazement he actually said he was okay with, without any prompting on her part. They finished watching the movie while they waited for Dawn to come home from her date. Susan was sleeping at a friends house and Brooke was already in bed, sound asleep.

The next week was a whirlwind of activity, Cassie had called and told Irene her and Gary were planning to get married that summer as well. Irene sounded panicky and asked her, "When, exactly?" Cassie took her apprehension the wrong way and started getting angry and accusing her mother, saying, "You don't like Gary, do you?" Irene told her, "Just stop it, I was only wondering because Jean and Rob are planning to get married in June." Cassie replied angrily, "Well, why didn't you just tell me that, instead of making me think the worst." Irene sighed and asked her again, "When are you planning on having your wedding?" Cassie said, "We were thinking of the end of July." Irene, enthusiastically, replied, "That sounds wonderful!" and asked, "Are you planning on having it in Winnipeg?" Cassie said, hurriedly, "Oh, no, Gary will be stationed at the base in Cold Lake, Alberta and we'll be moving there before July, so we'd like to have the wedding in Edmonton, if that's okay with you and Dad." Irene was stunned and asked her, "Are you two planning on a church wedding?" Cassie said, "Yes, we hoped so, we only want a very small reception though, mostly family, all of our friends are in Winnipeg, and we don't know anyone in Edmonton." She added, "Gary and I discussed it and decided we'd wait and have the wedding after he was settled in Cold Lake, we'll be moving in May." She asked, "By the way Mom, would you mind if I moved in with you and Dad for a couple of weeks before the wedding?" Irene told her, shaking her head, "Of course not, that will be fine."

When Irene told Roland that evening all about her conversation with Cassie, his answer was, "Wow, I guess we won't be doing much as far as vacationing goes this year. We have to pay for these two weddings." He paused and said, "I was thinking we could visit my family though, when we're in Ontario for Jean's wedding. We can drive to Sarnia the day after the wedding." Irene said, "Yes, that would be nice I think we should try to stay as long as we can." And added, "We'll have to start planning Cassie's wedding as soon as we return though." Irene gathered her thoughts and told him, "Cassie said it would only be a few people, mostly family, she told me, since their friends are mostly in Winnipeg and Regina." Irene said, suddenly frowning, "I don't even know if Maureen and Jean will be able to afford to come, since it would mean they would have to fly out here." Roland decided and shaking his head said, "Since its Cassie's second wedding, I'm not going to pay for that, if the other girls can't afford to come that's just too bad, I won't pay for their flights. These two weddings are already going to cost me enough," he reminded Irene, "As you know I had to pay for Maureen's just last year." Irene sighed and said, "I understand, the kids will just have to understand too and I'm quite sure when I explain it to them, they will."

Jean visited and brought swatches of fabric with her, she wanted Brooke as her flower girl and Dawn and Susan as bridesmaids. She wanted the colour of their gowns to match her colour scheme and said, "We have to make sure to get the colours exactly the same as the swatches." They shopped for four days straight, before finally finding not only the right colour of dresses, but the right style as well. Irene didn't want Susan to be in a dress that wasn't suitable for someone her age and most of the bridesmaids' dresses in the stores were designed for much older girls than Susan was. Thankfully they had no trouble finding a little white dress for Brooke to wear, the dressmaker who was shortening it for her had agreed to sew on little ribbons the colour of the bridesmaids dresses, she was going to give Irene some extra ribbon as well, so it could be fastened to the little basket of rose petals, Brooke was going to be carrying up the isle.

That evening at home Irene put her feet up and thought, finally, I think we have everything finished. The only thing she would have to do was have the girls satin shoes dyed to match the dresses and buy Brooke a little pair of white patent ones. She had to find a dress for herself as well and make sure Roland had a new shirt and tie that would co-ordinate with her dress; he was going to be wearing his new dark suit. She thought she could handle the rest of these things quite easily. She was glad she was finished shopping with Jean, the girl was so tiring. She knew exactly what she wanted and didn't rest until she found it.

Roland was sitting in his chair in the family room while Irene and the girls shopped for shoes, he was thinking about Alex and the fact that he needed to call her; he decided he'd do that tomorrow, from the office. Susan had reminded him again, of how Alex had stared at her all day that day. She'd made jokes about it, as she did about almost everything these days, Susan was becoming a regular clown, Roland thought with a chuckle. She could be so funny sometimes; he was constantly amused when she was around. He knew Irene was annoyed with her most times, she didn't think Susan behaved very ladylike and when he thought about it he had to agree, but he still found her to be very entertaining. Irene kept telling him not to encourage her so much by always laughing at her, but he couldn't help it, she really was quite funny.

Irene found a dress for herself in a lovely lilac colour at her favourite boutique, but she was having difficulty finding a shirt for Roland to match it. He was with her during her search and suggested, "I could wear a white shirt and then maybe we could find a tie that has the lilac colour in it, that might be easier." Sounding frustrated, Irene replied, "I only want to do that as a last resort." He hoped they'd find something soon, he was getting sick of going to all the men's stores trying to find a shirt in a colour that didn't seem to exist, he'd much rather have been home watching football on TV. They arrived home empty handed that day and Roland hoped Irene would give up and settle for the option he'd suggested of a white shirt and a lilac tie.

Irene found the perfect colour of shirt for Roland a few days later and called him at work to let him know, she said, "I've got good news, I found the perfect shirt but I'm not sure of the size, since it's a European make. Would you come home a little early, so we can make it to the store before it closes for the evening?" Roland rolled his eyes and started to object, when she pleaded with him, "I really want things to be perfect for Jean's wedding; you know how picky she is. Please, just this once, come home early and pick me up so we can make it to the store and you can try the shirt on." Roland relented sighing and told her, "All right, I'll be there as soon as I can," and hung up the phone. He sighed heavily as he picked it up again and called Alex, he told her, "I'll have to cancel our meeting, something's come up. I'll call you again to reschedule, but I have so many meetings over the next couple of weeks I'll have to call you when I can manage it." She sounded almost relieved that he couldn't make it and that started him wondering all over again. He sat there shaking his head once he'd hung up the phone thinking, that he had no idea what he would have said to her anyway. It seemed the more time passed the sillier this whole thing seemed to him, he thought I'm probably just imagining things when I think they all have weird reactions to the situation when I mention it to them. He decided to get back to work to take his mind off it.

On the plane on their way to Toronto, Roland remembered that he'd never called and rescheduled that meeting with Alex; he thought shrugging, it's probably for the best. Susan had taken to making jokes constantly about it and he thought now it was more because it annoyed her mother than because she was bothered by the incident, in fact she didn't seem to be bothered by it at all. The more he thought about, he was thankful now he'd never confronted Alex about it, after all. He knew he probably would have felt a little foolish anyway; he smiled thinking, funny how everything seemed to work out for the best

Jean's wedding was beautiful, everyone was there, even Cassie and Gary had been able to make it, they'd driven down from Winnipeg. Cassie said, happily, "We took turns driving, it was fun and it didn't really take that long at all. We wanted to visit some of our friends in Toronto anyway, before we move." The moving company had already picked up all their furniture and things. They'd been staying with Gary's brother in Winnipeg for a few days before they'd arrived in Toronto for Jean's wedding. They hadn't wanted to move to Cold Lake until after Jean's wedding, they knew Jean and Maureen probably wouldn't be able to come to their own wedding because that would mean they'd have to pay for flights to Edmonton and Cassie knew her sisters wouldn't be able to afford it. She wanted to see them, before they moved though and since Gary didn't have to report for duty in his new posting for a while yet, they'd been able to come to Jean's wedding.

Irene and Roland rented a car and along with the three

younger girls drove out to Sarnia to visit his parents. They'd been at the wedding; they'd driven up with Melissa and Howard. Roland had been shocked at how frail his Dad looked, he'd tried to talk to his Mom about him but she'd only say, "We'll have plenty of time to talk later, let's just have fun at Jean's wedding." Roland was telling Irene all about this during the car ride to Sarnia. She said, "I've been worried about him too, I saw Dad go out to the car to lie down during the reception. I found that rather unusual." She said, frowning, "Mom said much the same thing to me when I asked her if he was okay." Roland looked over at her; they shared a look that said they both knew that he was not well and Mom and Dad hadn't wanted to talk about it.

They arrived in Sarnia and pulled up in front of Mom and Dad's house and just as they were getting out of the car, Irene noticed Melissa hurrying towards them. She was crying and Irene ran to her and held her; she asked gently, "What's the matter?" Melissa managed through her sobs, "I've been waiting for you to arrive, Dad was rushed to the hospital this morning." Roland made it around the car and was now at their sides, he'd heard what she said and asked, "How is he?" Melissa said, "He isn't good, he never wanted anyone to know, Mom told me this morning in the emergency waiting room that he has lung cancer." Roland's jaw dropped and his legs felt as if they wouldn't hold him, he made it to the porch steps and leaned against the railing, he asked, "Did they say how long he has?" Melissa started crying again, she said, "Mom wouldn't talk about it anymore and just told me she didn't know. I don't think he has too long, though." She tried hard to stop crying long enough so she could speak, she finally said, "The doctor at the emergency department in the hospital told me it would be a good idea to gather the family together." Roland could feel tears welling up in his eyes. He asked Irene, "Could you ask Dawn to stay with the girls? You and I have to get to the hospital as quickly as we can."

Irene talked to Dawn and Susan, who unfortunately had

heard only snippets of the conversation, once she'd filled in the parts that they hadn't heard and answered their questions, she said, "I'm going to trust you two to talk to Brooke, and do it gently, please." Dawn said, quietly, "Mom, of course we will and I'll do my very best to explain things as gently as I can to her." Susan who was standing with a frightened look on her face simply nodded. Irene patted her head and hugged her, she said, "I'm trusting you too, you know." Susan simply nodded again.

Irene and Roland arrived at the hospital and had to wait outside Dad's room because the doctor was with him. When they were finally allowed into his room, they were not prepared for what they saw. He was hooked up to a respirator and Mom was at his side holding his hand. She looked at them with tears streaming down her cheeks, the deep pain she felt was evident, in her face; Roland was having difficulty not breaking down himself, at the sight of her. He didn't want to break down, he wanted to be strong for Mom. Irene couldn't help herself and started to cry as she held Mom's hand. She leaned over Dad and kissed his cheek, he was not awake and Irene worried that the machine might be the only thing keeping him alive.

Roland asked his Mom, "What happened?" She told them everything, she said sighing, "Dad has had cancer for quite some time, but he only found out a few months ago. The doctors told him then; he didn't have much time left." She said, holding up a hand, "Before you ask, he didn't want sympathy; he just wanted to enjoy what time he had left. He was so happy to be able to be there at Jean's wedding, he'd been so afraid that he might not make it and he didn't want to ruin her wedding day."

Roland hung his head, he went to his father's side and took his hand and told him, "I love you, Dad please try to take it easy." Dad opened his eyes, he couldn't speak because of the machine, he looked directly at Roland, sort of half nodded, and then he closed them again. Roland was afraid for a second, but was relieved when he realized Dad had simply fallen asleep, again.

He had the strangest feeling that that look Dad had just given him had been "goodbye."

That night around eleven the hospital called and told Roland, he'd passed away. Roland couldn't stop the tears that were coming in torrents; he knew he had to tell his Mom but he was afraid of what her reaction would be. He knocked softly, on her bedroom door, she answered quickly, startling him, she said, in a sad, soft voice, "Come in." When Roland opened the door, she was sitting in the chair beside the bed, fully dressed. She slowly looked up at him and said, "Its okay, I know, he's gone." Roland looked puzzled, she told him, looking at the floor, "You can't live with someone for all these years and not know, he was my life, but I didn't want him to suffer, I loved him far too much for that." Through her sobs, she said, "I had to tell the doctor, what Dad had told me, back when he was first diagnosed. Dad said then that he didn't want to be hooked up to a machine that would breathe for him or keep him alive." She continued softly, "I didn't want that for him either, but I hadn't told the doctors that yet and I was shocked to find out that they'd had to revive him yesterday. That's when they put him on that machine. When they finally let me see him again I didn't know what to do, I felt like I'd betrayed him. I hadn't been expecting him to have any trouble yesterday." She said, looking at the floor and explaining, "Of course I understood he was very ill, but he told me he felt good and he desperately wanted to go to the wedding." She took a couple of staggered breaths and told Roland, "Once I had the opportunity to explain everything that Dad wanted to the doctor. He understood about the respirator and told me he would unplug it and let him slip away, peacefully. He said he would need to get clearance from the hospital, though."

She looked so small Roland wanted to help her in anyway he could, he listened as she continued in a soft voice, "The doctor asked me if I wanted to be there when they unplugged the machine, I told him I couldn't. I was afraid that if I was there,

I might not be able to let them do it and that would have been very selfish on my part," as she spoke fresh tears rolled down her cheeks. Roland went to her and held her. He assured her, "Don't you worry Mom, you did the right thing, you did what Dad wanted." He pulled her gently to a standing position, saying, "Come on Mom, let's go out to the kitchen and I'll make you a cup of tea." She followed blindly, holding onto his hand, once they reached the kitchen, Irene was already there and she ran to Mom and took her hands in hers. Roland noticed she'd already put the kettle on the stove and she had the tea on the counter, along with a small plate of cookies. He thought she knows Mom so well, she knew she'd want to have a cup of tea; she always did when things were bothering her or she needed to think. Roland loved Irene a little more, at that moment, for being there for his mother.

The funeral was short and unbearably sad, Irene watched Roland and Mom and it broke her heart. She'd never known a family to be as close as theirs was, it was hard to imagine Mom without Dad. Melissa leaned over and whispered to them before the service began, "I'll take care of Mom, you won't have to worry." She lived only a few blocks from Mom and didn't work outside of her home. She told them, "I'll make sure to check on her every day." She continued and said, "Mom could sell her house and live with us if she wanted to, I spoke to Howard about it and he thought it was a great idea." Irene thought that was a wonderful gesture. She'd asked Mom, herself if she would consider moving to Edmonton and living with her and Roland. Mom had thanked her, but said, "I need to have my friends around me, and I want to be in familiar surroundings." She had shaken her head and added, "I just don't think I could manage such a complete change at this stage of my life." Irene had told her that she understood.

A week later, Roland, Irene, Dawn, Susan and Brooke were on the plane on their way back to Edmonton. All of them were silent, even Brooke, who was thinking about Grandma and how she was going to be lonely in her house all by herself. Irene was thinking about all that had happened in this past month and she knew Cassie's wedding was coming up as well and they'd have plenty to do to get ready for that. She wondered if Mom would feel up to coming out for a visit and attending the wedding. She turned to Roland and started to ask him and noticed he was looking at her and he'd just started to say something to her, but she hadn't heard what he'd said. They both smiled and Roland said, "You first," Irene said, smiling, "No, you can go ahead." Roland told her, "I've been thinking of asking Mom out to Cassie's wedding and asking her if she'd like to visit as well." Irene looked at him in surprise; she said, "That's exactly what I was going to ask you." They chuckled at that, it was funny that at times they seemed to think alike, it was kind of refreshing, after so many years of problems. Irene looked at Roland and smiled; he picked up her hand and gave it a gentle squeeze. They were happy together, in spite of the turmoil of the past few days.

School was finished for the year by the time they returned to Edmonton. Irene had telephoned from Sarnia, the day after Dad passed away and informed the principals of the schools the girls attended, what was happening and explained that the girls wouldn't be able to make it back before the end of the school year. She'd taken them out of school three weeks before school was to end for the year. She'd fully intended to have them back in school for the final week, but when Dad passed away, that had become an impossibility. Both principals had told her not to worry about it, they said the kids had all done well throughout the school year and they'd all be moving on to the next grade in September.

Irene now had them all at home, the only one who wouldn't be, was Dawn, she was going to be starting a job for the summer, at the Safeway in the shopping centre located right in their neighbourhood. Irene was going to have the chore of taking her to work and picking her up afterward, but she decided it was a small price to pay since Dawn would be learning valuable lessons by working. Roland thought she needed to know how hard it was to earn money; he thought Irene spoiled them far too much with the things she allowed them to buy. Irene didn't agree, she thought it was important for them to have nice clothes and things, even if they were only going to school. What would people think of her, if she didn't make sure they all had nice things? She shuddered at the thought that someone might think they were poor. Irene just couldn't bear the thought of anyone thinking anything derogatory about herself or her children.

Cassie's wedding was lovely and Mom did come out to attend it and to visit, after all. At first Mom had thought it might be too long of a trip with her arthritis, which had them worried that she might not come. Roland decided though to see what he could do and informed the airline, when he made her reservation that she had difficulty sitting for long periods of time due to arthritis and their response was terrific. They assured him they'd pass the message along and that one of the flight attendants would assist her in moving around the cabin periodically, he was thrilled and so was Mom when he told her and she'd finally agreed to come. When she arrived, she'd announced proudly, "I was treated like royalty on my flight, they were so attentive to my needs, I was amazed at how easy the flight was on my legs, compared to the last time I flew." She said, smiling, "They helped me walk up and down the aisle a couple of times and it really helped ease the pain and stiffness."

Cassie was disappointed Maureen and Jean couldn't afford to be there, but she knew they didn't have a lot of money to spare and flights were so expensive, but she hadn't given up hope that they would somehow find a way to be there. Cassie and Gary decided not to have a honeymoon, since money was a little tight for them as well. When the wedding was over Cassie hugged her Grandma and told her, "Thank you for coming, having you here meant so much to me." She hugged her Mom and Dad as well, saying, "Thank you, Dad", then looked at her Mom, and said, "Thanks for helping me plan everything, Mom." She knew that her Dad had said he wasn't going to do much since it was her second wedding and he'd already paid for her first wedding, but Cassie knew her Mom made most of the arrangements and that her Dad hadn't objected. She smiled at that thought; she knew her Mom could accomplish almost anything she set her mind to, she knew she wasn't a particularly clever woman, but she was stubborn and she knew how to manipulate people. Cassie had watched in quiet amazement, some of the things her Mom had accomplished over the years, she smiled thinking to herself, I know I've witnessed a skill in my mother, that I probably won't see in anyone else.

Mom was leaving today and Irene felt a pang of guilt and really didn't know why, she'd asked her to stay numerous times and Mom had always said the same thing, "I have my friends and my house back in Sarnia." Irene thought maybe there was something she could do or say to change her mind, but she just couldn't think of anything else and Irene knew Mom needed her friends and the familiar surroundings of her home, she remembered Mom explaining that to her when they were in Sarnia.

Brooke and Susan loved spending time with their Grandma and they were going to miss her. Dawn worked most of the time and when she wasn't working she was busy with her boyfriend Allan, but she managed to make Grandma feel special in the short time she did spend with her. Irene had been impressed watching her with her Grandma. Roland seemed happier with his Mom being there when he arrived home from work. It really was a shame that she was leaving.

They all piled into the car to take her to the airport, even Dawn came with them, she'd traded shifts with a co-worker at Safeway so she could say goodbye to her Grandma. Irene thought that was really sweet, Dawn seemed to be such a wonderful young woman, she was very thoughtful and kind.   Irene was a little worried about Susan, she was showing signs of being a little selfish and Brooke was still a child albeit, a very spoiled child, but Irene thought that was normal, since she was the baby of the family.

Grandma hugged and kissed everyone and walked slowly down the hall and through to the gate, with the help of an attendant from the airline. She probably could have managed on her own, but Roland thought, why take the chance of her falling when the airline staff is there to help. She had a cane, but she could still be unsteady sometimes and since she now had tears in her eyes, he was especially concerned and had approached the counter at the check-in with Mom and asked for someone to assist her onto the plane. They watched her disappear into the hallway on her way to board the plane and then moved to the observation deck, outside and watched her plane pull out of the gate. They waved to her; she was seated in a window seat close to the front of the plane. Roland had purchased her a first class ticket, to help ensure she'd be comfortable. She was waving frantically, as if they could have missed her when she was sitting with her face pressed up against the window. They all smiled excitedly when they saw her waving, but watched sadly, as her flight took off, and when they couldn't see the plane any longer, they slowly turned and walked back to the car.

On the way home, they chatted about how nice it would be for all of them, if she could come and live with them. Irene explained to the kids, when they asked why she couldn't live with them, "Grandma has her friends there, in Sarnia and she needs that," she added, "Imagine if you were her age and didn't have your friends and familiar surroundings, how would you feel?" They fell silent and stayed quiet the rest of the way home, Roland and Irene exchanged looks that said without words, they knew the kids understood.

thirty-two

UNEXPECTED PASSING

Roland was finishing up in a meeting, when the receptionist paged over the intercom, "Urgent call for Mr. Petersen, pick up on line one." Roland frowned looking a little worried and quickly excused himself. He hurried down the hall to his private office and took the call. He picked up the phone and was just about to answer when he heard Melissa's voice, she sounded frantic. He started shaking his head; he couldn't understand a word she said. He asked, loudly trying to be sure she would be able to hear him over her own voice, "Melissa, calm down and tell me what's wrong!" She sobbed again and clearly said, "Mom's dead!" Roland who had been standing behind his desk, sat down heavily, in his chair. His mind was racing, Melissa continued ranting uncontrollably and he still couldn't understand what she was saying, finally when she paused to take a breath, he was able to ask her, "Where are you?" Between sobs she said, "I'm at home." Roland then asked, "Is Howard there with you?" When she replied, "Yes he is," he said, "Put him on the phone." Howard came on the line saying, "Roland, I'm so sorry." Roland replied, "Thank you," and explained, "I was having trouble understanding Melissa, since she wasn't able to stop crying long enough to speak coherently." Howard told

372

him softly, hoping she wouldn't hear him, "She was the one who found her, she discovered her when she went over to check on her. She found her, in a pool of blood, on the bathroom floor. She'd apparently fallen and hit her head on the edge of the tub." Roland gasped. Howard continued, "The doctor, at the hospital said she'd died instantly. Harold continued explaining, "Melissa went into shock. The police called me at work and when I arrived at Mom's she was hysterical, a paramedic was trying to calm her down, I heard him telling her, "She's gone and has been for quite sometime." He was doing his best to explain to her that rigor mortis had already set in, and that they couldn't revive her." He continued in a soft voice that Roland had to strain to hear, "Melissa was screaming at the top of her lungs, you have to try to save her! You haven't even tried! Please!" He said, "I tried my best to comfort her but she was hysterical, the police suggested that I take her to a doctor and get some tranquilizers for her." Howard said, "I did take her, but she refused to take any of the pills until she spoke to you." Roland told him, sadly, "Tell her I'll be there, just as soon as I can, and tell her to take the damn pills!" I'll check on flights right away and hopefully I'll be there sometime tomorrow." Howard told Roland, whispering so Melissa wouldn't hear, "Melissa's blaming herself for Mom's accident; she says she should have insisted on Mom coming to live with us." Roland told him, "Yeah, I gathered as much, I'll talk to her when I get there." He asked Howard, "Could you make the arrangements to have Mom's body moved from the hospital to the funeral home?" Howard replied, "Certainly. The same one we used for Dad?" Roland told him, "Sure I think that'll be fine and thanks, tell Melissa, I'm on my way," and hung up.

He sat there feeling numb for a few minutes trying to comprehend all he'd just heard, he then picked up the phone and called Irene. He told her briefly, what had transpired and then wanted to know, "Do you want to come with me?" She said with resentment in her voice "Well yes, of course. I think that would be a good idea if I did, don't you?" Roland heard the injured tone in her voice and decided he just didn't care one way or the other, right now, if she thought he'd said the wrong thing. He hadn't meant for it to sound hurtful, he was simply giving her a choice because of the kids, couldn't she give him a break just this one time, his Mom had just died, for heaven's sake. She interrupted his thoughts with, "I'll have the neighbours on both sides of us check in on the kids while we're away." She was silent a moment and said, "I'll also talk to the kids when they get home from school and if they want someone to actually stay here with them, I'll ask my friend Karen's mother, the girls always liked the woman whenever Karen came over for coffee and brought her along, remember? She even insisted they call her Grammy." Irene was sure if they needed anyone they would want it to be her. Roland told her, quickly, "I'll make the travel arrangements; I'll see you when I get there." He couldn't bear to stay on the phone with her a second longer, listening to her babble, she hadn't even told him she was sorry, in fact she hadn't offered him any condolences at all; it was his mother for God's sake, what was wrong with her? He forced himself to put her out of his mind, asked his secretary to take care of his and Irene's airline reservations and car rental, and walked back to the boardroom to wrap up his meeting. He wanted to get home as soon as possible.

Irene hung up the phone and quickly wrote a note to the girls telling them she would be home soon and pulled on a coat, grabbed her purse and took off; she needed to find a black suit for the funeral. She knew she had one in her closet already, the one she'd worn to Dad's funeral, but she also knew everyone had all ready seen it and that would never do. She would have to find another one quickly, along with a blouse and a pair of shoes as well. She pressed the gas pedal a little harder, as she headed for her favourite ladies store, it was a little boutique-type store located in the mall, fairly close to their home. She was sure she'd find the perfect outfit there. The place even sold the accessories as well as the shoes and purses to match the lines they carried. She loved it, it was one stop shopping, a little pricey, but well worth it, the store only carried a few sizes of each item, so she was fairly certain she wouldn't see anyone else in the same outfit no matter what the occasion was.

Roland arrived home looking for Irene, Dawn told him, when he started hollering her name, "Dad, she left us a note; it says that she had to pick up a few things at the mall and will be back soon." Roland thought, that figures, she most likely thought she had to have a new outfit for the funeral. He shook his head and told Dawn, "I'm going upstairs to change." He asked her, "Do you have any plans tonight?" She looked at him funny and said, "No, why?" He replied, "Because, as soon as your mother gets home, we need to talk to you and your sisters." Dawn looked at him strangely again and asked, "Okay. Is anything wrong, Dad?" He simply told her, "Your Mom and I will talk to all of you together," and continued up the stairs. She looked puzzled but shrugged and replied, "Okay, we'll be here."

Roland was upstairs changing his clothes when Irene came running into the bedroom with her packages. She kissed him on the cheek and told him, "Sorry for being so long." She explained, "I had nothing suitable to wear for the funeral so I had run out to get a black suit." She went on to say, "I needed to have it altered a little, so I had to wait for the seamstress in the store to finish it." She told him, smiling, "Do you know the shop stayed open just for me, wasn't that nice of them?" Roland looked at her unable to believe what she was doing. He was thinking, I could use a little compassion, but all she can talk about is herself and what she bought. He said in a sad voice, "We need to talk to the kids." She replied, as if she had forgotten, "Oh yes, lets go do that," as she hung up her new suit on the door and looped her bag with the shoes and purse and accessories on the doorknob. Roland asked on his way out of the room, "What's in the bag?" She made a clucking sound with her tongue and replied rolling her eyes, as if he should've already known the answer, "The accessories I need, to wear with the suit I bought." He rolled his eyes as well and shook his head. She answered him by saying sternly, "Did you want me to show up at your mother's funeral looking like something the cat dragged in?" He told her, "That'll never happen as long as there are stores and credit cards." She just gave a disgusted click of her tongue and started down the stairs.

When they reached the bottom, the kids were already waiting for them. Dawn had told her sisters already, that Mom and Dad wanted to tell them something.

They told the kids about their Grandma's death as gently as they possibly could and they cried as Roland answered their questions the best he could without going into too much detail. He didn't want them to have nightmares, about their grandmother lying on her bathroom floor in a pool of blood, as he knew he was certainly going to. He suddenly noticed Irene looking at him holding her head slightly to the side with a puzzled expression on her face. He realized he hadn't told her the details, either, but in all fairness she hadn't allowed him the time to, she'd been too busy shopping and then babbling about what she'd bought. He figured he'd talk to her when they went upstairs to pack. Their flight was leaving at noon the next day.

Irene cried when he told her what happened to Mom, she said, "We should have insisted she move here and stay with us." He told her, "That's what Melissa is saying too." Irene looked stunned, and Roland corrected himself, he said "No, not with us." He explained, "Melissa is blaming herself and feels she should have insisted Mom sell her house and move in with her." Irene said, clucking her tongue and shaking her head, "Their home is way too small for Mom to have lived with them, ours would have been perfect." Roland went to her and held her, he told her, "You can't blame yourself either, that same accident could have just as easily happened right here in our own house." Irene said, "I know that, but maybe we could've done something to help her, one of us might have heard her fall." Roland told her, "Don't think that way, it's over now and we have to deal with it the way it is and not worry about what ifs." He looked at his watch and said, "We better get packed and you need to call your friend, Karen so she can have her mother on stand by just in case the kids do need someone to stay with them." She realized she also needed to call the neighbours on both sides to alert them that the girls would be alone in the house. She hadn't expected to be so long at the mall, and because she was she hadn't had the time to do all the things that she needed to do. Dawn thought they would be fine on their own, but she'd agreed to call Karen if anything should happen or if they needed Grammy to stay for whatever reason. Irene made sure the spare room had fresh sheets on the bed and fresh towels sitting on the dresser, just in case.

When they were on the plane that afternoon, Roland was doing his best to concentrate on the newspaper he was reading and Irene was sitting beside him with her eyes closed trying her best not to think of poor Mom lying, bleeding on the floor in her bathroom. She wondered if it was even possible for doctors to know for sure if people felt any pain at all when they, supposedly died instantly. She knew she was driving herself crazy thinking about it. She also knew that all the worrying in the world couldn't change the circumstances or bring her back. Irene thought with a sigh, she'd truly loved Mom; she was such a sweet person. She knew she was going to miss her terribly.

The plane landed and they entered the terminal, Roland left Irene to claim their bags, while he went off to the car rental booth. He was back at Irene's side before the baggage had even come down the ramp. She jumped when he suddenly appeared beside her and draped his arm around her shoulders. He said when he felt her start, "Sorry for startling you." She asked him, "How in the world did you rent a car so quickly?" He told her half smiling, "I cheated, I had my secretary make the arrangements, I just wanted to be sure the car will be ready, when we are." She smiled saying, "You're always so efficient, even when it must be difficult for you, you still manage to take control and get things done." He smiled back and said, "I'm not all that organized, I only wish I was." They heard the signal and noticed the light had begun flashing on the baggage ramp, they knew it was just a matter of minutes before their bags would be coming down the conveyer ramp. Roland leaned in to get a better view of the ramp and told Irene, "I can see them coming down the ramp now." He moved closer so he could retrieve them quickly, as soon as they reached where he was standing. Once they had their bags in tow, they walked to the rental car counter.

Roland handed his receipt over to the attendant, who read it and picked up the phone and checked with one of his coworkers, he turned back to them and announced, "The car's all ready, they're bringing it up for your inspection." Roland helped Irene inside the car as soon as it arrived and quickly completed the required inspection, making note of any scratches or damage. He signed the form, put their bags in the trunk and thanked the attendant.

They drove out of the airport, they had to find a hotel to stay in, they wanted to drop off their bags and then call Melissa. They weren't sure if Howard and Melissa would've made all the arrangements for the funeral. In the event they hadn't, they knew that they would need to take care of it as soon as they arrived in Sarnia. They found a room in the same hotel by the river where Irene had stayed when she'd come to Sarnia for her mother's funeral. Roland only realized it as they were walking down the hall on the way to their room, when Irene mentioned, "This place looks exactly the same, I stayed in this room, right here," and pointed to a door. He looked at her, wide-eyed saying, "I'm so sorry, I didn't even think that your memories might be too painful and that you might not want to stay here." Irene told him, shaking her head, "I'll be fine, it's just a hotel." They dropped their bags in the room and immediately called Melissa. Howard answered the phone and told Roland, "Melissa's finally lying down." Roland replied, "Good" and asked him, "Have any arrangements been made yet for the funeral?" Howard replied, "I'm sorry Roland, the only thing I've done so far, is arrange for Mom's body to be moved from the hospital to the funeral home, I've been so busy with Melissa." Roland asked, "Does she want to be there at the funeral home with me to help make decisions about the funeral and the casket?" Howard told him, sadly, "She said she just couldn't do it." Roland looked down and trying to keep the emotion out of his voice, told Howard, "Okay, tell her I'll do it myself and tell her not to worry, okay."

When he hung up the phone, Irene asked, "Are we going to be meeting Melissa at the funeral home or are we supposed to pick her up?" Roland reiterated what Howard had told him. She replied, frowning, "Melissa needs to be there," shaking her head, she said, "It isn't fair of her to expect that you will make all the painful arrangements. I never wanted to have to do that for my mother, but I found it actually helped me to come to terms with the fact that she was gone." Roland sighed and told her, "I agree, but Howard seems to think otherwise, he doesn't want Melissa to be any more upset than she already is."

When they arrived at the funeral home, the director was very kind, he remembered Irene from when she, along with Donna and Jake had arranged her mother's funeral. He expressed his sorrow and got right down to business he guided them through the whole process and explained everything to them. He led them down to the casket room, so they could choose one for Mom. He took notes about the insurance coverage Mom had and told Roland, "I don't want you to worry; I'll take care of making sure the insurance company receives the death certificate." He added as if it was an afterthought, "The funeral home can be paid directly by the insurance company, if you'd prefer that. I'll only need you to sign a few papers giving them express permission to that effect." He led them back to the office and Roland signed all the necessary paperwork. He already knew Mom's financial affairs, she'd always made certain he was aware of her personal finances and she'd also made sure that he knew where her personal papers were kept. She'd even named him executor of her estate. She didn't have much, but she'd wanted things to be taken care of properly when the time came.

The funeral was a beautiful service, it was held in the quaint little chapel inside the funeral home. Roland had run an ad in the Obituary Column of the Sarnia Observer newspaper to notify people of Mom's passing and all Mom's friends and acquaintances attended. Even neighbours from all over her neighbourhood were there. Roland had been surprised at how many people Mom had actually known. She'd been quite active in the community, she'd volunteered at the hospital and she'd helped run the city food bank, she had even helped cook meals for the homeless at the shelter downtown. Roland was astonished at how much charity work she had actually been involved in, even with her arthritis as bad as it was, she had still managed to help so many people, he was in awe.

Once the service was over they proceeded to the cemetery, she was laid to rest next to Dad. Roland hadn't realized that she'd purchased the plot next to Dad's with some of the insurance money from a policy Dad had taken out for her, Mom had mentioned she might, but she'd never said she actually had bought it. He lifted his head and looked around at the many people standing around the grave and thought, noticing how many were openly weeping, Mom is certainly going to be missed by a great number people.

After the service at the cemetery, everyone was invited back to the church hall for refreshments. Roland was talking to as many people as he possibly could; he was doing his best to personally thank everyone for coming. One of Mom's best friends told him tearfully, "Your Mom was the kindest person I've ever met." Roland had been doing so well, but after that comment, he was having a tremendous amount of trouble keeping himself together, so much so that he finally had to leave and take a walk outside in the fresh air for a while. He was wondering as he walked, how you could know someone your whole life and still not really know them. He had no idea his Mom had done all the things these people were telling him she'd done. He began to feel guilty; he hadn't made any effort to really talk with his mother in a long time.

Irene appeared on the steps just as he was coming up the walk. She asked, "Where have you been, I've been looking for you?" He explained, "I needed some air." He looked at her, thought for a moment, and then asked, "Were you aware of all the things Mom was doing for the community?" Irene shrugged and said, "I only knew about her volunteering at the hospital." She said, "I was just as shocked to hear about the other things as you were. We took for granted that she didn't do too much, because of her arthritis, but boy, were we wrong." Roland smiled at her and took her hand and together they walked back into the hall to say goodbye to everyone, it was time to leave.

Melissa was getting a little better at holding back the tears, at least for a few minutes at a time. She said over her shoulder, as she walked away to say goodbye to another friend of Mom's, "I didn't want to appear like I was a zombie, so I didn't taken any pills today." Howard who was standing behind Roland said, shaking his head, "Her doctor assured her they wouldn't do that but you know Melissa. She said she wasn't going to take any chances."

Irene and Roland visited with Melissa and her family the next day and Melissa was almost herself, she was taking the pills the doctor had prescribed and true to his word, they didn't turn her into a zombie.

The following day after a brief stop at the cemetery, they drove back to the Airport to catch their flight home. They were rather quiet and subdued for most of the trip. They both felt they were all each other had now. Irene said almost dreamily, "It's funny, even though we have siblings, once our parents are gone, we feel like we're all alone in the world." Roland looked at her and nodded; he took her hand and held it for the rest of the flight.

The kids had so many questions when they returned. Dawn announced as soon as they walked in the door, "I allowed Brooke to stay up so she could see you, she's excited and she wants to know about the funeral, too." Irene and Roland sat down with them and answered all their questions, once the kids had exhausted the subject and ran out of questions, they tucked Brooke and Susan into bed. Dawn came downstairs with them and filled them in on how good both Susan and Brooke had been, she said, "I didn't have any problems at all, not with either one of them." She told them about the meals she'd prepared and when she finished Irene gave her a big hug and told her, "We really appreciate all that you did."

Dawn went upstairs to bed and Roland and Irene collapsed on the couch in the living room with martinis that Roland had made them. He said holding Irene's out to her, "I thought we could use these." Irene agreed wholeheartedly, taking hers from him saying, "Yes, thank you, we really do need them." They talked for a long time before heading up to bed themselves. They were beginning to feel close to each other again and it felt wonderful to both of them. They'd been at odds with each other off and on for so many years. It was nice to finally be close again.

thirty-three

ANOTHER HURDLE

Melissa's call came late one Thursday night, when Irene and Roland were just climbing into bed after a long day. Roland had had a tough day at the office, Irene had attended school meetings that had lasted until late into the evening, and both of them were bone tired. Roland picked up the phone beside the bed and before he even finished saying hello, Melissa started rambling, the only thing he could understand was, "I'll be out on the first flight in the morning." Irene could hear Roland say, "You're welcome to stay here anytime you want." He quickly added, frowning, "Is there something wrong though or will this just be a visit?" Melissa explained, "You remember my best friend Alex?" She didn't stop to wait for his answer, she continued in her usual babbling tone of voice, that happened whenever she was excited or upset about something, "Well, her brother, John, was killed by a drunk driver, last night." Roland sat up straighter and said, "Oh my God, I'm sorry to hear that." Irene, who'd been lying down looking up at him, bolted upright when she heard that statement, she tugged on his arm and mouthed, "What's wrong?" Roland covered the phone with his hand and told her quickly, "Alex's brother, John was killed last night by a drunk driver." Irene gasped, and then covered her mouth. She stole a glance at Roland to see if he was looking at her, he wasn't, thank God he was looking the other way and hadn't noticed her shock. She had to remember, she wasn't even supposed to know John. She'd have to be very careful from now on.

Roland hung up and told Irene everything he'd heard from Melissa. Irene asked, "When is she coming down?" Roland replied, "She'll be here tomorrow, but she isn't sure if Alex will want her to stay with her and she wanted to know if she could stay here in case Alex already has a house full. She said Alex and John have relatives who live in Regina and some from Sarnia, as well and they may be staying there."

Irene tried to comprehend all that having Susan's real father, dead, might mean to her and to Susan eventually. She'd had no idea if she should ever tell Susan, she didn't think she ever would now, unless she was left with no choice. She hoped Roland would never find out the truth. Roland had been talking to her when all of a sudden he realized she wasn't listening. He'd asked her a question about the guest room and she hadn't responded. He looked at her, she had a deep frown on her face and her eyes were huge. He asked her, touching her arm, "Are you okay?" She told him, "Oh, I'm fine," and covered her odd behaviour with, "I was thinking about how poor Alex must be feeling and about how I would feel if it were Jake. Did you ask me something before?" Roland smiled at her and took her in his arms, as he did he said, "Nah, don't worry about it. Oh, I just remembered I have meetings all day tomorrow, would you mind picking up Melissa at the airport?" She replied kissing him, on the cheek, "Of Course not, just give me the flight number and tell me what time it's supposed to arrive and I'll be there." She smiled and said, "Now we'd better get to sleep," and kissed him and rolled over. She heard him begin to snore and wondered if she would be blessed with being able to fall asleep tonight.

Melissa arrived the next day and Irene was at the airport to meet her. Irene asked her, as they waited for her bag, "Do you know if Alex made any arrangements for the funeral yet?" Melissa said, "I don't think she's had time yet. I'm not sure if the body has been released yet." Irene looked puzzled and Melissa explained, "He was hit by a drunk driver and apparently they require that an autopsy be completed since the driver is going to be charged with manslaughter and I guess they have to be sure there were no extenuating circumstances that could somehow mean that John was at fault as well." Irene looked sad and as Melissa watched her, she felt sorry for her. They picked up her bag and continued out to the car saying very little to each other.

Finally, Melissa asked, as they were driving out of the terminal, "Do you feel bad knowing that he's dead?" Irene sighed and said, "It was a long time ago and if I had it to do all over again I never would have done anything with the man." Melissa said, "Well, now that he's gone, you shouldn't have to worry anymore." She asked Irene, "Have you ever noticed the distinct resemblance between John and Susan?" Irene pulled the car over to the side of the road and stopped. She looked straight at Melissa and told her, "I have thought about it over and over again all these years," she started to cry and told Melissa, "If I could undo the whole thing I would, but I can't." She blew her nose and said, "Roland and Susan would both be so hurt if they knew." Melissa was crying too, she said, "I know they would be and that's why I'll keep doing everything I can to make sure that they never do know." Irene reached for her hand and gave it a little squeeze. Then she dried her eyes and pulled back onto the road. Melissa asked her, "Would you mind if I ask you just one more question?" Irene gave her a nervous look and asked, "What do you want to know, now?" Melissa laughed at that but asked her shyly, "Did Roland's affair all those years ago, bother you, at the time?" Irene's expression changed quickly, she glanced at Melissa, and told her simply, "Yes it did, very much so." Melissa was sorry she'd asked, she could see the raw pain in Irene's face and she could hear it in her voice and for the first time, she knew it was the truth. She thought, now I understand why Irene did what she did, it was just too bad about Susan being caught in the middle. Melissa asked Irene, "Would you mind taking me to Alex's house first?" She thought a moment then asked, "Will you come in with me?" Irene swallowed and told her, "Yes, I will, I really like Alex, so I will, I'd like to tell her how sorry I am."

Once they reached Alex's place, they parked on the street a few doors down. The driveway was already full and the street was filling up fast as well. They walked up the sidewalk and approached the house, when they were just about to knock, the door opened. Irene and Melissa jumped back surprised, the man standing there looking at them was the spitting image of John. He smiled and said, "Please come in." He introduced himself saying, "Hi, I'm Sidney, John's brother, from Regina." He took their coats and asked, frowning, "How did you know John?" Irene and Melissa exchanged glances before Melissa spoke up and told him, "Alex and I are best friends and this is Irene, my sister in-law, she picked me up from the airport. She noticed Alex and excused herself, she ran over to her, and gave her a huge hug. Irene followed her and as she hugged Alex she told her, "I'm so sorry, if I can do anything at all, please just ask me."

Alex looked terrible, she looked from one to the other and told them, "I've not been able to sleep for the last couple of nights, I'm the only one of my family who lives in town and I had to identify my brother. I can't get that image out of my mind." Fresh tears slid down her cheeks and she explained that fateful night to them, "John had been out for a walk that night, before he went to bed," she added, "He's been walking at the same time every night for ages and that night a drunk driver came out of nowhere and drove right up on the sidewalk and ran him over." She started to sob and Irene went to get her a glass of water while Melissa held her in a comforting embrace. Alex was distraught and Melissa was glad she'd come here first. Alex recovered a little and said, "Thank you so much for coming, can you stay here with me, tonight?" Melissa looked over at Irene and Irene told her, "Don't you worry at all Melissa, we all know you're not here for a social visit this time and you should be with your friend, she needs you." She went on to say, "I'll get your bags from the car and bring them into the house for you." As she was putting on her coat, Sydney came over asking, "Are you leaving already?" Irene answered, "I will be shortly, I'm going to get Melissa's bags out of the car for her." She explained, "Alex wants Melissa to stay here with her tonight." Sydney nodded his understanding and said, "She is pretty upset, I think that's a good idea." He opened the door for her saying, "I'll go with you and carry her bags for you." Irene thanked him and they walked out of the house together. Sydney told her, "My brother spoke to me about you." Irene looked shocked, she turned to him and asked, "What do you mean by that?" He told her with a sigh, "Don't worry, I know my brother was quite a womanizer, when he worked for the Fuller Brush Company in Regina." He said quite seriously, "You might be pleased to know though that he was heart broken when you refused to see him again." Irene walked with her head down; she was very embarrassed to have been confronted with this, especially by someone who was a total stranger to her. He may look like John, Irene thought, but he isn't John. He seemed to notice how uncomfortable she was and said, "I'm sorry, I didn't mean to embarrass you." He added boldly, "I can see why John was so taken with you though." Irene wondered just what he was talking about, she didn't look anything like she had back then, she'd gained at least twenty pounds and she hadn't aged well, she knew she was full of lines and wrinkles. It had been so long since she'd even thought of herself as anything but Roland's wife and her children's mother that she wasn't even sure if this guy was flirting with her or not. She thought if he is, he must be blind as well as stupid. She didn't think she was attractive at all, anymore. Irene remained silent, thinking that was the best way to deal with him. She opened the trunk and stepped aside as Sydney lifted Melissa's bags out and set them on the ground. He looked at Irene and asked her, "Why did you break it off with John?" Irene looked him in the eye and said tersely, "Not that it's any of your business, but it was because I was married and I finally came to my senses and realized that what I was doing was wrong not to mention idiotic, as well. I knew I loved my husband and I didn't want to lose him." Sydney just nodded and said, "I understand." He asked on the way back to the house, "Did your husband ever find out?" She closed her eyes, thinking will he ever stop but said after a moment, "No, he didn't and I hope he never will," she finished by saying, "I never want to hurt him that way." Irene feeling uncomfortable with the whole conversation, hurried into the house and found Melissa, she told her, "Sydney brought your bags in," and rushed on, "I'm going to go home now, okay? Take care of Alex." She told Melissa before she left, "Please call me if you need anything." Melissa said, "Thanks," and squeezed her hand. Irene hugged Alex telling her, "I'll see you soon, take care," and left as quickly as she could, she didn't want to run into Sydney again. She hoped she'd never, ever have to speak to that man again; she shivered just thinking about it.

When she arrived home, Roland was waiting for her, he'd hurried home as soon as he could in the hopes of seeing Melissa. Irene was surprised to see him so early, he told her, noticing her surprise, "I was worried that Melissa might be staying there, I wish I could have gone to the airport with you to meet her, but I couldn't get out of one of the meetings this morning but I managed to cancel all the afternoon ones though." Irene told him, "We stopped off at Alex's first and she wanted Melissa to stay there with her." Roland replied, sighing, "I understand, I guess I just hoped she'd be here." He asked, "Is there anything you want to do with the rest of the day," it was only just after lunch. Irene told him, shrugging, "I don't have anything planned." He walked over to her grinning and kissed her, and then kissed her neck before whispering in her ear, "I have a few things in mind." She laughed and kissed him back. He pulled her in the direction of the stairs and said, "Come on lets get upstairs, the kids aren't due home for hours." Irene couldn't help but smile as she let him pull her up the stairs.

When they reached the bedroom she started to unbutton her blouse and Roland stopped her, gently taking her hands in his, "I want to do that," he said. She looked surprised as he laid her on the bed and started kissing her while at the same time slowly undressing her. His mouth followed his hands as he removed pieces of clothing. Irene felt as if she were young and desirable again. She responded undoing his shirt and kissing him as she undressed him. She was surprised by the excitement she was beginning to feel, she'd thought it was long ago forgotten. They made love with almost the same amount of passion as they used to, years ago. When they were finally spent, they lay together with their fingers entwined; talking about how they wished they'd never lost that part of their relationship. They both agreed they'd try their best never to lose it again. They promised each other they would never again go to bed angry, they would, from now on, find a way to work things out before they went to sleep.

John's funeral was three days later. It had taken several days before his body had been released to the funeral home. The autopsy had to be completed and the family had been told his body would be released once all the tests were completed. They needed to make sure there were no alcohol or drugs in his system. Irene and Roland had read in the paper that the police had charged the driver with impaired driving as well as manslaughter.

The family couldn't believe that it had even been necessary to do an autopsy; to them everything seemed cut and dried. The driver had had too much to drink, he'd gotten into his car and drove, he'd lost control and ended up on the sidewalk where he hit John and killed him, it may have been an accident only because it wasn't intentional, but they believed that anyone who drank and then drove should suffer the consequences of their actions. Some of John's family, by pure coincidence had actually been trying to raise awareness of this dangerous act before the accident. It seemed to be happening far too often these days and they'd felt something needed to be done.

The funeral service was held at the Lutheran church. Irene thought, my God, I had sex with John for months and I never even knew him. I never asked him anything, not about his religion or anything else, all we'd ever done was have sex and when we finished we'd talked about the products he sold as if nothing had ever happened. We never asked each other anything personal. She felt so ashamed of herself, she closed her eyes and thought if she didn't stop thinking about these things, Roland, who had become so much closer to her lately would know something was bothering her. She didn't need that; she was once again enjoying all the attention he was lavishing on her.

The service was over and the pallbearers were carrying the casket down the aisle, one of them was Sydney, he had tears in his eyes as he looked over at her. She looked away quickly; she didn't want him looking at her. She just wanted him to go home, back to Regina and stay there. She never wanted to see him again. She still couldn't believe John had told anyone about her, least of all his brother, who looked too much like him, Irene thought. He'd even told Alex, she recalled.

Susan and Dawn were sitting beside them in the pew and as people starting filing out of their seats and walking down the isle, towards the door; Roland and Irene stepped aside and let the girls go first, since they'd been getting a little restless. Susan was first to reach the isle and was hurrying down it ahead of them, when she reached the steps she stopped and they finally caught up with her. Irene stopped beside her, looking out at everyone and enjoying the fresh air, when she noticed Sydney, he was staring straight ahead with his mouth agape. Irene suddenly realized, as a wave of terror seized her, that he was looking at Susan. She berated herself for allowing Susan to come with them in the first place, but she'd insisted and Roland had sided with her, saying that it wouldn't hurt if the kids came along. He'd said they wouldn't stay long afterward at the hall anyway. Susan had told them she thought it was nice to go to funerals of the families of people you cared for and she really liked Alex, probably because she adored Melissa and Alex was Melissa's best friend. Irene rushed over and stood in front of her blocking Sydney's view and led her down the steps, she steered her over to the side out of the way of the crowd and waited until Roland and Dawn made their way down to where they were standing.

The place where they were standing in front of the church was so crowded Irene felt safe, for the moment. She asked Roland, "Do you think we should go to the cemetery?" He nodded saying, "I think we should make the effort, we want Alex to know we care." Irene said, "I hadn't thought of it that way. I just didn't want to be in the way with the kids, that's all." Roland told her, "I don't think the girls will be any trouble." Irene said, knowing she was grasping as straws, "I've been worrying about Susan, I don't want her to have nightmares." Susan was rather sensitive and she'd had plenty of nightmares after her grandmother's death. Roland looked thoughtful and nodding, he said, "Maybe you're right. We'll take them home and then go back to the hall afterwards."

On the way home to drop the girls off, Irene was thinking about going to the hall, she was afraid Sidney would say something and Roland would hear. She wished she could come up with an excuse so they wouldn't have to go there either, but she couldn't think of anything that would be even remotely believable and she didn't want to raise any suspicions, not now, she couldn't risk it.

They talked to Alex and a few others at the hall and Roland of course talked with Melissa. Irene noticed a woman she knew from the kid's school, she was one of the mothers Irene had met at one of the school functions she'd volunteered for. Normally Irene would have ignored her, but she needed a distraction

now and made her way over to say hello. The woman, Irene
finally remembered her name, which was Sally, had noticed
Irene approaching and a look of recognition crossed her face.
They both smiled at each other and talked for a few minutes,
before Roland came up to them and asked, "Irene, are you ready
to go?" She introduced him to Sally and said, "Yes, I am," and
explained, "We have to get home to the girls." Sally smiled an
understanding smile saying, "Goodbye, maybe we'll meet at the
school again sometime."

They made it all the way to the door when Irene realized she
was holding her breath, she'd been hoping they could make a
quick exit and be done with this uncomfortable situation. They
were almost out the door when Sidney appeared out of what
seemed like thin air, and asked, looking at her, "Are you two
leaving already?" He said, "I haven't even had a chance to get to
know you and your husband." Irene was left with no choice but
to introduce Roland to him. Roland chatted politely to Sydney
for a few minutes as Irene stood nervously at his side and much
to her surprise, he told Sydney, "It was nice meeting you, but we
really do have to be going." Sydney smiled a sly smile as Roland
turned to leave. Irene quickly looked the other way and took
Roland's arm as they left.

She breathed a sigh of relief as they got into the car. Roland
looked at her and smiled, he asked, "What was that was for?"
Irene said, "I hate funerals and I'm just glad it's over." She asked,
"What did Melissa say? Is she going to be spending any time with
us before she leaves to go home?" Roland replied, "I asked her
that same question, but she said she wasn't sure if Alex would
want her to leave just yet." He told Irene, "I told her that she
could come by anytime. Is that was okay with you?" Irene
replied, "Of course it is." The balance of the drive home was
quiet; they both seemed to be in deep thought. Irene was glad
Roland was quiet; it gave her time to think. She hoped she never
had to see that Sydney again, she didn't trust him at all.

A couple of days later, Irene was walking into the house, having just arrived home from her hair appointment, when the phone rang. She rushed to answer it, shrugging out of her coat on the way. She was surprised to hear Melissa's voice and asked her, "How are you? Are you coming over for a visit?" Melissa answered, "That's what I was calling for, I wanted to know if we could come tomorrow evening, maybe for dinner?" Irene hadn't heard the "we" and told her, "Sure just come on over anytime. Do you need me to pick you up?" Melissa said, softly, "I was calling more, to ask if it was okay if I brought Alex with me." Irene closed her eyes and sat on the chair beside the hall table. She said, "Sure no problem, you know she's welcome, too," as cheerily as she could muster, she hoped it didn't sound too phoney. Melissa said almost as an afterthought, "By the way, I think Sydney will be gone, but in case he doesn't leave tomorrow, would it be okay if I bring him too?" Irene's heart was pounding, she thought it's bad enough that Alex will be coming with her; she didn't know if she could handle Sydney as well. She said as lightly as she could, "Sure," but she'd hesitated a little too long and she knew it. Melissa waited a beat and said, "He's probably not going to be here, but I'm not sure." Irene told her, "Oh don't worry, the more the merrier." She said, "Now I better go and figure out what to cook." Melissa laughed and told her, "Don't go to too much trouble, neither Alex or Sydney have been eating much these days, anyway." Irene commented, "That's too bad," and immediately realized that the statement had totally lacked conviction. The two of them chatted a moment longer before saying goodbye. As Irene put the phone down, she prayed that, that stupid Sydney, would be gone by tomorrow, she just couldn't fathom entertaining the two of them all evening, especially if both of them were eyeing Susan the whole time. She shuddered to think of it.

She racked her brains wondering if she could find a way for Susan not to be there and suddenly smiled as she called her best friend Karen and asked her, "Could you do me a favour?" Without waiting for her reply she asked, "Would you mind picking up Susan from school tomorrow when you pick up Katie? I need to know if she can spend the night at your place, as well." Karen said, "Of course I will, but I want to know what's going on, it sounds like something's wrong." Irene told her quickly, "I promise to explain everything, once we have a moment to ourselves, when no one else is around." Karen said, "Ooh, sounds juicy." Irene remembered and said, "Oh yeah, do you think you can make it sound like it was a request from Katie? I don't want anyone to know I asked you to do this, okay? Karen laughed and told her, "Ah, the plot thickens," then added more seriously, "Katie has been asking for days, if Susan could come over to play." Karen went on, "She'll be thrilled when she finds out Susan is staying overnight as well. I'll take her to school the next day." Irene let out a big sigh, and said, "You're a life saver, thanks so much." She smiled to herself as she hung up the phone.

She headed to the kitchen, thinking, now all I have to do is figure out what to serve, and that shouldn't be too difficult. She examined the things in the freezer and noticed a lasagne that she'd made a couple of weeks ago; she usually had something stashed away, in the event of an emergency, like this one. She said aloud, "Perfect, I'll stop at the Safeway store and pick up a French stick and then I'll make a Caesar salad, I'll also make that chocolate caramel ice cream dessert. That's pretty easy and everyone always loves it." She noticed some frozen shrimp in the freezer just before she closed the lid and thought; I'll serve shrimp as an appetizer with some cocktail sauce. I could also put out some nuts and pretzels to go with our drinks, before dinner. She glanced at her watch and noticed it was almost time for the kids to come home from school. She knew they didn't have any extracurricular activities tonight. Most nights they had something, like volleyball or reading club or whatever, but not tonight.

Susan was the first to arrive and was ecstatic to hear that she could spend the night at Katie's tomorrow, she said, "Oh Mommy, thank you." Irene told her, "Auntie Karen will be picking you up after school and she'll also be taking you to school tomorrow." Susan wondered aloud, "Am I going to have to take my pyjamas to school?" Irene smiled at her and said, "No don't worry, I'm going to be visiting Karen tomorrow and I'll make sure to take all the things you'll need over there with me." Susan said, "Everything?" Irene replied impatiently, "Yes, I'll take your pyjamas and your clothes for school the next day when I go over to visit. I'll even take the bunny that you like to sleep with." Susan kissed her mother, ran into the kitchen for a cookie, and continued running upstairs shouting, "I need to pack a suitcase." Irene hollered up the stairs to her, "That's fine, but I want to make sure everything you'll need is in it, so after you pack it I want to see what's inside, just to make certain you haven't forgotten anything, like your toothbrush or something. And don't run and talk with that cookie in your mouth, you'll choke." Susan folded her arms and tapped her foot as she listened to her Mom, then reluctantly agreed, saying, "Fine, but you know, I'm not a baby anymore." Irene thought, shaking her head, no that's for sure, but you sure aren't very responsible either. She knew Susan would forget her head if it wasn't attached. Roland was always defending the child, she thought, he just doesn't know her like I do.

Dawn came home next and heard Susan singing upstairs, and asked, "What's up with her?" Irene told her, "Be nice, she's excited about going to Katie's tomorrow for a sleep over." Dawn frowned and looked at her Mom saying, "Hello, did you forget tomorrow's a school night?" Irene smiled and said, "No, I didn't forget, Karen will take both Katie and Susan to school the next morning." Dawn was silent a moment thinking this is strange and said, pouting, "Huh, you never let me sleep over at my friends houses on school nights." Irene said, "I know that but that's only because you're older and have more homework to do." She added, "But just maybe I'll allow it the next time you ask, provided that your homework is done." Dawn's face lit up and she turned on her heel and raced up the stairs to her room. Irene smiled, slyly as she walked into the kitchen thinking, things just might work out all right yet. Not even five minutes later Dawn came running into the kitchen and excitedly, told her, "Carol just asked me to stay over at her place tomorrow night," she quickly added, "We're going to study our Geography together." Irene had trouble concealing her smile and said without turning around, "That didn't take you very long." Dawn replied, smiling, "I had to hurry I was worried that you might change your mind." Irene smiled back and told her, "Fine, you can go." Dawn looked amazed for a split second before she turned and ran out of the kitchen, she called out, "Thanks, I'm going to pack my stuff in my backpack, then I won't have to come home. I can just take the school bus to Carol's and then you won't have to drive me over there, okay?" Irene yelled upstairs in reply, "Okay, fine." She heard Dawn holler, "Yipee" and smiled. As she walked back into the kitchen she breathed a huge sigh of relief, as she thought now I'll only have little Brooke at dinner tomorrow and she's no trouble at all. She thought in the event the conversation takes a turn for the worse, I'll only have to contend with her and she's much too young to understand anyway. She hoped the conversation wouldn't be about Susan or worse, about John possibly being her father. Irene hoped and prayed that that little secret would always stay a secret.

Roland was home early, for a change that evening and when they sat down to dinner, both kids bombarded him with the fact that they would be at their friends homes for sleepovers, tomorrow. Roland looked at Irene and asked, "Is there some sort of school holiday I've forgotten about?" Irene laughed and said, "No there isn't but I allowed them to." She leaned over and mouthed, "I'll talk to you later about it." He frowned, but decided to let it drop, she usually knew what she was doing when it came to the kids and school, so he decided not to interfere. She mentioned as casually as she could, "Melissa called and asked if she could come over for dinner tomorrow night, she said she was going to bring Alex and possibly Sydney if he hadn't left for home already." Roland looked surprised, he said, "Oh good, I'm glad she's coming, we've hardly spent any time with her at all." He quickly added, feeling he'd responded, insensitively, "I know and certainly understand why, but I still wish I could have a little time with her." Irene suggested, "Why don't you take her out for lunch, by herself one day, before she leaves for home, that way the two of you can have a real visit, and you wouldn't have anyone else to try to entertain as well." Roland nodded, "That's a great idea." Irene interrupted smiling, "I do have the odd one." Roland smiled back at her and continued, "I'll ask her, if I can get her away from Alex for a minute, tomorrow, that is"

Melissa and Alex arrived in the afternoon the next day. Irene was ecstatic when she saw them coming up the walk by themselves. She opened the door, greeted them with hugs, and asked, "How are you?" She continued on, asking and hoping, "I guess Sydney left for home?" She nearly fell over when Melissa replied, "Oh no, he hasn't yet, he's going to be coming as well. He'll be driving his own car though because apparently he's not staying for dinner, he wants to get back home and he says it's quite a long drive." Alex looked at Irene and said, "He said he wanted to drop something off to you before he left for home." Irene wondered what that could possibly be, and said, "Oh, wonder why he couldn't have just given whatever it is to you to bring?" Melissa shrugged and looked over at Alex who was blushing slightly and looking at the floor, she said quickly to Irene, "Oh who knows," and gave Alex a gentle nudge in the direction of the living room.

They sat in the living room and chatted, Alex talked about growing up with her two brothers and had tears in her eyes as she spoke, so Melissa started talking about some of the funny things that happened growing up with her only brother, Roland,

to try to ease the pain she could see on Alex's face. Her ploy
worked because Alex actually laughed a couple of times at the
funny things she recounted. Irene could relate to most of the
situations because she'd grown up with her brother Jake as well
as her sister, Donna.

They ate shrimp and drank martini's that Irene had learned
from Roland, how to make. They went out to the kitchen together
when Irene went to stir the sauce. They decided they needed
another martini and had just come back with fresh drinks and
were once again seated in the living room when the doorbell
rang. Irene walked to the door with what felt like lead feet, she
peered through the sidelight window at the front door and felt
an icy fear creep up her spine as she opened the front door to
let Sydney enter. She'd hoped against all hope that it was only
a friend, but she knew she hadn't been expecting anyone else
and it was way too soon for Roland to be home, besides, he had
his own key and certainly wouldn't ring the doorbell. Sydney
rushed right in as soon as she opened the door; he gave her a
quick hug and asked, "Is Roland home yet?" Irene frowned and
told him, "No he isn't yet and he won't be for about another
hour and a half". Sydney walked past her, saying, "Good." He
followed the sound of his sister's voice to the living room. Irene
was following behind; she'd noticed the thick envelope he was
carrying under his arm.

He sat down and told them in a serious manner, "I'm only
going to stay a few minutes." He declined the drink Irene offered
and said, "I'm going to get straight to the point." He looked right
at Irene and told her flat out, "I read John's will; he set up a trust
fund for Susan." Irene looked as if she would faint. Sydney
continued, "My brother always knew Susan was his. He told me
he'd seen her quite often, from a distance, and he mentioned the
resemblance, that she bears to him quite often. He'd been so
proud of his daughter, Susan. I noticed myself, the resemblance
she possesses to both John and me the other day at the funeral."

He continued, "I know you blocked my line of vision that day, and walked her down the steps and out of my sight. I knew then that you knew she was John's."

Irene realized she was holding her breath and exhaled loudly. Melissa ran to her and held her hand telling her, "Don't worry Irene; we'll keep your secret, if that's what you want." Irene could only nod, in response. She closed her eyes willing herself to gain control of her voice, and asked, "When will the trust begin to pay out." Sydney said, "According to the will it should begin regular payments, through the Lawyer of course, on Susan's twenty first birthday and will continue on for the rest of her life, John wanted to provide for his daughter, even though he knew he couldn't see her." Sydney said, sadly, after an awkward moment, "I do believe he planned to meet her and tell her the truth, just prior to the first payment of the trust, at least that's what he told me, several years ago."

Irene had been listening to him with wide glazed over eyes; she looked to be in shock. She recovered a little and pointed to the envelope he'd placed on the coffee table and asked, "Would you mind telling me what's in that envelope?" Sydney seemed to have forgotten about it altogether, he picked it up and handed it over to her. She opened it and found a photo album of John's family. She looked up at Sydney, as he said, "John had been working on this, he was trying to make sure Susan would at least know, what the other side of her family looked like, even if she could never meet them." Irene paged through the album and noticed how much Susan looked like her father's family, even the baby pictures of John, could have easily been pictures of Susan at the same age. Irene closed the book; tears were streaming down her face. She said, "I don't have the heart to tell either Susan or Roland, both of them will be heartbroken." Sydney nodded and looked down, all he said was, "I'm very sorry." He stood and kissed Irene's cheek and hugged both Melissa and Alex. He said, "You are welcome to come and visit me anytime you want."

He gave Melissa his business card with his phone numbers and address printed on it; and was handing one to Irene, when he paused and gave Melissa a second one saying, "Tell Irene she can call me anytime, if she needs someone to talk to." He felt sorry for her; she looked to be in a considerable amount of pain. Alex was crying as he left, she missed her brother and wished he could stay longer. Melissa put her arm around her shoulders and led her back to the living room.

Irene was still sitting in her chair staring at the album. Melissa looked at Alex, then back at Irene, and said, "Irene, maybe Alex should take the album home with her and you can have some time to decide what you want to do." Irene's eyes filled with tears. She whispered to Melissa, "This will destroy my family." Melissa looked at her, she could see the raw pain Irene was feeling and felt sorry for her and told her as gently as she could, "Maybe you should put off telling anyone for a while." She continued saying, "Susan is still young, she doesn't need to know right now and Roland doesn't either." Irene sniffed and Alex handed her a tissue, Irene looked up at her and Alex smiled at her, her face filled with compassion and she told her, "Your secret is safe with me and I know it is with Melissa as well." Irene gave both of them a hug saying, "Thanks, you two, I don't know what I'd do without you." Melissa suggested, "Why don't we put the album back in the envelope along with the letter from the lawyer." Alex said, trying to help, "I'm going to see the lawyer, myself in a few days and I can tell him all about this situation for you and ask him to keep things quiet until further instruction, from either me or you. Are you okay with that, Irene, or do you want to take care of things yourself?" Irene sighed and answered, "No, I'd really appreciate it if you did that for me, thanks Alex." She hugged both of the women and thanked them again.

Melissa finished stuffing everything back into the envelope and wrote "Alex" in large letters on the front, she held it up so they could see Alex's name written on it and told them, "This is just to ensure that no one will open it by mistake." She put it by the front door with their shoes and returned to the living room. She suggested to Alex and Irene, "Let's go into the kitchen and make ourselves another martini. Then let's sit down in the living room and talk about more pleasant things." She reminded them, "Brooke and Roland will be home shortly and we don't want either one of them to think that anything is wrong." Melissa looked at Irene, slightly alarmed and asked, "How is Brooke getting home today, if the other girls are at sleepovers?" Irene told her, "I made arrangements with one of the other mothers to bring her home; I did that yesterday, after you called and told me you would be coming for dinner." Melissa shook her head and said with a smile, "I should have known, you've always been so organized." Irene laughed. They trudged off together to the kitchen to make their martinis, they really needed another drink to help them make it through the evening, Melissa thought.

Brooke burst through the door and came running into the living room shedding her coat, gloves and backpack in a trail along the way. She ran straight to Melissa and hugged her, and then she walked over and kissed her mother. She said a slightly shy, "Hi" to Alex. Then when Melissa asked her about her day, she told everyone about the games they played at recess and in no time had them all laughing.

Roland walked into the house a little earlier than expected, he said, eagerly, "I just couldn't wait to see my little sister and gave Melissa a hug and kiss on the cheek." He shook Alex's hand and then gave her a hug too. Alex apologized, saying, "I'm so sorry for hogging Melissa all this time." Roland told her, "Please don't feel bad, I was just kidding before when I made reference to not seeing her too much on the day of the funeral." Melissa said loudly, pretending to be angry, "I'm here now so stop fighting over me." That made everyone laugh.

Brooke asked, "Mom, where are Dawn and Susan?" Irene reminded her, "Did you forget, that they're sleeping over at their friends houses?" Brooke looked disappointed and stuck out her bottom lip pouting. Roland noticed and smiling told her, "You're pretty lucky, because you can tell your sisters that you got to visit with their favourite Aunt and Alex, too. How about that?" Brooke smiled looking brighter and raising her head said, "Yeah, neat."

Dinner was uneventful. They chatted about harmless topics and Irene was grateful she knew she couldn't have kept up the pretence otherwise. Melissa and Alex helped immensely, both of them noticed the toll the afternoon had taken on Irene and tried hard to keep Roland busy talking and listening to them in the hopes he wouldn't notice how melancholy Irene's mood was. They even steered the conversation making sure they didn't discuss anything too serious.

When Melissa and Alex left and the dinner dishes were washed and put away, Roland asked Irene, "Why have you been so quiet tonight? I noticed you were very serious all evening and I was wondering why." He said, "I didn't want to ask you about it with Melissa and Alex here." He was watching her as she said, "I'm just extremely tired, that's all." He wondered if there was something else, but decided to drop it, in his experience with her, which was plenty; he knew he'd get nowhere badgering her, not until she was good and ready anyway. He'd never been able to drag anything out of her, if she wasn't ready to tell him. He looked at her once more and wondered again, what the problem could possibly be.

thirty-four

THE CALL

A lex and Irene kept in touch and spent time together as often as they could manage. Alex would invite Irene over to her place for coffee or sometimes they'd simply shop together and then return to either her house or Irene's and make dinner together or just sit and chat.

Alex had inherited John's house and over the years had made some wonderful changes. Irene had helped her chose paint colours and she'd also helped her choose all her new furniture. The house truly looked like a home, albeit, very feminine décor, but warm and inviting, just the same. Irene loved visiting Alex now, her house felt so cozy, kind of like a beautiful, comforting blanket, she thought. She knew Roland would never allow her to decorate their home that way. He hated anything in the house that looked too feminine, and whenever Irene talked to him about it, he'd say something like, "I just don't feel comfortable with flowers and such," or "I can't relax in a frilly environment." Irene thought shaking her head; I can't even have a floral quilt on the bed. She sighed and looked over at Roland, he'd listened rather intently to all her ranting about how beautiful Alex's place was now and how she'd enjoyed helping her decorate it. She'd just been out for a visit that day and was telling Roland all about it. He'd been watching her as she told him and said, as if hearing her thoughts, "I know you always wanted a place decorated like that, maybe we could compromise a little, I could try and live with a little femininity, I guess." They both laughed and he continued, "Just, promise me that you won't turn our home into a "woman's home" please." She poked him and promised, "I will consult with you before making any changes, okay?" He agreed, saying with a shrug, "I know we need to make some changes, now that the kids have grown up."

Dawn had gotten married the year before and Susan was now twenty-one and living on her own. She was a nurse at the University hospital in Edmonton and they were extremely proud of her. The only child at home now was Brooke and she was growing up quickly.

They had bedrooms that Irene wanted to turn into guest rooms. She also wanted to use one as an office where she could go to write letters or pay bills, she'd been telling Roland all about her plans when, Brooke suddenly burst into the room, she'd just answered the phone when it rang a few moments ago. She had a puzzled look on her face as she told her Mom, "Some lawyer's on the phone and he wants to know if he has the right number. He's looking for the guardian of the trust fund for Susan Diane Petersen." She questioned, screwing up her face as she asked, "Do you guys know what he's talking about?" Irene's eyes widened, she swallowed and without uttering a single word, took the phone. She glanced at Roland who was looking at her in complete shock. Irene walked out of the room, with the phone held to her ear, asking, "Who's speaking, please?" The voice on the line told her his name, which Irene missed completely, she did hear, though, "I'm the lawyer who has taken over her case and I need to speak with the guardian of the trust fund or Susan herself." He continued briskly, "It is imperative that we set up a meeting as soon as possible." Irene asked, "What happened to the other lawyer?" He told her, "I'm sorry to say he passed away several months ago and I'm looking after his clients and his practise now." Irene thought, what did he say his name was again, Arthur something, she couldn't remember. She tried to regain her composure and asked in what she thought was her best business-like voice, "Could you please give me your number and I'll call you back on Monday." She added, "I wasn't aware that lawyers even worked on Saturdays." Arthur something, replied, "I usually don't but since I've taken over this practise my work load has doubled and I don't have much choice. I look forward to speaking with you on Monday," and he hung up.

Irene swallowed the lump in her throat, as she returned the phone to the hall table. She was staring down at it, afraid to move when she heard footsteps behind her. Roland asked, "What that was all about?" Irene told him, "The lawyer had the wrong information and I needed to clear it up." She said, "I'm going to speak to Susan and have her call to clear things up herself, since she's an adult now." She told him, "Apparently this lawyer has taken over a practise of another lawyer who recently died and I think he's made a mistake." Roland looked sceptical, but Irene walked away and called over her shoulder, "Would you like a cup of coffee? She said trying hard to keep her voice even, "I feel like some, so I'm going to make a pot."

Irene walked to the kitchen, fully expecting Roland to follow her and ask more questions. She was so nervous, she knew she had to tell him, but she had to tell Susan, first. The old lawyer had been very understanding of her situation and had agreed to keep things a secret. She hadn't heard a thing from him when Susan turned twenty-one, a couple of months ago. She remembered when she'd met with him, he'd said he didn't like the deception but had relented and he'd even said he understood, he told her at the time she could hold off for a little while, but that she'd have to tell Susan eventually. She wondered now if he'd fallen ill and that was the reason he'd never called her back. She thought with a shudder, now this new Arthur guy, is going to ruin everything. At least he wouldn't know that she and Alex had been responsible for delaying the payment of the trust to Susan. He would only think that the old lawyer had not done his job, he'd said as much during their short conversation on the phone.

Irene breathed a sigh of relief when she heard Roland and Brooke talking in the living room. She knew she was in the clear for the time being. She waited for the coffee to finish and willed her hands not to shake as she brought in a cup for each of them, the three of them chatted until bedtime.

Sunday morning Irene called Susan, she knew the girl's schedule and knew that she was off, both today and Monday, and asked her, "Can I visit you in your apartment, tomorrow?" Susan frowned and said, "Sure, what time were you thinking?" She was a little preoccupied, wondering why in the world Mom wanted to visit, she certainly had not made a habit of visiting her, since she'd moved out on her own, in fact she could only remember her being in her apartment twice before. She heard her Mom say, "Around nine?" She put her thoughts on hold and responded, "Make it ten." She laughed and said, "A girl needs to catch up on her Z's sometime, you know." Irene chuckled and replied, "Okay ten it is then see you tomorrow," and hung up.

On Monday morning, Irene was so nervous, she walked into the building Susan lived in and tried her best to calm herself by taking deep breaths and letting them out slowly, she soon gave up, it simply wasn't working. She buzzed Susan's apartment. Susan answered and told her in her usual cheery voice, "Come on up." Susan had changed so much since she'd moved out, she used to be so grouchy all the time, but now she was fun to be around, she laughed and joked and told funny stories about being a nurse. Irene enjoyed their visits, she liked them better when Susan came home though, she didn't like to come to her apartment but she thought it was best today, under the circumstances. As she walked off the elevator, she noticed Susan standing in her doorway waiting for her; she lived only three doors down from the elevator.

Susan noticed the tension on Irene's face immediately when she walked through the door. She told her, "Sit down" and offered her something to drink. Irene told her after swallowing hard, "Just a glass of water will be fine." When Susan came back with a glass of ice water, she handed it to her Mom, sat down next to her, and asked, "So what's up?" Irene took a deep breath, looked at Susan and told her, "There's no easy way to say what I have to tell you." She asked Susan, pleadingly, "Please don't hate me." Susan looked panicked, she gasped and asked, "Mom what's wrong?" Irene took another deep breath and told her everything, how she'd had an affair years ago and had gotten pregnant, and how she had not known for sure who Susan's real father was until a paternity test was performed several years later. When she finished her story, she told her, "I'm so sorry, I've kept it a secret all these years because I couldn't bear to hurt either you or your father." Susan just stared at her, she was dumfounded, she finally asked, breathlessly, "Why are you telling me this now?" Irene explained who her paternal father was and told her all about the trust fund he'd left for her. She told her, "The lawyer called on Saturday and wanted to know where to make the payments." She explained how there was a different lawyer looking after the trust now, because the older lawyer had passed away.

Susan became thoughtful, she looked at her mother and asked her, "Is this the reason you were never as nice to me as you were to the others?" With her temper rising a notch, she continued, "You were really mean to me at times, especially the things you said to me. I can understand why you wouldn't want anyone to know about your dirty little secret, but didn't you think I had a right to know who my own father was!" She said it more as a fact than a question. Irene started crying. Susan ignored her tears and asked, "Does my father," then corrected, "Oh excuse me, does your husband know about this?" Irene looked horrified at that, she felt as if she'd been slapped, her head snapped up and for the first time she saw pure hatred in Susan's eyes, she lowered her eyes and shook her head in answer. Susan walked across the room seething; she opened the door and hissed, "Get out!" Irene walked swiftly out the door and as she was hurrying down the hall Susan told her, a little too loudly, "Tell your husband because if you don't, I will." She added, "I'll be talking to him tomorrow, so I guess that gives you tonight to tell him yourself." She watched her Mom get on the elevator with her head down. There were others in the hall, but Susan thought it serves her right, she should be embarrassed and walked back into her apartment and slammed the door, she hated her mother for this, she just couldn't believe that she'd lived a lie all her life. The sisters that she thought were hers were really only half hers. My God, she thought, and said aloud, "Alex is my Aunt!" She cried most of the day and when she finally stopped, she thought and said aloud with a vengeance, "I'm going to make sure she pays for all the heartache she's causing both me and Dad." She started to cry even harder when she realized once more that Dad wasn't "her" Dad at all.

Irene called Roland at work, she told him, "We need to talk as soon as possible." He replied annoyed, "Irene, I'm working, can't it wait I'll be home tonight, you know that." Irene told him closing her eyes, "No, it can't." Roland was about to tell her not to be so dramatic, but something in her voice told him not to and he simply said, "I'll be home as soon as I can." Irene hung up and sat down in the living room to wait for him. She sighed, she knew this was going to completely ruin her family, she'd always known though that she couldn't keep this quiet forever. She said, aloud, "Oh God, I can't even cry anymore, what am I going to do?" She felt dead inside. She knew she'd committed the worst sin possible.

Roland walked in and saw her sitting there and as he walked over to her, he could tell that something really awful had happened. He sat down and took her in his arms and she started to cry, she knew he wouldn't forgive her and she was going to miss his comforting embrace and the wonderful relationship they had now. He sat and held her until the sobbing subsided and she was able to speak again. He gently asked her, "Irene tell me what's wrong." She told him, with tears glistening in her eyes, "You're going to hate me." He was beginning to feel a genuine fear, but said, "I could never hate you." She said, "Yes you can and you will, when I tell you what I have to tell you." He let go of her and sat up straighter. She told him everything and as she spoke, she watched his sober expression change to one of complete horror. She could see the shock and then the pain registering on his face and she felt like her heart was being wrenched from her chest. He said nothing; he listened without interrupting her. When she finished, he simply stood and told her, his voice void of all emotion, "I'll be moving to a hotel until I feel that I can deal with all of this." He left the room and swiftly walked up the stairs. Irene could hear him opening and closing drawers and then the closet, within minutes he walked, calmly back down the stairs with a suitcase and a suit bag, he took his coat from the closet threw it over his arm and left without saying a word.

Irene had no idea what to do. She sat there on the couch, as if in a trance, she hadn't moved at all until she heard Brooke come in the side door. It took her a few seconds to realize what was going on; when it suddenly dawned on her, she thought my God, I have to tell Brooke. She looked up just as Brooke entered the room. Brooke dropped her things on the hall table and ran to her mother, who looked terrible. She noticed that she was as white as a ghost and trembling as well. She brought her the afghan from the family room and wrapped it tightly around her. She asked, "Mom, are you feeling okay?" Irene patted the couch beside her and told her, "Please sit down beside me, there's something I have to tell you." As she relayed the story to Brooke, she watched the tears forming in the girl's eyes. She felt as if she was tearing Brooke's world apart and she was only seventeen. Brooke sat back on the couch, she didn't say anything, she seemed to be thinking it over. When she spoke, she asked, "How did Susan take the news?" Irene said tearing up again, "Not very well, I'm afraid," and proceeded to tell her what had transpired. Next, she asked, "What did Dad say?" Irene lowered her eyes and said, "He only said he was moving to a hotel until he could deal with it and he left." Brooke asked, shocked, "Do you know which one?" Irene realizing she didn't simply shook her head. She told Brooke, after a moment, "You can call him at work tomorrow and find out though." Brooke seemed to accept this. She asked, suddenly, "Do Dawn and all my other sisters, the ones from out of town, know?" Irene shook her head again. She said, "I haven't told any of them yet." She admitted to Brooke, "I really don't know how." Brooke leaned over and held her mother, she offered, "I can help you tell them, if you want me to." Irene looked into Brooke's tear streaked face, she reached out and touched her cheek and told her, "I'm so sorry, I never wanted to hurt you or your Dad or Susan or any of your sisters." She said, "Thank you for offering to help me tell your sisters, but I think this is something I need to do myself."

Brooke walked upstairs feeling like a zombie; she thought my wonderful family is falling apart. She couldn't believe Susan was only her "half sister." She started thinking about her and wondered how she was. She put her things down on her bed and called her. Susan seemed okay, she talked to Brooke for a while and told her, "I thought about it and it doesn't have to change anything between us." The two of them had become quite close, since she'd moved out on her own. Susan told her about the trust fund and how, at least financially, she wouldn't have to worry now. She said, "I'm not sure of the exact amount I'll receive, but that lawyer I spoke to told me it was a substantial amount. He said I would receive a lump sum to make up for the missed payments." She explained to Brooke, "The fund should have started to pay out monthly when I turned twenty one and it didn't so I guess there will be a check to cover those missed payments and then a monthly cheque after that and apparently this monthly payment will go on for the rest of my life." When Brooke said, "Wow, this whole thing is unbelievable," Susan agreed. She said after a moment, her voice portraying the sadness she felt, "I guess I'll get over the hurt one day. I'd rather have Dad though then all the money." She added in a strange almost far away kind of voice, "I'm so afraid that Dad may not be willing to act like my father anymore, now that he knows he isn't my real one." She laughed a phoney laugh but Brooke could hear the hurt in it. Brooke said, "Hey Susan, don't talk like that. Dad loves you and you know it, I'm sure that isn't going to change." Susan said, solemnly, "I sure hope you're right."

Irene had such trouble living with this new guilt. She'd buried this whole mess so deeply for so long that she'd almost convinced herself that it was just some sort of dream. She'd never actually let herself see it for what it was, now she had no choice, she couldn't lie her way out of it anymore. She wished she could, she hated feeling this way. She wondered if Roland would ever come home and if he didn't, she wondered would he have to pay for her support, he'd always handled all their accounts and investments, including her inheritance from her mother, she didn't even know how much of that still remained intact. She was extremely nervous about it; she didn't know where to turn. She virtually had no marketable skills. It had been years since she'd worked, and she had no idea what she was going do.

She called Cassie, Jean and Maureen, one by one and told them the whole story. She'd thought of flying each of them home, but had changed her mind. They'd only want to know about their father anyway and they'd probably spend most of their time with Susan and him, she was aware she'd never taken the time to build a close relationship with any of her children and felt remorseful over it now. The conversations went much as she'd thought they would. All three of the girls had listened and then had each come up with their own excuses why they couldn't stay on the phone with her any longer. She knew she didn't matter to them much anyway these days. They rarely called her anymore. There was a time when they'd called often, she thought with a slight smile at the memory, but the past few years they hadn't bothered, except on special occasions such as her birthday, Mother's Day or Christmas. She wasn't sure why, they didn't, she was still their mother, they should be more attentive, she thought, especially now, didn't they understand that she was hurting, she wondered.

Irene lived on edge each day for the next week, waiting for some kind of response from Roland. The man still hadn't said a single word to her and he was still living in the Coast Hotel, downtown. She cleaned and cooked for herself and Brooke; however, except for necessary trips to the grocery store she didn't leave the house. She spent her days sitting on the couch, knitting and waiting for the phone to ring or for Roland to walk through the front door, but wish as she might, that hadn't happened. She was beginning to wonder if he would simply stay away and never come home. She hadn't heard from any of her girls either, even Brooke was distant, now. She'd mentioned to her the other day, that she'd made the calls to tell her sisters and she'd wanted to talk to her about it, but Brooke had only shook her head and told her, "I can't talk about it, Mom," and she'd run off upstairs. Irene thought sadly, I've never felt so all alone in my whole life.

thirty-five

ALMOST NORMAL

Roland finally walked through the front door after almost two weeks of being away without once contacting Irene. Irene had been sitting on the couch as usual, knitting, when he walked in, she looked up at him nervously but to her surprise, he said nothing. Her heart was pounding, she had no idea what to expect, she noticed the blank look on his face and quickly looked back down at her knitting. She decided that since he hadn't even glanced at her, she was just going to pretend that nothing was out of the ordinary. She watched him from the corner of her eye, while appearing to be concentrating on her knitting and almost jumped when she noticed he'd looked at her briefly and then quickly turned away and went straight upstairs without saying a single word to her. She could hear him opening and closing drawers in the dresser and the closet as well and wondered if he'd simply run out of clean clothes and had only come home to pick up a fresh supply.

She sat there nervously and kept on knitting, she had no idea if she was even following the pattern anymore and she didn't care she needed the busy work. She was terrified of whether Roland would leave again or if he would stay and of what he might say to her if he chose to stay. He finally came downstairs and with her heart hammering inside her chest, she dared to steal a quick glance at him, he didn't have any bags with him, she thought breathlessly, that might be a good sign, at least it looks like he plans to stay for a while, but suddenly felt nauseous wondering what he'd say to her, she swallowed and tried harder to concentrate on her knitting.

He sat down in his chair and for a time said nothing, making her even more nervous. Finally, he said, evenly with a tinge of resentment in his voice, "We need to talk." Irene nodded her agreement thinking, he certainly could treat me a little kinder, but before she could respond. He asked, "Do you want us to separate?" Her eyes grew wide and a cold fear gripped her, she shook her head and told him in a voice that was almost a whisper, "No, I don't, I've never wanted that, that's why I never told you anything. I've always been afraid of what your reaction would be." She almost pleaded, "Roland, you have no idea how sorry I've been all these years." He sighed a ragged breath, looked down at the floor, and as if what she had just confessed was immaterial, said, "I thought since Brooke is still in school and living at home that we should stay together for the time being, it will make a more solid home for her." He continued, "She's not quite grown up yet and I think she still needs the comfort and security of a good home." Irene nodded, she was stunned and decided not to say anything even though she wanted to throw herself at his feet and beg him to forgive her and tell him how much she loved him, but as she watched him sitting there telling her what he thought and not even asking for her opinion, thought I have my pride too, and said, smugly, "Yes, I agree." Roland picked up the paper and began reading; he said nothing else to her. She watched him for a second thinking; I may be able to remind him that he loves me if I try. She knew she had to try; she didn't want to lose him.

When Brooke came home from school that day, she was ecstatic to see her Dad sitting in the living room. She raced across the room, threw herself into his arms, and told him, "Oh my God! Dad your back! I missed you!" She sat with him for a while, they talked about her day at school, and when she finished she told him, smiling, "I'm going up to go to my room to call my sisters! They'll be so happy to hear that you're back." She kissed his cheek, raced upstairs, and called each one of her sisters to tell them the news.

Irene and Roland lived like strangers; they were civil to each other, but nothing else. They managed to sleep in the same bed without ever touching, not even so much as a simple kiss goodnight. Irene spent countless hours crying, she felt as if their life was nothing but a charade, these days. It had been almost two years since Roland had come back home and they had never even so much as kissed each other and they'd never been out anywhere together. Roland went golfing and bowling and she had her bridge club and book club, but they never went out as a couple. She'd never in her life felt so empty inside.

Brooke's graduation was coming up in another month and she hadn't even given a single thought to what she was going to wear to the ceremony. She thought I must really be losing it if I don't even care about what I'm going to wear, that never would have happened to me before. She realized for the first time in her life and astonished, said aloud, "I don't care about "things" anymore, I just want my husband back, he means everything to me. I love him so much." She lay down on the bed and cried succumbing to the crushing pain of realizing she was losing both him and her family.

Brooke's big day came and she looked beautiful. Irene and Roland went together to the ceremony. They actually smiled at each other for the first time in ages, but Irene's heart wrenched when she noticed that his smile never reached his eyes, she knew he was simply trying to keep up the appearance of being a normal family for Brooke's sake. She felt like such a fool. She'd been stupid enough to believe, for almost 2 years now, that his coming back home could be the start of mending their lives, together. During that time, she'd never once given up hope, no matter what happened between them. She was having great difficulty not crying as she came to the full realization that their life now was nothing but a front on his part. She looked at him as he smiled a phoney smile in her direction and thought angrily, he should win an academy award for his performance. She felt lucky that she could use the excuse of being proud of Brooke as an explanation for the tears that she simply couldn't stop and were now streaming down her face. She looked around and took comfort in the fact that some of the other mothers were crying, as well.

Roland noticed her tears and couldn't bring himself to be moved. He thought of all the times he'd tried so hard to make her happy and all she ever cared about was herself and what other people thought. He was beginning to wonder if she'd ever really loved him at all or if she'd only loved the things, he gave her. He'd also spent some time thinking about his affair with Sharon, all those years ago and how Irene had played the injured wife when she discovered the truth, when all the while she'd been having an affair herself. He hated her for that. Why hadn't she just told him the truth, he would have forgiven her for it then. He could have even forgiven the fact that she'd gotten pregnant, he knew that was something she couldn't have prevented. He realized now, that his beautiful wife had always been deceitful only he'd been too much in love with her to see it. He recalled years ago Melissa telling him, she didn't trust Irene, he wished he would have listened to her. He had no idea what he was going to do now, but he knew he couldn't stay with her much longer, it would drive him crazy.

He was thinking of taking the retirement package the Company had offered. He thought maybe he'd move down south somewhere and spend his retirement playing golf. He shook his head; he had so much to figure out. He was going to wait until Brooke moved out of the house, in a few months, she'd told them she wanted to live with Susan, while she went to college, since Susan's apartment was within walking distance to NAIT. He thought with a smile, she'd been accepted into the Dental Hygienist program at NAIT and was excited about it, she'd wanted to be a Dental Hygienist since she'd first entered high school and she'd worked hard to realize her dream. She'd even had to repeat one semester in order to bring her grades up so she could apply to NAIT. He was so proud of her.

Brooke noticed the tension at home and one evening while she was visiting with her sister, Susan, she told her, "I can't wait to move out of that house. I hate watching them trying to pretend that things are normal, I know they're only doing it for my sake." Susan raised an eyebrow and replied, "Well, you could move in here early if you wanted to, you know." Brooke looked at her, her eyes widening in excitement, she jumped up and threw her arms around her neck, saying, "Oh, thank you, thank you." Susan laughed and told her, "I hope you know CPR because I can't breathe and I'll soon be on the floor." Brooke laughed and let go of her and still laughing, said, "I'm sorry, was that a little too tight?" They laughed about it a bit more and then got down to work planning Brooke's move. Susan said, "I have a friend with a decent sized truck, so you'd be able to move your bedroom furniture and clothes all at the same time instead of making two trips." Brooke said, "I don't have any other furniture or large items, except my bike and my skis. I was going to ask Mom if I could leave them at the house until I figure out where I can store them." Susan told her, "You know we could enquire about getting a storage locker in the basement of the building for stuff like that." Brooke said smiling, "You're so smart, let's go and see." They left Susan's apartment and went down to talk to the building superintendent.

When Brooke left Susan's place she felt like she was walking on air. She couldn't wait to get home and tell her parents the news. When she arrived, she found her mother in the kitchen making dinner. She told her, excitedly, about her plans and immediately felt guilty, when she noticed Mom was crying. Brooke told her trying her best to sound positive, "Hey Mom, I'm grown up now and I can't live at home forever." Her mother told her dabbing at her eyes, "I know but I was hoping you wouldn't go so soon. I think you'll be able to study better here anyway, it's quiet and you won't have any distractions, to interrupt you while you're studying." Brooke told her, as gently as she could, "Mom, I'm going to be moving as soon as Susan can arrange for her friend to bring the truck over." Irene started to cry harder and as Brooke turned to leave the kitchen, she grabbed her arm and turned her around to face her, she begged her, "Please, don't go, I'm afraid that if you move out your father will move out too." She continued, sobbing, "He's only been staying because of you."

Brooke looked at her with wide eyes. She pulled her arm from her grasp, turned and ran upstairs. She ran straight to her room, closed the door and called Susan. When she told her, through her tears, what had transpired between her and Mom, Susan sighed and said, sadly, "Brooke, don't let that deter you. Mom is using you so Dad won't leave her." Susan sighed again loudly this time and continued, "I'm going to make the arrangements to move your stuff, as long as that's still okay with you. You still do want to move in with me, don't you?" Brooke said, crying, "Yes I do, but now I'm going to feel bad about it." Susan rolled her eyes and told her, "Good God Brooke, you're not responsible for keeping Mom and Dad's marriage together." Brooke was silent for a moment and giving this some thought she decided, "You're right Susan, I know you're right," then giving her head a shake to clear it, said, "Go ahead and make the arrangements for the truck, and thanks for the advice, I knew I could count on you." Susan replied, smiling, "What are sisters for."

When they sat down for supper that night, Brooke told her Dad, "I'm going to be moving out this weekend." Irene looked shocked, she almost chocked on her food. She got up from the table and went down the hall to the powder room, where she splashed cold water on her face trying to bring back some feeling, she felt completely numb. She looked in the mirror as she dried her face and said to her reflection, "If Roland is going to leave me, which it seems he is then I can do absolutely nothing about it. I've tried everything possible over the past two years and nothing has worked." She tidied the bathroom thinking, I cooked his favourite meals, I kept the house spotless and I tried my best to have interesting conversations with him. I even researched some topics I thought he would be interested in, but he mostly just ignored me.

She walked back to the dinner table, thinking, I'm going to have to make some changes in my life, as well. He's not the only one who can change. She thought, I've made a fool of myself, if he doesn't want me anymore, then I don't want him either but she sat down at the table and watched Roland as he talked with Brooke and felt a stab of longing for him. She quickly looked away silently willing herself to remember that she didn't care about him anymore.

The next weekend Roland helped Brooke and Susan's friend Bob, move Brooke's furniture and clothes into the truck that Bob had parked in the driveway, the truck even had a ramp, which made loading it easy. Irene and Roland both hugged and kissed Brooke goodbye and watched her climb into the truck as she waved goodbye to them. She was so excited, she was actually going to be sharing an apartment with her sister, she'd been dreaming of doing that for the past two years.

They walked back into the house in silence as soon as the truck carrying Brooke and all her belongings was out of sight. Irene went to the kitchen and Roland to the living room. Irene wondered what would happen now. She busied herself baking a cake; she couldn't think of anything else to do to keep herself occupied.

Roland was sitting with the newspaper. He wasn't actually reading, instead he was planning what he was going to do now. He'd accepted the early retirement package and he would be retiring in just three short months. He wanted to live here in the house until then. He was planning to tell Irene about his plans and ask her what she planned to do now. He'd made it clear to her 2 years ago, that they were through and he'd said as soon as Brooke moved out, he wanted them to separate. He was struggling with the idea of separation though because he still believed that marriage was for better or worse. He knew that the church allowed for divorce on the grounds of adultery, but he also knew and felt pangs of guilt thinking about the fact that he himself was guilty of that particular sin too and she hadn't divorced him all those years ago. He sighed heavily thinking, as guilty as I feel; I can no longer keep up the pretence. He wasn't sure right now if he even loved her anymore and he knew he was having great difficulty forgiving her for what she'd done. He shrugged, he suspected she didn't love him anymore anyways, who knows, he thought sadly, maybe she never did.

They ate supper without much conversation; they'd exchanged a few thoughts on having no children at home, but nothing more serious than that. Irene was a bundle of nerves, she was positive Roland was planning something, but she had no idea what.

A few nights later, as they were finishing dinner, Roland told her about his retirement package. She asked nervously, "Are you considering taking it?" He answered, "Yes, as a matter of fact, I already have." She looked hurt; he hadn't even had the decency to tell her before he'd actually accepted it. He looked at her and asked, "What do you have planned for yourself, if you don't mind my asking?" She took a while to answer, trying her best to come up with something that sounded exciting, but she couldn't think of anything so she simply said, "I haven't given it much thought, because I don't know what my options are." Roland told her, after a moment, "I understand, you haven't worked in a long time, but you don't have to worry about that." He noticed the blank look on her face and added happily, "My retirement package is more that enough to look after both of us to a ripe old age. And we have our investments as well." He noticed she wasn't joining him in his attempt at joviality, so he assumed a more serious tone and asked, "Do you want to stay in the house?" Her breath caught and she looked up at him with a panicked expression and said, "I don't want to go anywhere else," then added, thinking she may not have a choice, "Not yet anyway." He smiled, trying to let her know it was okay and told her, "Relax, you don't have to, you can stay in the house as long as you want." She let out a breath and asked, gingerly, "What plans have you made?" She cringed when he said a little too cheerily, "I'm thinking of going south, I'll probably buy a condo in Palm Springs in California, some of the fellows at work have been there and they tell me the golfing is fantastic." She gasped in surprise and answered, "Oh my, that's so far away." He told her, "Well, as you know, I always said I wanted to golf more when I retired and that's the perfect place for it. And as you know, I've also always wanted to move back to the States one day." She looked down for a moment, then told him, "Don't worry, I'll look for a smaller place eventually, I guess." She paused, seemingly at a loss for words then added, "But I need some time, to think, I'm not sure what I want to do." He felt a slight twinge of guilt as he looked at her but he repeated, "You can take as long as want." He reminded her, "Remember, this house is paid for, so we only have the taxes and upkeep to pay for now, which doesn't cost all that much, so stay forever if you want, that's fine. It would probably be more expensive for you to move somewhere else anyway." He added, "But you can do whatever you want, I'll continue to pay for all your expenses." She was relieved; she didn't think she could deal with losing her house as well as him and her family all at once. Roland seemed to understand and she was glad for that. They finished their meal in silence.

When they were cleaning up the dishes, Irene asked, "When will you be retiring?" He said smiling, "In just three short months, I can't wait." His smile turned to a frown as he said, "I forgot to ask you, if it's okay with you, if I stay here until I'm able to make the move to the States." She replied, with a sigh, "That's fine, Roland." She added a second later, "I guess you're glad now, that you never became a Canadian Citizen." He just smiled a half smile, nodded in answer, and began putting the dishes in the dishwasher.

Irene somehow made it through each day, she felt as if she was waiting to die. She had no idea how long Roland was going to be staying, he moved into the guest room the same night Brooke had moved out. She thought the man rarely speaks to me, except to thank me for making dinner or for doing the laundry. He does remind me constantly though that I don't have to do those things for him anymore. She thought with a blank expression, he has no idea that I have to, I simply can't imagine not doing those things, I've done them for so long now. She sighed, and said aloud, as if doing so would force her to realize once and for all, "I'm going to have to get used to the idea of not being needed anymore," and had to work hard to prevent herself from crying as she said the words. She felt so used these days, but she knew it was her own fault, doing things for Roland was what she'd always done and no matter how much she told herself to stop, she couldn't. She knew in her heart she should have told him "no" when he'd asked if he could stay until he found a place in the States, but silly me, she thought I keep hoping he'll change his mind and then scolded herself saying, "I should paste a "Doormat" sign on my forehead."

Roland spent his last day at work saying goodbye to everyone, he knew he was going to miss the place, not so much the work itself, but the people. He'd made some good friends over the years.

Roland and Irene had gone together, to all the retirement parties. Irene recalled she was quite surprised that he hadn't told anyone of his plans to move to the States or of their impending separation. She'd had trouble answering questions posed by his co-workers and their wives. Everyone had asked her about their plans, now that they were officially retired. She'd only smiled and said, "We aren't sure, just yet" or sometimes she'd simply said, "We'll see," and flashed a smile that she hadn't felt. By the end of each party, she'd been exhausted from smiling and pretending. She'd mentioned this to Roland on the way home from the last of these parties. She sadly recalled that conversation, he'd asked her, "Would you prefer that every one of them know the truth?" She'd looked at him and shook her head saying, "It's just hard pretending, that's all." She remembered his sudden anger at that statement and he'd blurted out at her, "I've been silent for years, but now I'm finally going to tell you." He'd paused to regain his composure and continued, "Irene you've been pretending for most of our married life, why the hell is this so different? I would think this simple deception, would be easy for you." She recalled she'd looked down at her hands in her lap she'd had no reply. She'd kept quiet the rest of the way home and looked out the window without actually seeing anything; she remembered being lost in her pain, wishing things could be different and that somehow they could be happy once more.

The next morning, Roland came downstairs with a suitcase and left it in the front entranceway. He sat down after pouring himself a coffee and said as if it was a common occurrence, "I have reservations on a flight to Palm Springs and...," he checked his watch, "I'll be leaving in about an hour." When she didn't look up, he continued, "I've arranged for the Airport Limousine to pick me up." She lifted her head slowly and he saw the look on her face, he couldn't figure out the expression of utter shock that he was seeing; he thought she had to know this was coming. He'd told her not all that long ago that he'd planned to move to the States, he decided to ignore it and simply said, "I'm going to be looking at property there and with any luck I'll find a condo that I like. I'm hoping to find one I can take possession of immediately, and if I do then I'll move down within the month."

Irene quietly let out a long breath; she hadn't even realized she had been holding it. She didn't say anything to him; she picked up the paper and started reading, or at least doing her best to read. She was having trouble digesting what he'd just said, but she didn't want to show it. She was tired of this whole thing and just wanted it to be over. Roland didn't love her anymore and she knew she would have to face it sooner or later. One thing this whole mess had taught her was that she truly loved him, she hadn't been so sure for the past little while, but now that their marriage was ending, she knew for certain that she loved him. She swallowed the lump in her throat thinking of the irony in it all.

She began reading an article about some politician she'd never heard of and wasn't even interested in, but it was better than sitting there, listening to him tell her of all his wonderful plans, plans that didn't include her. She'd love to go to the desert with him; she only wished he would ask her. She'd been looking forward to his retirement before all this mess happened, she thought angrily of how she'd imagined their life together, with no children, for years. She recalled she had always dreamed of travelling and having fun. Shopping had always been something she loved to do and she remembered now she'd even dreamed of possibly buying another home, somewhere warm, for the winter. Now, she thought sadly, Roland was going to be doing all those things without her. Her eyes stung, she couldn't wait for him to leave, she didn't want him to see her cry, again. She knew she'd feel humiliated if she did because she knew he would probably just sigh heavily, shake his head and leave the kitchen. He'd done that to her before and she didn't want it to happen again. He'd told her several times, over the past couple of years that she'd made her own bed and now she had to sleep in it.

She kept reading, still not absorbing a single thing and willing herself not to cry, when suddenly she heard a horn honking and Roland jumped to his feet and rushed out of the kitchen, he hollered back, "I'll call you, to let you know that I've arrived in the desert." Irene wanted so badly to tell him not to bother, but she wanted him to call, so she ended up saying nothing at all. She loved just to hear his voice and she hoped that he'd change his mind about this whole separation thing, once he was down there alone.

She heard the door close and put her head on her arms on the table and totally lost control of her emotions, she let it all out. She sobbed and blew her nose for most of the morning. When she thought she was finally cried out, she went to the powder room and splashed cold water on her face. She caught sight of her reflection in the mirror, her face was puffy and red, and she immediately started to cry again. After a few minutes, she stopped abruptly and looking into the mirror again, suddenly yelled at her reflection, "Stop it!" She knew she had to stop; Roland was gone. She splashed her face with cold water repeatedly until her face felt numb then she dried it saying defiantly, "I have to make a life for myself, if he's doing it alone, so can I. I am sick of crying and worrying about what other people will think. Maybe it's not too late for me to just start telling the truth." She picked up her comb and combed her hair saying, to her reflection, "I don't want to lie anymore, it's too painful when the people I love find out the truth and it seems they always do one way or another." She shook her head thinking of how she'd truly thought she could keep Susan's paternity a secret forever. She remembered how she'd felt the day that lawyer had called about the trust account for Susan and how it had frightened her when she'd realized that she had no choice but to tell Roland, because she'd known that if she didn't, Susan would once she'd told her the truth.

She hadn't realized how long she had been standing in the powder room thinking, until the phone rang. She walked out to the hall table and as she picked it up to answer it, she noticed the clock; it had been four whole hours since Roland had left. Her best friend Karen was on the line and Irene simply couldn't help herself and started to cry. She was blurting out all that had happened when Karen said, "Irene, please, calm down!" She added when Irene stopped talking, "Just sit down and make yourself some tea, okay? I'm on my way over, and you can tell me everything then, okay? Can you do that?" Irene managed a meek sounding, "Okay, but hurry please, I feel as if I'm falling apart."

thirty-six

THE DESERT

Try as he might, Roland couldn't stop thinking about Irene, he'd tried reading, he'd even tried to concentrate on the in-flight movie, and nothing worked, he could escape for only a short time and then his thoughts would inevitably return to her.

He thought about Susan and about how he felt in his heart, that he was her father even if he wasn't biologically. When he'd gone to visit her he'd told her that as far as he was concerned he was her father, because he loved her and he knew she loved him, he remembered saying, "I may not be your biological father, but I'm your father in every other way." When he'd left that day, he was sure she knew he loved her and always wanted to be her Dad. She was smiling when he'd said goodbye to her in her apartment.

He'd gone to see Brooke too; he'd dropped in on her at school, she'd been so happy to see him. She'd said she understood why he was leaving her Mom. She was sad, but had said she was okay with things.

Biting his top lip and looking out the window of the airplane at the passing clouds, he recalled his visit with Dawn; she hadn't been quite as forgiving. She'd reminded him in no uncertain terms, that marriage was for better or worse. He'd told her, as gently as he could, that adultery was different. The way she'd looked at him, he'd wondered for the first time if Irene had ever actually told the girls about his own infidelity. He wasn't sure if she did or not, but he knew her and he thought if she hasn't yet, she most likely will, she always had to lay the blame on someone else, he recalled shaking his head, things could never be her fault. Roland had finally told Dawn that it wasn't just the adultery; he'd said he could forgive that, but that he couldn't forgive her for keeping it from him. He told Dawn about the paternity test that she'd had the doctor perform years before and knew for sure that he wasn't Susan's father, but she still hadn't told him. He'd said that's why he couldn't live with her anymore and added that he hoped she would understand someday. He'd looked at her, before he left; she was scowling, not wanting to meet his gaze and he knew she didn't understand. He'd stood, walked over to her, kissed the top of her head, and told her he loved her and left. He remembered sadly, that she'd never even said goodbye.

His thoughts turned to earlier in the day, he thought of Irene and her attempt to read the paper this morning. He wondered now, if he remembered that day clearly, when she'd first told him about her affair and Susan's paternity because, he thought frowning, he couldn't recall if she'd even said she was sorry. He remembered the searing pain he'd felt that day and thought maybe she had said it; maybe he just hadn't been listening at that point because the pain he'd felt was overwhelming. That day was still a nightmare for him and he thought it most likely always would be. He still had nightmares about it.

He got off the plane at the Palm Springs airport, he felt the sun on his face as he stepped off the plane and smiled, it felt good as he walked towards the terminal. He loved this airport, almost everything was outside, there were shade tarps covering things, here and there, it was so refreshing. He'd been in many airports, but none as nice as this one. He thought smiling Irene would love it and immediately stopped himself; he knew he'd need to make a conscious effort from now on not to think that way anymore. He had to remind himself, he wasn't with her any longer and that he didn't care what she would or would not like, not now or in the foreseeable future. He started thinking as he looked around for the baggage pickup, I still have to call her though, and since I promised her I would, I will. He shook his head and sighed, then figured, okay I'll allow myself to do only that and then I'll try my best not to think about her anymore for the duration of this trip.

He retrieved his bag and his golf clubs from the baggage carousel and headed out to the curb to hail a cab. He was going to be staying at a hotel right in Palm Springs. He was planning on meeting with the Real Estate Agent tomorrow; she'd promised him she would line up some nice places for him to look at. They'd already discussed his needs as well as the price he was willing to pay over the phone. Roland thought, it should be easy for her to select the right properties to show me, now that she knows what I want and I should be able to find something relatively quickly, I hope. He whistled as he picked up his bag and walked towards the taxi stand.

He called Irene as soon as he reached his room at the hotel and told her quickly, "I'm staying at the Marriott Hotel" and gave her the number to call in case of an emergency. He didn't ask how she was. He only asked, "Do you need anything?" She said as coldly as she could manage, "No, I don't and what could you possibly do from all the way down there, if I did." He noticed her tone of voice and said in reply, "I have to go", and hung up. He sat on the bed for a long time; he thought he detected a distinct coldness in her voice. Oh well he thought, it's probably better this way. He had to admit, though he felt lost. He realized he'd never been single, except in high school and he didn't have a clue what to do. He finally got up, took a shower, and decided to get out and do some exploring.

He asked the clerk at the front desk, "Where can I rent a car?"

To his surprise, the clerk told him, smiling, "Right here," and then proceeded to ask him all the necessary questions. When he finished, he said, "We'll arrange everything; we should have one here for you in about thirty minutes, tops." Roland returned the smile saying, "Thanks, I'll be in the café," and headed across the lobby.

He was sitting having a sandwich and coffee, reading the local paper, when the clerk approached him and gave him the keys. He said, "The inspection has already been done, so whenever you're finished with the car or when you checkout of the hotel, you can simply return the keys to the front desk. Enjoy." Roland thanked him and took the keys. He noticed the car was a grey Audi, according to the tag, he thought, that shouldn't be too hard to find. He finished his meal and went out to the front parking lot. He was surprised to find four grey Audis in the lot. He glanced at the key, noticed the license plate number, and started looking for the plate on the car that matched the number. He found it almost immediately, climbed in, and started it up. He thought as he drove out of the hotel lot, admiring the smooth handling and richly appointed interior of the car, I could really get used to this.

He drove around town, familiarizing himself with the place. He drove into residential areas looking at homes with for sale signs on the lawn, wondering how much the ones he liked were asking. He'd never bought a home on his own before, he wasn't sure if he even knew what he wanted. He'd told the Agent he wanted three bedrooms at least and three bathrooms. He also told her he wanted a modern kitchen, but he really didn't know all that much about cooking, so he wondered if it really mattered about the kitchen. He also said he wanted a nice large living room with a fireplace that's for sure, he thought nodding his head, because he knew nights in the desert could be chilly. He also knew he would need to have central air conditioning for the daytime and he figured the home would probably need to have some kind of humidifier, since he was in the desert and it was extremely dry. He eventually gave up his search for properties, since he really didn't have a clue what he was doing anyway and returned to the hotel.

He had a quick drink in the bar and went upstairs to his room. He was getting tired; he thought the drink would help relax him so he'd be able to sleep. He wanted to be fresh tomorrow, so in the event he saw something that he liked, he'd be able to buy it immediately and feel good about it. He also wanted to get in a round of golf, if time permitted. He'd noticed a gorgeous golf course in his travels earlier in his rental car and was looking forward to playing it.

The Real Estate Agent was very efficient. Her name was Audrey Simmonds, she was a middle-aged woman, with a husband and five children, that she insisted kept her extremely busy, "Busier than my full time job," she'd joked. Roland laughed and told her, "I have six girls myself." She said, "Oh, poor you, but it must be fun." He smiled and told her, "I love it." She looked at him smiling; she could tell that he meant it. She smiled to herself, she liked this quiet man, she wanted to find him a nice home he could be comfortable in and one that he would be able to have his girls come and stay in comfortably as well, when they came down to visit.

She showed him the first three homes on her list, they were all in gated communities and the condominium fee in each one included membership at the on site golf course. Roland loved all the golf courses, but not the homes. There was always something missing that he felt he couldn't do without. Audrey told him when she noticed the discouraged look on his face, "Be patient, I'm just getting started." Roland looked at her and decided to relax and trust that she'd find him the right property. She showed him one more home but it needed too much work. She said, "I didn't think it was a very good buy anyway, but I wanted to see what you thought of the floor plan." She told him after they'd inspected the last home she'd booked for the day, "I'll have more to show you tomorrow." Roland looked forlorn and asked a little impatiently, "How long do think it will take to find me a property that's suitable?" She explained with a sympathetic smile, "Now that I've met you and have shown you a few properties and listened to the comments you made about each one, I have a much better idea of what it is you like and want in a home." She smiled again and told him, "I'll pick you up at the hotel tomorrow, shall we say eight thirty?" She saw the worried look on his face, and said, "Don't worry, please just trust me, I'm pretty good at finding the perfect house for my clients." Roland looked at her and decided he did trust her; he returned her smile saying, "See you at eight thirty tomorrow."

Roland managed to get in his round of golf that afternoon, he'd had a great game and a wonderful dinner with the two guys he'd teed off with at the golf course. They were all good golfers, including Roland, and they talked for a long time after they finished their dinners. Roland finally looked at his watch, stood and said, "I better get going," he explained, "My Real Estate Agent is picking him up early tomorrow, to look at some more properties." They exchanged phone numbers and agreed that they'd play as often as they could, before Roland left for Canada again. Roland told them smiling, "You're on," and left whistling a happy tune, he'd had an exceptionally good time today. He loved to golf and they did too, which made it all the more enjoyable.

The next morning the first home they viewed was the one Roland knew he wanted. Audrey told him, when she could see that he was becoming anxious, "Let's just look at the others for comparison and also because, you never know." She said, "Don't forget I selected these homes based on your comments from yesterday and there just might be one you'll like better than the first one." He inspected each home and thought, this woman is fantastic, she really listened to what I said, yesterday. He looked at all the homes, but told her, "I still like the first one the best. Would it be okay to go through it again?" She answered, shrugging, "It's vacant, so I don't see why not, but I'll check to be sure." She made a call on her mobile phone and as she hung up the phone, she told him, "We can go right over now if you like." He inspected the house again and imagined the furniture he would buy to put in it. He knew exactly what type furniture he wanted; he even knew the colours he wanted. He thought with a smile Lord knows how many times I've been dragged out furniture shopping by Irene, so I should have a pretty good idea of what I like and what I don't like, by now. He finished his inspection and found it to be just as perfect as the first time he viewed it. Audrey told him, "Let's go to my office and write the offer." Roland agreed, he said, "The quicker I buy the place, the quicker I can move in." He asked her, thoughtfully, "Do you think I can close and move in within the month?" She replied, "Let's give it a try, I would think since it's vacant they'll want to give possession as soon as possible, but of course you never know, so we'll ask for the date that you want and see if they accept it and if they don't we'll see what date they counter with." Roland nodded and waited for the contract to be drawn up and ready for his signature.

He golfed and did some site seeing, he met more people on a few of the other golf courses he'd played and decided happily, that he really liked Palm Springs. He couldn't wait to move into his new home. Audrey met him for lunch a couple of weeks later and handed him the keys. He looked at them and felt a thrill of excitement, he was going to be starting a whole new life here, and he was really beginning to like the idea. He felt like a kid again, buying his first home and smiled at the thought.

He spent the next few days shopping for furniture and all the necessities he would need to start living in his new house. He had an excellent view of the swimming pool and the hot tub from his patio. He thought as soon as soon as my furniture is delivered and I've made the bed and put away the kitchen things

I bought, I'm going to head down and try out the hot tub and the pool. He smiled as he looked out the patio door and noticed that most of the people who lived there were his age or older, he liked that; he knew it was going to be a nice quiet place, which was exactly what he wanted. The golf course was only a block away from his front door, Heaven, he thought.

He had all new appliances, they'd actually come with the place, and he thought maybe he should get some cold drinks and put them in the fridge. He was painting while he waited for the furniture to arrive; the place was a little tired and had needed some sprucing up. He'd gone to the paint department in the Home Depot store and told the girl the colours of the furniture he'd bought and she'd helped him select the paint colours for the walls and ceiling. He'd already finished the living room and was just starting on the kitchen, when the bedroom furniture arrived. He waited for the men to set it up making sure they left everything out a ways from the walls, so he could paint that room as well, then he returned to finish the kitchen, it didn't take much time, it wasn't very large. He managed to finish painting the bedroom and half of the bathroom, when his living room furniture finally arrived.

He was exhausted, when he finished the painting, it had been a long time since he'd done any himself. Over the past decade or so he'd always been too busy to do things around the house himself and had always hired others to do the work. He decided to leave things out until tomorrow so they'd be handy in case the place needed a second coat. He hoped it didn't, because then he could move out of the hotel and into his new home that much sooner. He was actually excited and smiled to himself thinking, hopefully tomorrow I'll have time to try out the hot tub and pool, he yawned thinking, I'm just too tired tonight.

He locked the door, got into his rented car, and drove back to the hotel. On the way he thought about buying a car of his own, he also toyed with idea of driving the one he already owned that was sitting in his garage in Edmonton, down when he returned. He'd have to think about which would be better. He still had to bring some more clothes and things down with him when he returned. He suddenly thought he'd need to ask Irene if he could leave a winter coat at the house. She might not mind, and if she decided to sell the house, he'd have to go back anyway to help dispose of the extra furniture and things, so he could pick up his winter things then, if he thought he needed them.

He arrived at the hotel practically dragging his feet; he went straight to his room, ordered a sandwich and a beer from room service and ate while he watched the news. When he finished eating he barely made it to bed, he was so tired and fell asleep as soon as his head hit the pillow.

The next day he picked up breakfast to go from the Café located just off the lobby, which consisted of a bagel and large coffee. He checked out of the hotel and drove the short distance to his new home.

He'd arranged to keep the car through the rental company and was told to simply return it to the branch near the airport when he left; they'd even given him the driving directions to their location near the terminal. He'd decided this morning in the shower that he didn't care if his house needed a second coat of paint or not, if it did, he'd just have to do it while he was living there. He didn't want to spend another night in the hotel; he needed to move into his house because for him it meant the beginning of his new life. Staying in the hotel he felt like he was living in limbo, he needed to feel that he was moving forward, he thought living in his new house, and meeting his new neighbours would do that for him.

He pulled up in the driveway of his home and immediately felt a sense of pride, I'm like a kid with a new toy, he thought with a chuckle. He noticed as he looked at it through the windshield, the place was really quite beautiful there were flowers and trees and he noticed that they were all in bloom. He could see the golf course running through the residential area and thought, nodding happily, this place feels right to me. The guards at the gate already seemed to know who he was and had opened the gate for him, waving and smiling. As he'd driven to his house he'd noticed people out walking and still others playing golf. He'd also driven by the tennis court and even it was occupied, and there were more people chatting happily while they waited for a free court. He smiled, he was sure he was going to fit in nicely here.

He pushed the idea of Irene, loving it here, out of his mind she kept popping into his thoughts at the strangest times, and he had to constantly remind himself that he was tired of being deceived by her because if he didn't, the guilt of leaving her would begin to creep in, again. He asked himself the same question, over and over, why didn't she own up to her own affair when he'd owned up to his all those years ago, he shook his head to clear it and got out of the car trying hard not to think of her and entered his home.

He surveyed his work from the previous day and noticed that the paint he'd applied yesterday was looking pretty good. He put his bagel down on the counter and inspected it a little closer, he stood looking around nodding his head and smiling, he was pleased that it didn't need a second coat.

He started moving the furniture to where he wanted it. He walked into the bedroom and moved the dresser back and then pushed the bed up against the wall, he placed the lamps on the night tables on each side of the bed. Then he opened the packages of new sheets he'd purchased and made the bed. He'd bought a duvet and a duvet cover; he'd even bought the pillow shams to match. He stood back admiring his choices and his handiwork. Then thought, with a groan, I still need to install the new blinds, thank God there are only five windows, one in the master bedroom and one in each of the guest bedrooms, as well as the huge sliding glass door in the living room and a small kitchen window. He thought I'll just do the master bedroom, the living room and the kitchen right now and leave the other rooms for another day, that should give me enough privacy for the time being, I don't plan on walking around naked anyway, then thought with a little chuckle, I wouldn't want to frighten any of my neighbours.

He remembered he still had to shop for groceries, as he opened his empty fridge. He got back to work making his house a home, he placed towels on the towel bars and put out soap from the hotel, in all three baths. He fetched his suitcases from the car and put away all his clothes. He looked around and smiled, he really liked the place; it was shaping up nicely, he thought.

He picked up his bagel that he had noticed lying on the counter and took a big bite, he'd forgotten about it while he worked. As he ate he watched his neighbours around the pool and the hot tub, they seemed to be having a pretty good time. He opened the door and stepped out onto his patio. He jumped when he heard a voice, say, "Hi," he turned and found himself facing a man about his own age smiling at him, the guy said, "I didn't mean to startle you, sorry." Roland reached out his hand to the man and introduced himself, saying "Hi, I'm Roland Petersen and don't worry about startling me, at my age I need that once in a while just to make sure my heart's still pumping." The man shook his hand and replied laughing, "Yeah I know what you mean, by the way I'm Alvin Boland, Al for short, I live next door," and used his thumb and his head to indicate the direction. He asked, inquisitively, "You live alone?" Roland hesitated a moment, he wasn't used to saying he was alone, but replied, "Yes, as a matter of fact, I do." Al told him, "I'm on my own too, it's nice to have another neighbour who's single, there aren't too many of us single guys around here," and smiled. They chatted for a while and discovered they had very similar interests, Al had only moved in last week, so they decided they could discover the place together. They both liked to golf and neither one of them had played tennis since college, but decided they might like to give it a try again.   Al said, "We should get together once you're all settled and have time." Roland suggested, "Why don't we get in a round of golf later this afternoon, I only have to get some groceries and then I'm free." They agreed on a tee time and ducked into Roland's place to call the clubhouse to reserve their tee time. They said good-bye and Roland left for the grocery store.

On the plane ride back to Edmonton, Roland reminisced about his trip. He considered himself truly blessed, he had found the perfect home and he had met his new best friend. He really enjoyed Al's company. They'd discovered they were both Engineers, Al was an Electrical Engineer and had only been retired for six months, he shook his head as he remembered the jokes they'd told each other about engineers. He'd made several other new friends as well in the short time he was there.

He was planning to make this trip back to Edmonton a quick one. He wanted to pick up the rest of his clothes, except for his winter things, which he hoped he could leave in the house in Edmonton, and return to the desert just as soon as he could manage. He was looking forward to playing more golf and he'd already made plans with Al to play tennis next week too, he made a mental note to buy himself a racquet and some tennis balls, the shoes could wait. He figured he'd just wear his runners until he found out if he still liked the game.

thirty-seven

ALL ALONE

I rene wasn't able to coax herself out of bed in the mornings. Her house was far too large now and unbelievably quiet; she was finding the silence unbearable. The kids, she noticed lately simply weren't interested in spending much time with her. Dawn had invited her over to dinner a couple of times, which Irene thought was nice of her, but the amount of time she'd stayed each time was too short and she'd always had to return home, and home was beginning to feel like a tomb to her.

She'd tried to keep up with the things she'd always done, such as playing bridge and visiting with neighbours and friends but found that being with her friends was embarrassing. Everyone knew that she and Roland had separated and she felt as if they all pitied her, so she'd called and told them she wasn't feeling well the last couple of times she'd been invited and hadn't bothered to go out since. She had to admit that she felt bad about it though because she knew she needed the outing.

She forced herself to get out of bed and noticed she didn't feel quite as bad once she was up and mobile. She padded to the bathroom, funny she thought, I never noticed before, just how much these floors squeak and groan and smiled thinking, a house full of kids, with their music and chatter could muffle almost anything. She washed her face, brushed her teeth, then

439

looked at herself in the mirror, and said, sternly, "You have to get over these feelings of self pity you're having and get on with your life! You're acting like an idiot."

She walked back to her bedroom with a purpose, stepped into her slippers and pulled on her housecoat, knotting the belt on her way down the stairs to the kitchen. She put on a pot of coffee, found a pad of paper and a pen, and placed it on the table. Convincing herself of what she needed to do, she said aloud, "I'm going to sit here and make a list of the things I'd like to do and the places I'd like to go and then I'm going to force myself to do at least one of the things from my list each day." She poured herself a cup of coffee and made some toast; she buttered it and found some apricot jam in the fridge. As she slathered the jam on her toast she thought about the fifteen pounds she'd lost in the past little while since Roland had left; her clothes were hanging off her now.

She sat down with her coffee and took a bite of her toast, racking her brain, trying her best to think of something she could put on her list, that she wanted to do. She drank her coffee as she thought and was finally able to come up with two things. The first one was cleaning up the house, which she hadn't done in ages, and the other was shopping for new sheets and a comforter for her bed. She knew she needed to get rid of the things that reminded her of Roland. Suddenly, she sat up straighter in her chair and her eyes widened as she thought of something else, and immediately added it to her list, she wrote, "get rid of Roland's chair" in large letters. She started day dreaming of what she would do with the empty space it would leave, she decided after giving it a great deal of thought, I'll buy a wing chair to compliment the couch, I've always loved wing chairs, it was Roland who never wanted one. Defiantly, she said aloud, "That's exactly what I'm going to do, I can have anything I want now, and I don't need his approval for anything." She looked at her list and even though there were now only four things listed on it, she was beginning to feel like she was making progress. Taking a closer look, she noticed that one of the items, would be too depressing to do right now, it was "cleaning the house," and she scratched it off, thinking, the things I list and do must involve getting me out of this house, I don't want to do things that will keep me in the house. She put more lines through the "cleaning the house" item and read over the other ones again. She was getting excited about the idea of shopping and was anxious to get started, she thought smiling, I can finish this list another time, right now I need to get started on the items I've already listed. I'll tuck the pad of paper into my purse and if I think of other things when I'm out I'll jot them down. She thought who knows this could be a whole new beginning for me.

She finished her toast and ran upstairs and showered, she put on one of her favourite outfits, it was a little large now, but she still liked it, it was a red suit with a blouse to match, it seemed to perk up her colour the moment she slipped it on. She found the shoes that matched it perfectly and combed her hair, she even put on some lipstick and then frowning at her image in the mirror, decided she could use a little mascara as well. She looked in the mirror again once she'd finished and smiled at the result of her efforts. She actually felt good about herself, for a change. Her smile widened as she gathered her purse and keys and left the house.

The air outside felt wonderful, she couldn't remember the last time she'd been out of the house. She drove to The Bay, her favourite department store singing along with the radio. The Bay carried a wonderful selection of home furnishings as well as home fashions and accessories. She parked a little ways from the entrance, she wanted to walk outside a little and enjoy the sunshine. When she entered the store, she was already in the furniture department. She looked around and couldn't believe her luck, right at the entrance to the store, in one of those displays that department stores always set up so nicely, she saw the chair that she knew she simply had to have. She admired it and tried it out, as she sat in it she thought, it's so comfortable, it's perfect. She found a saleswoman, and told her, "I'd like to buy the chair near the entrance." On the way to the counter to pay for it, the saleswoman told her, "I don't know if you've seen it or not but, we have a couch and loveseat that match that chair, and..." she drew out the "a" sound in the word and, "We also have a heavenly coffee and end table ensemble displayed with it, there's even a sofa table to match." Irene was just about to say that she was only interested in the chair, when the saleswoman stopped in front of the most lovely living room grouping she'd ever seen. "Her chair," the one she was buying, was part of this gorgeous grouping. She stared wide eyed at the whole set, she couldn't help herself; she looked at the saleswoman smiling and said, "I'll take it all, the whole grouping." She produced her credit card and the saleswoman told her, after checking that it was in stock, "I can have it delivered for you in two days. Would that be okay?" Irene was thrilled and replied, "Yes, thank you."

She walked into the linen department with a smile on her face she was proud of herself for getting out of the house. She hadn't realized how much she missed shopping. She walked around looking at all the lovely things and finally settled on a duvet and duvet cover set. She also purchased all the matching pillows as well, thinking to herself, Roland always hated having throw cushions on the bed and thought defiantly, now I can have as many as I want, and tossed a few extra ones on the counter, feeling a bit naughty as she did and smiling just a little wider. She went to the drapery department and ordered new window coverings. She picked up a few other miscellaneous items in other departments in the store, as she passed them. She had to ask the store clerk for help to get it all out to her car. She was elated.

She stopped at Karen's place on her way home, to show

off her new bedroom ensemble and to tell her about the living room suite she'd chosen. They chatted over coffee and decided to go out to lunch the next day. Karen was raving about a place she'd been to with her husband, and said, pleadingly, "We just have to go." Irene had laughed and agreed.

When Irene left Karen's house she was smiling, as Karen watched her walk down the walkway and out to her car, she even noticed that she had a spring in her step again, she was glad her friend was beginning to feel better. She thought Irene needed to get on with her life and was happy to hear of all the things she said she wanted to do. She thought with a tinge of excitement, she even told me she wanted to take a Caribbean cruise and had asked if I wanted to come too. Karen thought smiling to herself, wild horses couldn't keep me away from that cruise, it had sounded wonderful and Irene had actually sounded like her old self as she'd told her about it and Karen had watched her add it to her list of things she wanted to do. She smiled thinking of Irene and her list, but she thought it was a good idea; it seemed to be working for her.

Irene was tidying up the living room; she'd already made the bed with her new duvet ensemble. The drapes she'd ordered for the living room and bedroom had been installed this morning and the new furniture had been delivered, as well. She was standing back smiling as she admired her new living room grouping, when she heard a knock on the door. She walked over to answer it thinking happily that it was probably Karen or maybe even Alex stopping over for a visit.

She panicked when she caught a glimpse of Roland standing there, through the sidelight window at the front door; he was waiting for her to answer. Her heart leapt into her throat, she felt like a schoolgirl. She opened the door, hoping against all hope that he'd come to his senses and had come back to her. She said, "Hello," and stood there looking expectantly, at him. His face was expressionless and he asked in a flat serious tone of voice, "Can I come in?" She nodded in answer; she didn't trust herself to speak. He pushed past her gently and told her, "I need to go upstairs to get the rest of my things." She felt like the floor was giving way beneath her, and grabbed the wall in the entryway. She finally found the courage to speak and replied, keeping her voice as even as she could manage, "Sure, go ahead, do whatever you need to do," and quickly looked away, busying herself with closing the door, and looking through the window towards the street.

He watched her without saying anything more, then turned and went upstairs. He packed up his things; it took him all of about thirty minutes. He walked downstairs and noticed the new furniture in the living room; he smiled and said, "I like the changes you've made." Then added, "I noticed the bedroom as well, I bought a similar set for my new home in Palm Springs." Irene sighed and asked him, "So, you found a condo?" He told her about his new place and all about the new friends he'd made. Irene thought sadly, I'm such an idiot, I actually thought he might be coming back to me when I saw him at the door, when instead he couldn't wait to tell me about his new home and all his new friends. He only came back because he wanted to pick up his things. Oh God she thought, I have to make a life for myself, I've wasted so much time hoping we could somehow save our marriage, but I realize now there's no hope, I have to find a way to move on.

He asked her a question and she had to ask him to repeat it, she was so wrapped up in her own thoughts she hadn't heard what he'd said, he repeated, "Would you mind if I kept my winter things in the basement closet, for now?" She thought that would be a good idea, it would give him something to come back for, who knows, she thought, he may actually want to come back eventually, she could only hope, then was immediately upset with herself for even thinking such a thing, she thought, will I ever learn to just let him go. She said, finally, "I guess it won't hurt, there's plenty of room." He casually asked thinking he needed to make conversation, "So, what have you been up to, these days?" She lied and told him, "Oh, the usual, going out with friends, playing bridge, shopping," and she did a sweeping motion with her hand, indicating the new living room. She told him, "Oh, by the way I've decided to just stay put, here in the house for the time being." Roland told her, nodding, "I thought you might, so I took the liberty of hiring a landscape service, are you okay with that?" He quickly added, "If you're not, I'll let them go and you can hire anyone you want." She told him as she looked out the window, "I really don't care who takes care of the property as long as they do a decent job, I don't want to live in a run down dump." He rolled his eyes behind her back, thinking she never changes. She practically lives in a palace; this is certainly one of the nicest homes on the street. She'd made sure of that when they'd originally purchased it years ago. It now had an almost regal look to it, it was just one of those properties that looked better with age, and it was so far removed from what she called a "dump." She really didn't know just how good she had it, but then again, he thought, she never had. He could finally see that now and wondered why he was never able to see it before.

He gathered his winter coats, gloves, scarves and boots and struggling not to drop anything, carried them downstairs to put them in the basement closet. She never even offered to help him carry anything, not even the scarves or gloves. She just sat in the living room with her nose in the air. He shook his head; she truly did think she was something special.

Roland had just picked up his suitcases and was heading out the door, when she asked him, "Are you going to file for a divorce?" He put the suitcases he was holding down, turned around and stared at her; that was a question he'd never expected from her. He asked, "Is that what you want?" She replied flippantly with her head held high, "It doesn't matter one way or the other to me," then added, hoping to make him think, "At least not at this point, anyway." Roland looked upset and told her, "I wasn't even considering such a thing!" He reminded her, "Did you forget that we're Catholics!" She thought the fact that they were Catholic was possibly the only thing that might save her. Just maybe she thought, when Roland had more time to think about things he might come to his senses and realize, they should be living together, they were married, after all and they were Catholic.

Roland loaded the last of his things into his car and drove off. Irene had cried and tried her best to console herself, with the idea that he'd eventually come to his senses, but was immediately angry with herself again for thinking such a thing. A little voice in the back of her mind, kept telling her, "Don't be so silly, he won't be coming back and you'd better get used to it."

She managed to keep herself busy; she and Karen started volunteering at the hospital. Irene couldn't stand being around so many sick people though, she was deathly afraid she'd catch something. She switched from visiting patients to helping out in the hospital gift shop, at least there; she dealt mostly with healthy people who were only there to visit friends and family. She washed her hands incessantly though, just in case. She and Karen were excited about the cruise they'd booked, it was sailing next month and they talked about it constantly. They'd shopped together and bought tons of clothes and bathing suits for it.

She had visits from the older girls who came with their kids, although not as often as she thought they should visit. She had five grandchildren, now, she couldn't believe where the time had gone sometimes. Maureen had been the first to have her (legitimate) grandchild. Irene never counted the other "unfortunate incident" as she called it. Jean was second and Cassie was third. She often thought it was funny how that happened, the oldest child was the last of her three older girls to have a child and the youngest was first. Susan and Brooke visited occasionally. Brooke had warmed up to her a little more, but Susan remained distant. Irene wondered if she would ever change, in her feelings toward her, she had to admit though, of all her children, Susan was still the one she had trouble feeling close to and the mess they'd gone through these past few years, had made things even worse. All of the girls were very close to their Dad though, even Susan.

thirty-eight

AN UNANSWERED PRAYER

One day almost three years from the day Roland had moved out, Maureen called and without even giving her mother a chance to speak said, "Mom, I think you should know about Dad." Irene had been shocked when she told her Roland was ill and had been for several months now. Maureen had also informed her that she'd been down to Palm Springs several times in the last year and so had Susan. They'd both tried to help him as best they could. Maureen told her, sadly, "Mom, he has nurses round the clock now, to look after him, we couldn't handle things by ourselves anymore." Irene asked reluctantly, becoming alarmed, "What's wrong with him?" She held her breath waiting for the answer, not sure, if she could handle it. Maureen paused and told her, "Mom, he seemed to be fine, he complained quite a bit about what he called, "just his arthritis," but when the pain worsened and he couldn't stand it any longer, he finally gave in and went to see a doctor. He'd said he wanted to find out if they could give him something to help ease the pain." She paused and asked, "Mom, are you sitting down?" Irene told her, "No, but just a second and I will, something tells me I better." Maureen continued, "They took x-rays and finally did a bone scan to confirm what the doctor

448

said the x-rays had indicated, Mom, they discovered he has bone cancer." Irene gasped and asked, "And he didn't know that?" Maureen answered, "Mom, according to what the doctor told us, he apparently had had prostrate cancer that went undetected, for several years and it finally spread to his bones, the doctor said that's usually what happens with this type of cancer. He said it's aggressive." Irene's mind was racing, what could she do to help. Then thought why didn't I know about this before and asked in a shaky voice, "Why didn't one of you tell me?" She could hear Maureen take a deep breath, "Mom, Dad asked us not to, he said it wasn't fair, he said he wanted you to continue to get on with your life and not have to worry about him."

Irene thought, my God, they kept it from me, I can understand Maureen or the older girls not telling me before, since we rarely speak to each other these days, but I can't understand why Susan or even Brooke, never told me. She was hurt and saddened as well, thinking about it. Didn't her kids understand that she had a right to know, she'd spent years with their father, and they should have told her? Irene was shocked; she was still trying to absorb the seriousness of what Maureen had told her. She'd prayed asking God for Roland to come back to her one day; it was the only thing that had kept her going when he'd first left. Now she had to admit that she rarely thought of it anymore, she'd given up hope long ago. She had plenty of friends now, the ladies at the Hospital Auxiliary and her bridge club, but she knew she was still very lonely and she missed her family. She had often thought that if she could start all over again, she would certainly change many of the things that she'd done in her life. She also realized now though that she could make a life for herself and do things that were fun, without needing a husband to do them with, she thought of the cruise that she and Karen had taken a couple of years ago, although she would have preferred to have Roland there, she had fun without him. She was looking forward to the next cruise she and Karen were taking; they were leaving next month. Her thoughts snapped back to the present and she asked Maureen, "What can I do to help?" Maureen replied, "All of us are flying down, Dad's paying our fares. When he was first diagnosed and was told he wouldn't have more than six months left, he gave me the money to pay for the flights to bring everyone down, when the time came." Irene sobbed and asked, "Do you think it would be okay if I meet all of you there?" Maureen told her, "I think that's a good idea, Mom, that's why I called you, I thought you'd want to be there." Irene could only say, "Thank you." Maureen told her, "We're all meeting at the Marriott Hotel, is that okay with you?" Irene replied, "Yes, anywhere will be fine. I'll see you there and Maureen, thanks again for letting me know." Maureen said, "Okay Mom, I'll make your hotel reservations for you, since I'm making them for everyone else anyway." She added before hanging up, "I love you, Mom, see you there." Irene responded, "I love you too."

Irene rushed to pack and then realized she hadn't even arranged for a flight yet. She punched the numbers 411, for directory assistance, into the phone and asked impatiently, "Can you give me Air Canada's number, please?" She telephoned the airline immediately and as quickly as she could, explained the circumstances to the reservations clerk; she was put on hold for a few minutes and when the clerk came back on the line, she told her they could get her on a flight later today. Irene gave her a credit card number and hurried to finish packing. She realized she was throwing things into the suitcase, haphazardly, but she also realized she simply didn't care what she brought with her, for once. She could only think of poor Roland. She thought, my God, he's been sick and dying in his home in Palm Springs and I never even knew he was ill. She had to make it to his side before it was too late; she wanted him to know that she loved him.

On the flight she suddenly understood that she'd been a fool, she had been so busy all her life, caring about what everyone else thought about her, sometimes to the point of not even caring for her own family properly. She now knew that most of those people she had been so worried would think poorly of her, hadn't really even cared what she did, or didn't do for that matter. She knew she'd been utterly foolish to think they ever had, most of them had only been interested in gossiping. She knew all the people who had truly cared about her she had hurt. She knew she'd hurt her children, just as she knew she'd hurt Roland. Roland was so important to her. She couldn't understand why it had taken so long for her to come to her senses and understand that. She wished she understood that when they were together. She thought of the last time she'd visited with Melissa, they'd discussed that very same thing, Irene had felt close to her that time, she seemed to be so caring and sympathetic of her situation.

She hurried off the plane and quickly found her bags. She got into one of the cabs that was waiting at the curb at the airport and told the driver the name of the hotel she was to be staying at and was surprised by how quickly they reached it. She'd always pictured Palm Springs as a larger city than it actually was.

She paid the driver and the porter took her bags. She rushed into the lobby and noticed her girls were all ready there; they were walking through the lobby headed in her direction. They looked up, noticed her, walked over to her and each greeted her with a perfunctory kiss on her cheek. Cassie spoke up and said, coldly, "We're heading over to Dad's place." Susan shoved a piece of paper at her, saying, "Here's his address, we'll see you there, try not to be too long, he isn't doing very well."

She took the paper and watched them leave, her heart shattering. She realized as she watched them pile into a cab, they don't even want me to go with them. She turned and walked to the front desk to register. The gentleman behind the desk, felt sorry for her, she was crying. He took care of her registration as quickly as possible and handed the key to her room to the porter, who escorted her up to her floor and down the hall to her room, where he placed her suitcase inside the suite and quietly closed the door. Irene cried as she tried her best to freshen up, she splashed water on her face and then left her room and raced down the hall to the elevator, she was thinking of what Susan had said about Roland not doing well and to hurry.

She arrived at the address Susan had given her and was shocked at the sheer beauty of the place; it was an absolutely gorgeous gated condominium community, complete with golf course, swimming pools, tennis courts and restaurants The list went on and on, she was at the front gate sitting in the back of a taxi, waiting for the guard to open the gates and let the taxi drive through. As she waited, she couldn't help but notice the list of amenities listed on the gatehouse and had been reading them. She was getting anxious because it seemed to be taking too long for the guard to open the gate; she hoped Roland hadn't left word that she wasn't permitted to visit. Just as she was beginning to panic, the gates swung open. The driver followed the directions the guard had given him and found Roland's place without any problem. Irene paid him and stood on the curb as he drove off. She couldn't believe that she was actually afraid to go to the door; her stomach was in knots.

All of a sudden, the front door of Roland's house burst open and Maureen was hurrying down the walk, she told her, taking her arm, "Hurry Mom, Dad doesn't have much time left." Irene gasped and hurried into the house. She raced over to the bed and her hand went to her mouth, as she looked down at Roland, noticing with a gasp that he looked like a skeleton. His skin was white as the sheets he was lying on and he was so terribly thin; his lips were nothing more than thin lines tinged with blue. He opened his eyes and for a second he seemed to recognize her. He smiled ever so slightly and closed his eyes again. She smoothed his forehead with her hand and whispered, "I'm here Roland, I love you, I'm so sorry you had to go through this." His eyes flickered open and she thought he was trying to say something.

She looked frantically at the nurse, who only answered, shaking her head, "He can't speak, the respirator prevents it." She patted Irene's hand in an effort to comfort her. Irene watched as he closed his eyes again and it was as if he had waited for her to arrive before he left them for good. She watched his features relax as the monitor behind his bed sounded an alarm and the green line flattened out. Irene cried and called to the nurse, "Please do something!" The nurse quietly said, "I'm sorry, his heart has stopped, he's gone." Irene held his hand for a long time; she was looking at him with tears streaming down her cheeks. She kissed his forehead and told him once again, "I'm so sorry, I love you Roland, I always have."

The girls watched their mother; they were amazed at the way she was behaving. Cassie whispered to Jean and Maureen, through her tears, "I've never seen this much emotion, not ever from Mom." Maureen said, quietly, "Maybe she's changed, maybe she sees now, what she never saw before. Maybe she knows now that Dad really loved her." She added, sadly, "Dad told me he'd spent years wishing she would come to her senses, maybe she finally did."

Irene kissed each of the girls and before she left the house, she noticed Melissa sitting in the corner of the room. She looked over at her and as their eyes met and she saw the pain in Melissa's eyes, something inside her felt as if it gave way and she felt a flood of sorrow. She lowered her gaze and left house.

She got into the cab that she'd asked one of the nurses to call for her and asked him quietly, "Please take me to the Marriott Hotel." She looked out at the scenery as they drove. She was glad Roland had had the opportunity to live once again in the Country he loved so much and had served so many years ago. He was an American through and through; she had always known that, she was the one who had insisted they live in Canada, her Country. She admitted to herself now that she was the one who hadn't wanted change, not him. She thought wringing her hands in her lap; she'd been a selfish individual. She had always taken advantage of the fact that he would do anything to make her happy, even at the expense of his own happiness. He'd been the "perfect" husband; she knew she'd been far from the perfect wife that he'd so deserved to have.

She walked into the hotel and rode the elevator up to her room; she opened the door and heard the telephone ringing, it rang three times, but stopped before she'd been able to enter the room and answer it. She straightened, closed the door, dropped her purse and room key on the table by the door and walked directly into the bathroom; she knew what she had to do. She opened the cosmetic bag she'd brought with her, spilling some of its contents onto the counter in her haste. She removed the little bottle of sleeping pills and poured them into her hand; she quickly washed them down with water from the tap.

She walked over to the desk by the window, withdrew some paper from the drawer, and picked up the pen. She knew she wouldn't have much time so as quickly as she could she wrote a letter to her girls. She wrote, "I want you to know that I love all of you. I am so sorry for all the pain I caused each of you throughout your lives. I wish there was some way I could make it up to you. I love your Father, I always have, and I always will. I want to be with him now. I know that I can't go on living without him. Once again I love you." She signed it shakily, "All my love forever, Mom."

She walked over to the bed and lay down, she was already beginning to feel dizzy; she started thinking about her life. She wished she could have a second chance to make things right. She knew now, just how selfish she'd always been. She'd learned so much from the ladies at the Hospital Auxiliary, they were so happy all the time, they'd explained to her when she'd asked, that their happiness came from helping others. She'd realized when she'd heard them say that and thought about what it meant that she'd always been miserable because she'd only ever been interested in helping herself, her whole life, she'd never cared about anyone but herself, she felt so ashamed. She knew she never deserved to have a man like Roland as her husband. She said aloud, "I'm feeling so sleepy Roland, it won't be long now and I'll be there. This time I promise to be the wife you deserve." Her thoughts strayed back to her children and she hoped they would understand. She thought of Roland again and wished she hadn't hurt him, so many times over the years.

She began talking to God, saying, "I'm so sorry for all the things I've done." Her mind drifted again and she found herself thinking of the little prayer she'd taught each of her children when they were little, it was called "Now I Lay Me Down to Sleep." She felt like she was floating now and began to recite it, she whispered, "Now I lay me down to sleep; I pray the Lord my soul to keep; if I should die before I wake; I pray the Lord my soul to take. She finished it and as she did, a smile crossed her lips and she said with such love in her voice, "Roland" as everything turned black...

~~~

LaVergne, TN USA
24 October 2010
202060LV00004B/21/P